NEW BRIGHTON

HELEN TREVORROW

RED DOG
UK

Published by RED DOG PRESS 2022

First Edition

Hardback ISBN 978-1-914480-99-7
Paperback ISBN 978-1-914480-97-3
Ebook ISBN 978-1-914480-98-0

www.reddogpress.co.uk

For Ruby

ONE

THE WEATHER IS a sharp slap of wet and cold. I'm an hour late already, and even from this distance, I can sense that Vincent is furious. I wave in earnest, but he doesn't see me. He hates to wait. I rush towards him leaving behind me a sky that is lit up by an ominous indigo cloud.

I love the smell of a storm. It smells like freedom, and I want to be free more than anything in this world. My name is Robyn Lockhart. Fully inked on my university application, I am Robyn Elizabeth Lockhart which sounds to me like an old grandiose lady, or someone I don't know. If I was in a movie then I wouldn't be the star. I'd be the best friend, the slightly geeky shadow who gets murdered, or even worse, never gets laid.

Tonight, I'm wearing a ring on each finger, and the thumb (yes, the thumb) of my left hand. The silver and gold metals pop against my black nail varnish. I can feel the powerful sensation when they brush together. I clatter and prickle along with the impending storm. I can't wait for Summer. It seems like we've had a never-ending Winter and I am desperate to feel warmth on my face.

I tilt back my head and inhale deeply through both nostrils. I can smell the pungent storm, fresh like spring. I open my eyes and glance back at the sea, and through the fog I glimpse that indigo sky starting to boil with distant thunder. I wonder how on earth that could smell like fresh linen.

Vincent looks like James Dean, standing with one foot up on the brick wall behind him. He wears a second-hand denim jacket with creaking seams and a sprout of frayed white cotton above the right-hand pocket. One hand is shoved inside the jacket and the other holds a cigarette.

I am about to shout 'Vincent' in an apologetic tone, but I am startled by a moan in the alleyway on my left. I hear the sound of high-heeled shoes on scratchy cement. I trace the blended outlines of what I struggle to see through the mist; it's a Teddy Boy and a woman. He wears a long, dark trench coat with thick, white-soled shoes shuffling between her high heels.

The Teddy Boy parts her fur coat. They look like two wild bears embracing. Her arms go up around his neck, and he fumbles around his own waist to undo his belt. Then he lifts her, pinning her to the damp, decayed wall, her bare thighs open around him. I stop to watch, mostly wondering if I have ever felt like that, or frantically done what they are doing now.

There's a lot I can't recall. But I intend to remember everything.

In black and white lettering, the name of the night's disco, 'INDYGOTH' illuminates through the mist.

"Robyn! You left me waiting!" Vincent shouts, stepping out from under the Astoria's wide awning and running a hand through his perfect quiff. He drops his arms open to his sides acting deliberately confused. He could fly into a rage at any moment, but even so, I just want to ask him if we've ever done it outside in an alleyway? Because right now, racking my brain, and searching my fragile memory, I can't remember. It's like it's on the tip of my tongue.

I'm breathless from running and watching the Teddy Boy prise open that woman's legs. I glimpsed a fraction of her creamy white inside thigh.

"Vincent, have we ever…" I begin to ask him, because I have to know, and it's starting to freak me out that I can't remember this specific detail. But he's too irritated, and so I instinctively change my approach. "I was looking after Alice, so I couldn't leave her on her own."

It is not a lie. Technically, I'm always looking after Alice—my poor, sweet sister, and the person that I love the most in the whole wide world. If I had one wish and one wish only, I'd give it to her to make her better. She's frail, and always poorly, not like me. I'm average height for my build, but I've never met a jar I couldn't open. Vincent sulks by turning his back towards me and not meeting my eye.

"I didn't mean to make you wait," I say. Vincent stubs his cigarette out under his boot. He rearranges himself compulsively, tucking his shirt into his trousers and centralising the metal buckle of his belt. "Have you seen the weather?" Stupid comment, I know, as he'd been standing out in the weather for almost an hour because of me. I quickly change tack again. "The forecast is awful," I say, leaning into him, snaking my fingers between his, thinking about the Teddy Boy and the woman going at it just yards away. If I had more guts then I would pull Vincent into that back alley and go at it next to them my face spattered by the rain. I kiss Vincent, pushing myself against him. It's not as good as a back alley tryst, but it's enough to make him forgive me for being so late. Still saying nothing, he leads me inside.

Brighton is like this; elegant Victorian facade giving way to dingy back alleys lit only by the reflection of a streetlamp in a puddle. So, naturally, the Astoria is a grand Victorian theatre turned jaded nightclub, reeking of beer, vibrating with bass, and dripping with red velvet.

For a mere five pounds entry you also receive a free drink. Vincent and I spill downstairs into the main auditorium. He is far too good looking to be my boyfriend. Everyone stares at us, or rather at him, I assume, and his pheromone inducing eyebrows.

I don't even know how we got together. We just are.

"I didn't think you were going to bother to show up," he says, reaching over to take my free drink token to buy *me* a drink. He has issues: abandonment issues about women, on account of his mother. It makes him tricky to manage. I honestly don't mean to be nasty to him but it's too tempting. It's likely that he brings out the worst in me, and I in him.

A path to the crowded bar opens in front of him and I follow in his slipstream. The bartender is a striking girl with spiky blonde hair, and she asks Vincent what he wants to drink. She has a bold, creaturesque tattoo crawling up her neck, its body hidden under her cut-off plaid shirt.

"Two pints!" Vincent shouts holding up two fingers over the noise of the weird Goth band playing. He never says 'please'. I don't like that about him. I feel myself finishing his sentences, shouting "please", and "thank you" at the blonde bartender.

I've got my drink. I've got my boyfriend. I turn to face the stage. The music is so loud and aggressive. I nod my head to the beat. In the shadows, I spy a man in a long black coat that I have seen before. I suspect that he is probably a drug dealer. A sudden exciting urge descends on me; the possibility that Vincent and I could get high. I make eye contact. The man catches my eye, holds my gaze and raises one sinister eyebrow. But he's not who I think he is. He's something else entirely, worse, and much more dangerous. I quickly look away.

Best to forget it. After all, Vincent's Mum loved drugs more than she loved him. The bartender still stares at us, and so I slide my arm around Vincent's neck, claiming him. I push my body against him and she moves away to serve someone else.

"Shall we get some coke?" I whisper, brushing his ear with my lips. It just slipped out! I was trying to be sexy, but he immediately pulls away, repulsed.

"No!" He says, narrowing his eyes. I've called it wrong again.

"I just want to have a good time, don't you?" I say, but his entire body has stiffened to my touch. He's trembling with rage.

"You keep me waiting in the storm for an hour, and now you want to buy drugs?" He asks. That is exactly what has happened, yes, but I'm in no mood to be submissive. He straightens his jacket, tucks the shirt into his trousers and puffs out his chest, again.

"I was joking. Forget it. Let's start again. Let's dance," I shout, taking his hand to lead him to the dance floor, but he flicks me away. People are watching, preying on us, hoping that sparks will fly.

"What's the matter with you?" he shouts.

"Me? What's the matter with you?" I shout back, and our faces are so close that I see my spittle land on his cheek. In that moment,

I feel wretched and unleashed. I don't want to apologise, I want to fight. I am able to touch it—the anger that I keep down—it's bubbling right there, all the time, just waiting to explode. It's the only thing I am really sure about.

"And you use your sister as the excuse?" He teases, his quiff wobbling as his head bobs up and down. Intense heat rises within me. I know that if I looked at my chest it would be bright red.

"Don't talk about my sister," I say. I want to add a threat, but I'm frightening myself. How dare he bring her into this. I just want a fucking break for one night. I just want to be free. I want to have fun. I could easily say something about his mother, but I never would. My body reacts and I feel my legs trembling, I feel weird and giddy. I'm embarrassed now, he's made me feel ashamed about wanting drugs when my sister has to take so much medicine from the doctor.

"You don't realise how lucky you are with *your* Mother and *your* sister, and all you want to do is get off your face all the time. I wish I had a family like yours. I wouldn't take them for granted," he says. In my head the world slows down, the room spins around me like I'm drunk. From inside, I watch my eyes blink. I raise my hand and strike fast with an open palm and slap Vincent across the face. (Not the hand with all the rings I might add, I'm not a total bitch).

Now he feels the sting too, like I do from his words. When eventually he turns to face me, there's a silky lustre in his eyes that I realise are tears. A hard slap can do that. Trust me, I know. But even so, I might have taken things too far. It's probably too late to say, "sorry," but it tumbles, mumbled from my lips.

"I'm going. Have a good night on your own." He says, and as he turns, his shoulder brushes me, and I inhale a mouthful of his scent—the leathery back seat of an old car, engine grease and aftershave—and then he's gone. I didn't want that to happen. I get a sad, fizzy sensation that I am going to cry.

I blink back the tears, and I scan the faces of the Goths and the Indie Kids, and I feel them staring. To them I am the crying girl abandoned by her boyfriend. How sad. I turn my back on the room and stare behind the bar. The bartender bends to capture my gaze. I blink up at her.

"That went well," she says. "I hope it wasn't the first date." She waits for my reaction and, when she sees me smile, she laughs at her own joke, and I do too.

"I think it's more like a last date," I reply. She has big, wide, kind eyes. She leans on the bar with her elbow and holds onto the beer pump with the other hand. She wears a tight, checked, buttoned-down shirt with the arms cut off and black braces. She makes me suddenly feel better.

"Are you going to go after him?" she asks, and I get a sudden prickly rush, an intense sensation that I know her. I shake my head.

"I've seen you somewhere before?" I say, as a man tries to get her attention. She makes an art form of ignoring him. She moves like a cat, controlling her eye contact, evading and locking on when it suits her.

"Hang on," she says, and serves the impatient man next to me. She places another beer on the bar for me.

"It's on me," she says.

"Thank you," I say, but she's on the move. "I don't even know your name?" I shout after her—cheesy! I watch her moving behind the bar. She knows I am watching her. She dances, pours drinks, smiles at people, and then she comes back to me.

"Tiffany," she says. *Tiffany.* I roll it around in my mind. Her name smells like sweets, and specifically with her accent, (which, incidentally, is American), like sugar candy.

"I'm Robyn Lockhart," I say, like I'm five years old and just learnt my own name.

"Lockhart, eh? Strong, gutsy," she says. "Have you got a lot of heart?"

Woah! What am I meant to say to that? I'm relieved that she moves away to serve someone else, giving me time to excitedly mull over the perfect retort. And no, I'm not gutsy, I have very little heart and, apart from my ability to open jars, I am not strong.

I can see her tattoo now that she is up close. It's a map. It curves around her body, waiting to be read. I wonder where it leads. What shall I say to her next?

"I love your tattoo?" I say, knowing it is weak and that she must hear that all the time from pervy men lined up on this bar, so I add, "Where does it begin?"

"People usually ask where it ends," she says.

"Well, I'm an optimist," I say, and she laughs.

"I've got an excellent memory," she says, "I would never forget meeting you."

I'm so embarrassed, I feel heat in my chest and cheeks. The corners of my lips turn up into a smile. I look away, I look down, and I open my handbag to rummage through it as a diversion.

My bag is more of a canvas military satchel than a woman's handbag. It contains black eyeliner, mascara and red lipstick. I carry a small, dark purple bottle of perfume with a crystal skull head. I've got a purse with thirty pounds and my ID, and my mother's business card. The corners are full of dust and what feel like pencil sharpenings (whose origins are a total mystery). I carry a notebook in which I write down where I've been, what it smelled like and what I ate. There's also a ridiculous sprung metal hand exerciser with a worn rubber grip that mother insists on making us use (five hundred a day). I give it a familiar squeeze, and then another out of habit.

The row with Vincent still burns. I should retreat home to nurse my broken heart, and I promise myself that I will, just as soon as I have spoken a little more to Tiffany. I drop my shoulders, and face the band. I nod to the beat of the music and try to act cool, but my eyes keep coming back to her. For me it's like the bar is now the stage and she is the show.

I stand there, drinking, continuing our conversation through stolen glances and smiles. I want to know everything about her. The bar begins to empty and so I lean over to speak to her, but as I do there is a loud bang, followed by silence and sudden submergence into pitch-black darkness.

My hand searches in the dark to find something solid to anchor me. It finds warm sticky comfort on the wood of the bar. Someone clicks a lighter and I'm drawn to a speck of an orange flame. Another person shouts: "What the hell was that?"

A girl screams, and the dim emergency lighting flickers faintly into life. I can smell harsh electrical burning. There is a plume of smoke over near the stage.

I feel his grip before I see his face. His fingers curled around my arm, his body too close. His breath on my neck is hot and decayed. I wretch from a fast, intense rush of adrenaline. It's the man in the long black coat. The man in the shadows that I thought was a drug dealer. The one who had raised an eyebrow at me. I feel his firm touch, his meaty hand around my elbow. He smells gamey, like freshly killed birds still warm in their feathers.

"Robyn," he whispers, "I'll take you home."

My hand finds its way protectively to my neck, and my ear. He talks as if he knows me. I've got to get away from him. The lights brightly flicker. I twist out of his grip and he holds up his hands and stands back. Though I want to, I can tell he's not the kind of man to slap. His mouth is small, and rodent like, a little tongue moistens his pink lips amidst his stubbly beard.

"Come on," he says. "You know me."

I'm shaking because I don't know him and, even though I might have seen him before, I don't know who he is.

Tiffany is talking to the manager on the stage. She shouts instructions because the microphones have stopped working. "There has been a power surge," she says. She keeps shouting "Don't panic," in a way that makes everyone panic.

"It's Montpelier Road, isn't it?" he whispers. "If there's no one at home, I could keep you company?" I get a sudden physical drop in my stomach. I'm frozen to the spot. I've had a lot to drink, but I'm suddenly stone cold sober.

The crowd seems to splinter into two groups—one half heading for the emergency exit and the other retreating back up the stairs towards the main entrance. Tiffany sprints across the dancefloor towards me. She sees the man, and I shake free of his grip and step away.

She looks from him to me, and me to him.

"It's the power. There's a black out," she says, taking my hand. She pulls me away, and I go willingly. I'm terrified, but her fingers are electric. I let my thumb stroke her wrist, as if by accident. I fix my gaze on her and her alone. "My boss has let me go early."

"Yes," I say, without hesitation and without being asked. "I'm coming with you."

We leave together, and I look back to watch the masses file out in thick, rubber soled boots and pink frilly skirts. The tattooed and the pierced. The man in the long black coat is nowhere to be seen. He has disappeared back into the shadows.

TWO

TIFFANY'S APARTMENT IS only five minutes away, but after thirty seconds, we are soaked to the skin. Branches fly across the road from nowhere. A ton of slates tip down off a roof and smash onto the street. She takes my hand, slipping her fingers between mine, and we start to run.

We race under the canopy of Tiffany's flat. The plaster has peeled back in patches, and the large brass knocker is pitted with an orange fungus. It gives off a pungent smell of wet clay. I can hear the shrill drumming of pebbles being thrown up onto the promenade by the waves. The weather makes her more agile, her eyes have dilated into big, black saucers, like a prowling feline awaiting the storm.

"Ignore my flatmates," Tiffany says, turning to look at me as we fall in and wrestle the door shut. I can still hear the wind screaming and seagulls squawking madly. The place smells like my grandmother's face powder, sweet and chalky and musty all at the same time. Old fashioned. There are five floors in this cavernous building. At the very top of the stairs, a man steps out of his room and onto the landing.

"You're home early, Tiffany," he says. "Who's your friend?" But on seeing me, his face drops. "Oh," he says, "it's her," as if he knows who I am. Astounding, but I assume he might have been inside the club, and saw me arguing with Vincent and even slap him. Awkward.

He leans in the doorway with an arm up on the frame and, as I get closer, I can see that he is wearing make-up and his head is in a mesh net as if he has just removed a wig. He sees me looking and so I smile at him, not knowing what else to do. As he turns his back on me I see his suspenders and fine legs through his Japanese silk dressing gown. There is a small tattoo of a black beetle at the base of his neck.

"That's Gloria," Tiffany says. "Ignore her."

Tiffany opens her door. It is big and ornate, but someone has bolted on a simpler modern lock with a smaller key. She flicks on an orange lamp giving the room a warm glow. We can hear the storm outside. There are rows of records in a bookcase, but my eyes are drawn to a map on the wall.

"Come in," she says. It is a world map but different. I'm not sure how. It seems to be drawn upside down or from a different perspective. The shape of the continents is recognisable, but the starting point is wrong, as if the centre is at the South Pole.

"I have to live by the sea," she says. "I get very claustrophobic when I can't see the sea."

I nod but everything she says makes me feel like I've heard it before. Her voice, those eyes, this room. You know when you go back somewhere that you used to go to as a child, and everything's familiar, but smaller and different. I have that feeling in Tiffany's room. As if I have been here before.

"Appropriate," she says, and I hear the music and a chill runs up my spine. There are goosebumps on my arms. It's the Eurythmics, *Here Comes The Rain Again*.

Tiffany moves around lighting candles with a box of long matches. As each catches, it seems to illuminate another map. All different sizes, some in ornate frames, and some without. Behind a big red chair I see a pile of rolled up documents, more maps, with frayed edges, and yellowed paper.

She disappears into the bathroom and comes back with towels for us both. Her bed is at the other end of the room. She's lit three candles next to it.

"Put this on, you're shivering," she says, handing me a black fleece hoodie. I turn away from her and take off my jacket and my T-shirt and even my bra! Naughty, I know! My skin is sticky and wet. I put the hoodie on. My heart races.

I bend forward and wrap my hair in the towel. Tiffany comes back wearing shorts and a red vest with Mavericks written sideways in swirly print. She opens a small patterned tin on the coffee table and pats the sofa next to her.

She lights up a joint and passes it to me, and after one burning pull my head reels and I am floating. It is like the top of my skull has come off. It is so sudden and so fast. I'm not a good pot smoker, but I want to appear cool. I hold the joint in front of my face to look at it, but I have to close one eye to focus.

"I don't usually smoke. Gloria left this here, but it's turning into that kind of night." She crosses her long legs, and rests them on the coffee table. Her skin is flawless and smooth.

"Who are the Mavericks?" I ask, forwardly pulling a thread from the frayed armhole and winding it around my index finger.

"It's for Portland, Oregon," Tiffany laughs. "Just like me." I give her the joint back and put my hands by my sides because they feel suddenly extremely heavy. Now that she is semi-clothed, I can see that the tattoo stretches all the way down her side, around her ribs.

The room feels hot and I feel myself sliding deeper into the sofa under Tiffany's spell. She is so American in her cut-off jock vest and tattoos. She pulls out a curl comb and runs it through her hair trying to flatten it with a side parting. Her black eye make-up is smeared around her eyes. I guess mine must be too.

"I'm jealous that you're just starting Uni. Your mind is going to be blown open wide."

"Yeah?" I ask, but my mind is already blown wide open. She licks her lips before she starts to speak.

"What's interesting about you, Robyn, is that you grew up here, and yet you still want to go to uni here. Don't you ever want to get away?" she asks.

"Leave here?" I ask naively, as if it had never occurred to me. But of course it has occurred to me, but I have never dared to imagine— not with my sister so poorly—that it could be a reality. "Why would you want to? Everything we need is here." I realise it's closed-minded to say that, and not even what I truly believe. It just seems to trot off my tongue like a preloaded response. A girl like me should be desperate to feel the metaphorical wind in her hair. But I don't. Or maybe I do. Oh, I don't know!

"You don't want to escape this town? Run away somewhere hot?" she says.

"I suppose I might," I say. "You came here didn't you?"

"I did. I wanted to. I want to see everything that's out there. I want to travel the world."

But I can't leave. I can't ever leave my sister. My mother controls my life. I don't say that to Tiffany. I don't want her to know that I'm far less in control than I appear.

"Sometimes, I think that I might never go anywhere," I blurt out. I never tell people this. It makes me sound powerless, but I know that something isn't right with my life. For reasons unknown to me, I trust Tiffany.

"If you think you're stuck here forever, you're not," she says, with smoke rising up over her face. "Robyn, nothing you thought was real, really is. We're living in a bubble."

I have the sudden urge to kiss her. I'm desperate to touch her. I want to imprint myself onto her. I'm all out of kilter, my body twisted, my arms too long and awkward. My breathing quickens. What on earth am I doing? I've got a boyfriend. In fact, I might still have a boyfriend if I telephoned and apologised. Still, I put my hand on her leg. She tenses her thigh under my fingertips. We both look at my hand. She puts the joint out in the ashtray.

Tiffany pulls up her red vest revealing the full extent of her tattoo and her breasts, round and firm. I hold my breath. I'm tumbling out of control. I can't breathe. She turns to the side and takes my hand, curls her fingers around mine and presses them against her side, against the outline of her tattoo.

"Do you remember? Do you remember anything? Do you even remember me?" she whispers. Her face has changed. She's earnest, eager, desperate even, and not to kiss me, it feels far more important, more urgent.

That which I can't remember is as real as what I can. Great black holes exist where my life should be. Sometimes a smell can trigger a new memory. I remember my first reaction on seeing her back in the club, thinking that I'd seen her before.

I run through the interlinking rooms of my mind, because I do remember something, but I don't know what. Or, perhaps I'm just high.

"I don't know if I've done this before?" I ask, confused, still running my hand over the outline of her ribs. What exactly does she want me to remember?

But it's when I smell her skin that I know for sure that I've been here before, and that I do know her. She smells of fresh soap and stone fruit—like peach or apricot. I know that sounds weird, but when I can't remember, I smell. It triggers me. I remember smells deeply, I don't forget them. I use them like a memory map. I'm breathing her in. My face is against her skin. That's when I kiss her, softly on her side and her goosebumps tickle my lips. She looks down at me and smiles.

"Hi," she says, as if seeing me for the first time.

The room lights up. For a light, bright millisecond Tiffany is illuminated. She is a beautiful painted girl. A work of art. But a crashing roar of thunder shatters our moment. It sounds like it is right on top of us and we both jump.

Tiffany runs to the window. It is the sort of sound that instigates flight. I get up and follow her. Her room is on a corner and she has French doors and a little balcony. She tries to open them, but the wind is so fierce it almost pulls them off their hinges.

We can't see a thing, not the road, not the beach, just some lights making their way through the mulch. The thunder roars on like metal against metal, ripping, screeching for twenty or thirty seconds at a time, and when it pauses for breath we hear only the comparative silence of the rain.

"What was that?" asks Tiffany. "It sounded like a building collapsing."

"I should go," I say, suddenly lucid, guiltily zipping up the hoodie. My sister is at home in the darkness of a power cut. What if she is worrying about me? What if Vincent is worrying about me? No one knows where I am. I feel the imagined trouble that I could be in. And the trouble I'd be in if I stay.

"It's awful out there," she says. "You shouldn't be out alone at this time."

"Tiffany, I can't," I say. "I have to go."

"But, it's dangerous," Tiffany says, though my mind is made up.

I keep the hoodie so that I'll have an excuse to bring it back. I gather up my things before I have a change of heart. I take the towel from my wet hair and hang it untidily on the back of the red chair. Tiffany snatches it and then wraps it harshly, folding her arms around it.

"Can I see you again?" Tiffany says, as she opens the door, annoyed.

"Yes, another time," I say, and I mean it.

"This *is* our time, Robyn," she says, and I linger, not sure how to say goodbye. Not understanding fully what has passed between us. I find it hard to move away, when suddenly Gloria, her flat mate, is right behind me on the landing.

"Did you hear that?" Gloria asks, much more agitated than either of us. "Brighton is falling apart," she says. I leave them talking in the hallway and slip away, Tiffany with no top on and Gloria in full make-up and suspenders.

THREE

TIFFANY IS RIGHT. It is dangerous out. But there is more to be frightened of than just the weather. It is dangerous inside too. I keep thinking about that grotesque, lecherous man in the club, telling me I knew him. I need to get into the safety of my own home.

Within moments I am soaked through again. I keep my hair out of my face with one hand, while the other holds my jacket across my chest. A large piece of board tears across the street, missing me by a couple of feet. People's bins have been blown over and household waste is strewn all down the road. Empty food packets flip across the pavement. A large, unruffled seagull flays ham from a plastic container.

As I turn up into Montpelier Road, the wind picks up and I have to struggle to keep my feet on the ground. A pub sign swings on its hinges, looking like it might snap off. I cross the street to get away from it. As I get higher, looking back out to sea, I think that I can see strange lights through the fog.

In spite of what I could have done with Tiffany, all I can think is, 'Bloody Vincent, leaving me like that.' It was easy to blame him for the entire episode, because if he stayed, then I wouldn't have started speaking to her. He can never be wrong. All of the things he said about my family while he is so easily hurt and then turns nasty.

I wonder what would have happened if I had stayed with Tiffany. My pulse picks up. I think about her side, her tattoo, and the smell of her skin.

The wind blows me into my house, and I struggle to get the door closed. I've been trying not to think about scary things but I'm jumpy, and anxious. My eyes search out every shadow, every dark place, for where that man from the club might be waiting for me.

Ours is the prettiest house on the prettiest street; Montpelier Road, with a fine, bowed window and balcony. There's a steep set of narrow stairs which run down to a second entrance to the kitchen, and I look there, always wary of someone lurking.

I open the front door. There's a loud silence. I hear the hum of dormant electricity fizzing, and the wind whispering through the letterbox, trying to get in. The house smells of the turmeric and chilli that I cooked for dinner. There's a sub-note of damp which always persists and, though not to everyone's taste, makes me feel at home.

I flick on the small hall light. It's late, so I don't want to shout but I need to check on my family. It's not enough to slope into bed without seeing them.

I descend stairs to the kitchen in darkness and open the fridge. It shines its light on me as I drink milk from the carton, spilling it onto my chin, and then I pick up a lump of cheese. It's the only thing I can find that I can put straight into my mouth. I sprint silently up the stairs, two at a time, it's a tall, slim house with four floors. My feet are light like a boxer's, I am well practised in navigating these stairs. I check my sister's bedroom. She is not there. My heart is in my mouth as I run into my mother's room and switch on the light. She's not there either. The bed is cold. The blankets are undisturbed.

I look in the bathroom. Nothing. I even drop to the floor to look underneath my own bed, mostly for ghouls and men who want to get me. I'm spooked. There's no one here except for me.

Downstairs in the lounge, next to the telephone, is a note in my mother's handwriting.

Darling Robyn,

Firstly, please don't worry, but Alice has had a turn and they are keeping her in to be sure. They are going to monitor her overnight. I'm sure it's just the usual and she'll be back home as soon as possible. Please don't worry. I'll call you first thing in the morning. Go to sleep and stay out of the storm!

Love you.

Mum x

P.S. We're in St Thomas's hospital

What the hell? It happens all the time. My whole life I am a bystander to my sister's sickness. I never really get used to it. Each time I get a sense of impending doom and the dread of it never being over. I feel like I live with disaster looming. But I am the lucky sister. I'm the healthy one and Alice is getting worse.

No one knows Alice like me. That morning, we'd watched TV together as usual. Her on the right side of the couch, under a light blanket with her feet propped up on me. I tickle her toes, not too much as she can't stand it, more a gentle massage. Her toes get pretty cold—a circulation issue or just never ending winter in our damp house near the sea.

We watch, but we talk non-stop throughout. That's what people don't realise about Alice. She acts shy with other people, but when she's with me she's verbose. Never stops. She's funny too. And gross. She looks like a mermaid and farts like a walrus.

We watched the original Superman movie with Christopher Reeves. Alice loves the bit where Superman goes to the Arctic to find his father and he throws a shard of ice into the snow and then an ice palace forms and he finds out who he really is. I think she liked it because she could remember it from before, from when she could see it properly. I didn't have to describe every scene. She remembered it.

Mother took her to the hospital. I would have gone. I should have gone. I wanted to take her but Mother told me to go out and have a good time with Vincent. I dawdled in the shower. I thought of cancelling. Eventually, I had to run out of the house because it was too late to cancel Vincent.

It might seem petty now, after the fight we had but in all honesty, some time ago, I had planned to split up with Vincent. I listed all the reasons why; he is irritable and has no patience; he is obsessively compulsive about his appearance; and he has failed every exam he has taken. But when I saw him with my sister, I changed my mind.

She was having an episode where she had lost all strength in her limbs. She couldn't walk. He picked her up and carried her into the playground where he put her on a swing. It was gently spitting rain, it had that beautiful, grassy, hard to grasp smell of fresh rain, and everyone had cleared out of the park. He listened to her. He gave her time.

That night I had sex with Vincent for the first time. It was sort of like a thank you. Since then, Alice has gotten well and then gotten sick all over again. We dare not to think about the future, hers or mine. We hang around together every day when I'm not working in the cafe. I deferred my university place two years in a row to be with her.

But I should never have gone out with Vincent tonight. I should never have left Alice. I should be with her now. I'm so selfish. I screw up the note and throw it at the wall. I should go to her.

I go upstairs again, and strip off my wet clothes and take a hot shower. I'm jumpy and so I leave the shower door open and water pools onto the floor. I decide that I won't say anything to Vincent about Tiffany. I'll apologise and try to make things up. It would upset Alice if Vincent suddenly wasn't on the scene anymore. Going home with Tiffany was a mistake, albeit a glorious mistake that I would make again tomorrow.

I put on pyjamas and take a blanket to the sofa next to the telephone. I'm strung out. I'm hearing noises, wooden beams contract and make me jump. The wind outside is playing percussion. I'm going to wait for my mother to ring. My sister's not even in Brighton anymore. St Thomas's is in London.

I write in my notebook. I write my life down to remember and to tell my sister. The burning plastic of the Astoria, Vincent's jacket, the old lady face powder, and wet clay of Tiffany's building. Tiffany's freshly soaped skin (I'll keep that one just for me).

I must have slept.

I jerk awake for the first time and try to focus on the digital clock, flashing red. 2:33 a.m. The back of my head is soaked with sweat, and my hair is slick to my neck. I was in the middle of a dream. I was with Tiffany on the pier. She had different coloured hair. Then it cut to a hand—a balled fist against a pane of glass. My mother is there and she says;

"This is where we'll work."

FOUR

I AM WOKEN by the telephone ringing. It smells so fresh. The storm must be over. I am still half asleep, still dreaming, so I say, "Mum?"' when I answer the phone. But it's not Mother.

"It's me, Vincent." There are gulls in the background and traffic. He's in a phonebox somewhere near the seafront.

"Oh," I say, disappointed.

"Did you get home safely?" he asks. It's too early to argue, and I'm far too sleepy to issue a witty put-down. I'm usually never too tired for a fight, but I feel guilty and I want to make up, just like he does. This is how we work. We'll never speak of the fight again.

"What time is it?" I ask.

"Almost six," he says.

"Are you kidding me? You're phoning at six o' clock in the morning?"

"Listen, you've got to see this. It's incredible."

IT IS ONLY just light. There's a familiar cushion of protective grey clouds lining the sky. Clearing over the sea, the sky pops in blue. It is pure cold with an unexpected bite. It takes ten minutes to walk to the seafront. I am wearing a red woollen jumper beneath a see through (yes, see through as in transparent) plastic waterproof coat of Mum's. The smell is clear rich, oxygen surprisingly underlined by sweet metallic rust.

Vincent runs up Little Preston Street to meet me, waving and giddy. His hair is flyaway and his shirt untucked. I've never seen him like this. He takes my hand, kisses it and makes me run with him. It's pretty cute.

"That's nice," I say, meaning the hand-holding and general positive demeanour. I want to ask if he's still drunk, but I daren't broach the subject of intoxication.

"I was wrong to leave you last night," he says, and that suits me because I'm happy to forget all about it. We are running close to Tiffany's flat and I start to prickle with nerves. I don't want her to see me in this coat of Mother's.

"Look," Vincent shouts. Right there in the middle of the beach, between the two piers, sits a ship.

It's as tall as a church steeple and sharp to a point, and has made a solid wave of stones either side of its bow. We weave between the cars, open mouthed, making our way towards it. Vincent and I grip each other's hands as we get up to the green railings of the sea front.

The ship is copper-coloured, and dusty with rust. I can taste it in my mouth. It's in the air, we are breathing it in. It sits tilted over to the right and I can't understand how it didn't collide with the West pier. People must be able to see it from several streets behind.

The tide has sucked back out, leaving the vessel's rotten barnacles exposed. The hull is full of dents and what paint is left on the starboard side flails off in pieces. A ripped flag in faded red and green has wilted at the stern.

This was the noise that disturbed Tiffany and me last night.

I look up behind me to where Tiffany is now standing on her balcony, drinking tea from a cup. She watches me and salutes me like a soldier. I squeeze Vincent's hand and stare at his face to make sure that he hasn't seen.

"It's a ship, Robyn. It's a ship, right here in the city," says Vincent, breathless. I've never heard him talk so much.

The police are already here. They point and shout, pushing people back. They have erected a cordon of blue and white tape. A policeman bangs on the bonnets of cars, getting people to drive away. A TV news van has arrived and cameras pan around, recording the scene.

The kids have got through, their faces rubbed red with cold. Where the ship's metal bow has embedded in the stones, they write their names on the hull with lumps of white Brighton chalk.

Out at sea, a lifeboat balances on top of the waves, impotent. Through a tiny window up inside the ship, I see a shadow. I shiver. It is the vague outline of a tall, thin body, seen through just a slip of glass. Maybe nothing. Large seagulls circle above, perhaps it was just the shadow of a bird.

Sirens start up all over the city and get closer, from east and west more people arrive. The police are stopping anyone behind us. A man dressed as Elvis Presley stands agog in the middle of the road with a can of beer in his hand.

"Move it," says a policeman. Vincent slips his arms around me, protective.

"Where's it come from?" asks Vincent.

"Safety measures in place now please, ladies and gentlemen. Back to the other side of the road." They start to funnel us back and away from the front. We quickly become gridlocked, us and the kids and Elvis. We shuffle back in turn, necks bent, eyes fixed on the ship.

A convoy of green army trucks splits the crowds open like an axe through timber. When they stop, they come alive with soldiers carrying machine guns spilling out from behind the tarpaulin at the rear.

"What the fuck is happening?" Vincent says, his mood shifting. My heartbeat picks up. We all start moving away faster, and I notice that the way we are being marshalled is taking us straight past Tiffany's building. Right on schedule, the door opens and there she is.

"Robyn!" she calls, and I instinctively put up my hand. "Come inside!"

I move towards her off the path, out of the melee and into her hallway. I drag Vincent with me, ignoring his protestations.

"This is my boyfriend, Vincent," I say quickly, and they shake hands as if this is a business meeting. If he recognises her from the Club last night, then he doesn't say.

"Come up," says Tiffany, for the second time in twelve hours, except this time there are four of us. Vincent and me, Tiffany and a trembling, verbose Gloria. I worry that Gloria will say something. I hold her back in the corridor.

"You won't say I was here last night, will you?" I ask.

"I never do my love," Gloria replies, and marches up the stairs.

In Tiffany's room, I notice my best bra hanging on the back of the chair. I leave it there, I don't even acknowledge it. Tiffany opens the balcony doors and there we stand, staring, huddling in the small opening of the corner balcony, all half a metre of it, thirty feet above the rust scabbed railings. Secretly, Tiffany reaches over and squeezes my hand.

A large articulated lorry arrives. It is made of the strangest metal that I have ever seen. As it comes closer, it looks as if the metal has been melted and then scooped back into place, like a licked ice-cream.

"We'll never leave this town," Gloria says, shaking her head.

Out of the metal truck men in white uniforms walk stealthily across to the boat. They put up flags along the promenade with three interlocking red rings which read 'Biohazard'.

"Oh, my," says Gloria. "Earth, sea and sky." There is someone on the deck of the ship. More than one. Strange looking figures, tall and dark, but people, clear as day, waving at us. They are thin, emaciated even. Suddenly my stomach drops. Something's wrong.

Gloria senses my panic. She puts her hands up to my neck and holds my head to face her. I can see the colouring of her irises, green feathered with hazelnut brown like honeycomb.

"Of all the artificial memories that you are brainwashed with, please remember that this is real. Write it in your notebook," Gloria tells me. I hear the roaring drone of an aeroplane's engines approaching.

"Not now, Gloria," Tiffany says.

I'm confused.

What does Gloria mean?

The approaching aeroplane gets louder and louder.

I can't hear myself think.

"You'll never stop us!" Gloria screams out of the balcony to the soldiers and white suits below.

The plane flies overhead. It is way too low. I can see the screws, almost read the instructions written on the undercarriage. The noise is deafening. It trails thick fumes. They blanket us. It is as if, suddenly, the fog from last night has returned, more toxic than before.

As we all fall to the floor, all I can think is; remember this is real. I grip Vincent's hand.

"Remember this is real. Remember this is real," I tell him, but lying on the floor of the apartment coughing up our guts, we can see nothing at all.

FIVE

TIFFANY AND I sit in my kitchen. Vincent is upstairs, slumped—as if lobotomised—in my mother's leather reclining chair. He has fallen silent. His skin is blotchy and red from the constant rubbing of his own hands against his face. His shirt is ripped and his hair dishevelled.

The white-suited army emptied all the buildings along the seafront. The fog became so instantly dense that we couldn't see the beach anymore. We were told to leave, but Gloria refused angrily and hid inside Tiffany's large, antique French wardrobe.

Vincent coughed so badly that we took him to the first aid tent on Western Road. We waited while he spent thirty minutes on a nebuliser.

Tiffany's eyes wander around my kitchen shelves looking at pictures, studying objects and measuring me, I guess. She lingers on Alice's walking sticks.

"What exactly is wrong with your sister?" She asks, but I can't recall ever telling her about my sister. She can see us in the pictures. I shrug my shoulders.

"Lots of things," I say. I don't tell her that there are constant scans, diagnosis and re-diagnosis, and that there are episodes of exhaustion and paralysis. But actually what it is—the definitive reason—has never been told to me and I've although I have asked, mother has always evaded answering.

I run the cold tap and open my mouth under the faucet to drink, washing my face as I do so.

"There's a glass right there," says Tiffany pointing. I fill the glass.

"Why did Gloria hide?" I ask, because she's not just Tiffany's flatmate. She feels like someone important. My limbs still tremble with adrenaline. I'm wired.

"But your sister's in hospital, right? She must be pretty sick," Tiffany says, opening the refrigerator. She can't possibly be hungry with this going on, but she tells me she's starving. She holds up a babyish cheese triangle in a foil wrapper. "I love these. Do you still love these?"

"She's always been ill, a genetic disorder, or something,"

"But you're okay?"

"Yes," I say. "I'm the healthy one."

"Gloria's an artist," she says, with her mouth full.

"An artist? Like a painter?" I ask.

"No, more of an artiste. In clubs, on the stage, jokes and singing, mostly," says Tiffany. I wipe my mouth, there's water trickling down my chin. "But she's political too. I guess you'd call her an activist."

"For what?" I ask.

"For freedom," she says, deadpan.

"She told me to remember what is real. She was really determined. Is she a psychic, or a hypnotist?" I ask. She unwraps another cheese triangle (that's the whole packet) and puts it in her mouth. Tiffany turns on the radio and the presenter, Sarah Phoenix makes no reference to the ship, nor the gas. Instead, they play a pop quiz. Tiffany bends over and rests her ear close to the speaker to listen.

"She can get inside your head, that's for sure." Tiffany takes a pen from the kitchen worktop and writes a number on her hand.

My throat is sore and I can't stop sneezing. There is plenty of medicine in the cupboard. We both take Oxycodone and Tiffany coughs so hard she doubles over. I give her a bottle of cough syrup, that she clutches swigging from it like it was whisky. She takes another strip of Oxycodone, thirty tablets in a foil packet, and puts them in her pocket 'for later'.

Tiffany picks up a photograph of my mother, and with a downturned mouth, puts it back where it was. She runs her hand over the front of a tatty old cupboard.

"What's in here?" Tiffany asks, tugging at a small lock on the cupboard. It's a mechanical code lock, like you'd have on a bicycle.

"Tiffany, have we met before?" I ask.

"You and I?"

I think I know these people. I think I know Tiffany. I've known it all along. I just have to figure out how.

There's a shadow from the road upstairs and a knock at the front door. Tiffany puts her fingers up to her lips and slides backwards to hide behind the locked cupboard.

When I look through the window I see a small, weasel-like man up at the main front door. It's David Sykes, my mother's personal assistant, or trainee or whatever you call a forty-year-old male secretary in the Council. His eyes swivel down at me. He knows I'm here.

I go up, Vincent still stares blankly at the TV, anxiously waiting for the story, but the news says nothing except for a traffic report and a piece about last night's storm. Not even a mention of the ship. I open the door. I can't help but look over David Sykes's shoulder and further out into the street. It is ominously quiet.

"Hello, Robyn," he says, as he looks at my breasts. I adjust my stance and put a hand over my chest and he straightens up and coughs. I sneeze hard in return at him. I don't cover my mouth or apologise.

"She's not here," I say.

"Is your phone off the hook?" he asks. "It's only your mother's been trying to call you and she can't seem to get through. She called me instead and asked me to come around and check on you." I look through the gap in the door, to the sideboard next to Vincent and see that the telephone is indeed 'off the hook'.

"Oh!" I say, Vincent has been playing with it, picking it up and putting down indecisively. "It is. Thank you. I'll put it back on."

"My pleasure, Robyn. My absolute pleasure," he says.

"Thanks," I say, trying to close the door.

"Do you want to invite me in?" he asks.

"I'm in the middle of something," I say. I'm desperate to talk more to Tiffany. She knows what this is all about. It's as if we are just on the cusp of something important.

"Your Mother called me, and I was at home doing some preparation for a meeting on Monday and I thought, no problem, I'll pop around and make sure that Robyn is okay."

"Well, I'm fine, thank you, David."

"Are you on your own?" he asks, trying to look around the door and then slipping off the path into a flower pot while he cranes his neck to look through the front bay window.

"No, my boyfriend's here," I say, and I notice David's eyes flicker and I know what he is thinking. I find it easier to fend men off with the threat of another man.

"Boyfriend," he repeats, and it takes a moment before he regains full control, so I know that in his mind he is imagining me with a boy. He licks his lips. He's looking over my shoulder. I don't think he believes me. I'm desperate to get back to Tiffany.

"Bye, then," I say.

"I really do think it would be better if I came in," he says, and he puts his thin outstretched arm on the wood of the door to prevent me from closing it. His fingers spread like a spider's legs. I shiver.

"It's not a good time," I say, and close the door.

Downstairs, Tiffany plays on my sister's walking sticks, as able-bodied people often do.

"I should leave you to get back to your boyfriend," she says, I think she's overheard me upstairs exaggerating.

"But, we've got stuff to talk about," I say. It's the reverse of the night before with me begging her to stay. "I know there's something going on—with me."

"You could start by opening that cupboard," she says, flicking the lock. But I don't know the code. "You think you don't know the code, but you do." She stands back and gestures for me to take the lock from her. I put up my hand and take it. I'm up so close to her that I can see her world map tattoos forging their way up her neck.

"You've got to tell me what Gloria meant," I said.

"Put in the number," she says.

"I don't know the number,"

"Put in the number."

"This is stupid," I say, grinding the mini-wheels in the lock around to my birthday, ten-thirty (1-0-3-0).

"You would never believe me," she says, shaking her head. "This is something that you have to find out for yourself."

"Tell me," I say, and my hand goes up gently around her neck. South America is pulsating. My fingers fit snug around her muscles. The lock opens and slips off the door, we step back as the cupboard doors open. Tiffany holds them closed with her hands.

"Are you sure you want to know?" she asks.

"Yes," I say, and she lets the doors fall slowly open. I hold her hand. I don't know what's inside. It's a small cupboard. It's dark in there. I don't know what I am expecting. As my eyes adjust to the darkness, I can see that there are piles and piles of little books. They are all random shapes and sizes. Some look new, hardly used, others are crinkled and well-thumbed. They are notebooks, not reading books.

"They're yours," Tiffany says.

"Mine?"

"Your life, all written here, by your own hand," she says. But I don't remember, or perhaps I do remember that one with the ripped brown cover, its spine swollen. I don't want to touch them in case they bite.

"Did I put them here?"

"No, your mother did."

"Why?" I ask, but there's a noise upstairs. Vincent is on the telephone. He stands up and stumbles around. Tiffany heads for the door and the narrow stairs back to the street. She's trying to leave. Not now. I need her. I follow her grabbing arm.

"It's all in there," Tiffany says. "You write it down to remind yourself."

"But why can't I remember?" I ask. Tiffany unlocks the bolts of the door. "Please tell me."

"Right now, today, is your sister in a hospital in London?" she asks, slowly removing my hand from her arm.

"Yes," I say, cautiously, I'm anxious about what this would have to do with my sister.

"Have you been to London before?"

"Yes, of course I have," I say. Our eyes are only inches apart. I am incensed by the stupidity of the question. Suddenly, I don't feel in control of my emotions, there's that angry unpredictable person inside of me again.

"I remember the first time I went to London," Tiffany says. "When I was seven, I went on a school trip to the Natural History museum. We went on a white coach. The coach had an apple on the side. A red apple with a green leaf."

I remember that coach.

I remember it clear white with the apple on the side. What is she doing? Was she there too?

"It was freezing," she continues. "And while we were inside the museum, there was a sudden cold-snap, and it started snowing, and when we went outside we had a snowball fight on the grass. The entire class, and the teachers too."

No, this isn't right. She's talking about my school trip.

This happened to me.

"You mean my school trip," I say. "That happened to me. I must have told you. You must have read it in these notebooks."

"No, it's mine," she says. "I was seven years old. It was amazing snow, the best snow I've ever seen." But I remember that snow, so light and fluffy, evaporating on my tongue. What is she doing? Telling my story like it's hers?

"That happened to me. That's mine," I say.

"I had a chequered scarf," she says. "A hat too, a matching set."

"No, I did," I shout. "What are you trying to do?"

31

"In red and black," she says, but it's my memory of the sometimes scratchy wool that became old and thin and slick from use.

"This is my fucking story," I say, furious, shaking with rage.

"No," she says, and she touches my neck, and she runs the knuckles of her fingers against my clavicle and puts her fingers to my lips. I shiver. "It's mine too. You need to see for yourself."

Vincent interrupts us shouting down the stairs, rambling incoherently about the ship being moved to Shoreham—how the tide has come in and the army and the coast guard have boarded the ship. How it is being moved under guard to be kept in a secure dock.

"The ship's in Shoreham Docks," Vincent shouts.

"Then we're going to Shoreham Docks," I shout back.

"You should go to London," whispers Tiffany. "What you need to know can't be told to you. And it's not on the ship. Which hospital is your sister in?" My head spins, beginning to sear with pain.

"St Thomas's," I say, realising that I'm trying to grab hold of her again.

"Don't stop," she says. "Don't ever give up. Find your sister and you'll learn the truth." Then she kisses me, the most intense goodbye kiss, as if we may never see each other again, and she's gone.

Maybe it's not me who is the healthy sister after all. I'm angry, but sure that something has happened to me. Something unspeakable, something sticky and hot. Something that hurts me—a virus or an accident? Something is blocking me, stopping me from remembering my life.

But I am going to remember everything. I will.

SIX

HOURS LATER, I'M at Shoreham Docks with Vincent. I am insistent, entranced with this rust-bucket ghost ship and I'm about to make us do something crazy. I should be sweating or trembling with nerves, but all I can think about getting it over and done with, and getting back to my notebooks.

It's dark and freezing cold. The far side of the dock juts out into the sea, creating a deep, safe channel for ships to moor. On top of this plateau, the Council has built a huge hanger. It has a tall chimney with a red light on the top that you can see from miles around.

Ben is Vincent's friend, sporting the badge of the Shoreham Docks security detail glittering on his ample shoulder. He wears black utility shorts adorned with baggy pockets and badges. I have never seen him wear long trousers, even in our unrelenting winter. His legs are covered in small, bright-coloured tattoos that pop-out from amongst his hair. There seems to be no design or uniting theme: a red octopus; a mandala; and a black beetle. He smells like a gymnasium.

Vincent smokes a roll-up—not his usual choice—and he flicks it, only half-smoked, into the sea and looks at his watch. It is midnight. His incessant watch checking, twisting his arm back and forth, lowering his head, and pulling back his sleeve is already shredding my nerves.

Before we left, I had only moments to rifle through my notebooks. I know they're mine, not only because they're written in my hand, but I recognise a familiar path that I know I've trodden before. Not to sound crass, but very much in the way that you know your own bad smells.

I could not find the facts that I am looking for. I flicked through two notebooks and I couldn't see any real clues—just lists of the foods I'd eaten and detailed conversations with Jan, my boss at the café.

Ben's role is to oversee the ship while the Council's inspectors—or the army, police or whoever the fuck gassed us this morning—change rotation at midnight. Ben will be alone patrolling the hanger for only half an hour at the maximum, possibly even less, just enough time for Vincent and I to satisfy *my* curiosity.

Ben has instructed us to shut up and wait. Vincent lifts his arm to check the time once more. I grab his hand and push my fingers between his.

"It's thirty seconds since you looked the last time," I say. He lifts my hand to his stubbly mouth and kisses it.

"I'm nervous," he says. He's a drip at times. He better not fuck this up. He's worryingly just as confused as I am about the ship, and about Gloria.

"Do you remember the first time you went to London?" I whisper.

"Yep," he says.

"How old were you?" I ask.

"Dunno," he quips, and I'm massively relieved, and my chest visually drops. I feel sheer relief, but then he shifts on his feet, puckers up his mouth acting whimsical. "Actually, I was seven. I went to the Natural History Museum with the school." I try to speak, but I stutter. I put my hand up to his lips. My skin suddenly tingles with perspiration. I don't want to hear anymore.

The hangar door opens with a tinny creak. It swings inward into the interior blackness of the vast space—a tiny mouse-hole in a monolith. Somewhere inside, a small drip echoes and amplifies. Ben's face appears in the darkness. I almost scream. Vincent puts his hand over my mouth.

"You've got to be kidding," I say.

"You've got to be silent," Ben whispers. "Completely fucking one-hundred-per-cent silent. I could lose my job."

The floor is an immense concrete slab given traction by a smattering of crystallised salt that crunches delightfully under foot. A channel of sea-water runs through the centre of the hanger. When I first see the ship, she is in shadow. Her gingery pallor now faded brown through lack of light. She really is a rust bucket, gnarled and lived-in, but looking small and vulnerable inside this huge building. The torn flag is colourless in this dark light, but I know it is nothing I have ever seen before. On the dockside, the authorities have erected a table with torches lined up in rows and boxes of kit, sprays and gauze.

"They've already swept it for forensics," says Ben. "Or whatever it is they look for." Vincent picks up a torch and tests its weight in his hand. He jigs from foot to foot and smooths down the front of his shirt. Every wrinkle in his clothes makes him feel more exposed.

"Where's it from?" I ask. Ben looks at me and his eyes narrow. He stares at me like I am being silly, like I should already know and then he nods his head in the direction of the sea.

"Your guess is as good as mine," he says, as he takes my hand and leads me to a wide plank serving as a gangway leading across into the boat. I can smell her, rich like menstrual blood.

"Well, you must know. Someone must know. It can't just appear out of nowhere," I say.

"I just guard the docks," says Ben, handing me a small torch. "Angle it down at the ground, like this. Don't go flashing it around for all to see. Okay?" I nod.

Amidst all this, and with my heart racing, I notice something quite tiny and inconsequential. There, sat on the table-top, is an intriguing cube of metal. I'm drawn to it. It's bigger than a dice in size, but small enough to hide entirely within the fist of a hand. It sits peculiarly on a table of familiar things, looking extremely out of place.

It stands out boldly but then disappears.

"Come," says Ben, and I look again. It's rather as if I thought I saw a cube of metal on the table. It drew my eye certainly, but when

I look again it has gone. I am like a magpie drawn to the shiny object, only to realise that it is a mirage, just the reflection of the sun.

I cross the plank onto the ship. The ship gently sways. Ben is close behind me. I glance back toward the table and, sure enough, for only a second the cube is there and when I look again, it has gone.

"We haven't got much time," Ben says. "If something goes wrong, or if you're caught, then you don't me. Okay? You say that you came in here on your own. Understood?"

"Yes," I say.

"We'll be quick," says Vincent. "In and out." He doesn't know what we're searching for.

"Hurry." Ben says, waiting at the entry hatch leading into the ship. The deck is sparse. "They've moved a lot of stuff already." I can see the bubbles of rust wrestling paint from metal. I want to ask about the cube, whether it came from the boat or somewhere else.

Vincent stalks straight through the hatch. It's my turn to go inside. The hole looms like a horrific gateway into the unknown. Vincent's silhouette stretches then flickers as he disappears down the corridor further inside the ship.

"Wait," Ben whispers after him, and then he too is gone, following Vincent. I hear their feet on the stairs, but I am left all alone. I go to the hatch. I have goosebumps all over my body.

For the second time in only twenty-four hours I find myself cursing. "Fucking Vincent! Leaving me on my own." I venture in, one foot at a time. The corridor is a dark musty green. To my surprise I can smell food. The sort of long-lingered aroma of abandoned kitchens—bland steamed rice and putrid oil. There is something aromatic too, a spice maybe? Perhaps it's ginger?

The control bridge, I guess you'd call it, which is not impressive in size or design, is falling apart. A rectangular windowed room where the wheel is housed, and where I suppose the Captain must have stood. It is old and decrepit, yes, but someone has been through with a crowbar, and has pulled out the insides of the instruments and left wires hanging like veins, cupboards ripped slack like open wounds.

I turn and back away into the corridor. There are small black flies dancing above my head. The light blinks off and on, flickering like a horror film climax.

I can't wait alone. I have to go down the stairs after Vincent and Ben. I grip the handrail, and duck my head. It is more of a ladder than a staircase. The heat is stifling below decks. My wrist sweeps against a pipe and it burns me sharply. I pull away. The ship is alive, wanting to expel intruders.

I pass a cabin. A sleeping bag is unravelled across the floor. The cabin is dilapidated and blemished by years of sticky dirt piling up in its corners. A green and red piece of cotton material is strung up across the middle, perhaps to partition the room.

It is a hollow indistinct sound at first, but I am sure that I can hear music. I let go of the fabric. I follow the sound. I go back out into the corridor, and it grows more audible. I pass three more cabin doors. There is no trace of Ben and Vincent. The dim, green light flickers. I can see the shadow of my outstretched hand feeling its way along the wall.

The rooms are empty, stripped bare of any artefacts, anything personal or distinguishable is gone. In two of the rooms, the thin mattresses from the bed have been ripped open and lay across the floor with their stuffing spewing out.

I sneeze. The music stops. I am lost, with no signal to tell me where I should be looking. I should call out under my breath for the boys, but I don't want to make a noise. I need to find the source of the music.

It sounds like Brighton pier music. It's up-tempo, and sprightly but with more drums. The music starts up again and I can tell that it is actually coming from inside the wall itself. I press my ear against the wall. It is sticky.

I run my fingers across it. It is panelled in a rough tongue and groove. I bend down and square my fingers around a rectangular panel and I realise that it opens. The music is louder.

I search for a gap to lever the panel open. I can't do it with my fingers alone. If only I had something useful about me to open it but I have nothing. I need to tool up. I need to start carrying.

I glance around, compelled to see what is inside. On the wall, just a few metres along the corridor, an emergency glass cupboard is smashed and hanging open. The contents remain; a small axe. It's perfectly kept inside its cage. With both hands, I grab it and then put my boot up and pull. The whole slim axe comes off in my hands.

I get up and wedge the axe into a small gap and pull it back and straight away it pops open. My heart throbs in my mouth. I pant like I've run a marathon, and wipe a bead of sweat away from my eyebrow.

The opening to the hatch is no bigger than a TV screen. It is a cupboard. I climb inside. They must have missed it when they swept the ship. They could not have heard the music. They must have thought that it was nothing.

I turn on my torch. I am careful. It is a small space with a sloped ceiling that must be the underside of another set of stairs. I sit on soft material and when I lift it up and hold it in front of me, I put the torch in my mouth and handle it with both hands. It is a little girl's coat.

The coat is soft and red and padded, and would fit someone at infant school. Scrawled in handwriting on the label is 'Mika'. I turn the name over in my mouth.

The walls are adorned with pictures drawn only in three colours—red, blue and green. She has drawn the things that we all want; a house; a sister; a pet. The remnants of the crayons are underneath me, worn down to the stub.

There are a series of photographs scattered against the wall, some have fallen face down, others still upright. Pictured are three little girls. I wonder if this is Mika, the artist. The girl in the picture looks happy: cuddling, smiling, laughing.

The music is coming from a little doll. Half-human, half-bunny, the plastic toy has a sweet face and rabbit's ears. She has left it behind. It stares at me blankly, its mouth pert, while its warped song slows and speeds up at random. Its batteries are fading like the pigment in its round droopy eyes, old and worn out. It's a second hand toy, or perhaps third or fourth hand.

There is a bang on the wall and scuffling in the corridor. I pin myself back into the corner, petrified, clutching the doll as Mika might have once done.

Ben's face appears. He puts his index finger on his lips. It is tattooed with a black beetle. I have never noticed it before. It's like Gloria's.

"We need to go," he says. "Now." He drags me out of the cupboard, with his hands grabbing me under my armpits. I can't get my feet out and I fall onto the sticky floor on my hip. He still doesn't let me go. It hurts. He pulls me up and marches me up the stairs.

I lose the doll. I want it so much. I want to give it back to Mika wherever she is. I want the photograph of her smiling with her sisters. I want that picture of her happiness so that I can keep it with me forever. I love her smile. Where is she now? What has happened to her?

"Wait! Hang on," I say.

But Ben is through the hatch, with me, and back out onto the deck. He gestures to Vincent with his fingers.

"They've gone back out, over there," Vincent points in the opposite direction from the tiny hanger entrance that we entered through.

They're here.

"We've got to go now, mate. Move, go, go," says Ben, pushing me by the shoulders in front of him. Get your hands off me, Ben!

We cross the deck in three steps. Ben's stride is longer than mine, and my feet hardly touch the ground. I feel small being moved around like this. This is fear—not mine, but Ben's. He is at risk, and it feels like he isn't just at risk of being in trouble at work. Sweat pours off him. He is wet to the touch. We go over the plank, over the dark water, and I see the cube again.

The metal cube sits visible on the table.

It calls to me.

Forget the doll.

It's this Cube I really want.

I want to have something from here, from this ship, from this hangar. I want to take something to remind me. I don't want to be cheated out of it.

I look for the Cube, and it's gone. Ben pushes me past the table and I glimpse it out of the corner of my eye. I reach for it, patting the air, then landing on it. It is in my hand. I can feel it.

Vincent is ahead. He gestures for me to follow, repeatedly turning to call me with his hand. Ben lets go of me. I grasp the Cube between my finger and thumb. I feel it sizzle, either ice cold or scorching hot. It's an intense sensation like I've banged my fingers and they are throbbing.

We are fast-walking, moving back to the exit. Ben is gone. He is going to intercept whoever interrupted us and create a diversion. I take the cube out for one second. I don't look directly at it. I look ahead at Vincent and see it in my peripheral vision.

There is a light coming from the cube, a slick translucent beam that is difficult to see. Before I can react, it seems to release a thin red light straight into my eye. It happens so fast. I shut my eyes tight but it's too late.

One minute I am with Vincent in the blackened hanger, and the next, I am…

I am lying in bed.

There is a humming noise, a type of electronic purr. It's the blinds. The blinds are retracting into the ceiling. I am in a fancy bedroom. The sheets are so soft that I wonder if they are real silk, because I have never slept in sheets like this before. The room flushes with light. I can hear the ocean. I can hear the birds and sense the heat. I can't smell anything.

A woman lies with her back to me. I put my hand out to touch her.

But it isn't my hand.

It is a man's hand.

The fingers are stout, and my new thumbs are like lollipops. There is thick brown hair on my arms. I wear a gold ring on my wedding finger.

I'm here, but I'm not me.

The woman's back slopes down towards my waist. She is slim, with pure white skin. Then I think;

'I could see she was not Elizabeth, even in my waking stupor my mind would not allow me the luxury of that mistake.'

But it's not my thought, I didn't think it, although I can hear it. It is not the voice that I hear in my own mind. It is a man's voice. I am hearing, and feeling someone else's thoughts.

I am overcome with a sudden and deep sadness. I feel like I have ruined my life. I feel that no one can truly love me, that if I can't be with Elizabeth, (whoever Elizabeth is!), then I might as well die.

The woman in the bed stirs and wakes up. She feels me touch her and she recoils from my hand. His hand.

Then suddenly Vincent is in front of me in the darkness, and I'm back in the hanger. I'm overcome with the smell of sea salt and rusty metal. My cheek is hot and stung. Vincent has hit me.

"What's wrong with you? Hurry up!" he says, and I shove the Cube back inside my pocket. He takes my hand, and we run fast across the hanger and away through the boxes and crates stacked around Shoreham Docks.

SEVEN

EARLY THE NEXT morning, Brighton train station is silent. On Sunday mornings it waits patiently to attend to the city's cumulative hangover. Not that I would know about the comings and goings of the station. I used to walk to school and back every day, but that wasn't far. I go out in town at the weekend. I often work in a café on the seafront with my kind boss, Jan.

Tiffany told me to go to London and see my sister, so that is what we are going to do.

My eye twitches, telling me that I need to sleep. Once, right after Alice collapsed unexpectedly, I went into shock and fell asleep on the sofa while the paramedics were still in the house. Can Vincent see my eye twitching? I doubt it, he's never attentive at the best of times, and right now he strides ahead, not looking back.

For Vincent, it is all about *The Ship* now. But for me, it's all about *The Cube*. He's with me, we're both searching, but he's slightly behind. He's certainly not ready for the Cube.

Have you ever seen a spider, in the twilight, run across the floor? You can only see it when you're not looking at it. Try to pinpoint it with your eye and it's gone. Look away and you can see it at the sides of your vision. The Cube is like that.

The shops are still boarded up from the night before. It is freezing cold. Homeless men wrapped in sleeping bags are dotted around like sea lions. Vincent looks up at the travel boards. He walks around me in a circle with his arms open.

Red.

Red.

Red.

"The trains are cancelled," he shouts. A man in a trilby plays a Nina Simone song on the piano in the centre of the concourse.

In a corner a dozen or so people wait to board a train that is pulling in. I take Vincent by the hand and rifle up to the guard at the barriers.

"We're going to London," I say, as he disregards me. He looks like a shaven father Christmas. "I said, we are going to London."

"Not today you're not," he says, turning to face me. His voice is deep, though not jolly. "All trains to London are cancelled."

"When will they be running again?" I ask, and he checks his watch. His face screws up in a way that says Vincent and I are crazy—as if we were coercing him in a childish game.

"Possibly tomorrow. The line's been ripped up by the storm, a tree pulled electric cabling down Friday night. It's a bloody disaster to be honest, love. I'm sorry. If you've already bought a ticket then you can get a refund at the ticket office. Over there," and he points to an office near the taxis.

"Where are they going?" I ask, pointing to the crowd of people at the other side jostling to get in position. We must be able to start traveling and connect somewhere else to another train.

"That's a charter train to Bognor Regis," he says.

"A charter train?" I ask. I've heard of a charter flight but never a charter train.

"A fucking charter train?" Vincent shouts. The guard hears Vincent but chooses to ignore. Another outburst and we'll be cautioned. "Bollocks."

"Thank you, love. That's enough," he says, dismissing me.

"Vincent, let's go to Bognor instead, change trains to London from there," I say, pulling his coat sleeves. We must look, to passers-by, like drunken, troublesome youths. I am finished with being good.

"It's a pre-booked conference, sadly, otherwise we'd all be off to Bognor wouldn't we? On you go," the guard says. On you go? He is driving me on as if he is a policeman, when all I want to do is go to London to see my sister.

"I need to get to London," I shout, and everything echoes. There's the clear sound of shoes walking, the sound of an umbrella tip splitting the cold hard pavement. The wind cuts me and chases me around the corners of the station. The sudden cold snap is so sharp and extreme that I instinctively pick my hand up to inspect for blood.

The guard turns his back to the wind and hauls his shoulders up murmuring; "We both know there's no trains to London, Robyn, so stop playing silly buggers. I don't want to have to call your Mother," he whispers, and I need to sit down because I feel wobbly. I look around for a seat, but my legs are cement—fixed rigid to the spot. Everything slows. The guard's hair is blown back against his head. Rubbish sweeps itself along the floor, collecting in the corner of the ticket barrier.

Everyone knows me, but I don't know them.

Vincent pulls me away and we run out of the station. A taxi speeds around the corner, dangerously close. I can feel its engine vibrate within the tin ribs of the bonnet.

"We'll try something else," Vincent says, dashing into the morning air past a queue of waiting white and green Brighton taxis. I don't know who these taxis think they're here to collect. There is a smell of coffee and bread. A homeless man has woken up and begs from the middle of a coiled, paisley-pattern sleeping bag. He winks at me. I wonder what he knows?

Vincent pulls me down North Road and then through the North Laines. I can smell incense and pot. Vincent is captivated by his mission. He talks to himself, in swear words.

Everything seems ugly and unknown. The streets that I regularly walk are trying to smother me. The church bells at St Peter's church ring out. At the end of the street, a woman wrapped in red and green fabric wheels out a rail of second hand clothes. A seagull lands in the middle of the road with a gentle swoop. I think about Tiffany and the way South America pulses on her neck.

We fall out into a tall, whitewashed square behind the casino. Bins rattle full of Saturday night's excesses and the engine of the National Express coach reverberates.

"We did it, we're getting the bus," shouts a euphoric Vincent who lets go of my hand to punch the air. There is not a soul around, except for us. The front of the bus says 'Brighton Coach Station'.

"It says Brighton, Vincent," I say.

"No, he must be changing it to go back," says Vincent, as he bangs on the door with his fist. It makes me think about the time I went to London with the school on the apple coach. Something about that bus is different. This coach is a familiar white, red and blue. The one in my memory is not as real, not as factual.

The apple coach is faded sepia, just a memory from my childhood that I can't quite grasp. I can't see the whole coach as one, only snippets. I can't feel it vibrate in my chest like this one in front of me now. I can touch the furry velvet of the orange seats. I can see it so clearly, but I cannot hear it. I cannot feel it. I don't know what it smelled like.

The coach driver wobbles. He has a bad leg and carries too much weight. His black shoes are thick soled. His company branded fleece is bobbled over his man breasts from repetitive friction. He reaches into his pocket for a packet of cigarettes.

"Are you going to London?" Vincent asks, striding up, towering over him. I reach out to pull him back. The coach driver is startled. His eyes widen and he looks around with a dumb smile on his face. It's as if he thinks someone is playing a trick on him.

"No, mate. You've missed it. No more buses to London today." He lights his cigarette.

"Fuck! You've got to be kidding me," Vincent says, and he kicks the side of the bus with his boot.

"Eh! What do you think you're doing?" the driver says, and he pushes Vincent away from the bus. Vincent barges his chest into the coach driver. His fingers flex in and out of fists. Vincent's eyes have filmed over with a veil of tears.

"Oi," he shouts. "Get your hands off me, you greasy little shit bag. It's an offence to abuse a public transport official." The trauma of the past twenty-four hours is unravelling Vincent. His shirt is half untucked and smeared with black dirt. There's a speck of blood on his collar and a yellowish liquid stain down his front.

It takes all my strength to pull him away. Vincent points, spittle frothing from his mouth, cursing the coach driver.

"You ain't right," the driver shouts and to me says. "You haven't been third spliced. I can see by the look of you. I'm going to report you."

I pull Vincent into an alleyway leading back to the Laines, and when we round the corner into the street where a row of motorcycles are parked up, I let Vincent go.

"Calm down," I say, and when he's still pacing and then frantically adjusting himself, I put my arms around him and kiss his head. "Calm down."

What does he mean, 'third splice'?

"Since when are there no trains and no buses to London?" Vincent asks. He's still full of adrenaline. He wants to go back and fight the bus driver.

"It's a Sunday," I say.

"I don't give a fuck if it's fucking Christmas day, this is bullshit, Robyn." Vincent throws his hands up in the air, putting them on his waist, rubbing his forehead. The street starts to fill with tourists and people out for breakfast. A man on a Vespa pulls up to park.

It is a beautiful vintage scooter with a Union Jack and at least eight headlights stacked at the front. It carries shiny metal badges and has a metre high radio aerial. The man who gets off is a Mod. He wears a khaki green Harrington bomber jacket. I have seen so many in the café where I work with Jan that I know the brands and see lots of men like him.

He takes off his helmet and his hair has a sharp, straight, girlish fringe and long sideburns. Someone inside the coffee shop waves at him, attracting his attention. He doesn't notice Vincent and me standing silent on the pavement. He walks off at pace across the road. It is like an invitation.

Vincent lifts up his leg and stamps his boot down across the handlebars in one violent motion. The steering lock pops open. He takes out a hinged pocket knife, popping a panel out from the inside of the scooter. He straddles the seat. I stand in front of the scooter, obscuring the view from the Café.

There is a spark. The engine revs. Vincent manoeuvres the bike backwards.

"Get on," he says, and I do. We ride off. I put my hands around his waist and we take off rounding through the Laines, coming full circle and reaching the seafront. We roar along, Vincent's quiff redolent, streaming in the wind.

We drive by the West Pier, past Tiffany's apartment, and the spot where the ship ran aground. We pass The Grand Hotel, the Royal Albert Hall, and the Palace Pier where Vincent takes a left up the Old Steine.

I look at the Astoria, where we argued on Friday night and Blenheim Place, where I saw the Teddy Boy and the girl. Vincent opens the throttle and we roar out of town, northbound, heading for London.

EIGHT

I AM NOT wearing a helmet. The cheeks of my mouth balloon and ripple with the force of the wind. A tear streams horizontally out of the side of my eye. I don't know if I have been on this road before, but it's exhilarating.

It only takes ten minutes to get out of Brighton, and straight away we are in the Sussex countryside. Grassy motorway banks sprout with coarse, waist-high tufts of juicy grass. We are going uphill. The bike slows and the engine gives a deep cough.

On either side of the motorway, where the grassy bank dips, I catch glimpses of mile upon mile of white-domed tunnels. I don't understand what they are for, but the tunnels are vast and the domes themselves are misted up with the opaque sheen of polythene.

I wasn't expecting to be going so obviously uphill. My ears compress and flirt with popping. Vincent's body is sliding back into my lap. I can feel his core tense and I lean forward. I hold onto him tight. We've never been so emotionally engaged. There is no other car or bike on the road. In both directions we are now the only traffic.

Vincent points to a flashing sign. I can't drive a car. I'm incompetent, I know that. Mother has never taught me and I have never had lessons.

We drive under a bank of flashing signs. Even in my ignorance, I understand that the red flashing 'T' shape means that the road ahead is closed. To underline this, a big yellow triangular sign comes into view.

'ROAD AHEAD CLOSED'

Another sign reads, 'TURN AROUND IN THE BARRIER GAP'

Vincent's swearing is ripped out of his mouth by the wind. On we roar. We should slow down. We don't know what is up ahead. I want him to slow down, but just as I'm starting to shout at him the road flattens out.

A sign reads 'CAUTION'.

Ahead there is yet another series of signs;

'ROAD CLOSED'

'ROAD CLOSED'

'ROAD CLOSED'

As we near the conclusion, yellow cones with flashing red lights taper us off into the outside lane gradually slowing us through a widening circle that becomes a U-turn back onto the opposite carriageway.

It's like being brought around the track of a children's ride at the pier. You set off with excitement and anticipation of where you are going, and end up being shepherded back to where you started.

Vincent stops the moped. He kicks out the stand and parks us. The ring of fancy headlights droop like a wilted flower.

The tarmac under my feet is pristine. The road is not just closed. It does not go any further. It just ends. The only way forward is a loop that will turn us gently around and send us back to Brighton. The hairs on the back of my neck stand up. My heart beats fast and I fight for breath.

There's no more fucking road.

There is no London.

We are being kept here.

We can't leave.

We are being lied to.

I have to sit down for a second, otherwise I am going to fall. I'm breathing too shallow, too quickly. I feel nauseous and my vision squeezes and I see tiny stars. I'm going to pass out. I hang my head down over my knees.

"We had it so good," Vincent says. "We should have had a laugh on Friday night, had a few drinks, gone back to yours. We'd have slept in late. We'd have missed the ship. We wouldn't have known fuck all about it. We didn't know how lucky we were."

I breathe and try to stop myself from passing out or vomiting. I let my mind wander to Mother. I am specifically thinking about a conversation where my mother showed me a letter from Brighton University deferring my entry for twelve months. I had not requested the form. I said that I want to go this year and while Mother did not say I couldn't go, she shook her head and rubbed the back of my hand, and I signed the deferral form. I did very the same the following year.

"One thing I know already, Robyn," he says. "My mother found out about this. I know it. It all makes sense now. It drove her mad. The things she used to say."

Vincent climbs over the barrier and starts scaling a fifteen metre high bank of grass and coarse shrubs. He is going to be cut raw smashing through those thorny bushes. Above the bank is a line of trees that start abruptly and stretch as far into the distance as I can see, or make out before I can see no more. I feel as though we have come up high and that the forest of trees is going higher still.

I am startled by the cold. It has seeped in without me noticing. Night is coming with a bitter, alien frost that bites sharply.

I call after Vincent, quietly at first and then screaming. He yells back at me. I can't hear myself. I can hear his swearing and shouting and the noise of him ripping up clumps of grass and long strands of sharp thorny bushes.

Eventually he collapses down onto his backside.

"You must have driven this road before?" I shout. I mean he must have. I must have. We have barely been on the road for thirty minutes. I have driven on this road. Yet I can't remember when. I can't put my finger on an exact time, recently, when I have been on this road, the M27. I must have been on here to go to Gatwick airport, and all of the times that I have been to London.

"I have to see," Vincent says, turning back to scale the bank. "I'm going to see what's over this ridge."

"Wait for me," I say, and I start to scramble up the bank. I must see too. Vincent takes my hand and we push on through the brambles, through the long grass and into the trees. I can see the light tantalising us from the other side of the wood. In those strides I am calm and Vincent, being taller sees it first.

Now he falls to his knees.

It's like we've opened a box but there is nothing inside. We are looking towards London yet all we can see are thousands and thousands of white polytunnels reflecting the light. They look like sweeties laid out crisp as far as the eye can see.

Yet beyond there is something else. Something that I can't quite understand. A strip of white, like a thick icing drawn along the entire horizon. It rises high into the sky like a luminous flat mountain.

"What is that?" I ask.

"Where are we?" Vincent says. "What's real, Robyn? Where has everything gone?"

London, if it's out there at all, is nowhere to be seen.

NINE

VINCENT FALLS ON top of me, stumbling over my toes, while bundling a sleeping bag into a rucksack. The porch is dark and full of stuff. It smells like wet grass. Everywhere I put my foot, I seem to stand on something. The porch is a lean-to entry recess that runs along the side of Vincent's farmhouse. The roof leaks loveably and there's a dip in the floor where the stone has worn smooth from water.

The house is farmhouse filthy encased in mud and humming with man smells. Vincent's room however is an island of sanitisation, and which he cleans and arranges compulsively maintaining immaculate order; folded pants, ironed trousers on hangers; freshly laundered socks, balled. I've frequently heard his father say to him, "you clean like a woman." I am appalled and offended, and flick Vincent's Dad my middle finger under the table, while Vincent silently accepts it as a compliment.

Vincent throws a jacket at me. It's a blue padded women's coat for working on a farm. It was his mother's. Her cigarette papers and her lighter are still in the pocket. I'm wearing his mother's coat. I don't ask him how I look. He's lost any trace of the tiny sense of humour he had in the first place. I rummage deep in a pile of shoes and find a pair of walking boots that fit me. They smell of dogs, though there are no dogs here anymore.

Vincent has hidden the stolen moped in the barn under a thick tarpaulin. I rode it back myself with Vincent clinging on to me, petrified. I heard him breathing deeply, still in shock. I rode fast, hatching my plan, explaining to Vincent what we are going to do next.

We need to work fast before his father returns. Vincent throws me a pair of socks and then goes outside to leave food for the animals.

"You'll need proper socks with those boots," he says.

"I know," I say. He's handy I must admit. I do need him to help me. He's got the tent compressed into a small papoose that he ties to the bottom of his rucksack. His chin is now covered in stubble that is half a centimetre thick. Over his leather jacket he's thrown a khaki waistcoat with many pockets. It is frayed at the collar and speckled with pin pricks where the thread has caught on gorse bushes and thorns.

I take another rucksack and open it on the work surface in the kitchen. I rifle through the cupboards. I pull out a few cans of soup and half a loaf of white bread. Thank goodness there's chocolate. I open the fridge and drink milk from the bottle, and it runs down my chin. It's like we're burgling the place.

Minutes later, I stand in the lean-to and notice the locked cupboard with the glass doors. I could just break the glass with my bare fist, but that would be sharp and painful. Instead I call Vincent to bring me the key and he doesn't argue. He opens the cupboard and takes the shotgun out and puts it into its own black canvas case.

I wear it over my shoulder while he stuffs the pockets of his gilet with red shotgun cartridges. He carries a thick hunting knife with a serrated blade and a photograph of his mother.

We leave by the back door. We cross a row of decrepit sheds. Like Vincent's family, this place has seen better times. We cross the wide cement yard. There's a low wall that we climb over easily. We push through the bushes to a waist-high barbed wire fence that is supposed to stop cows from coming into the house. Vincent throws a blanket on the wire and I hold his hand while I pull up my foot and launch myself over.

He follows me and we're out into the open countryside. I know this field and the next one over, but after that I don't have a clue what is out there.

TEN

WE ARE IN the space behind Brighton where I thought Burgess Hill was. Isn't there supposed to be Crawley or Gatwick Airport? Well, there's not. It is pretty and alien. There are rows and rows of white polytunnels sparkling as far as I can see in all directions. I have the most awful gut wrenching feeling that this is their world and that Vincent and I are just visiting.

There are people out here; three lorries pass us on unpaved roads. They are unremarkable trucks and, inside one, we see potatoes in thick dusty brown sacks. We duck and hide each time one passes.

We have agreed the following three things; We won't be caught and picked up; We won't accept their explanations; And we won't be sent back.

"They've been lying to us," Vincent says.

"Who?" I ask, because I believe that we've been lied to, but I don't know by whom. Wasn't it Mother who told me that they had gone to London? She wrote it in her note.

"Everyone. Fucking everyone," he says. But not Tiffany, she was trying to tell me.

The light here never fades entirely. It is always daylight with a few shaded hours of dusk. It's when we feel these darker hours approach that our tiredness reaches out to pull us to the ground. Vincent puts up the tent in a small copse of trees. The floor is spongy where little husks have fallen to the ground over and over again and lay here crunchy and undisturbed.

I drink lukewarm water from a flask. I look at the trees that surround us. I don't feel scared with Vincent and a shotgun so close by. What I feel is unease that all of the trees that I have ever seen (in my life) are small and young. They never look like the mighty oaks that I have read about in books.

I run my hand against the silvery trunk of a plane tree that stands perhaps twenty feet tall. How many years does it take to grow to this height? Where are all of the old gnarly trees?

We eat the bread. It is hard and dry, and wouldn't have lasted another day. We duck down into the small tent and zip up the door. Vincent needs the dark and quiet to sleep, but the red canvas spreads a glow over us. It's like we're inside a giant red balloon.

We do not speak. There's a growing unspoken understanding between Vincent and me. We are working in tandem, one knowing what the other is thinking. We're getting on better than ever before on this bizarre and petrifying journey.

We take off our boots and a sour smell of sweat fills the tiny space. I unzip the door and see a small brown mouse running across the spongy floor. I anchor our socks down with some stones to air them.

If we were in bed at home I would kiss Vincent, probably more, putting my hand over his mouth to silence him, but it doesn't seem right here, and he doesn't try. I can feel the shotgun in its canvas case digging into my buttock. Vincent starts to snore. I don't know if I want to kiss him anymore. It feels like we've passed that. Tiffany slips into my mind and I think about kissing her instead.

I wiggle around to get more comfortable, careful not to disturb him. Then I feel another metal. It's small and pointy and it's jabbing me in the ribs. It's the Cube in my pocket. In all the chaos, I had forgotten about it. I take it out.

I hold the Cube in my hand, and it feels like a dice. It has soft corners and is heavy like a gold wedding ring still warm. I hold it up to inspect it and unbelievably, when I look at it directly, it disappears and the feeling disappears too. It just isn't there— there's a gap between my fingers where it should be.

Looking away and catching it to the side of my vision, the soft warm Cube returns its impression to my palm. I hold it for a while and nothing happens. It could be a mirage, a hallucination reaction to stress. I was petrified in that dock, maybe it fried my brain. It can't have been real, it was an anxious illusion.

How had I been holding the Cube? It was specifically between my thumb and forefinger. I move my hand into that position and the Cube suddenly changes temperature. It is searing—either hot or cold, I can't tell.

There is a surge of red light.

It sends my heart racing. It's like nothing I have ever encountered. It is tinged with magic, and tastes phosphorus. It must be mirrors, or magnetics? There must be an explanation for what it is.

Suddenly I am back within the Cube.

ELEVEN

I AM IN bed. Or rather, *he* is in bed. This is either my dream or his memory. I've heard about people regressing into a previous life. A girl in my school told me she had been a racing car driver in a previous life and that she'd been killed in a high-speed accident. Now she hates cars.

This must be my dream. I'll speak like it is my dream although it's through someone else's eyes. I've never dreamt like this before and I don't know whether I am awake or asleep. Vincent might be lying here next to me or perhaps I am somewhere else.

I don't know whether my eyes are turning like my sister's, into something less than perfect. Is this what she sees?

The sheets are grey silk. I am with a woman. She is extraordinarily beautiful. She is slim and her skin is perfect, not a blemish nor a pimple. She is sophisticated and older than me, though not old. She has long blonde hair that pools onto the pillow.

If this was my dream then I would like to touch her hair. But my hand, his hand, is moving towards her back, just like it did yesterday. I can hear the ocean. Wherever I am—wherever they are—it's hotter than Brighton. The electric blind is opening. The room is filled with light. I try to touch her hair. I can see she is not Elizabeth. I don't know an Elizabeth, but I'm thinking, saying to myself, that even in my waking stupor, my mind will not allow me the luxury of that mistake.

I feel devastated and sick with guilt about her—whoever Elizabeth is—and I feel like crying. In this place, in this dream, I know two things:

The woman in the bed is not Elizabeth.

And this is not my dream. I'm watching something that I'm not in control of. I can stop and start. I can play and pause, but I am watching someone else's story.

There is a knock at the door and he pulls his hand back. The woman pulls the sheet up over her shoulder. For an awful second I think it might Elizabeth catching him in the act. I hear his voice.

He's American. He shouts; "Wait a second!"

There are children on the other side of the door. I can hear them giggling. The woman gets up. She's naked. She looks like a model, just perfect, almost too perfect.

She doesn't look back. She ignores him, she certainly doesn't touch him. We, he and I, watch her walk across the room. She bends down to pick up the clothes that are strewn across the floor. She doesn't speak. She goes into what must be the en-suite bathroom because I hear water running. She closes the door.

Now she's gone, he sits up in bed and calls the children in. He makes an effort to straighten out the sheets. There's a stain, some kind of sex residue. It's gross. He puts a pillow over it.

The door opens and the kids run in, shouting; "Happy Birthday, Daddy."

There are two boys aged around eight and a smaller girl.

The girl sits up on his lap and he kisses her head. I can see the little head close up—the wispy strands of flyaway hair like little butterflies fluttering. He keeps his face there on the top of her head. He likes it. He feels happy and I feel happy too. This is what it must feel like to have a child. It feels like the sweetest, purest feeling of love I have ever felt. He loves the child so much.

One of the boys smacks him around the face with a pillow. The boy is under-ripe and wants attention. He hurts his Dad. The pillow was not as soft as it might have appeared. Perhaps it was the zipper or the sharp end of a duck feather. It has scratched the skin and left a stinging itch.

The little girl lifts her finger to trace it along his cheek where there must be a red welt. He pulls her finger away and kisses it. She giggles. With his right arm he swipes at the boy missing on purpose, just enough for him to get away. The little girl screams in delight and jumps up onto her feet. Within a couple of seconds the other boy is up banging him over the head with another pillow.

At that moment, the woman walks out of the bathroom wearing a short, strapless mini dress with stiletto sandals tied criss-cross around her calves. We watch her. How does she walk in those? I am wearing metal toed boots and Vincent's mother's coat! She is kind of like a prostitute, but not. I hate it when women say that about other women, but you know what I mean; glossy and trashy.

The children go silent. Their three heads swivel like little owls, blinking. This isn't good for them to see. The woman lingers at the door.

"Ciao, Ivan," she says. "I'll be in touch."

He's called Ivan, this man I am. He is wearing a wedding ring, a thick marital band, but she is not his wife.

"Daddy," says the little girl. "Who is that lady?"

"Just a friend from work," he says.

"Does Mommy know her?" The middle boy asks.

"You'll have to ask Mommy if she knows Kelly from Marketing," he says, getting out of bed. A nanny comes over and herds up the children. Ivan and the nanny talk about having a birthday breakfast together on the deck.

"I invited your Mom for my birthday breakfast but she couldn't make it," Ivan says, pulling on a mint silk dressing gown.

Echoing from the ceiling of the room, something says; "Good morning, Ivan." I know straight away that it is not a person. Something about the tone of the voice, the pitch, or the pace. It just isn't human.

"Good morning," Ivan says. "Can you get the Professor on a call, please?" He picks up a picture of a woman and stares at it. He wipes the glass of the picture frame carefully with his robe, and places it back onto the side board.

A circle of dots appear on the wall. The electronic blinds come down again. The room is changing itself. I hear a telephone ringing.

A picture suddenly appears on a projected screen. Ivan is going to have a conversation with someone on a screen on the wall.

The image is of a high wooden bench and metal shelves with clear glass beakers stacked up. Perhaps a school science room. A man appears in the centre of the screen. They are friendly, matey, and jovial. In the way that men, other than Vincent, are to other men. But I have seen this man before. Ivan calls him The Professor. I know him as something else.

He's younger here than the way I know him. But I recognise his wide nostrils and fleshy jowls that look strange on him as a younger man.

I've never heard him speak and so it's beyond weird to see him occupy the screen fully alive, his rubbery lips filling the camera's width. He has the poshest, most stereotypically English voice I have ever heard. It doesn't fit somehow. Like Sir Laurence Olivier reciting Shakespeare from the mouth of Al Capone. I can't help but laugh.

"We're going on a little trip, Ivan," The Professor says. "I hope you've got your sea legs?"

"They signed it?" asks Ivan.

"Yes, Ivan. You are now the proud owner of five thousand hectares of prime frozen wasteland."

Somehow I am thrown across the room. I can hear Ivan yelling and celebrating but all I can see is where the marble floor tiles meet the silk draped off the side of the bed. Ivan is jumping around. The Professor says:

"Steady on, old boy."

Ivan picks me up, his stout fingers raising my viewpoint up to his face. I know now that I'm not looking through his eyes, but through a pair of spectacles that he is wearing. It must be a recording, but from where, and from when I don't know. How on earth I am now watching it, through the Cube, in my head, is mind-boggling.

"There are three PhD students I think we should approach to bring on board. But more of that later. I must go, Ivan. I've got to get to the airport."

"How long is your flight?" we ask, Ivan and I.

"Thirteen hours from Heathrow to Buenos Aires, I believe, and then another four hour flight down to Ushuaia. It's a bloody long trip! By the way, Ivan, thank you for sending me business class. It's very generous of you."

I hear Ivan's voice in my head again. He says to himself; 'I can't wait to show you, Elizabeth, what I am creating.'

TWELVE

WE'VE BEEN WALKING through the network of polytunnels for the past two days. It's all open land. Anyone can wander into it, but no one seems to, except for us. Vincent wears wide, dark sunglasses, the kind that old ladies with cataracts wear. I am being driven blind by the constant glare of the sun against the sparkly white outlines of the tunnels. We can feel the weight of the landscape closing in on us. We are narrowing the distance to the broad band of white mountains growing bigger with each step.

If London was there, we'd be in it by now.

I send Vincent out in front to lead the way. If I go ahead, he becomes listless and complains. Better to keep him busy, and with the illusion of control. We are so engrossed in our walking, and looking mostly at the ground because of the glare, that we go for hours without any conversation. I have been messing around with the Cube in my pocket. I've figured out that it is reading my fingerprints when I hold it a certain way. I realise that I can also be engaged with the Cube while I am walking along. It feels like being in a daydream.

I roll it in my hand. It is so weird to feel it in my pocket, but then I look inside and see the Cube isn't there! If I lose it, I'll never find it again. Honestly, if I drop it, it might be gone forever. It's so fragile and perilous. I will have to be very careful with it. Vincent has no idea what I am up to and I'm not telling him.

I take out the Cube and hold it gently. The red light comes on. I am still following Vincent and I am able to turn the corner to walk around the outside of a tunnel. I am able to change my direction to avoid a hole in the grass that might roll my ankle.

I can do these things but at the same time I am in his world. Ivan's world. I hold the Cube up in front of my face. I don't look at it. I look towards the white horizon and see it in my peripheral vision.

I go. I am both here and there at the exact same time.

Ivan is in a hotel room. It has floor to ceiling windows, and far across the scraggly rooftops of a town I can see flat-topped mountains, peaks dripping with snow. I can't breathe there, but I get the sensation that the air is crystal clear. I can't dream of this. I've never seen anything like it.

In my world, I trip over the root of a tree and fall. The Cube is thrown out of my hand. Vincent hears and calls back to ask if I am alright. I'm not alright. I need to find the Cube, my Cube.

I scramble around on my hands and knees looking over the grass. I am panicking. Where the fuck is it? I need to get it back. I need to get it back!

I fix my eyes on a tree ten yards away and scan the outskirts of my vision. I look away to my right and then there it is in my periphery. It had been thrown straight in front of me. I move to it. I look ahead, catch it in my peripheral vision and pick it up. I hold it.

There's the red light. I'm back in the hotel room. The Professor is wearing an explorer's hat—a worn brown leather panama. It doesn't suit him. There seems to be a black knitted beanie underneath it. It is a very strange look and perhaps he's wearing it to keep warm.

But Vincent comes back to help me up. Fuck off, Vincent.

"Leave me alone, Vincent," I say, because I am concentrating on the memory I am watching—that I am in. "I'm sorry, I just need a minute." He understands. We don't do niceties anymore. It's refreshing and a crucial part of our new found freedom.

"It's okay," he says. "Take your time." He goes over to the hedgerow to take a pee.

The Professor has swagger.

"No one is supposed to know that we're here," Ivan says, and The Professor fills a tumbler with whisky or brandy and looks up at Ivan. He raises an eyebrow.

"Everyone in the town is looking at us, Ivan. They can see we're important." Ivan doesn't like this. He bristles. Prefers to be under the radar, like I do. He doesn't like people knowing his business. He's going to say something about the Professor asking an assistant to find a prostitute in town. Ivan is fuming. He turns back to the mountains, and I see his chest lurching up and down with deep breaths.

Ivan thinks that the Professor has been letting his eyes linger on the waitress' backside. The Professor has been showing off, attracting attention, and being inappropriate with almost every woman they see. Ivan doesn't like it. There's so much friction in the room between these two men that the hairs on my arms are standing on end.

"You should try colonic irrigation in the spa, Ivan. I feel wonderful," The Professor says.

The thread jumps, because suddenly there are three other men in the room. Ivan feels happy, full of energy and excitement. He's gone all giddy. It's bubbling inside him. I can't help but smile.

The Professor shakes hands with a man who looks like an old-school wrestler, all his surfaces are rounded except for his forehead, which is as flat as an anvil. He is introduced as the British foreign attaché to Argentina and the Southern Isles. It is a tricky role. There's a history of conflict. The Professor knows that, prior to being the foreign attaché, this chap played rugby for England. The Professor is now giddy too.

They've met before. They've had dinner in the best restaurant in Ushuaia. That's where they are. Ushuaia. Near the Southern tip of Argentina. He wants Ivan and The Professor to watch a rugby game together. Ivan tells him again that he married an English girl and that he knows all about rugby.

They laugh about their wives, but whenever Ivan thinks about Elizabeth he gets a painful knot in his chest, like indigestion. Oh no, he is losing himself, he is coming out of the conversation into a slough of regret. He's staring out the window. I want to shake him.

"Ivan. Ivan," The Professor says, and he snaps his head around.

"What that's you say?" Ivan says, but the story jumps again and there's someone new. The foreign attaché introduces him as the Ambassador. There is a secret service agent, a sort of James Bond-esque figure with him. He has a wire around his ear and a gun pressed inside his lean frame.

In the hallway outside are many people. Ivan's entourage, a team of assistants and engineers. They buzz around the entrance. Their eyes on stalks whenever the door opens.

Ivan signs a document with a fancy ink pen. It is the British Official Secrets Act. He can't stop smiling. It's covert, a bit like a movie scene.

Once they've all signed the document, the ice breaks. The Ambassador takes Ivan by the arm. For a second, I think they are going to kiss. Ivan is thinking, you give them a whiff of Empire and they jump at it. He is delighted they are working together with the British and not with the Americans or the Russians.

The Ambassador holds up a glass of champagne. There are tears in his eyes as he toasts Ivan and the Professor and wishes them 'the very best of luck'. He gives Ivan a gift of a framed black and white photograph of Captain Scott reaching the South Pole in 1912. The five-man expedition crew is assembled like a ghost sports team on snow in old-fashioned animal skins and goggles. It is a gift from The Prime Minister of Great Britain.

This is what powerful men must be like. I'm not used to it. I'm used to powerful women. I find it amusing. I find it basic and unsophisticated.

The Ambassador and his staff leave to meet the helicopter, which they will take back up north to Buenos Aires.

Ivan and The Professor stand face to face. Ivan is going back to California, but The Professor will stay down here. Ivan thinks, 'he's never coming back.'

The Professor is never coming back.

THIRTEEN

I JERK AWAKE covered in sweat, thinking about my mother and my sister. I should have gone back to Brighton and tried to contact them first. They will be worried about me. My sister will be petrified. I need to find a telephone. I need to call her.

Having exhausted our meagre rations and desperate for a drink of water, we crouch down and wait by the outer plastic of a polytunnel. With so many to choose from it is pot luck what is inside. I think I've seen the outline of a vine that reminds me of Mother's tomatoes but I can't be sure.

Vincent pushes his hunting knife into the outer shell expecting to carve a straight open line but it does not pierce. Instead it stretches and the sharp tip of the blade can't penetrate the skin. Vincent takes off his glasses and slashes at it over and over, but he cannot make an incision.

"What is this?" I ask, as he pushes his fingers into the wall and watches it bend and stretch. It's a fabric, a kind of plastic. A feeling of abject horror overcomes me. I should know what this is, shouldn't I? In our normal world, this plastic wall should rip and tear. I am more than a little nervous.

"I've never seen anything like it," he says. Sick with hunger and nerves, we go around to the front of the tunnel to examine the lock. There's a panel made of metal, bearing a number grid, which is now rusted and broken. It must have once been a keypad to gain entry. In its place is now a regular lock that hangs in tattered aluminium.

I grab the shotgun and slip it out of its canvas holder. Vincent shakes the lock a few times with his hand. We are so deep in trouble already that another trespassing incident seems little to worry about.

"It'll make a noise," says Vincent of the gun, but I've already got it aimed at the lock. "Keep the butt in your shoulder."

Vincent takes a step back to allow me to blow the lock off its chain. What does he know about shotguns? I narrow my eyes and squeeze the trigger. My feet come up off the floor. I am expecting a kick, but I don't get one. I get a smell of burning instead, and fiery stinging hands as if I'd slapped someone's arse too hard.

"My mother was a good shot," he says, and kicks the remnants of the lock away with his boot, the door swings open and we march inside. I know the smell, my mother's tiny greenhouse in the garden at home; green, earthy and sweet. It's the smell of tomato.

Inside is gloriously tropical and deceivingly big. Strung out in linear patterns are rows and rows of tomatoes. We are lucky because they are just ripening—some still hold onto the firm tinge of green. The harder, not quite ripe tomatoes are ideal for stashing in our rucksack.

Vincent's beard drips with tomato juice and pearly oval seeds. His eyes spin about wildly and he stretches himself into a long banana shape, his head far out in front of his body, as he tries to contend with the mess. He spits out the hard pithy tops where the stalk attaches to the fruit. Pink and blue butterflies flutter about our heads.

It is beautiful here. It's cocooned and feels strangely natural. I could stay in here for a long time.

"Do you think you get a bad stomach from eating too many?" Vincent asks, pushing another into his mouth.

"I don't know. I've never eaten this many before," I say, shoving another glorious tomato into my own mouth. I realise just how hungry I am. Vincent bends to uncouple a hosepipe that is plugged into an irrigation system on the floor. Water spews from the hose and Vincent holds it up to his mouth, licks it, fills his mouth and spits, and then he takes more, swallowing this time.

"It's okay to drink," he says, and offers the hose to me to do the same. "It's just plain water."

"Are you sure?" I ask, tasting it too, of course—I have to check it for myself.

I bend to drink and I hear a metallic click above me. Vincent hears it too and drops to the floor. I follow him. I see a spider, gangly and swollen bodied, crawl and hide beneath a leaf. I pull away. I put one hand onto my shotgun. I should have reloaded it. We freeze in silence. We wait. Suddenly right above us the sprinkler system bursts into life, spraying us and the tomato plants in a warm mist.

I stand up with my hair soaking wet, plastered to my face and neck. Oh, the relief! We laugh. Vincent undoes his waistcoat and jacket and takes them off. He pulls down his jeans, throws them to the side where he thinks they will stay dry and stands directly under the sprinkler. We are stark naked like Adam and Eve laughing in a fertile garden.

"I'm having a wash," he says, and I too can smell my own sour underarms (I've never smelled this bad before, I swear it!) and so I unzip my clothes and join him. I rinse my knickers and rub the fabric under the arms of my T-shirt. We will smell of ripe tomato now instead of sweat. I stand naked in front of Vincent and kiss him, feeling him get hard against me. For the first time since the ship ran aground, I feel happy.

But something triggers my senses. I don't hear an alarm, but I open my eyes and search around me, and I catch a red bulb flashing solidly above the entrance. I point it out to Vincent. He can't see it. His eyesight is terrible. He doesn't know what I am talking about. He tries to kiss me more.

Am I aware of a high-pitched frequency? I can't hear anything. Or rather, I'm not sure but I can feel that red, flashing bulb screaming in silence, telling somebody we are here.

Am I paranoid? Yes I am? We're naked and we're trespassing, and literally everything is weird enough already.

"I think we need to go," I say.

"You never want to anymore," Vincent says, still trying to kiss my neck.

"Someone's here," I say, and Vincent freezes. Is there another noise? We jump, and suddenly Vincent gets it and moves fast.

We gather up our belongings and stash our wet clothes in the outer mesh pocket of Vincent's rucksack. My coat is still dry. My trousers are too. We emerge half-naked from the entrance tunnel. It is startlingly colder and lighter outside so we do not see them at first as our eyes adjust.

Shit.

They are sat on three large quad bikes, waiting for us. Easily recognisable, seven or possibly eight men all with blonde hair. I have seen them before in town, causing fights on the seafront. They are itinerant travellers. Gypsies.

"What the fuck do you think you're doing?" the tallest one shouts.

"We weren't doing anything wrong," I say, and he looks me up and down. I don't even think to apologise, even though we were trespassing and eating the produce. I want to ask them what all of this is.

"We haven't got anything left to eat," Vincent says.

"We were starving," I say.

The largest man uncrosses his arms and puts a finger up to his lips in a gesture for me to be quiet. I stop talking. This is bad. I'm frightened. Slowly, he meanders over to stand in front of Vincent, elongating his head to the right hand side as if he's stretching the muscles in his neck.

He spits on the floor and it leaves a thick translucent streak like an opaque bird dropping. He is wearing a red tracksuit with two white stripes down the arms. He does not pause, he keeps moving slowly, and then viciously in one perpetual motion he lurches forward with a fist clenched. Turns out that Vincent's handsome jaw is made of glass. He knocks Vincent out cold with one punch.

FOURTEEN

I KICK. I SCREAM. Eventually they bring me to a small house with two rooms. There are four such houses in a square arrangement with porches opening up to face each other. Outside, two grey horses are tethered to a front bench. They chew grass from a brown hanging sack and eye me cautiously.

The horses are right to eye me like that. I have never ridden one. I have never even had so much as a pet cat. Not with my mother working so hard and being a single parent of two girls—one with special needs. When I was a child, I desperately wanted a dog.

I wish that Tiffany had come with us. She's savvy. I sit alone with a man called Erik. He has a white-blond mullet with a ballooned face, bronzed copper from the sun. He wears two gold-hooped earrings and a necklace with a long white tooth. We are shelling peas. (Yes, as in preparing to cook a meal! I know how bizarre this sounds.) The sun is low and keeps lighting up the ends of his hair from behind. The tooth is his own; a difficult extraction he tells me proudly, without anaesthetic.

"Not like that, like this," he says, showing me how to split the juicy pod along its vein by squeezing between his thumb and forefinger and then splicing them out in a swoop using the long fingernail of his other hand. His fingers are like sausages that have been squashed out of shape in the bottom of a shopping bag.

I can't remember ever shelling peas before. The smell is intense. The flesh is sweet, earthy and kind of floral. It's a unique smell I'll never forget.

I am not frightened of him. I feel quite safe. Vincent is in the house across the square with this man's wife. I can see the woman going in and out, carrying a basket of washing. They are not going to hurt us. They are worried about us.

I can hear the gang of lads who brought us here doing something outside to the engine of a tractor. When Erik saw Vincent's face he apologised, but then added the caveat that the boys were only doing their jobs. You do something wrong, you get a smack. I grimace, realising it's the same side that I'd already smacked on Friday night. Doesn't it come in threes? Vincent's going to get hit again, that's my prediction.

They are guardians of the land, Erik tells me. They move from place to place harvesting the fruit and vegetables when the time is right. His family has always done this. They do not abide by the rules of the city and the Council. They are free, whatever that means.

"You don't know about geothermal energy?" he asks.

"No, I don't," I say, feeling foolish.

"It's direct from the ground, it's especially good for tomatoes."

"What are the greenhouses made of?" I ask.

"The structure? It's a kind of plastic resin. It's imported. We can't make that ourselves. We do things differently up here. The women carry our own babies. No interference." He says, proudly, how weird. Doesn't every woman carry her own baby? He grabs his blond hair by the front tuft and leans forward.

"See, our hair is blond. Pure Viking." He pulls down his bottom eyelid and leans forward to show me his eyeball. "Perfect vision. 100% perfect."

His wife walks in carrying a metal pot with a lid. It steams and smells deliciously of onions and garlic.

"You hear that, Lena? They walked from Brighton!"

She smiles at me, and then makes a hissing sound with her mouth, a sort of 'tut' and says to Erik; "They are lapsellinen."

It's in another language, but I hear her clearly.

Erik draws his face back into his neck like a turtle. He raises his eyebrows and shakes his head. He mutters something in a language I don't know. Lena raises the pot onto the stove, talking quietly so that I have to strain to listen.

"You didn't finish school yet?" he asks, holding up another pea, willing me to improve. I feel like they are recruiting wives for their punchy blonde sons. I mean, what else could go wrong?

"I finished school. I have a place at university," I say.

"You are too big for starting university? Look at you! You are a grown woman. You ought to be starting a family." See what I mean about the wives thing? I am startled that he keeps being rude about my age. I laugh. What does he mean? I'm young. Lena is talking fast now in the other language.

Earlier, when we first arrived, I smelt Lena opening a bottle of lotion—was it camphor? Maybe menthol? She told Erik and I to leave her alone with Vincent. She had made the boys lay Vincent out on a single bed covered with a hand-embroidered eiderdown. She spent nearly two hours alone with him patching him up and talking in whispered voices. She washed his clothes. Vincent's jeans, T-shirt and boxer shorts are hung up now on the washing line outside.

She asks me to take off my clothes so that she can wash them. She hands me an orange tracksuit two-piece and a pair of knickers. The knickers are her own, she apologises, but they are immaculately clean. I have no doubt they are. They are sturdy as hell, and make me feel safe.

I put on the fresh smelling tracksuit. It's made of a cotton material but it seems to stretch, again it feels rather like a plastic. It shines and there are no seams, and no stitching. I make sure that I move the Cube, and I zip it safely inside the pocket of the tracksuit trousers. On the wall are photographs of Lena and her brood of young blond men.

They look so different to everyone I know, so light and so pale, their jaws are squared, their eyes are blue. Their features hang from their bulky, muscular frames. Vincent is so dark and swarthy. Everyone I know is dark, brown eyed, thick dark hair. Even my mother.

But it makes me realise that I look different, to everyone, including my mother.

"You are right, Lena," Erik says, putting down the peas. He clasps his hands in front of his rotund stomach. "We can't take you back until tomorrow morning. You'll have to stay here for the night."

"I'm not going back." I poke out my head from behind the screen.

"I'll send a message. We have a satellite phone. I'll let them know you're okay."

"No. Absolutely not. It's my belief that if you telephone them, my mother and possibly her team will come up here and take me back."

"Yes, that's the point."

"Against my will. I don't want to go. I won't go."

"You go any further from here, and it's just dangerous, I'm afraid. We don't even go, perhaps occasionally for hunting, but it's not safe."

"We're in the middle of something important," I say.

"Important to you, but not to me. We know everything already."

"I need to see for myself."

"You could stay here a few days. You could help Lena." I see Lena carrying my washing. I don't think so. He sits back in his chair. He curls his fingers around his stomach and taps it, and then opens his hands and flattens his palms and calls Lena over as if to deal with me.

"Lena," he says. "You explain please."

"I'm going to see my sister. In London," I plead, I have already told him this, but I need to appeal to Lena's sense of family. I stand out from behind the screen in the orange tracksuit and they both nod their heads in appreciation.

"That's much better. Trendier than what you had on before." Erik says.

Lena dries her hands on her apron and then takes my hands. She curls a finger around my hair and tucks it behind my ear. She speaks softly.

"You are a strong woman. I can see that. Your name is beautiful, like the bird. We don't get robins here but I've seen them in pictures," Lena says. "Now then, let me be very clear with you." Erik guffaws.

"I keep telling you, Lena, she's not a child. She might talk like one, but she's not, she's a grown woman." Erik says, while Lena turns to chastise him.

"We're sick of listening to your voice," she says. She turns slowly back to me. If I could stay here with just these two forever then I think I might. "But out here, Robyn, up the bank, we are the last stop. Out there is just wild rock and ice. We're not lying to you. There really is nothing else to see."

FIFTEEN

BUT I DON'T stay. I keep on and on, and eventually they agree to let us go on and tell us that if we do not return within three days, then they will alert the police to come and find us. The same boys who brought us here now drive us on. I sit on the back of one quad bike and Vincent on the other. I hold onto my driver's waist. He is thin in the hips but broad and bony shouldered. I can feel his ribs through his tracksuit top. He has shaved his blond locks into a severe flat-top haircut. I can see each strand of his tightly cut hair.

The third bike carries our supplies—the tent; a new sleeping bag that they've given us (rather more technologically advanced from its weight and material I'd say. I'm obviously having that one); sandwiches made by Lena, (cheese and ham); a large selection of biscuits and a canteen of water.

The shotgun is slung happily over my shoulder. It is fully loaded and I have a pocket full of cartridges. I like its weight, and it goes without saying that I love its smell (pure cold metal). Erik made us practise shooting beer cans from forty feet away. Turns out I am a much better shot than Vincent. I'm not entirely surprised.

We have a map. We are to follow the trail and not deviate. There are—get this—crevasses in the glacier into which we could fall! Like, never to be found again. It's happened before.

We stick to the trail. There's a shepherd's hut in which we can shelter once we get up there. That's only *if* we get up there. If the weather closes in, we're to come back immediately.

There are animals up there. We're not to leave food out as they are attracted by smells. If we shit or urinate we're to bury it deep in the snow and cover it over (nice!).

Erik tries to give us a dog; a black and tan Alsatian with a pointy face, but sadly neither Vincent or I know how to control a dog.

"What if it falls in the crevasse?" I ask.

"Don't be ridiculous! It's highly intelligent, it will alert you and scare away animals." Erik said defensively. But dogs were always going over the edge in Brighton. Regardless, Lena doesn't think we'll be gone for long. From the intensity of her goodbye, I know that wherever we are going we will not return the same. I'm petrified and if I don't find my sister at the end of this, I am going to find something else unexpected.

Lena never says, 'London'. She never mentions it.

I know from her eyes that London isn't there. She frequently repeats;

"They should have been told this before!" and "It's not our job to educate them!"

When I push her to tell me what she means, she just ignores me and carries on with the many household chores that having a husband and seven sons produces.

But her eyes do not lie.

We moved rapidly towards wherever it is we are going. The bikes hum, flicking up mud and clumps of grass in our wake. The rows of polytunnels finish and disappear first behind us and then below us, eventually turning into tiny dominoes in the distance. The ground beneath us hardens to rock. The air suddenly fills with the smell of juicy watermelon.

"Can you smell that?" I ask the boy

"Nah," he says, and ignores me.

One of the boys stops at a small building that looks like a brick post box. He opens a panel and enters a code to deactivate a security system. We cross a cement river. It's a canal, clearly human-made and wide, with sloping grey walls and a deep channel of luminous, clear blue water running through the middle. There are tall watchtowers dotted all along the canal and, as I move, I can make out its seemingly endless shape stretching into the distance.

The water gushes through and it is the clearest turquoise blue I have ever seen. It looks like it would taste like raspberry slush puppy. It is moving fast and I can see tips of white spray. There's a ford where we can cross and we burst over it on the quad bikes. I love the sensation of being on the bike. I love being in a gang like this. The boys do this often, I can tell. They know their way instinctively. I am sprayed with the water and it's so cold that it stings.

The sky is light blue. My skin tightens with the cold. I see my breath in front of me and watch the earth rise up in a gigantic hill.

Higher and higher I rise. We have travelled no distance, but enough for a tangible change in the landscape. A change of season done horizontally. The cold shocks me, excites me and takes my breath.

SIXTEEN

THE BOYS LEAVE us and I plunge into an anxious state of loss and excitement. We're alone out here. No one's coming to save us. Not for the next three days, anyway.

The big boy that punched Vincent shook his hand now, and pulled Vincent into a hug. They had a primordial emotional charm, those rough boys. I think it might be called honesty. We should have stayed with them. Vincent and I could work with them. We could be genuine—working the land, having a purpose.

But as we start to walk on alone, I think about my sister again, and I wonder what else my mother has kept from me, and I remember my purpose. I walk faster and stronger, with my eyes looking forward.

Behind us, the boys sat draped across their bikes watching us go on, mystified. In their rainbow coloured tracksuits and blond mullets they looked like a weird editorial from a high-end fashion magazine.

Now, I find it hard to breathe. I have to draw in huge gulps of air. I remember a fitness trainer at school once telling me to draw in breath through my nose and my mouth at the same time, so that's what I do. It adds to the noise in my head, though we walk in silence. I concentrate on putting one foot after the other.

I am walking on snow.

It crunches.

What can I see? I don't know what it is. It's so vast and white, as if I am looking up at a great wall of sea, frozen in the midst of a tsunami.

Vincent holds his hands around his eyes to shield them from the brightness. He's whining, as if in pain. His breath pours out like steam from an engine.

"Stay on the path," I say. I say it over and over again. "Stay on the path."

The Finnish gypsies had given us warm lined jackets, but I still shiver. We've pulled the hoods up and tied the drawstring around our faces. The temperature has dropped so quickly. It's like being in a swimming pool that suddenly gets deep. The intense cold is shocking and I struggle to adjust.

My teeth are banging together. It is still light, but I feel so very tired. Our shadows are so long now. Every footstep is achingly uphill, and soon it's so steep I am moving with my hands too, climbing like a child up a set of stairs, and just to see Vincent I have to look up at the soles of his boots. It's slippy and sharp, it glows blue in places and I have to be careful not to stumble.

"Stay on the path!" I shout.

I can't go on. I'll have to sit here and sleep. I hear the little chirps of birds. There are no birds here. Vincent shouts down to me.

"Don't sit. Let's get you up."

He's agitated. He's at the top. There's a building.

He comes back down to offer me his gloved hand. We emerge over the top together to see.

Ahead is a building and in the far distance just white tipped mountains with grey faces.

Nothing else.

Absolute nothingness as far as the eye can see, and from here I can see for miles and miles and miles. London is not here. London is not out there in front of me. Nor is it behind me. I am dizzy.

I am sick. It can't be. It can't be true. I turn around and look back at where we came from, and I can see the concrete canal semi-circling thousands of polytunnels which disappear into the distance under a thick swell of white-grey cloud.

Vincent rubs his eyes underneath his sunglasses. There is frost on his moustache, an icicle drooping from the end of his nose. Is he welling up?

I fall back into a heap of snow. If London is not here, then where is it? Where is my mother? Does my mother know all of this is up here? I suppose she must. Does Jan, my boss, know? Vincent's friend, Ben? Does he know? But how the fuck do I not know?

What does it even mean? And where is Alice? My sister. Where is she? My heart races. I am dizzy.

Vincent paces back and forth. He doesn't want me to sit down, and he's right, because as soon as you stop moving, the cold gets into your bones.

"Get up and move, keep moving," he says, and pulls me up. "I know where we are."

He takes off his dark glasses and cups his hands around his eyes to scan the horizon. He looks back and I can tell he's thinking that we should go back, but the route looks very steep from here and I am so weak that I know that I would fall. What we are wearing is so cumbersome, I feel like an astronaut on the moon, lumbering slowly in acres of gear.

"I think we should go inside, get out of this cold," I say.

"We're not in—" Vincent stops and spits at the ground. He is struggling to explain. "Robyn, we're not even in England. I knew, I knew there was something wrong. I always knew. She wouldn't have just left me like that."

"We should get warm for a second. We can't think straight in this cold," I say, using everything I've got to power myself up. I take his arm.

The building is brick red with turned out corners like you would see in Asia. Each corner of the roof rolls up like a snail shell. The colour is diluted now but from the remnants of paint left the roof must once have been yellow. Multi-coloured streamers are strung from the roof and as the wind starts to get up they billow in red, blue, green, yellow and orange.

We stare at them, mesmerised, moving freely in the frozen landscape, but seeing them agitating is an ominous sight. I can smell it.

"A storm is coming," I say. We can't go forward.

"Can we make it back in time?" Vincent asks, and I shake my head. We are too tired, shocked and scared. We have to wait it out—up here.

My cheeks sting. Water from my eyes has fallen and frozen, salty against my cheek.

Vincent stops suddenly and crouches low to the ground. I watch and he jumps back. He starts rubbing the surface. I waddle over to him.

"Here," he points to a darkness in the snow. He hunches over something black poking through the ice. He pulls it and it starts unravelling in his hands. String. Damp and dirty, more of it coming out of the compact snow. He's completely bent over, scratching around the hard ground to get a purchase on it.

The string reveals a form under the snow. I can see that it is long and black and frozen into the ground. Vincent takes off his sunglasses and throws them into the snow. With his gloved hands he frantically digs out the compacted snow around the black shape, and I realise that it is not black at all but burnt orange darkened by water.

There's a smell of a butcher's shop. It is the odour of blood and meat on the turn.

As Vincent huffs and puffs he starts to carve out the shape of the black form—a clear outline, top to bottom, of what, or who, they were.

When he's finished digging there are six forms in total—human figures, partially buried. Their bodies are laid out in the snow only roughly wrapped in material. Their arms are crossed over their chests.

For a minute I think of my sister and I'm overcome with a desire to vomit, flee and run. I turn over in the snow. I'm crying, but I'm so cold, so incapable of movement that I let my eyes hang open.

It takes some time for Vincent to fully uncover all six, enough time for the weather to come in hard. We are showered with fresh snowflakes. The wind blows them sideways across us. If I let myself go limp. I am sure I will be blown off the side of the mountain, right back down to Erik and Lena.

"These are people," he says. "Do their families know that they are here? They'll have people missing them." His mood, his solemnity, he's always thinking about it, always looking for his mother. Each body that he is carving out, to Vincent, could be his mum. I start to shiver from the cold but I am petrified, literally frozen to the spot. I can't look at the bodies. I try to pull my shaking head away. I have never seen a dead body before. It can't be real.

"Vincent, we have to get inside now. Because if we don't, we'll end up like them."

Vincent has never been religious, but he is wasting time praying over them. I want to get in, and out of the wind that will kill us. Perhaps we've stumbled into a graveyard. Perhaps the ice here is filled with preserved remains. I glance around me, but the weather is so stinging that I can't see far. Vincent puts his hand up to his forehead, then his chest and then his stomach in the sign of the Elements.

"Earth, Sea and Sky," he says.

Vincent swipes one more time at one of the bodies and pulls the material off the face. It is a picture of abject horror. The mouth is open in a scream. The eyes open with no eyeballs. The skin frozen yellow and pulled taught over the cheek-bones of the skull. Hair stuck out like strands of straw. He stumbles back, bends over to vomit into the storm, but nothing comes out, only strings of bile.

I scream. All I can hear is blood rushing up into my head and then Vincent screams too. Then the next second he faints. He tries to stand up but his knees have buckled. I am filled with adrenaline. I can feel it fizz in my eyeballs. We have to fucking move.

"Get the fuck up, Vincent," I say. He's reacting to the height and the cold, to the exertion of hiking up here.

I dry heave and some vomit rises into my mouth. I bend down and gather Vincent's lanky body around my shoulder to lever him up. He's all off kilter, like a boxer who has been knocked out.

"I'm alright," he says, but his speech is slurred. The face he has exposed is not someone who died peacefully in their sleep. The contorted face carries the horror of a final scream. Of eyes plucked or mauled. The wind roars into my face.

I can't open the door with Vincent in my arms. I lay him down on the side. Everything takes longer, everything is heavier, every breath I take is laboured, and I can't seem to get enough air into my lungs. I can't blink. My eyelids are completely frozen, it takes incredible effort to close them. These gloves are too big to control.

I kick the door open. It is thick dark wood, maybe mahogany. It is not locked. It flaps open giving me a glimpse of the darkness within. Inside or outside? I have no choice. I enter into the darkness.

I lead Vincent inside. He mutters under his breath. His breathing has become shallow. His brow is furrowed as he silently argues with himself. I need to open his coat to let him breathe.

"Where's your sister?" he asks. I grasp his hand and try to pull him inside but he won't budge. In the distance, through the snow, I see something move.

I tell myself it's nothing. That it's just a shadow, but I am bundling, pulling Vincent inside now, fast, because I get the odious feeling that we're not up here on our own. He moves like a sloth. He's lost all impetus.

There is a snapping sound. I hear it again. I get a sudden cramp in my stomach. I don't want to look, but in the snow I see a shadow over the area where the bodies are.

I take a step backwards.

Vincent is delirious now and mumbling about his mother.

I close the door as much as I can. There's a sliver which won't fully shut because it is jammed open with snow.

I put my hand over Vincent's mouth. My hand shakes, jerking wildly up and down. The cold and the exertion have gone to his head. I get a grip on his shoulder, underneath the strap of his backpack and pull him backwards. He helps me by using his legs to push himself in. I look him in the eye and put a finger up to my lips.

"Please be quiet," I whisper.

Something towers over the bodies, ripping at them. Their smell must have got up and out into the air.

I angle myself so that I can't see the bodies, or the thing. It's as if the dead bodies are calling Vincent and me to go outside and lie with them in the open, until we sleep for a long time and freeze hard into their arms. Their curses are on us. They have slept undisturbed until our stupid enquiring minds opened up their rib cages to this.

I never pray, but I bless myself—head, chest and stomach, 'Earth, Sea and Sky.' I try to close the mahogany doors again, but they won't budge and I am so petrified of making any further noise that I start to urinate. I feel it hot and I tighten to stop myself, but I'm so cold and the sensation is so warm. A stream of light perforates the darkness.

I can hear the thing chewing.

I pull my head in. I want to shield my eyes and ears. I tremble. I cast my glance inside.

There are burnt out candles littering the floor. I look in to avoid looking out. I try the door again. In the fading light, my fingers trace the outline of the bolt, I'll have to give it a very gentle lift. I'm so cold I can hardly move my fingers. I'm so sluggish.

In the middle of the room there's a raised platform. The statue sitting in the middle tells me it's an altar. The statue is of a bald man with thick bands of fat around his arms and waist, and a smiling face. My eyes adjust to the darkness. I see more carvings in the walls; a thin man with a pointed hat and women with long bodies wearing pointed head-dresses. All of their faces look peaceful. I wish I had their peace. I only have fear.

I've almost closed the doors.

I push Vincent onto his side. He's a lumbering, giant turtle with his backpack still attached. I won't take it off him. It will make a noise. He mutters, shivering.

I manage to pull the bolt shut. It's almost black inside. I can hardly see my hand in front of my face.

I slip back behind the altar. This place was a church, but it's not Elemental. It has a different feel altogether, the strange emphasis on these statues. There is no inscription of the Earth, Sea and Sky as there always is in Elemental churches.

There is something at the door.

It is sniffing around—its big wet black nose jammed in the gap.

I don't move.

I don't breathe.

It must have smelled us.

It sneezes or coughs, makes a sputtering guttural noise. I wait, paralysed.

In the silence that follows, I realise that it isn't leaving. That this is life or death. That it's the thing out there or me.

I have a shotgun.

I drop it off my shoulder, but I hardly have the energy to pick it back up.

I snap off my gloves. My hands are a whitish blue, luminous in the darkness. I'm already a ghost.

I put the gun on the altar and unzip it from its case. It's the longest fucking zip. A draught from under the door blows up some stones, some grit, frozen debris trickles across my feet.

The doors look as though they are breathing. They pulsate in and out. It is such a natural movement, that at first I don't realise what is happening.

When they swing in again, it is fast and violent and the bolt splinters into two pieces, and the building is filled with such a deep, low roar, that I hear it in my belly.

In the doorway, illuminated by the light outside, stands a polar bear. Her fur glows like a halo. Her mouth is dirty—blood red—and she stands up on two feet. She is so fiercely beautiful. Pure, raw, power.

Vincent stirs, tries to stand, but she pounces, batting him to the other side of the room with a swipe of her paw. There's a noise from

Vincent's body like the wheeze of a piano accordion. She slashes at him with her claws. I feel Vincent's blood hit my face.

I stand frozen, watching.

The gun. Get the fucking gun!

I fumble, all fingers and thumbs. He's face down and she's on top of him. She's got her snout inside his backpack. Seeing me, she backs off, but she has Vincent and she's going to take him away. She's three times the size of him. She's trying to pull him away out the door.

I have a terrible thought; If she takes Vincent, then I might make it back alive.

I stand still. She looks into my eyes as she backs away, making a silent pact to let me go.

No. She's not taking my Vincent. I would rather die.

My impotent hands come into life.

He might be dead already. But she's not having him.

I raise the shotgun and blast. The noise ricochets around the building. She drops Vincent.

There's blood on her fur. She whines, screaming in pain—a huge bellowing roar that descends into a whimper.

She steps back outside. She's on all fours now, trying to run away, but I'm fast behind and she is wounded. I step over the mound that is Vincent and out into the snow. I have one shot left. I have to. I have no choice. It's me or her. She looks behind me and I shoot again.

Her tongue is long, it hangs out of her mouth as if to lick the snow. Her eyes are open. She is beautifully dead. I am terrified and disgusted. Something chemical is surging inside my body. Adrenaline. Euphoria. I have a blood lust. I smell it—the burn of shot and the rich iron of lashings of fresh blood.

It is suddenly silent. But I take up my gun and reach inside my pockets to find two more cartridges and crunch them into the barrel.

I turn back to Vincent. I've seen doctors taking my sister's pulse enough times to know what to do. I push two fingers into his neck.

There's a flap of skin open across his jaw and I can see through his cheek to the teeth inside his face.

I don't know where else he is hurt. I take off my coat, and the orange tracksuit top that Lena and Erik gave me, and I wrap it around Vincent's neck. I don't know how long he's got.

I take off my T-shirt and press it into Vincent's wounded face. I go outside. The building is flanked with snow. I am able to step up onto a wood store and climb onto the roof. Icicles snap off the guttering.

I think about Vincent's warm, dirty body on mine only days before. I think of the strength of him, my arms around him on the scooter. He's going to die. It is windy up on the roof, but I tie the tracksuit to a post that sticks up. It billows in the wind, bright orange, the two arms shaking ferociously up at the sky.

SEVENTEEN

I AM CURLED around Vincent. I'm not sure that he is alive. I shiver. I'm aware I am trembling because I have trouble holding the Cube. It is locked onto my eye and the hope of being taken away into another world is keeping me conscious.

It also feels final. I imagine this is what taking serious drugs must be like. One burst and I am transported into another, better world where none of my problems exist. But I don't know if I am coming back.

I am riding a red Ducati motorbike. I am going fast on a quiet road through fields and woods. The sky is blue and dotted with white fluffy clouds. Of course it's not me, it's Ivan, but it feels like we are one and the same. I hear him think;

"When my mother dies, I won't have any reason to come back here."

Ivan parks the bike on the driveway of a modest house. The road has the wide proportions of American suburbia, the kind of street you would never find in Brighton. A rusting basketball ring tells me that this was once bubbling alive with family. Now it calls out with sadness that the children will never be seven years old again.

Ivan can smell something cooking. It's so alluring, so emotive, it makes him forget he's a grown man, and the boy in him heads straight for the kitchen. The pot hisses on the stove so Ivan goes over and turns down the gas. There's a noise outside. A high-pressured scorching blast followed by a tinny bang. A small person is bent over an old tin bath. The bath has been cut in two and this person is welding it back together. A battered gas cylinder chugs. Ivan thinks;

"She likes to patch and fix."

She is wearing a huge welder's visor and dirty red overalls. She is short in height, but I feel a tremendous force coming off her. It's in the way she stands. She is commanding. Ivan is in awe of her. She pulls up her visor.

"I'm making my own pizza oven," she says.

"Hi Mom," says Ivan.

"I could hear that bike of yours coming up the road." Light reflects from the glass of her visor and they close in slowly and hold each other, and it fills me with emotion. I am crying now, watching them, wondering if, in fact juggling, fighting off the thought that I won't see my sister ever again. Knowing that Vincent might never reconcile with his Mother. That this is it. These are the last things I will ever think.

I get a sense of her car mechanic smell. She is soft around the mouth, her skin is plump and pink. She inspects Ivan's face, looking at him all over. She must have done this when he was first born, perhaps lifting him up by the legs to inspect his tackle, and to count that all of his fingers were there.

She looks up at the sky and asks Ivan if he thinks it is going to rain. When they decide it isn't, they agree to leave her work in progress out in the open so that she can continue later. They inspect flower heads, she holds one down to show Ivan some crawling aphids and then she squirts them with liquid from an old washing up bottle.

I count four cats, two goats, a pig and a llama. She says that she's not ever getting another dog after she lost Einstein. The scene fuzzes with static electricity.

In reality, I see the lump of Vincent. I am beyond cold. If I could move I would reach out to him. I must try harder. My eyes glance outside but the glow of white is sharp and pointed. Large birds are swooping down to peck at the dead polar bear. They pull out some long red sinew which twists in the wind like a fish on a hook.

I'm back at Ivan's Mom's table. On the stove is a beef stew with red wine and shallots. They are her own vegetables that she has grown. Ivan's phone buzzes, but remarkably, he switches it off and puts it away in his pocket.

There's a llama in the doorway.

"Get away!" she screams. Ivan bought her the llama because she wouldn't replace the dog, but he understands now that they are not the same thing. He apologises and suggests rehoming it on a farm. His Mom immediately dismisses the idea. He buys over-elaborate gifts. He's rich and desperate to be loved.

He sits at the table and his Mom dishes up a pile of potatoes, mashed with real butter. Ivan is starving for her food. He's had months of Californian vegan hell.

She cracks open two beers, one for Ivan, and one for her, but I jump when she turns around because she's not Ivan's Mom, she's turned into a huge polar bear.

I'm trembling. If I concentrate I can detach. I can watch both. I can see a healthy polar bear, over eight feet tall serving dinner and talking in Ivan's Mom's voice, and I can see her dead on the ground outside being devoured by several large albatrosses.

She drinks the beer. It's the wrong shape for her mouth, too pointy, and beer trickles down her furry chin. She wipes it away with a napkin.

"Have you been up into space again?" Ivan's Mom asks, carrying the ketchup to her son. She spoons out the stew for both of them.

"Well, I've been up three times now into what you would call near space."

"The Mesosphere? Really? Oh, I think you've been a little bit further than that?" She holds out a plate of buttered slices of bread. Ivan takes one, folds it in half and dips it into the stew. Ivan squirms. He doesn't want to tell her where he's been or where he is going. He's her only son.

"You know I'm not allowed to say," he says. She raises her eyebrows and chews a piece of beef. It goes quiet for the first time and I can feel the tension between them. Ivan feels he has to fill the silence. "Okay, I was 6,000 miles above earth. It's an airplane really.

We didn't dock with the EVA space station but we were close. I wouldn't be allowed on board anyway. I'm not an astronaut."

"I'm worried about you, going up there. Everyone knows why they didn't go back to the moon, don't we?"

"Tell me the story about watching the moon landing in '69," Ivan tries to change the subject, get her talking about a story that she loves to tell.

"The government redacted the files, Ivan, those astronauts were developing all sorts of cancers."

"We're looking at that," he says, and dips another slice of bread into the gravy. Just then it pops into my head. Ivan's Mom is a force of nature, just like my mother. She is a Physics teacher. She trained as an aeronautical engineer and then worked as a Physicist for thirty years.

"As with any new technology, just because you can do it, doesn't mean that you should."

"Really, you don't think that because we can, we should?" They are picking up energy, they are tussling. He likes it, to tussle and argue with someone that doesn't have to worry about their job afterwards.

"What concerns me, Ivan, is the long term effect of radiation. You're proposing to send people up for how long? Forever? A six-month trip to your proposed colony is going to exert a thousand millisieverts on the human body."

"I'm a businessman, Mom, not a scientist."

"To my mind," says Ivan's Mom. "The main area of development should be in preparing and protecting the human body against radiation."

"Improvements are being developed all the time," Ivan says, angrily, loading more potatoes onto his plate.

"It's the clothing, new materials are needed to protect against UVA, certainly consider developing an anti-radiation medication to be taken in advance to protect blood and organs from inside. Have you thought about that?"

"You want a job, Mom?"

"You need to tell these scientists that work for you that this is where the real problem is." She takes the dishes back to the sink, but when she drops them in the noise is deafening. It sounds like the coarse dub-step of a helicopter. She turns around and she is the polar bear again. "It's fine now, Ivan, but when you get to my age, you'll know. Mark my words." She opens her mouth and roars and noise carries completely over me. I feel it in my chest. My whole being is vibrating.

The snow outside is being blown up into a frenzy. The birds fly away.

It really is a helicopter.

People!

We're saved!

I try to stretch a leg to kick Vincent. He doesn't move. I don't know if I am moving.

"Vincent, we're going to be okay," I say, my mouth feels frozen stiff.

People are hunched over the dead polar bear. They are uniformed. Hats pulled low, broad linear shoulders. Soldiers. Shit.

People are coming into the building. They become frantic when they see Vincent and me lying on the floor. One is waving back outside calling more people in. Another has taken off a glove and has his hand inside Vincent's clothes.

There's another light in my eye. This time white. It flicks away. Then back, away, then back. The light is shutting out Ivan. I want to stay here with him and his Mom.

A voice says;

"She's conscious."

Ivan and his Mom are by the front door. It's time to go. She holds him and he holds her. I get that lovely smell of car garage and flowers, perhaps a floral perfume that smells familiar?

"Is that where you're going now? Space?" asks Ivan's Mom. They are slipping away. Someone else has come into the building. A woman. It's her I can smell, the perfume. I know it. I know her. She's right up in my face, but I can't quite see her. She has glasses and a coat that zips up to her nose. She undoes the zip of her jacket.

Ivan shakes his head at his Mom. He doesn't want her to worry. He's not going into space.

"Actually, Mom, I'm working on something entirely different. It is incredibly exciting and very soon I'll be able to tell you all about it…" They flicker, breaking up. I'm losing them.

"Ivan, you tire so easily! What about the space race?" She's holding him by the shoulders.

"I haven't forgotten about that."

"Just remember honey that when you lose interest in something, you drop it like a stone. That's just the way you are."

They are gone. Dropped. Fizzed away, and I am back in the building and the woman smelling of perfume has unzipped her coat and her face is inches away from mine, and she screams at me.

"Robyn! Robyn!" There are tears in her eyes. She is angry.

"Mother," I say. "How..?"

"We've got you," she says, and her arms are around me. "You're going to be fine." Then I see another hand, and a needle, and a pinch in the base of my neck.

Then everything goes black.

EIGHTEEN

I STROKE MY DOG. He is small and black and he sits upright on my lap, enjoying being stroked. My hand lifts and draws down on his silky fur. Then he is gone. My hand still moves, stroking the empty air. I am in hospital. Waking up. There is a nurse, a cream coloured wall, and a clear liquid hung up in a glass bottle trickling into me.

I don't have a dog. I don't think we ever owned a dog.

I miss it intensely.

Then I go back to black.

NINETEEN

I AM WOKEN by an approaching noise. It's a trolley, or another metal object on squeaky wheels being pushed along the corridor outside. Whoever is doing the pushing stops to talk to someone else. Their conversation is only a mumble. I strain to listen, but my head is too foggy. I can't concentrate or hold my thoughts for long. Soon they move on again and I am left in silence.

I need to get out of here. I need to find my sister. Find Vincent.

I am in a hospital. The smell is menthol antiseptic. It's too harsh to be comforting, in fact it's scary. The room is more like a hotel. A built-in acrylic panel sweeps along the main wall. It's all white. There's no TV, no magazines, no clock. I paw at the medical equipment—a stainless steel bowl, wires, a bleeping monitor and bundled gauze resting fatly on the table top.

As I turn my neck there's a baby pain in my head. The numb sensation in my buttocks and lower back tells me that I have been asleep for a long time. I lift up my hand. My nails are cut flat and squat. I don't keep my nails like that.

My hands are dry, but the same familiar veins bulge. I am a whiter, paler version of myself.

Where the fuck am I?

I try to get up. Oh, my head! I pull two suckers off my chest. There's a long beep. The room spins and I feel nauseous. I lie back down. My head is bandaged. I get up again and onto my bare feet. I am wearing a white hospital smock.

I have to get up. I have to get moving again. I have to speak to Mother and find out what's happening.

There is a bathroom. I go in and see a toilet and a bath with a shower but no mirror. I realise that I am wearing a nappy under the gown. It feels thick between my legs. I try to take it off. It's clean, not soiled. The hospital gown gapes. I'd prefer to keep it on than have nothing on at all.

I look behind the door for a mirror. Nothing. I come back out into the room and turn to the window. I open the curtain and there's nothing there. It's only a panel of light. With the curtain in front it looks like a window, but it's totally sealed.

I feel a vomit inducing sense of panic.

Where am I? How long have I been here?

I go to the door. I'm expecting it to be locked, but it opens. The corridor is completely white and filled with artificial light. At either end is a set of double doors. My legs are wobbly. I assume because I haven't walked around for a while. I feel light, a bit giddy. My head hurts.

Both ends of the hall look exactly the same distance away from me. I lean my weary body towards one and then the other. I go to the right. My left side feels out of kilter. I need to run. To walk. To do something fast, like now. I'm obviously not dead. Where's Mother?

My gut tells me there is something not quite right.

Wherever I am, they don't know that I am awake yet, and that gives me a chance. I try to walk at pace towards the double doors, but I sway from side to side. What day is it? Where's Vincent? Where's my sister? There is no fucking London.

There is no London

Everything I have been told is a lie. I'm going to find out where I am, and why they've been lying to me and exactly what the fuck they've been giving me to make me forget everything.

I need to find Tiffany. She won't have a clue where I've gone. She's probably moved on to someone else. She was trying to tell me, trying to help me. I have to see her again. She's the only one who was willing to help me find the truth.

I feel a pain in my temple. I remember searing cold and I hear a bear's roar holler down the corridor, and a shot, and I jump out of my skin. I crouch on the floor and maybe I shout because the door opens and a nurse stands in the doorway.

"Good. You're awake," she says, smiling. She's plump with rosy cheeks. She wobbles slightly. She peers down at me. "Can you stand up, Robyn?"

I nod. She knows my name. Her thin, wiry glasses slip down her nose as she bends down.

"Where am I?" I ask.

"You're in the hospital." She says.

"Where? In Brighton?"

"Not exactly Brighton," she says. It's all hazy.

"Vincent?" I ask. "Is Vincent okay?"

"I've got a surprise for you," she says, "I think you'll like it." She puts her arm around me and we walk through the double doors. I can feel her warm flesh against me. It makes me want to cry.

There's a desk, a nurses' station where she must usually reside. She settles me into a wheelchair.

"I don't need that," I say, but she's stronger than me.

"There," she says. "In you get. That's better."

She pushes me through another white corridor. It's sealed. The air conditioning is cool and drives a tickle in my throat. All the doors are closed. I assume that there must be other patients here. I can hear a television, multiple televisions playing in different rooms.

As she wheels me, my mind spins around again, going over Vincent, my sister, Tiffany, university. I feel like I am floating up out of the wheelchair. I even catch myself tapping my foot to imaginary music. I've done enough drugs in the past to realise that I am high. Really high, and smoothly so. I'm fully medicated. My arms tingle. There's a stiffness in my jaw. I want to talk. My pain is subdued, I only feel its residue.

I breathe a deep sigh and then let it all out. The nurse has been chatting to me all along but she comes around to the front of me now and takes one of my feet and plants it on the floor.

"Here, now," she says, and does the same with the other foot. My jaw is locked, giving me the most terrible headache on the front left side.

Then I remember the Cube. Perhaps it was back in my barren room. Maybe they've taken it. I don't think I can trust them, even this nice nurse who smells of talcum powder. She's helping me up.

"Where's my mother?" I ask, but the nurse is busy opening the door. Her eyes have widened and she stares at me intently. Everything about her has become even more pink and rounded and soft.

"Someone has been waiting to see you," she says, her chubby palm fully spread as she holds open the door. It must be Vincent. Her other arm is around me, helping me get up out of my chair. I don't want her help, but she is so lovely and comforting that I have to do what she says.

She makes me think of hot chocolate, of piping hot Sunday dinners and gravy. She takes me into the room and then takes a step back urging me to go forward. The room is very much like the one that I woke up in.

Someone is lying on the bed. Her back to me.

Because it is a girl. It reminds me of waking up with Ivan and that woman in the bed, but I am further away. The body is more fragile. I walk towards the bed. I reach out with my pale thin limbs. Both hands touch her, because I know who she is.

My sister, Alice.

I can smell her. I can tap into the energy that zips between us. I push my face into the back of her hair. She smells of coconut—always the same. It's tinged with a medical disinfectant here, but still clearly her smell. It's from a set that I bought her for Christmas.

"Alice," I whisper, and she jumps, but realises it's me, and she reaches around to touch my face with her hand. I put my arms around her and we cuddle like that, big spoon and little spoon. I need to tell her that we are not in Brighton, that there is no London, that we are somewhere else, that they've moved us somewhere unknown, and for what, I'm not sure.

"Robyn," she says. "At last."

My sister! I have finally found my sister.

She wiggles around to see me and we are forehead to forehead and she is smiling, but when she sees the bandaged side of my face, her mouth drops.

"Your poor face," she says, and she cries. I feel sad when we should be happy to be back together. This is what I've wanted all along, to be with my sister. I don't know how long we've been apart, it might be a weekend, or a week but it really does feel much longer than that.

As we pull away from each other, I realise she has changed. One eye is opaque, as it had slowly become when she lost her sight, but the other is staring right at me. It is red and bloodshot, but it's wrong somehow. I realise that she can see me—fully and clearly.

Instinctively, I pull away, because I know that eye. I know it because it's mine.

"You don't know. You don't know, do you?" asks my sister, but she's like a weak, raging toddler. Her little body vibrates with anger, but she has no way to release her power. "They said you knew. They told me you knew!"

I reach up to the bandages on my face and pull, and they start to pluck away like feathers from a bird.

"Where's a mirror? I need a mirror," I say, frantically screaming. I push open the door into her bathroom and there is a large mirror the width of the sink. I go to it. The light flickers bright blue over my head. My face is pale and washed out.

I open my eyes and see that it is gone. My left eye is gone. All that is left is a black hole where my eyelids hang like vaginal lips.

TWENTY

I LOVE THE smell of the sea. I don't think I'll ever get bored of it. I get up in the mornings and go to work in a café called Lucky Beach. I get Mondays off and a half day Tuesday. I ride the bus, all two stops along the seafront.

My boss is called Jan and she's the loveliest woman. She likes to sit down and have a chat at any opportunity. She has blonde curls that get set by her hairdresser weekly in a long, glossy style. She's always hugging me, can't keep her hands off me. Mother often remarks snidely; "No children of her own." She sings along to most songs on the radio but rarely knows the words. She's got a beautiful little dog, he's a pug, and she brings him into the Café where he drinks milk from a saucer and howls at the noise of the till.

There's a penguin that I like. He's very tame. He's been coming to see me each day. I give him a blueberry muffin. I know they're not meant to eat those, but he likes it. He throws his head back with the muffin in his beak and gobbles it down in one. I call him Bruce. He's tame. He comes close to me, he wants to see what I've got. He's got terrible eyesight.

A juvenile albatross—a feisty teenager—swoops overhead trying to get some of the muffin. There's talk of a cull. They're getting more aggressive. It's the only thing that gets Jan angry. She's worried that the abundance of large sea birds is encouraging the 'wild animals' to come into town foraging for food. There's much talk of 'beasts' these days.

"Someone's going to get killed," she says, shaking her head. No one actually names the 'wild animals', as though addressing them by their proper name will bring them to your door. But they're big, and vicious, and should not be here in the first place. Jan's having a community meeting about it in the Café next Thursday. There's a homemade flyer stuck to the front window.

'RE-ZOO THE BEASTS'

People are scared, but I'm not. Mother has me on medication. Advised by the doctor and I've agreed to it. I need it. So, I see everything, but I don't really feel anything. So whilst I appreciate that there's some sort of danger, I'm not actually scared. I've got my own problems to deal with. Occasionally I get a pain in the side of my head. I bang into things. The drugs make me dizzy, and only having one eye doesn't help. Weirdly, I can't seem to balance on a bicycle anymore.

Jan and I listen to the radio. It mumbles away in the background, charting the progress of time throughout the day. Jan likes Sarah Phoenix, the radio presenter with striking red hair. Jan likes her voice and her no-nonsense, Mumsy manner. She's been into the Cafe and Jan keeps a photograph of the two of them smiling forever above the till.

Three boys on bicycles pass the café, perfectly balanced—pulling up their front wheels into wheelies. I feel a sharp slap of awe, jealousy and sadness.

"I used to be able to do that," says the only customer in the café. She usually sits outside alone at an aluminium table. She comes in nearly every day and always leaves me a tip. Once she asked me when my break was, which was strange. She must be lonely, because she's always trying to make conversation.

I give her a leaflet about Jan's 'Re-Zoo the Beasts meeting'. She reads it diligently, taking time to consider the issue, while I move on to wipe the next table. She looks up and asks in a formal tone; "Are you going to be there?"

Mother's taking care of those kinds of things at the moment. She's being very strict about ensuring that I get enough rest and organising my engagements. Mother tells me that 'the beasts' are nothing for me to worry about. But that just makes me more inclined to find out.

"I'm not sure," I say. "Are you going?"

"I'll go, if you're going," she answers directly.

"Okay," I say, "I'll go." She looks delighted. In fact she stands up and I think she's going to shake my hand, but when I recoil, she just nods her head and starts to leave. She has blonde spiky hair and a bold tattoo climbing up her neck.

I mention the meeting to Mother. I have to seed things in advance to plan my escapes, or else she wouldn't let me do anything, she wouldn't let me go anywhere. I've started stopping off places that I want to go on the way into work. I leave the Cafe early and walk around Brighton. I'm searching for something. I'm not sure what, but it's starting to become clear.

But as my mother rightly says, there's a whole army of Conservation Rangers—hundreds of them—whose sole job is to deal with the 'Beast Situation'. From the reports that she has seen, at least one third are now safely back in the zoo, and the rest will be efficiently dispatched. These are thorough and hardy experienced men and women. We shouldn't meddle in things that we know nothing about.

I don't go to the meeting.

After I don't show up, the blonde spiky customer doesn't come into the café half as much as before. However, I see her a couple of times. One afternoon I pass her on Western Road and she doesn't see me, so I stand inside the doorway of the Charity Shop and watch her. She queues to get money out of a cash point, listening to music, tapping her foot, and blowing bubble gum. She holds herself more confidently than I'd ever seen her at the café.

Another time, I spot her sitting on a wall under a tree at a bus stop across from my house. She stares across the road for an hour or more as if she is in a trance. I have to go upstairs to watch her from Mother's bedroom. I have a crazy thought about going out and asking her what she is doing, but I don't.

I follow her when she leaves the café. I'm freezing and I still have my apron on but I don't care. I need to know who she is. She walks around smoking a lot. She meets a very tall woman and they go into some elegant flats on the seafront. I think she lives there, high up in a little flat with a balcony overlooking the sea. I often go past on the bus and I always crane my neck to look.

Every day, I wait for her to come into the café, but she doesn't. I should have gone to the meeting.

Instead, Mother has decided that I am recuperating well and that the time has come for me to get 'out there'. She has set me up on a date with a junior team member whom she works with at the Council. He's called David Sykes. He's older than me, like twice my age, but Mother thinks it will be good to help me get over my break-up with Vincent.

I am so late to meet him.

I can't remember breaking up with Vincent. Apparently it was traumatic. Mother says that my medication is subduing painful memories. We decide that I will defer my place at university for another year so that I can get back on track. I need to return my strength after my donation. My sister is doing much better. Helping her is the best thing I've ever done.

I am meeting David in the Laines, in a pub called The White Rabbit. I've been warned by my mother not to drink excessively, and as soon as I see David again, I know why. I mean she's not stupid, my mother, she knows I'll have to sink a few to get through this 'date'. She kept saying; "Looks aren't everything." I assumed she was talking about David Sykes, but maybe she meant me.

I adjust my eye patch. It's black. I look like a pirate. I am wearing black boots. Mother took me shopping but I hate the clothes that she suggests; floral print dresses and so on—not that she ever wears anything of the sort herself with her interchangeable range of power suits. She wouldn't be seen dead in a floral dress.

David licks his lips and a little frothy saliva is caught in the corner of his mouth. Sitting across from David, I don't think I have ever been so un-attracted to another human being, male or female, in all my life. He looks like everyone else, with his brown eyes and brown hair, except he is so scrawny he must weigh half a person. I think that even in my own fragile state that I could lift him up myself.

Mother has some cheek. I know I've got a patch but, for fuck's sake, is David is all that I can be matched with? Is this now what Mother genuinely thinks of me? There is someone for everyone, they say. Well except my mother, who is perpetually sexless and single. She must have had sex to have my sister and I, but based on her behaviour since, never more than twice in her life.

I recall thinking at one time in my life that Vincent was so good looking that I must be okay—I mean attractive-wise—to pull him in the first place. Well, more than okay, I must be reasonably attractive to have been with him. But David Sykes! I don't mean to be nasty, and who am I to talk when I can't fasten my jeans. Let's not forget. I have no eye.

Mother says I'll get used to it and that every knock should be a reminder of my selfless act of charity. Of course, I can't fucking remember my selfless act.

I feel a flutter in the pit of my stomach. Nerves? Or I am alive after all. The flutter is not for David in that way. But I suppose that it might be for someone else. I have an appetite. I have desire. I could just have sex with David, I suppose, get it over and done with. But I would need to drink a lot more wine. If I had sex with David, it might sort of appease Mother and get her off my back. That sounds really fucked up, but I am looking for my freedom, searching it out, and I think I might do anything.

David tells me earnestly about his job and his plans to introduce a new traffic light system to reduce congestion along the seafront. I nod and listen, and I realise that I have finished a whole large glass of wine and he has hardly touched his. Would it be rude to ask him, 'don't you want that?' Then I would reach across, take his glass and throw the lot down my throat.

I want to but I stop myself but there's a bad me, inside, that wants to repulse David. If I put him off enough then he might lose interest that way, and I could get free without having to fuck him?

"Your Mother is an incredible woman, Robyn." He says, and I realise I'll never get free because all his hopes and dreams belong to his imaginary relationship with me, and the subsequent greater access to his true heart's desire; Mother.

"That is one way of putting it," I force through a smile.

"Do you ride a bicycle?" he asks.

"With my eye? After what's just happened to me? Are you having a laugh?" I snap back at him. I wish I could ride a bike again. "I can hardly walk in a straight line." I suppose he's only trying to make conversation, but there's an angry me lurking underneath the surface, and she's gaining power (glorious anger and rage!). David looks shocked and picks up his drink.

"I didn't mean to…" he doesn't finish his sentence.

"Perhaps in a few months I'll feel a bit better," I add, to soften my response.

"Well, perhaps then I could help you learn to ride again," he says. At the back of the bar there is a mirror. Bottles of liquor are arranged all around it. In the reflection I can suddenly see her.

"No," I say. "I won't need help. You never forget how to ride a bike." It's her, it's the girl with the blonde spiky hair (from the cafe that I've been following!) and yes, of course she's looking at me. I realise I know her name. Tiffany.

"Be nice to ride out, one Sunday, just the two of us," says David, his mind already imagining the scenario of the two of us on another date.

"Tiffany," tumbles breathlessly out of my mouth.

"Sorry, what did you say?"

"Excuse me," I say. "I'm just going to the bathroom." David half stands when I rise and he fumbles, dropping his glasses and napkin onto the floor.

The toilets are at the back of the pub and down a dark claustrophobic staircase. The music becomes muffled as I descend, and I can only hear the bass through the floor, and through my chest. The walls are covered in graffiti and publicity posters for upcoming bands.

There are three cubicles in the ladies and so I go into the one at the farthest end. A poster is stuck to the back of the door.

Tomorrow night a band called 'South Pole' is playing in the function room upstairs.

Tiffany has come into the room. I can sense her. I don't need to go to the toilet, I never did. I stand there, inside my cubicle and then, for effect, I flush the cistern. I open the door. Tiffany is leaning against the sink with her arms folded.

I have butterflies in my tummy.

"I think we need another storm," she says. I don't understand what she means, but I'm totally into it anyway. I am tingling all over.

"Yes," I say.

"Do you remember the storm?" She asks, and I shake my head. I hold my head to one side shielding my patch. I don't want her to see.

"Do you remember the Old Steine? Last Summer?" she asks. I shake my head again. I've got to clear this brain. I've got to stop taking Mother's prescriptions. I've got to get free. I know she's part of it. She's my way out.

"Kind of," I lie.

"We've met for the first time, quite a few times," she says, but I still don't remember. I want to remember her. I go over to her and she takes my hand, only holding the little finger of my right hand. Her touch is delicate. She looks around the area of my patch. I feel like she is holding back from crying because her chest heaves up and she sighs. The lower rim of her black mascaraed eyes brims with tears.

"Do you even know who I am?" she asks. I nod.

"You're Tiffany," I say, and the only thing I know about her is the warm feeling that I get. "I've seen you around here before." This makes her laugh. Then I am laughing too. We stay there like that for some time, holding hands. We don't say anything because we don't need to. We only need to feel.

But I hear him on the stairs.

"Robyn! Oh, Robyn!" David calls. Tiffany lets go of my hand and moves into the cubicle at the end. She pulls back the door, so it merely looks empty. I stick my hands under the dryer. I know enough to pretend that I am on my own. David's gaunt face appears in the doorway.

"You've been ages," he says, merrily. "Everything alright?"

"Yes, everything is wonderful now," I say, knowing that she can hear me.

"Oh good," he says. "Our food's arrived." I follow him out back up to the table. He's ordered a whole Emerald Rock Cod, and its bulbous opaque eye is staring at me. I've ordered a steak. It's never on any menus these days and it's very expensive. He's paying, and besides I have a strange insatiable appetite for rare meat.

But I am too excited to savour the tender fillet and I chew aimlessly, afraid to swallow. David slices open the fish, and out of him slips a long story about his own mother. All the time I am on tenterhooks, waiting for Tiffany to come up the stairs. I am breathless with anticipation. I have to nod at David's story and chew when I am too exhilarated to catch my breath.

When Tiffany finally does appear she walks through the pub, picks up her coat from a table in the corner and leaves. She doesn't even look at me. She's gone and the tension suddenly snaps and disappears leaving me teetering.

David passes me a napkin. My eyes still cry. It's relief. It's in grief for what I have already lost, and all that I think I still have time to lose. A tear trickles out from underneath my patch and down my cheek.

I promise myself that I am never going to forget her again.

Tiffany. Tiffany. Tiffany.

TWENTY ONE

I FEED THE penguin. He is fat and his colours are vividly drawn against the sky and sea. He is two-tone black and white, but with a beautiful orange beak and a blue sprouting crest under his chin. We're all just silhouettes against this horizon. All of us fade into the shadow of this never-ending vista. It was here before us and will be here long after we have gone.

I call him Bruce, and he doesn't seem to mind. I give him two muffins today. Fuck it. I give him a blueberry and then a lemon with poppy seed. They're not real poppy seeds and they are not real lemons either. It's all chemical. Before he gollops the last bit down, I get the overwhelming desire to vomit.

I heave sharply and scramble to the bin where I vomit a tidy parcel of sick. When I finish, my brow is splashed with pin-pricks of sweat. Bruce is as surprised as I am. I see he's watching me and he rises up and flaps his little wings furiously.

I know what he's thinking.

"No, I'm not," I say, but I can't remember anything about my own body. I can't remember my eye, I can't remember my last period or the one before that. "I don't know, I just don't know." I undo the top button of my jeans. That's better. I had sex with Vincent lots of times. Exactly where and when is sketchy, but I can remember the flicker of his dishevelled hair falling on top of me, brushing my face as he grinds away. That's not something you can forget in a hurry.

Other memories surface in this sex compartment of my brain. I think harder which hurts. It is so painful to think hard that it feels like I am squeezing lemon juice into the sinews of my brain. The penguin likes this and squeak-cackles like a dolphin. There's someone else having sex with me. Taut, lithe, moving inside me, an altogether more fluid experience. I remember kissing a tattoo.

The penguin claps his wings in glee. Little pervert!

"Where is Vincent, anyway?" I ask Bruce, and he shakes his head. He doesn't know. I wish I had more food to give him. The thought of fish makes me feel sick but he has plenty of fish in the sea and it was the sugar he was really after. Who could blame him?

If it is true that Vincent has dumped me, and that it caused me to have an anxious episode like Mother says (a sort of breakdown) then I think that I would feel it more. Surely, I would hate him now. I'm sure that I would remember and I would try to avoid him, but he is nowhere to be seen. He would never just disappear forever. I suppose this might be it (anxiety or paranoia or disbelief). Maybe I can't except that he finished with me and that's why my brain is fried.

But, if I wasn't over Vincent, then I wouldn't be thinking this way about Tiffany, all of the time. I can't stop thinking about her. I wonder where she is and what she's doing. I hope that she might show up at any time. Bruce throws his head back and squawks.

"Shhhhhh!" I say, Jan will be out if she hears him. She thinks they encourage beasts.

Vincent and I argued and split up and got back together all the time. If he dumped me, I think we'd still be friends. If he dumped me I don't think I would care that much. One thing is certain, he would never leave my sister, never.

I have decided not to take mother's pills anymore. I keep them under my tongue, I practise a couple of times and am able to speak completely normally with three large and one small tablet hidden in the recesses of my mouth.

It was something about the way Mother patted David's shoulder when she dropped him home after our date at The White Rabbit. She picked us up at 10 p.m. and then winked at him and invited him for Sunday lunch. My own mother! She is trying to marry her one-eyed daughter to a junior bureaucrat from the Council.

Jan arrives from the Café with her arms folded against the cold wind that has suddenly descended. She claps her hands over her apron and roars at the penguin and he turns on his heel and dives into the sea.

"You shouldn't feed the penguins, Robyn." She says. "How many times I have to tell you?"

"Sorry," I say, but I'm already planning Bruce's next snack. Tomorrow I might try him with a Danish Pastry.

"You'll be sorry when one of those beasts comes down looking for its next meal, don't encourage them. Once they've eaten all the penguins, they'll start on us."

"Bruce, take care of yourself, buddy!" I shout after my penguin who has disappeared into the turquoise sea. "It's a jungle out there!"

"They—" she lingers sneeringly on the word 'they'. "They can sniff out penguins from miles around." She swallows, her sinewy neck bobbling. "They pick up the scent and then creep up out of nowhere. A whole penguin can fill them for a month." She looks up and down the coast. She's wearing a whistle. All of the seafront vendors have them. She's meant to blow it to let a ranger know if something roams into town.

"Jan, how long have we had penguins in Brighton? And beasts for that matter? Doesn't it strike you as a little odd?" I ask. She tucks my hair behind my ear gently as if I am a child.

"You could come and stay with me for a few days, Robyn. Your Mother mightn't like it, but it is actually my job to look after you." Jan is lovely to me. She's more like an auntie than a boss, or, I dare say it, more like a mother than Mother.

"Jan," I say slowly. "We're not in Brighton, are we?"

"That depends on how you look at it," she says, she's giggling nervously, and I sense that this might be beyond her pay grade. I bet Mother's told her not to discuss this with me.

"We're either not in Brighton, or I've completely lost my mind," I say. "So you better tell me the truth, because I'm going to find out whether you tell me or not."

"No, we're not my love," she says. "I'm sorry."

"Then where the fuck are we?"

"That's all I can tell you. You'll have to ask your Mother to explain the rest." I'll find out myself. I will find the truth.

"Jan, come on."

"But in a funny sort of way, Robyn, to me, we are in Brighton. We really are." I want to ask more, but suddenly my head is back over the bin and I'm spitting mucus and then evacuating my empty stomach of bile. With each retch I begin to think more clearly. I'm like a sobering drunk. I am starting to remember.

In a funny sort of way, Robyn, we are in Brighton.

I heave into the bin again.

TWENTY TWO

I AM AT Brighton train station. It is freezing today. The weather is changing. It's a sky that I do not recognise anymore. It is as if a giant has drawn his knife across the firmament and opened up incisions that blister with lightning. I've never seen lightning like this. It smells bitter.

"Not even on the night of the storm?" asks Tiffany.

"I don't think so," I say, because it was just rain and wind and thunder under thick rolls of cloud. Also because I am starting to remember things.

I asked Mother if I could stay with Jan for the weekend and she took off her glasses and put one arm of her spectacles into her mouth to help her think. She was reading a document called 'Forging New Relationships and Alliances; A Strategic Approach'. It was stamped 'Urgent' in red ink. I wondered if she thought I was bluffing, and that I was going to try and see David, possibly spend a seedy weekend with him in a bed and breakfast. Think again, Mother. I'm getting my mojo back. Anyhow, she put her glasses back on and said: "Yes". No caveat, no exclusions.

Perhaps she thinks I am no longer capable of pulling off a feat of independence. In spite of her great experience, she might not realise that we all have muscle memory. It's the bit that won't stop twitching long after the itch has been scratched; the bit that springs back into action when it gets merely a sniff of what it used to do.

I don't tell my sister, Alice, what I am planning. I don't tell her much anymore.

I asked Jan to lie for me and she wiped her hands on her apron and then cupped my face.

"Of course, my darling," she said, leaving a feather of flour on my check. "If I get into trouble with your Mother, then I just don't care. It's gone too far." She's still obtuse in a naive kind of way. She won't tell me what it is exactly that's gone too far. Perhaps she doesn't know.

Tiffany bought the tickets. It is best not to plan in advance she explains—spontaneity is the route to freedom, and using cash is also preferable. I don't know where we're going. I'm just excited to be alone with her.

But when we arrive, there is a problem with the line. All the trains to London have been cancelled. There is a row of red 'X's. We've only got two days. The jolly looking train guard is advising people to postpone all travel until tomorrow.

Tiffany is unperturbed.

"There's one train to Bognor Regis that is still running and we're going to get that," she says. Travellers siphon off in a fast moving line toward a smaller platform in the left hand corner. The train is smaller, older and shittier than the parked beast that should have taken us somewhere else, somewhere bigger and more important.

I have memories of trains, that's for sure. A steam train through the countryside when I was too small to reach up and see out of the window. Mother had to pick me up to look outside. Another time I was on a school trip. There were a load of us in a carriage, a worried teacher continuously counting us with a pointed finger.

My memory is doing that thing where the edges turn out like flower petals and the image rolls and drips off like a water droplet.

We speed out of town, ducking underneath bridges and tunnels and riding high on a viaduct. I grip the seat. They are made of red crushed velvet. It feels unusual to be propelled along like this at speed.

I don't believe that we are going to Bognor Regis. Tiffany hasn't told me our actual destination and I haven't asked. I wonder how I came to be led around by the nose like this. Why do I do what I'm told without hesitation? Then I remember that I am defying Mother and my heart swells with pride. I'm going to be free one way or another.

Behind Brighton, the fields start to fill with domed polytunnels. There are thousands of them, all sizes, in neat rows and scattered randomly at angles. I don't ask Tiffany what they are. I don't want her to know that I don't know.

We veer to the left and go inside a dark tunnel. Tiffany sits across from me and there's a table between us. Her leg brushes against mine. I won't move and neither will she. Her head is tilted, leaning against the window. She looks out in the darkness and when she notices me looking at her in the reflection, she holds my gaze. It's nice.

We pop out into daylight. It's a young forest with thousands of saplings, fifteen or twenty feet high, their little matchstick trunks increase in numbers and darken into the distance.

The strip lighting in the carriage has suddenly changed from glaring white to a soft orange and it makes the seats look as though they have changed colour to a rich brown. It's extraordinary.

"A bit of theatre," says Tiffany. Over the speakers, an American woman announces that we've just crossed the border.

"Welcome to the United States of America."

Now, I am going mad.

Everything feels different. The same carriage is coloured with a different hue. The accent is different. I must be losing time. It's like the air is warmer. I must have a brain tumour. I must be in a sort of psychotic state, or receiving intensive treatment for a brain injury sustained in an accident of some kind.

Or, maybe, I am dead?

The announcer walks through the carriage and stops at our table. She is of average height with blonde wavy hair that cascades over her shoulders. She's an older lady with pronounced crow's feet—from lots of smiling, I imagine. She seems real. I reach out and touch her and she is warm blooded and soft, a real living human hand.

"Hi honey," she says to Tiffany, while patting my hand with hers. Tiffany opens up a purse with documents, perhaps a passport and tickets. "That's perfect thank you. Say hi to your Mom now, won't you, Tiffany?"

"I will," says Tiffany. "Have a nice day." The announcer turns sharply, and stops to stick her fingers and thumbs out like two pretend pistols.

"You bet," she says, and moves off down the corridor to check more tickets.

"You know her?" I ask.

"America's pretty small, everyone knows everyone," says Tiffany. I feel extremely uncomfortable and confused. I realise I have wedged myself up and back into my seat. I'm petrified. I look around me. There's a man, and a couple holding hands. People are looking at me.

"America's fucking massive," I say.

"Okay, chill out. Relax," Tiffany says. "I'm going to take care of you."

"We only just met," I say. "Where the fuck are you taking me?" She stretches out her hands to hold mine.

"I'm taking you home to Portland. I'm going to explain everything to you, but you've got to trust me."

I look out the window. I hum quietly to calm myself and I try to focus on the trees, but the more I look, the more I realise that I don't recognise them. They're not like the trees at home. They are fir trees. We're in an air-conditioned carriage, so I don't notice what the temperature is like until we reach Portland train station and step out onto the platform and it is much, much colder.

It is like landing in America. I pull my coat up around my neck. It smells different—the diesel, the station smell is thicker, denser, a plume of smoke rises from a manhole cover. I mean it is America, like I imagine it to be. Or a theme park of America, but wouldn't you make New York? Or L.A.? Why Portland? I am not dreaming. I am one hundred percent positive that this is real.

We walk into a huge marble hall. The benches are made of polished hard wood and the high ceilings are vaulted. A shop sells row upon row of voluminous jackets in blue, red and white. Outside the cars are from the movies. There's a wide squat truck. A grey uniformed man empties garbage from a trash can.

"It's pretty cool," says Tiffany. I am walking in a circle, glancing upward. She pulls me by the lapel of my coat because I am rotating, still looking up and taking it all in. There's a queue of people waiting to buy tickets.

"Where are they going?" I ask.

"Back to Brighton," she says, and sternly, she places a reassuring hand on my arm. "There is only here and there." I grasp at the thread of my reality. Everything I know to be true is unravelling, slipping through my fingers. Again, I have a sudden nauseating sensation. I cough and dry heave. Tiffany rushes to my side but I shake her off.

"What do you mean, there is only here and there?" I ask, and she doesn't want to tell me out here in the middle of the station. She glances around her, biting her bottom lip.

"We can walk to my house from here," she says. "Let's get inside where we can talk properly."

I touch my head, and my hollow eye socket. I am awake. I am here, but nothing is as I think it is. Either I've been moved here, or I was never there. I don't know which, and I've got to keep hold of Tiffany because she's the one that knows, or rather she is the only person willing to tell me. I know that I am going to be told something terrifying. I'm too scared to ask any more questions.

We walk along the main road into Portland. Traffic lights thread across the street from building to building and back again. We branch off into a smaller side street. I see the forest thickening once more. Sunlight twinkles through the trees.

"This must seem so strange to you," Tiffany says.

"Do you think?" I ask, sarcastically. I don't want to be nasty to her but it's time to know everything. Tiffany tells me how she used to play in these woods when she was a small child. I've heard this before. I've seen these woods before. We turn a corner and, through a clearing, I see a colossal white ridge rise up into the sky. It appears from nowhere to dominate my vision and swallow up my mind. My view point opens and I can take in its full form and its vast height. It forms the entire horizon. We are just ants. I reel back, dizzy.

"What is it?" I ask.

"Mount Hood," she says. It seems to ionise the air, charge it with a primal energy. I breathe in deep through my nose. "You can smell it? Taste it? It's fresh, right?"

"Yes."

"I forget how fresh it is. The real Portland is a big, dirty city, this is just a model of the real thing. This is just a fraction of what Portland actually is."

I listen and nod, but I am staring at Mount Hood, it's more than a mountain, it is why I am here. It's why she has brought me here.

"You are going to love my Mom." Tiffany picks up pace now. Her homing beacon has been set off and she's ripping up the pavement to get back to her mother. I'm so twitchy. I realise that I need to take my pills. I try not to but I need them, and I can't stop thinking about them. It would be easier to digest everything that Tiffany is telling me if I had taken my pills. They are in my bag, but I don't want Tiffany to see me taking them.

"How close are we?" I ask, and Tiffany points out the next road on the left. It is lined with spacious bungalows with driveways and grass. One has a basketball hoop. The garage is open and two teenage boys stand in the centre of the space, fixing a bicycle. Life goes on all around me as normal. Do they know that you can get a train to Brighton? Do they know that we are not actually where we thought we were?

"Here we are," says Tiffany, pointing to a humble bungalow.

"I remember this house," I say, but it's an odd tinted memory.

"I've never brought you here before," she says. "I've wanted to."

"There was a man here," I say.

"They've made you remember certain things," she says. "Memories they've put into your head."

"I came up here on a red motorcycle," I say, pointing a line with my finger down the middle of the street and up onto the drive. "That's all I have."

"These streets are fabricated, one after the other, built on a grid, all uniform, all the same, it goes on for miles."

The door opens with a burst of energy. Out of the front door pops a little old lady, no bigger than five feet tall. She must be at least eighty years old. She must be Tiffany's grandmother.

"Tiffany!" she shouts.

"Mom!" They hug and the little old lady pulls Tiffany's face down and kisses her cheeks and her eyes. She puts her hands up and holds my face.

"So this is the famous Robyn. I've been waiting for you for a long time."

TWENTY THREE

THE INSIDE OF the house is labyrinthine and adorned with artefacts from the sea. It's the sort of place that you could live if there were no adults to enforce rules and make you tidy things away. Each surface, and every inch of wall is covered in art, objects, and old dusty bottles with ships inside. There are long, ancient images of sea vessels, there's a satin puppet hanging from the ceiling, and what looks to be a fully stocked mirrored bar underneath the stairs.

"My Mom is a collector," says Tiffany. My mother would have this place stripped bare and sanitised. We sit down to drink tea out of china cups with saucers.

"How do you like Portland?" Tiffany's Mom asks and before waiting for me to reply adds; "Please, call me Eleanor."

It turns out Eleanor was actually a sea captain. To be specific she is a retired Master Chief Petty Officer with the Coast Guard. She has a stick to help her walk, which she hooks onto the side of the sofa while she carries the tray of cups.

"I was late to motherhood," she says. "Sugar?"

"No, thank you," I say, and notice that she has cute little spikes of white hair sticking out of a mole on her chin. She sees me looking.

"Look at my old skin," she says. "That's from years out on the sea and living right here, under this gigantic thing." She points out the window to Mount Hood, which hovers dramatically over us.

But she doesn't look like Tiffany at all. Tiffany is almost a whole foot taller than her. The colouring is all wrong, the bone structure, the stature. Tiffany is long and thin, she's muscular like a long distance runner, while Eleanor is short and squat like a weightlifter. It is obvious to me that they are not biologically related.

Eleanor is so chatty and gregarious that I can't help but compare my own cold mother. She laughs, she's rude. She makes a joke about sex—more of an innuendo. It's about their postman carrying a large sack. I don't even get it first, as I'm so disorientated, so Eleanor explains it to me.

"So I said, you shouldn't be carrying such heavy sacks, like postal sacks but also he's got a big..."

"Mom," Tiffany warns.

"Bah! More tea?" Eleanor says. I drain the last sip of tea. She has refilled my cup three times and I've eaten two pieces of lemon meringue pie. We don't make them like that in Brighton. Tiffany and Eleanor take out the dishes to the kitchen. I don't offer to help. I sense she wants to talk to her Mom alone. I press my face up to the window and look across the garden and the fields to Mount Hood.

Tiffany and her Mother whisper in the kitchen. They are talking about me. This is reassuring. I trust them. I think that they are going to help me. After some time, Eleanor comes back and invites me out into the garden to see her herbaceous borders. Tiffany is popping next door to say hello to the neighbour.

Eleanor pulls down the head of a hollyhock and examines it for aphids. She shows me their black little bodies on the stem and then squirts them with a liquid from a spray. Her fingers are swollen at the knuckle, they bend at odd junctures and her skin is pink leather.

"You know, Robyn, we're living in a moderated environment so far as temperature goes. If we didn't moderate the temperature then it would be too cold for anything to grow. Nothing would grow, not a bean, it would be a frozen desert." I look at her blankly. She continues; "We'd be immediately plunged into a deep freeze and everything would die. Not that I need to worry now at my age, anything could kill me off."

"Was I brought here as a child?" I ask, wherever here is.

"Well, no, Robyn. I'd say that you were born here. I was." She's talking in a casual way, like she's an old lady showing me her garden, which indeed she is doing. I don't know about flowers so in a normal world I'd just be a bit clueless, bored like an average young person in this scenario. But what she is telling me is that everything I know is back to front, that the world is inside out.

"You follow?"

I shake my head, 'no'. She holds her hands out flat, palms down and lifts them up to impersonate an aeroplane. She is talking slowly now as if I am deaf.

"An aeroplane goes up into the sky and releases ionised particles, that's just one part of it. You follow?" I nod.

"Underneath our feet," she jumps like a toddler, "is geothermal energy."

"Right," I say.

"Have you ever felt it get suddenly very cold?"

"Yes," I say, thinking of the train station in Brighton and other times I can't quite place.

"When the system breaks down, we are plunged into freezing temperatures. You must have felt it go suddenly cold from time to time?"

"Yes," I say. What on earth is she telling me? A huge albatross flies overhead with a tiny baby penguin in its beak.

"Oh, that cruel old bastard!" she says. "Green vegetables don't mind the cold, so they grow well and abundantly, so there's plenty of greens to eat. They do it all in polytunnels, but I like to chance mine out here. Not a lot of sun, that's the only thing."

"Where exactly are we?" I ask.

"You got to time the vegetables right. No point trying to grow anything for the next six months. Ain't going to get light. It's going to be nearly all darkness, day and night."

"I'm not in America or Brighton or anywhere near there am I?"

"Robyn, have you been having problems with your memory?"

"Yes," I say. "I think so."

"Tinkering with people's minds," she spits, and she uses her walking stick to hook a stem of a bush. There are little red berries. "Here." She gives me a berry. It is the bitterest fruit I have ever tasted. The cheeks of my mouth ache with it.

"Too damn cold," she says, spitting it onto the grass. "When I was a girl, Mount Hood was twice as big as it is now. Twice as high. Its shadow covered all of this garden. Nothing grew at all. It was just rocks."

A huge crack rings out. I stagger back. It's a ferocious noise that vibrates through me.

"Don't be frightened," she says. "It's just the ice talking. It's alive. It talks to me, keeps me company when Tiffany's away. My husband was petrified that it would move, that it would slide right off like a jelly and squash us all into the freezing ocean." She tightens her scarf around her neck. "It can't happen, there's miles of sluice between us and the ice. It's designed to break it down, let it thaw, and the runoff washes through huge tunnels underground."

I look at the ground under my feet. "Robyn, you know all of this honey, I think you might just need some help remembering." In the distance a spout of crystal ice water gushes out of the side of Mount Hood.

I LIE ON the sofa in the front room. Eleanor shines the light into my eye. She takes my pulse by holding my wrist.

"Do you get any bouts of sickness? Vomiting?" she asks.

"Yes," I say.

"Dizziness?"

"Yes."

"Pupils are dilated, so you've taken something today, Robyn, right?"

"Yes," I say.

"Which one?" asks Tiff, examining my array of medications; white boxes and jars of little blue pills. They talk to each other as if I'm not there, discussing my tablets.

"I've stopped taking all but the pain killer," I say. Tiff holds up a white box.

"This concoction will make you feel very strange. When was the attack?" asks Eleanor.

"Attack?" I ask.

"The operation, Robyn, when they stole your eyeball." Eleanor says. No one stole it, I donated it to my sister. It was an act of pure love.

"I don't... I don't know," I say, touching my temple and then tracing the outline of my eyeball socket with my fingers. Eleanor leans me back on the sofa and she pulls up my shirt and sees that I've had to fasten my jeans with a safety pin. I am mortified in front of Tiffany. She sees and she looks away.

"Why didn't you fasten your jeans? Have you put weight on?" asks Eleanor. The clocks strike four and an array of cuckoos and bells start to chime. On a Swiss clock a man and woman appear from opposite sides and travel toward each other in the centre and mechanically bash two cymbals together.

"In my calculations," says Tiffany, "and I'm basing this on when she disappeared to when she started working back at the café, that it's only around seven weeks, Mom, maybe nine weeks since the operation." Eleanor prods my stomach with her fingers. She raises her fine, wiry eyebrows.

"Tiffany says that you had a boyfriend, Robyn. Were you having sex?" Eleanor asks. I don't really want to answer in front of Tiffany, but I'm lying here with my jeans unfastened.

"Yes," I say. "It wasn't great," I add apologetically in front of Tiffany.

"I don't need to know how good it was, honey. It still works the same, regardless of the quality, I'm afraid." She looks at a small, raised, one-inch scar low on my abdomen. Have I seen it before?

"She's always had that," says Tiffany. Eleanor zips up my jeans and rises onto her feet painfully slowly using the armrest of the sofa for balance. "Her appendix, maybe?"

"It's the wrong place and the wrong sort of scar. I'm not a doctor, but that looks like egg harvesting," she says, and I wince. What other terrors have happened to me, of which I have no recollection. Eleanor narrows her eyes and peers over her half-moon glasses. She takes my hand and rubs it between hers.

"Robyn, congratulations, you're going to be a Mom."

TWENTY FOUR

WE'VE EATEN MACARONI cheese. It was the most loving dish of food I have ever tasted. I think I love Eleanor as much as I love Tiffany.

"Love makes food taste better," Eleanor tells me. "Tomorrow, I'll teach you how to make it." But I think I already know.

We sit in the conservatory. It is still cold, but it has aspirations to humidity. Eleanor has grown a lot of plants in here. She says that it is an emergency room. She rushes things in, if she can, when the temperature drops. Some of the tips of the plant leaves are brown.

"We all know, Robyn. We are all complicit in this society," Eleanor says, lifting up a flaccid leaf to show me. "The question, Robyn, is not *what* you can't remember, but *why*?"

"Why?" I ask.

"Exactly why you are being manipulated, and by whom?" she asks, and I lean in towards a trough full of earth with a heated lamp hanging down above it, emitting a warm, purple-hued light. When I say warm, I mean hot. Tiny delicate green snowflakes top the long-stalks. "Carrots," she says.

I wouldn't recognise a growing carrot from the sprouting leaves of a potato. The only thing I've ever grown is my hair. And now a baby.

"It can get a bit monotonous living here," says Eleanor. "For certain people, especially the young—when they realise that there won't be any opportunities. It was once thought that the public might be hoodwinked into believing that they were on the mainland."

"Times are changing," says Tiffany.

"A kind of illusion was created, and it has been upheld for many years. The Council believes that our very existence would be threatened if we lived in an open society."

"They would lose their power," says Tiffany.

"They are frightened that society will fall apart." Eleanor says. "Simulation, illusion, our complicity in the pretence is holding us together."

We're all quiet for a time. It feels like they are weighing up how much to say, how much I'll believe or take in. It is extraordinary, but not entirely shocking now that I've been through so much.

"You're saying that this is some sort of a game?" I ask, but it's not a real question, it's a filler until they give me more information. The information that I need to become free.

"Oh, no, it's not a game. This is our reality, this is our one life and I've lived all my eighty years here. I was born here. I, who had a ship. I could have sailed away," Eleanor says. "The people who created this place wanted something purer, and more real. That was their intent. But what have we become?" Eleanor is indignant. She bangs her little hand down on the side of the chair.

"Are you following all of this, Robyn?" asks Tiffany. "There's a lot to take in." But Eleanor wants to press ahead with what she's got to tell me. She doesn't want to wait. She has waited long enough.

"People tend to fall into three camps here; the first know exactly where and who we are and conform, they uphold the simulation; the second choose to forget and prefer to live in the simulacrum and the third do not comply and become a problem."

Eleanor's mouth is still moving, but I stop hearing what she is saying. I look at her, but my eyes are closing. My mind and body need to shut down and process everything that I have heard.

"I've gone very tired," I say. It seems incredible that all of this information has made me need to sleep. But it has. I can't process anymore. I'm going to have a child. I lean back and within seconds I am asleep.

When I wake some time later, I am in a bedroom where the walls are peppered with hung clippings of art. There's a print of a well-known Master, now fading. There are some hand drawn pencil sketches, perhaps done by Tiffany herself. Of course there's a map. This one shows the underbelly of the world. A sprawling ice-covered continent: Antarctica.

TWENTY FIVE

ELEANOR CALLS IT "a tiny bit of pot". Tiffany calls it Ayahuasca, and is appalled.

"You should be ashamed, Mom. Tripping at your age," she shouts and slams a door.

"It's perfectly safe, dear," says Eleanor, knocking on Tiffany's closed door. "It's a key to the mind, that's all. It helps us to loosen up, and hell, we all need that, don't we?"

"I want to unlock my mind, Tiffany," I say, and she eventually opens the door.

Eleanor too has been implanted with artificial memories. What the Council refers to clinically as 'A.M'. Hers were implanted as a child, as I'm finding out most AMs often are. They pop them in as early memories so that we can't argue. There were holidays abroad (a common theme), and I keep remembering my own trip that we used to take every year to Marbella in Spain, a particular memory is playing around the fountain in the early evenings where I once bought a football strip from a street vendor.

Eleanor vividly recalls her grand, important visit to see the Philharmonic Orchestra in Seattle when she was twelve years old. She recalls a red knitted beret that would sag with rain, and the fascinating oval domes that hung from the ceiling.

Over a long period of time she came around to realise that these memories had not actually happened to her. She can't pinpoint the moment that she knew the truth.

"It was more of a slow realisation, like wearing in new shoes," she says. "After a while they soften and feel comfortable. They don't feel new anymore, they're just the shoes you've always had."

She grew up a few blocks down the road. She met her husband in college where they quickly fell in love. It was encouraged to pair up quickly back then, with low population numbers—as soon as you married the Council gave you your own house. They were so very happy, the two of them, in their life together that they went along with the status quo.

Eleanor trained in the navy and was recognised early as a leader. She worked hard, was happy and yet month after month when her period arrived she felt disappointed. Months turned to years and still no baby. One particularly cold November morning they attended the hospital for a series of tests. Their worst fears were confirmed. Eleanor would not tolerate pregnancy.

A bitterly cold snap ensued which lasted six months and kept most people confined to their homes by thick snow and blizzards. During that time Eleanor mourned the child she would never carry. She toughened herself and emerged to become the woman that she was always meant to be. She didn't challenge the status quo. She didn't question her existence. She loved her husband. She mourned childlessness and she grew in a job that she loved.

"What could we do? And why would we even object in the first place? Object to what? We had food, jobs, freedom. This is my home. I was born here." Eleanor says.

Tiffany has only one AM. It's the Natural History Museum in Kensington memory. It seems that we all have it, it's done en-masse so that all the children believe in London. AMs are input into the individual at the Pavilion, it's a painless procedure, the amalgamation of cognitive, visual, aural and virtual reality technology aimed at enriching the experience of those first colonists.

Early settlers were only too happy to believe that they had ridden a roller coaster, or been on a two week vacation to the Bahamas. Knowing that they would never leave the colony, they chose to implant themselves with fresh exciting and pleasurable memories to placate themselves against the enduring monotony.

Eleanor thinks that this might be my problem. That they have laid down too many AMs in my brain. As if they're trying to cover something over. It can work like that. One memory can be laid down over the top of another, like an old-fashioned tape recording. It's all still there, but it's buried.

In my case, Eleanor thinks I'm in danger of an emotional meltdown. She is worried that my mind might cave-in or something awful. She wants to know why those in charge want me to forget.

"Why do you think there's something else, maybe this is who I am? Maybe this is all I am," I ask, blankly.

"We've met before," says Tiffany, picking repeatedly at a thread on the arm of the chair. "Lots of times. You should remember. In fact I think you do."

"Tiffany describes you as being far less timid than this," Eleanor says. "The drugs are subduing you, keeping you passive. You've got to wonder why?"

Eleanor brings the tea. Mine has a small amount of powdered Ayahuasca in it. So has hers. A micro-dose she calls it. Eleanor is coming with me. Tiffany is nervous. She is going to stay straight in order to watch over us. The psychotic potion has been procured from a friend in the Coast Guard, its standard practice apparently for officers to siphon off some of the drugs brought in by the refugees.

"Are you sure this is okay, Mom?" asks Tiffany.

"It's fine, I do it all the time." Eleanor says.

"But she's pregnant," says Tiffany. I touch my belly. It's unverified, untested, the point of view of a strange old lady in a strange land but I know it's true, in the same way that I know it's a girl.

"It's fine in pregnancy. This stuff is absolutely one hundred percent safe. It's her mind we're after. Just because she has a baby in there, it doesn't mean that her mind doesn't function." She pours me a warm yellow brew into a delicate pink floral cup with a matching saucer. "After this you're going to feel so much better."

The tea tastes earthy with bitter notes. Tiffany paces around like an expectant father. Eventually Eleanor tells her she's going to creep us out and ruin the vibe, and that she should go out and procure dinner, and come back in a few hours.

It's just Eleanor and I in the conservatory of her little house. I wonder if something is happening because Eleanor's soft little round face suddenly looks very mouse-like. I don't mean that looks like a mouse, I mean it looks as if she's turning into an actual mouse. Her spiky mole has grey whiskers. Her kind eyes dilate and saucer, like a cartoon character. But I blink and she's back to normal.

"You felt something there?" she asks.

"No," I say. "Maybe."

"You've done drugs before, Robyn? You're from Brighton after all?"

"Maybe," I say.

"It's only mild, I haven't given you a strong dose. We just need to unravel those knots in your brain. Get you feeling you again." I hear a noise behind me. For a minute, I think it must be Tiffany coming back in, but I hear it again and it sounds like a quiet firework going off. I turn around. One of Eleanor's orchids explodes and fires up into the roof of the conservatory where it spectacularly bursts raining droplets of luminescent petal fragments.

"Oh, it's beautiful," I say, taken aback.

"Oh," says Eleanor, surprised. "It's working." I look behind me and another petal shoots up into the sky with a 'fzzzz pttt'. They explode all over the roof of the conservatory.

"Can I brush your hair?" asks Eleanor, coming at me with a round hair brush. I sit on the floor in front of her examining the colours of her plants, now suddenly illuminated. Where before there was the muted green of mediocre home planting, it is now a lush rainforest, red, orange, green. I can hear parrots, tropical birds and even a waterfall.

Eleanor is only brushing my hair but it honestly does feel like she has unscrewed the top of my head off and is cleaning my brain in the way a butler goes over the family silver.

"Close your eyes now," says Eleanor.

I think I'm alone.

I open my eyes again, one of the plants is moving, growing in front of my eyes, its limbs snake around the chair until everything is bright luscious green.

"Close your eyes." Eleanor says, still right there next to me.

I close my eyes.

I am standing in a field.

There is a white greenhouse. No, it's a polytunnel. It is like a greenhouse. The sides are opaque, but I detect condensation on the other side. My hand is in front of my face. I am seeing with two eyes. I can tell by the way I see my hand in the middle of my vision instead of being skewed to the side as everything is now. I used to see everything like this.

My beautiful eye is gone.

My palm is spread open. I put my hand out to touch the wall of the polytunnel. My hand pushes into the wall, not through, it moves with my hand. It's like rubber. No, water. Or something in between. It's like nothing I've ever touched before. My hand is in the wall, and the wall bends to meet it. I've never seen anything like it. Then I am falling. Into the wall, into the whiteness, the plastic springiness, falling.

I'm on the pier. I'm with Tiffany. We're eating ice cream. It is bracing. The wind slaps up with freezing salt. I shiver. We laugh about eating ice-cream in such cold weather. We must be mad. We're leaning on the rails. Tiffany's got jet black hair. She looks glossy and foreign. I remember this was how she looked the first time that I met her. I dot the ice-cream on the end of her nose. She pretends to be angry. I lean in and suck it off. Then I kiss her mouth. I'm falling. I'm in love with her. I melt into our kiss.

I'm on a motorcycle, riding to my Mom's house. I've got three children. The fourth didn't make it. I'm riding on a main road through a forest and the sun is speckling through the trees. I'm so sad. I miss my wife, Elizabeth. But this isn't me. This is not me.

I'm in an alleyway with a man. His coat is soft, I put my arms around his neck. This is the alleyway next to the Astoria. It's foggy. We are hidden. He parts my legs. I kiss him. Then this memory is gone. I look at his face. He's the man with the long black coat from the Astoria who tried to walk me home. He's saying my name over and over again; "Robyn. Robyn. Robyn."

I'm back in my own body. I'm with Vincent and with my sister. Oh, fuck, I'm happy. Vincent, how can I forget you! We're watching TV at my house. Vincent sits between the two of us. He wants to watch football but we won't let him watch that rubbish in our house. We want to watch Superman. Vincent lets my sister grab the remote control and she puts it on. I squeeze Vincent's knee with pride. I love him. He's so good with her.

I'm a girl.

I'm only ten. I recognise the T-shirt I am wearing. This is sometime around my tenth birthday.

"You're special, Robyn," says Mother. "You're not like the other children." She takes my hand and spreads my palm open and we put our hands flat together. Thumb to thumb and finger to finger. I ask if my hands are like hers and she says; "No, you are one of a kind."

I'm sad because I want to be like her, just like her. She holds my hand and examines my thumb and each finger on both hands. She squeezes them, "I'm testing the firmness," she says. "Now, open wide."

She places a swab into my mouth.

"Say ahhh."

"Ahhh," I say, and she moves it around a bit and then she takes it out and places it into a test tube. She puts the test tube into a white box, where it sits with a row of other test tubes. "There, now then, what do you want for your tea?"

There's a glass box. A glass box with a clenched fist inside. The skin of the fist is like tan leather. My scope opens and I realise it's not just a glass box, it's a whole room inside a glass box with two seats like dentist's chairs.

On and on it goes. Line after line, face after face, hour after hour of my life.

"I'm not like the other children."

Eventually, I fall out onto the ice. I'm at the top. I'm at the top of the glacier. There is something white, it yelps. I look up close. I can smell its feral pelt. It has hurt Vincent. It shouldn't be here. They should never have brought polar bears here. It's against nature. I pull up my rifle and finish it off with a bullet through the head. The shot vibrates through my arms, but I don't even flinch. There's bright red blood seeping into the snow, and splattered across my face.

I stumble back inside. Vincent is lying on the floor. There's a lot of Vincent's blood shining like crude oil. I kneel with him. I pull him to me.

"Can I move him?" I shout. No one is there to hear me. I'd never get him down that mountain. I want the Cube.

The Cube.

I remember the Cube.

I am crying. I'm falling, slowly, sleepily awake.

"There now, stop crying," Eleanor says, with all four-foot-ten of her towering over me. I am lying on the floor of the conservatory. The plants seem to have stopped moving. Their colours are once again muted with normality. There's a tiny jerk, a spark, like the stars you see when you stand up too quickly. That's all that is left. She offers me a glass of orange juice.

"Are you back?" Eleanor asks. Yes, I'm back.

"Thank you, Eleanor," I say. "I remember everything now."

In the distance the glacier cracks and roars.

"And your Mother? What do you remember about your Mother?" Eleanor asks.

I feel a sharp dagger of betrayal through my heart. It takes my breath and I gasp.

I shake my head.

Disbelief.

Mother.

"She's the one," I whisper, my voice trembling. "She's the one that makes me forget."

The spell is broken and I boil with rage, I drop to my knees so harshly that a sharp pain shoots through my joints. I open my mouth and let out a high pitched scream so that Eleanor stops, her mouth hung aghast staring at me. This land. My mother. My Vincent. Tiffany. These lies. I fall to the floor and, in pure frustration, I lash out like a child.

TWENTY SIX

CHILDREN ARE PLAYING. I hear laughter, and running. A game of tag, maybe? I curl around in my warm cocoon. My pillow is crisp white cotton—a triumph of Eleanor's laundering. What a woman! My limbs are stiff. I have been asleep for a long time. I stretch my body, but I feel entirely different. The power of knowledge is overwhelming.

There's nothing for it, other than to just be, and let the information simmer inside me, until I know instinctively what to do with it. The rage inside me is quelled. That energy appeased, I need to re-channel, and until I do, I wait.

My mind is refilling with memories. I am being pummelled with happy and sad recollections. Some of them arrive violently, woken and brought into existence, as if they are happening in real life right now.

"You are in control now," Eleanor warns me. But without context, everything I have ever done is flooding into my head. I must not drown in my new found freedom. For freedom is what it is. I've found myself. Am still finding myself, and everything I needed was inside all this time.

I look out of the window and see six red-headed children running like flames of madness around Eleanor's back garden. They play tag amongst the roses. So accustomed are they to Mount Hood looming overhead, that they do not even look at it.

Getting up, I am lighter on my feet. The weight of confusion that has sat on me is lifted. The muddy burden in my thinking is gone.

"Imagine what else she can do," I hear Eleanor say. She is marvelling in the curative properties of Ayahuasca. She says it has been unlocking people for thousands of years.

"Are you sure it was a safe thing to give her? If she is pregnant?" The guest asks. It is a familiar voice. I hear the delicate sound of cups on China saucers. Eleanor has got out the best crockery.

"Yes it is. Didn't I give it to you for the baby blues?"

"Yes, you did," she says. "I can't remember which one? Two of them I think."

"Your first and your third," says Eleanor. There's a bang and a scream in the garden.

"And look how they turned out."

"And look how you turned out. The mother of us all," Gloria says, balancing on the arm of Tiffany's chair. I haven't seen her since the wardrobe. I haven't thought about her since I've been able to think clearly. Now I know there's so much more to her and I, and we've met many times in the past. She's not keen on me. But I think she is amazing.

"There's much to do, Eleanor. We're in great danger now more than ever," says the guest, but on seeing me, quiets and stands up, followed by Gloria, Eleanor and Tiffany. They stand for me, as if I am a judge about to walk into court.

"Here she is," says Tiffany. Gloria gasps and puts her hand up in front of her mouth. I must look different.

"Robyn, don't concern yourself with our worries for now. You must get well," says the guest.

"She needs to put a prosthetic in the hole," says Eleanor, pointing at her own eye socket. "A glass eye. She can't go around like this. It's not good for her self-esteem." But my self-esteem has taken a turn for the best. I am bubbling, boiling over. I'm not the wall flower I was yesterday. I can smell the potential of my own capabilities, just as I can smell Eleanor's food cooking in the oven.

There is so much that I already know, that I didn't know I knew. I am surprising myself.

I can load and fire a shotgun.

I can kill a beast.

What else am I capable of? I can't wait to find out.

"You've been asleep for ages," Tiffany says, taking my hand and leading me to the sofa.

"She must be starving," Eleanor says. The guest sits in the middle of the sofa, drinking tea. She smiles broadly at me—I sense delight. She is in her late forties, or maybe fifty. The lines around her eyes speak of pain. I suddenly recognise that look now, it doesn't look like anything in particular, pain simply looks like ruffled hair or makeup not applied. It looks like an hour of sleep, not slept.

"Sorry to intrude when you're just getting up. Must be quite strange to find us all here. We should at least let you have a cup of tea and a slice of toast," says the guest. She's beautiful, this sad woman with untameable red hair. I know her voice.

"This is Sarah. You'll have heard her on the radio," says Tiffany.

"Sarah Phoenix?" I ask, tickled. We have only two radio stations that play a mixed jumble of rock, indie and dance music. There aren't many celebrities in our world, so someone like her really stands out. Even though I've never seen her face before, I feel I know her. I look at her striking red hair.

"MC1R?" she asks. "You've not seen a redhead, Robyn?"

"I have, but not close up," I say, and looking over her shoulder out into the garden where there are more people with her, a whole entourage of big men leaning against the fence drinking tea. One chases the children in their game. I can count five men and one woman. "Who are they?"

"We've got the red hair gene," Sarah says, ignoring my question. "It's very rare. Why do you think I've got six children?"

"Council incentivised breeding scheme," I say confidently (part of my recently recalled knowledge).

"See, I told you my pot works well," says Eleanor.

"Come and sit next to me," Sarah says. I feel like she wants to hug me, but holds back. I have the ghastly thought that they want to put me on the radio.

"I'm not going on the radio," I say, and Tiffany cracks up laughing. Eleanor too and eventually all of them. It takes the best part of a minute for them to pull themselves together.

"No, no, no," says Eleanor from the kitchen.

"What we talk about, Robyn, is absolutely not for broadcast on the radio. Everything we talk about is in strictest confidence. It is a secret. You can't tell anyone."

"I know it's a secret," I say. It's all coming back to me. How I know them. How they fit together. What I have been involved in. "I've woken up."

"You can't tell your Mother," says Tiffany. I sit down next to Sarah and Eleanor brings me peanut butter on toast.

"It's actually lunchtime," she says.

"Thank you," I say. "I won't be telling my mother anything." Everything that Eleanor prepares for me to eat tastes amazing.

"How is it?" Sarah asks,

"Delicious," I say, and she laughs.

"Not the toast. How does it feel to have all of those memories back?"

It feels like rejection and acceptance. My mother abuses me, but now I respect myself. I don't have a mother's love, but I have self-love, and it has happened instantaneously. In only one evening, I've come to see the truth.

Most of all, I am dismayed, and in fear of my life that they will come and try to take my mind once more and I can never let that happen. I have a new future now, and a different past. I chew the toast. I don't need to explain. The only person that I have to explain myself to is myself.

I hear the children playing. I see a crystallised Mount Hood spewing water from its sides. I remember that Mount Hood is not a mountain, and everyone knows it is not, although they pretend that it is. We sit between Mount Hood and the ocean. Precarious, yes. Madness, probably.

I remember the ship on the beach like it has just happened. I remember going with Vincent to sneak inside. I was petrified.

Reliving the nauseating sensation of fear was enough to make me cry with joy. It is a pure unadulterated feeling when I have been so numb. Adrenaline surges through me.

I think about the little hidey-hole where the stowaway must have hidden in the ship.

Then, I remember that I had sex in the car park of the Churchill shopping centre with a man. As long as it was not David Sykes, then fine. There are lots of sex memories flying through my head, all the time. Some are erotic, some are disgusting and some might be illegal. I can't look at Tiffany without blushing.

There is plenty of blurred imagery. There is much that I can't decipher, that I'll have to ask about. My feelings can't keep up. I can suddenly remember recipes. I can cook.

I remember my sister, Alice. There are lots of memories of Alice at all ages; with mousey pigtails and glasses. I broke her glasses and threw them in the back of my mother's wardrobe—where they are still yet to be discovered (to this day! really!). I will check if they are still there when I get home to her.

I need to get back to my sister. Though I'm not sure where she is and even if it's safe to go home. I can't just ring the bell, that's for sure. Not unless I want an immediate frontal lobotomy.

How could my mother hate me so much?

Then I remember my baby. In a clichéd moment I touch my tummy. Inside, I smile, in spite of everything. I hope this baby is mine and Vincent's, conceived out of love. If not out of love then out of sex—and nothing else. Not conceived of mother's conceit—some experiment or control.

I open my mouth to speak, but there's nothing I want to say. No words are enough and I don't owe these people an explanation. I remain quiet. I gather myself. Gather my thoughts.

"Overwhelming," says Sarah, nodding. "Overwhelming, I should imagine. Of course it is." She pats my knee. I crunch into the toast and chew while my brain spins. Even the taste of peanut butter sets me off in new directions.

"Tiffany says that we met once before?" Sarah asks. "In the Spiegeltent?"

"I remember," I say. I do remember, suddenly, in the tented bar in the centre of Brighton, drinking and dancing to music. How wonderful to be so naive.

"That was two years ago," Tiffany says. "And nothing has changed." It's a patchy memory, but in it Tiffany tells Sarah that I am the cog around which the wheel spins.

"Still, we have her back now, Tiffany?" Sarah says.

"Yes, but we're not quite there yet," says Tiffany, shifting in her seat. but I do realise that it isn't enough for me to remember what has happened to me, I need to discover why it has happened, and what does Mother want from me.

"You obviously still think that I'm the cog?" I say, and they all suddenly fall silent. Gloria coughs. I gesture with my empty cup for Eleanor to bring me more tea. A cog can't turn without lubrication.

"Congratulations, Robyn, I hear that you're going to become a mother."

I am going to have a baby. I feel the corners of my mouth turn up. I laugh. This is the purest joy I have ever experienced. But the fear is real too. I'm already worried that there might be something wrong with my baby.

"You don't have to humour me," I say. "I need you to tell me what you want from me."

"We'll come to that shortly. But first, Eleanor," Sarah says. "Why don't you tell Robyn about when you became a mum?" Eleanor sits back down in her chair and pushes her glasses up her nose.

"I was retiring from the Coast Guard," Eleanor says. "I like to say it was my last day. But the truth is it was near the end, a few weeks before I was due to finish work forever. I was sixty years old. I didn't have this stick. I was as fit as a fiddle. I could still run ten miles in those days. I had lost my husband, Frank, only the year before," she continues. "He was my life. You would have liked him. He made a fabulous clam chowder with spring onions. We didn't have any children. That was our dark cloud. Outside of him, I had my job and that was that, and then suddenly it was all taken from me. I'll admit that I was frightened of being on my own."

"I can't imagine you ever being frightened," Tiffany says.

"Well, I was. I wasn't meant to be working that day. I was covering for somebody else, I wasn't meant to be there. There was a refugee ship two miles off the coast."

"Bigger than the one you explored, Robyn," Tiffany says.

"There's been a hell of a lot of ships," Gloria says. A buzzer sounds sharply and we all jump.

"You really have to want to come here, it's not like you can ever go back." Eleanor gets up and potters back to the kitchen and opens the oven door. The house fills with a deep delicious smell of cinnamon and cheese. It's real cheese, I can tell by the way it makes my stomach rumble.

"That smells nice," says Sarah. I can taste this smell. It's so rich. I can smell the butter, the pepper and the bacon. I'm a super-smeller. I realise that I have a natural ability, yes, and that I exercised my smelling muscle to make it accurate. If I was living a normal life then I might be a sommelier, or a winemaker. But instead, I realised early on that my smell triggered my memory, that the two were so entwined that I could use smell to get back to being me. I know that if I ever go back to my lovely basement kitchen, that my secret notebooks filled with tastes and smells were all notes to remind me of the things that I might be made to forget in the future.

"We intercepted the ship and brought it into the harbour." Eleanor bends and puts a long fork into the cooking pie. Her voice sounds momentarily lost inside the cooker.

"Shoreham harbour?" I ask.

"Not Shoreham. There are three harbours here. This one was ninety miles up the coast. It's used exclusively by the Pavilion."

"The Pavilion?" I ask. Gloria stops filing her fingernails and looks up.

"We'll talk about Pavilion later," Sarah says, as Eleanor sits back down and makes herself comfortable on the cushions.

"The ship was drifting. The crew had gone overboard. They might have rowed the last bit to shore, there might have been an argument at the last minute, who knows. Anyways, it was abandoned. I had my crew go through it, there was no one there. Once we did all the checks, we declared her safe. I radioed in and I went up on the bridge. I gave the order and we set off to bring her into the dock under her own steam. Tugboats met us outside the harbour to guide us the last way on. As we started coming closer into shore I got this overwhelming urge to go down into the bowels of the ship. I was overcome, someone was calling to me. Now, this was a big ship. There are four floors and over one hundred cabins. You could be on a ship like this for weeks and you wouldn't have been in all its rooms."

"Fate, perhaps," Sarah says.

"I couldn't leave the bridge but something was drawing me down there and so, once we got into the safe waters of the harbour and the crew had moored the ship, I went below. I didn't know what I was looking for. My arms were covered in goosebumps. The hackles on my neck were standing up. I followed a narrow passageway and after five minutes or so, I heard crying. It was a child crying, I can only describe it as a wail. It went right through me. I can still remember it now. It sounded like the child must have been crying for a long time and had given up all hope of ever being heard."

"It is sometimes known on journeys of this kind that mothers hide their children. There is no doubt in my mind that the mothers do this, hide them, out of love and to protect them."

"No one would voluntarily give up their child," says Gloria.

"I've considered it," Sarah says, dryly, looking out into the garden at her brood of rowdy red-headed children.

"For whatever reason, the mother couldn't come back for this little baby. There was a panel on the wall. It was very warm and toasty, high off the floor. The crying was coming from inside. There are so many cupboard spaces on ships where things can be stowed and locked away. When I opened it I was overcome by the smell of urine."

Tiffany looks at the floor. Eleanor talks to her.

"You must have been frightened stiff. You must have been petrified. But as soon as I set my eyes on you, you stopped crying and your face lit up. You held out both hands to me. You were tiny. I didn't know anything about babies. I had never had one of my own. I came to realise that you were, at that time, around fourteen months old. I picked you up. You were able to speak a couple of words already, although they were not in a language that I understood. You put your arms around my neck and I loved you from that moment."

"You are a wonderful mother," Sarah says. "A mother to us all." Tiffany is one of them. She's someone who arrived here on a ship like the one that I found. She was all alone in a cubby hole.

"I should have told somebody. I should have surrendered you, but you were the greatest gift. I took advantage of my position. Later, I looked for anyone who came off that ship. There was no trace. There was no sign of anyone. I can only assume that your biological parents did not make it to shore. I knew that I would have to live at least another twenty years, because I was going to raise this child myself."

"You got away with it?" I ask.

"Yes, I did. I put you inside the black holdall that I took with me, and I wrapped you in my jumper. I climbed back up the steps to the bridge. I said 'Goodbye' to the First Officer and I walked off the ship with Tiffany in the bag." She giggles.

"But how did you explain it? What did people say, Eleanor, when you turned up as a sixty year old woman with a new baby," I ask.

"Nothing. I stayed home, and after a while, I started to tell people that I had you in secret. That I'd struggled to get pregnant, that I was embarrassed to try, at my age, and that I didn't want people to have expectations. Because of my age and my standing no one ever questioned me, they just accepted what I said."

"But where did you come from, Tiffany?" I ask. "Where was the boat from?"

"We don't know," says Tiffany. "It doesn't matter to me, my home is here with Eleanor."

But the maps all over Tiffany's body tell a different story.

"North Africa, we think, I've always been sure that you are part African. But, that also means you could have been born anywhere in the world." Eleanor says. I connect now with Tiffany. I catch her eye. The look she gives me tells me that she does want to know where she came from. The flutter in my heart tells me that I am going to help her find out.

The back door opens, and a swarm of Sarah's children with their adult guardians rush in.

"We should be getting back now," says one, a tall slender woman with a beetle tattoo.

"This is Nat," Sarah says. "Nat helps me with the children. And Nat, this is her. This is Robyn."

"It's my pleasure to finally meet you," says Nat, and she bends forward to bow. It is uncomfortable and disarming, but Nat has paid me some kind of reverential gesture. Sarah's children have turned on the television and they crowd around watching a cartoon. The noise is deafening.

"I'm hungry," says one of the boys, starting a domino effect and Eleanor gets up to go to the kitchen.

"No, Eleanor, they're going. They'll eat you out of house and home. We've brought packed lunches for the train. Nat will take the children back to Brighton and I'll stay here to talk some more with you and Robyn."

"Are you sure? I've made macaroni cheese?" Asks Eleanor, disappointed that she won't be catering for an additional thirteen people. Sarah holds Eleanor by the shoulders.

"Eleanor, once they've gone please show Robyn the thing that we discussed. Let's see what she makes of it."

Later, when the children have gone, and we've eaten and drank more tea, Eleanor dusts off a rickety old chest of drawers and beckons me to come and follow her. The chest is Regency, late 18th century judging by the bowed front decoration and the smooth polished finish. It might have been made from cherry wood. I run my hand down its flank. Fucking hell. To think I knew none of this yesterday. There is so much in mind. I'm not stupid, or forgetful. I know so much.

Eleanor and I peer into the drawer. She's gesturing for me to assist her in looking through the drawer because she's too small to lean over properly.

She offers me her grandfather's glass eye.

"I'll clean it up for you," she says. "He had it plucked out by a strand of winching wire while out at sea."

"That's very kind," I say.

"I don't need it," she says. "Neither does my grandfather!"

I laugh. I don't know whether to be flattered or grossed out. She jokes that it's lucky that they didn't bury him with it.

"Eleanor, I think I was bred," I say, suddenly. "Like Sarah's red headed children. I think Mother carried me, she gave birth to me, but that we were bred, my sister and I."

It's a feeling that I get, that tells me this is true.

I have overlaid the story of my mother with much more love than was actually there. I know what she is like, yet I want to tell myself that she is warm, that she gives love, that she is 'Eleanor-like' because if I say it, if I think it enough, then maybe it will become true.

I feel it in the way my mother loves me with a cold touch, the way you care for a stranger's child who falls in the street and cuts their knee. You care, you are concerned, but you don't love them with the intense self-sacrificing love that you have for your own child. The sort of love that I already have for this baby growing inside me.

Then I see it.

It is wedged into the corner of the drawer.

The Cube!

Eleanor's hand innocently brushes over the top of it. Well, of course, she might not even be able to see it, challenged as she is to peer over the top and, even if she could, would she know the trick of looking only with your peripheral vision.

The glass eye is in a tin and as she reaches in to take the tin, so I too reach in and take the Cube.

"You put that back young lady." Eleanor says, and I do, though I'm drawn to it in an addictive sense. The feeling of lightness, of leaving your own mind and going into another reality is breathtaking. I realise that I can't not have it.

"She wants it!" Sarah shouts. "I knew it!' Seems like they are second guessing my every move.

"I have a mind of my own, you know?" I shout back.

"But you want the cube though, don't you?" Gloria asks.

"These are strictly against the law," Eleanor says, holding it up. "How do you even know about it?"

I had one of my own. I took it from the ship. In turn, it must have been taken from me by my mother. They're not hard to hide. They are small and innocuous. I'd never seen one before and now there are at least two. I wonder if Eleanor is using it in the same way she is using her Ayahuasca.

"Do you use it?" I whisper.

"Nah, I can't get it to work for me, never have been able."

"Can I try it?" I ask, leaning over Eleanor again. I want her to give it to me, but if she doesn't, I'm going to take it anyway.

"It won't work for you." Eleanor says. "It was my grandfather's. Eternal charge. They are made of pure Tantalum. They store a current inside forever. They never run out."

"Let her try," Sarah shouts.

"If I hold it just for a second, Eleanor, you'll know whether it works or not, won't you?"

"They are only ever synced with one person. It's not the fingerprint that it recognises, it's the actual DNA of your body." She tries to close the drawer. I jam it open. I pick up the Cube and the beam immediately locks onto my eye.

"Holy shit!" says Eleanor, jumping backwards, leaning on the back of a chair for support.

"What the fuck was that?" shouts Tiffany from the other side of the room.

"Rather interesting development," says Sarah. "As we suspected."

I wobble. It's not as clear cut with one eye. I can't see them, but I can hear them. Eleanor and Tiffany are frantic. I'm worried one of them is going to hit me with a broom in the way you are supposed to hit someone who is being electrocuted.

"It's only supposed to synchronise with one person," Eleanor says. I can hear them incredulous, questioning and possibly even jealous. They are impressed, but I don't care about impressing them, I have so much more important work to do. I have faith in the Cube and what it is teaching me.

"You were right, Tiffany. She is special," says Sarah.

"No wonder her mother has gone to so much effort to control her," Gloria says.

I sit back in my chair, and feel the power that the Cube gives me surging through my body. I am in control now.

"Spectacular!" Sarah says, and she begins to clap.

Then he's here.

He's back.

Ivan.

Tell me everything.

TWENTY SEVEN

IVAN SPEAKS TO ME. I hear him, but now and then I can tell by his lack of emphasis, or the quickening of his voice, that I am hearing his inner thoughts. It is not always obvious which is which, but I can see what he sees, sometimes feel what he feels, and I know he is showing me for a reason. He talks to himself like I do.

"What a place this is," he says out loud, but it is meant for me only—or whoever he is recording these messages for. I wonder whom he is telling? He stands on a high metal walkway between a ship and a dock, disembarking after a long trip. He is thinking; "According to the United Kingdom, under whose sovereignty we operate, this is categorised as a scientific experiment. A necessary incursion onto a piece of land that has lain under a mile of ice for more than thirty million years."

Ivan has secured a tiny plot, but it is big enough to fit in all of his dreams. He arrives at this piece of land in the evening—although it makes no difference here right now because it never gets dark. To Ivan, this is unusual, remarkable in fact. He has never experienced anything like it. To me, of course, in the now, this is normal.

"I'm doing it for you," he says. I don't think he can mean me, but rather the true intended recipient of these messages, whoever that might be.

Ivan is struck by the lack of ice. Out at sea, he has seen so many huge cliff-like bergs sheared off the glacier and floating. In the distance, to both the north and the south, he can make out the white-tipped mountains covered in snow. The temperature is moderate. He considers that the technology must be working well because the rocky earth is free of ice and snow.

He thinks that Antarctica is more than sixty times the size of the United Kingdom. More comparable in size with the continent of South America. He thinks that we have no idea what fossils might be found or what life once lived here, but we do know that it was not always covered in ice. We know that soon enough, perhaps even in his own lifetime, it will not be covered in ice once again.

Ivan asked for four thousand square kilometres. They awarded him one thousand square kilometres with a two thousand kilometre 'dead zone' around the settlement where the environments transition from terra-firma to its natural ice state.

He waves, overcome with excitement and emotion. There are fifty people waiting for him on the dock. It makes him think about ships returning to New York filled with sailors peppered with red, white and blue streamers—stars and stripes. He is romanticising, his heart has turned tender. His throat constricts, he chokes back tears of pride and sadness. How amazing it would be to have Elizabeth waiting for him here to circle her arms around his neck, kiss him, and then whisper that they were starting again, right here—starting over.

The memory jumps. I feel my body clench and tighten. I feel like I am fast forwarding Ivan's memories. To what? Something more important.

During the good years, Ivan and Elizabeth had driven from Death Valley to Las Vegas in a Ford Mustang. They had watched the Las Vegas strip rise up out of the desert, like children's building blocks. The same is happening now, though Ivan is sadly on his own. A building rises out of the land from nowhere. As we drive closer to it comes into focus.

The Professor is excited. When I see him he looks so familiar; the thick brow, the dark eyes. I realise he looks like Vincent. He asks about a woman; a Dr Joy Forster, and I feel Ivan's predatory anger bristle.

"She's a very attractive woman," the Professor says. "And newly single..." and the driver swerves around a boulder that has settled in the middle of the road, cutting him off. The Professor shouts at his assistant to have it removed. It has rolled down in a water flow. Debris still makes its way down in trickles or streams, all desperate to get back to the ocean.

"It is a wild country, Ivan," he says. His explorer's hat has loosened and fallen down in front of his eyes. We park in the middle of a vast flat expanse. Behind us is the sea. A cold aqua is spliced onto the horizon against the baby blue sky. Above us the clouds are thick; a feature that the colonists will have to get used to. A long spell of clear sky will push them back into a freeze.

"She's a widow," Ivan says. "In tragic circumstances I understand." He's saying it to deter the Professor.

To our right there is nothing but the flat expanse of land. To our left, in the distance, the red tipped cranes of the harbour silently work to empty a container ship. The Village, a small collection of 3D printed homes where the crew, builders and engineers live, is somewhere up there, where the hills begin to swell.

There are no trees. Nothing grows. No natural marks on the land save two shallow valleys that The Professor has worked into his designs to identify the Old Steine and Hove. The ground is desert like, compacted dirt, bare and unknown.

Ivan gets out of the black SUV. This feels abstract, like we're in a painting. We are in a vast expanse of nothing. We walk to the edge of the visible earth. We are fifty feet above the sea. I hear his thoughts. The beach is wider than he anticipated and pitted with rocks. It's not like he imagined, and certainly not like the geography of Brighton. The Professor orders his driver to balance Ivan;

"Let him see below," says The Professor. The driver holds us, and we lean out over the side, revealing a long drop onto the shale beneath. He leans us over the edge. I recognise this seafront as my own. Even with nothing there, I can tell that it is going to be Hove lawns.

"It will be landscaped, Ivan," the Professor says, recognising our anxiety.

"You've got to work with what you've got," Ivan says, feeling like he has walked into a dream. He's thinking that maybe all of this is too much. That maybe they should just have gone for a blank canvas from scratch. What's the point in honouring Brighton?

"That's the art," The Professor screams.

The Professor tells us that all of this will be railed in the traditional Brighton livery with mint green paint and gold regency lanterns. We hang out over the edge again. Ivan's life in the hands of The Professor's driver. We can see that under the sea wall dotted along in a line every sixty feet are circular drains. They are pumping out the clearest turquoise water that Ivan's has ever seen. This is the normal colour of water to me. What colour must the water have been like in the real Brighton? The Professor explains the process for the run-off from the glacier.

The new city is to be built above a network of tunnels primarily to handle the run-off of the ice that has been cleared but also to handle the run-off from the billions of cubic metres of ice, compacted in the glacial sheet that covers Antarctica. Without the tunnels the entire city would be washed away into the sea. The project would be doomed.

The driver pulls Ivan back and he turns inland to face the building. It is Regency in style and very tall. The scale of such a building rising out of the flat barren landscape is breathtaking. Even though I know that The Professor built it, it still feels like they have uncovered a lost civilisation hidden here for Millennia under the Antarctic ice sheet.

We all walk toward it across the expanse. The Professor wafts his hands out to his sides.

"This will be all laid to lawn," he says, and as we walk further he runs a little in front and darts to the side, opening up his arms to indicate a line. "And this will be a row of those lovely little beach huts. There's nothing that says 'English seaside' to me more than those little huts, Ivan."

We nod to agree with him, but the building looms large, getting closer and closer and we are awestruck with it and in turn with our endeavour.

"I had to build it first, Ivan," The Professor says.

They are in front of it. It is eighty feet tall at least. Up close, we can see that the houses have basements with stairs in the Victorian style. There are traditional railings, carvings and arches. The attention to detail is staggering. It is perfect, better, cleaner and more pristine than the real thing. It feels utterly weird to see it here in the middle of all this nothing.

"It's remarkable," Ivan says, holding the railings, shaking them for sturdiness and peering down into the basement and then back up to the balconies. He doesn't know this exact building, but he knows the sense of it, the idea of it that is so true to Brighton.

"It's almost a replica," he says. "But better." The Professor explains that the bricks are made from a 3D printed clay and polyurethane resin mix. The building will last forever. It will never decay. "I've always fancied living in an apartment in one of these buildings, and now it's going to come true."

TWENTY EIGHT

WHEN I OPEN my eye, Eleanor, Tiffany, Sarah, Gloria and two large men (Sarah's security) are watching me. I'm not sure how long I have been in the Cube, but Tiffany is wearing different clothes. A musty old glass eye stares at me from the centre of the table, dull and lifeless. Our bags are ready by the front door. The men don't speak and they are not introduced. They sit at the table, heaving spoonfuls of Eleanor's macaroni cheese into their mouths. Wherever Sarah goes these men go with her.

"You've must have done that before," Sarah says. There's a sponge cake on an old-fashioned cotton doily in the middle of the table. "You are magnificent."

"Who are you really?" I ask. "And what do you want from me?" I'm beginning to realise that the knowledge I am amassing through the Cube, and the information that is awakening in me, is very powerful, and much more than they know. I am starving again. Eleanor has cut some triangular slices of cake and I seize one and load my mouth full. It's got raisins and crumbly biscuit sponge, quite traditional actually, like a real grandma might make, and with real ingredients rather than chemicals.

"I'm someone who wants a better tomorrow, Robyn, for everyone in this community. For my own children, and for your child and for all the children yet to be born. There are other ways of living."

"And my mother," I say. "Where does she fit into this?"

"Your mother and I want different things," she says.

"Does she know about you?" I ask.

"Oh, I rather think so. She knows about us, and she knows that there are people who work silently for the good of our community, and she will stop at nothing to exterminate us."

"Exterminate?"

"On the radio, I hide in plain sight. I'm too well known to have disappeared. The people will rebel if she touches me. She has nothing to hold against me, and I exist outside her scrutiny."

She's still my mother, good or bad, I still love her. No matter what they do, or how good or bad the relationship is, they are still your parents.

"What do you see when you go inside the Cube?" Sarah asks.

"I see the start of all of this," I say. "I see the beginning of this place."

"Fascinating," she says. "I've never done it. Not many people ever have."

"Do you know how it works?" I ask, holding out the Cube. I daren't put it on the table in case someone snatches it away from me. Sarah moves her head and casts her eyes from side to side until she catches a glimpse of the Cube in her peripheral vision.

"It's a quantum computer," Sarah says, standing up to touch the tiled kitchen wall which is in a mosaic made up of tiny ceramic squares. "You see the way this mosaic is made up of many tiles, thousands of them making up the whole?" I nod. "It's the same way with a quantum computer. There's only one computer, like there's only one wall, but it's made up of thousands of these tiny little computers which are all linked, all part of the same bigger thing."

"How does it disappear?" I ask.

"It's a mystery. One of the characteristics of quantum is that the same object can exist in two places at the same time. But if you look at it directly, then it disappears. The same with these cubes, essentially, there's only one Cube but it appears in multiple locations. The brains behind these machines don't exist here in our world anymore. They've long since gone, unable to explain to us how to use them properly."

"Why can I use it?"

"Robyn, there are no computers here, there's no technology apart from telephones, TVs, and radios. This is all the Council allows us to use, and yet and all the time these quantum computers have been quietly, secretly operating right here beneath our noses without us having the ability to even see that they are here." She takes my arm, and pulls me closer to her, I can feel her breath. "There's a reason why you alone are able to access the Cube."

"Why?" I ask. One of the security men stands up from the table, wiping his mouth on the napkin.

"We need to go now please, Sarah," he says.

"You should go back to Brighton, and you should explore the Cube and learn from it. You should tell me when you find out anything useful."

"What about Mother?" I ask. I will be dealing with my mother, but it seems prudent that I am fully armed with all knowledge before I do so.

"You'll stay with Tiffany. Gloria is at your disposal night and day. Jan at the Cafe will make an excuse for you. No harm will come to you." Gloria winks at me.

"No *more* harm, you mean? I don't know if you can promise that, but I promise you I'm not having my mind erased again."

"I'll look after you," Tiffany says, and I think about her red-walled apartment, full of maps overlooking the sea, and remember clearly the night of the storm, and other times before that.

Sarah doesn't sit down again, she indicates with a finger for one of the two large men to bring her coat. He holds it out for her, and she slips her arms inside.

"What has become of the boy?" Sarah asks, and Tiffany bristles, and looks annoyed.

"Vincent," I say.

"He's in the Village," says Gloria. "His mother lives in the Village. She's rather, shall we say, active there."

"Tiffany, I have something important for you to do," Sarah says, doing up the last button of her coat.

"Yes," she says reluctantly.

"I want you to find the boy, Vincent," says Sarah. "We can't leave him there to rot. I'll give you some helpers. We'll look after him. Bring Vincent back to us."

TWENTY NINE

WE ARE GOING back to Brighton. Eleanor has made us a packed lunch of cheese and mayonnaise sandwiches for the journey, which is good because I am starving. She won't stop moving, pacing back and forth.

She is frightened for what is to come.

I have the future laid out in my mind as if it has already happened. The memories spill out of my head, I can't keep them all, I can't process them all.

Eleanor says she likes to pretend that her Portland Philharmonic recital memory is real and she filters out the bad colouration to make it more believable. She lets it slide because she enjoys it so much. It's one of the happiest moments of her childhood.

I have to control myself. The anger is going to swallow me up. The lies that my mother has told me. She has made me impotent, I'm not even capable of free thought. She has stolen my mind; and my life. She has stolen every relationship that I have ever had, she has stolen my sister from me and then she stole my eye.

How do I know that my sister's even sick? Perhaps it is part of the same experiment that she's been doing on me. Maybe she's making her sick. The deliberate sickening of her own child.

Now all these memories flood back and there is no memory of me agreeing to donate my eye. I'm going to have to be careful, because she is the police. She's the Council. She's got her claws into everything and if I'm not careful, she could make me disappear. Or worse, she could make me forget again.

And all I ever wanted was for her to love me.

The Cube is heavy in my hands with the weight of its potential. I know that this Cube might give me more power than I ever knew possible. The power to put everything right.

My mind is racing. I struggle to keep up with all the new information that I have received. But for the first time in my life, I can trust what I know is real. I have to trust what I know is real.

I am going to have a baby. I feel the bond with my child already. I know when and where she was conceived. I know who the father is. I remember the day, the hour, Vincent's dirty body against mine. Vincent is my baby's father. He has to be. The alternative is far too scary.

She's my future. She's been sent to save me and I will kill to protect her. I can't wait to meet her, to hold her. I touch the sides of my belly, 'Please be alright, little baby,' I think. Please be healthy, please don't let what is happening to me hurt you.

To protect her I need to always remember her. I'm going to have to make sure that she doesn't get erased from my memory. I can't forget her. I won't. The story in the Cube is not a simple distraction, I think it's a clue, a trail left to help me find my way.

As I sit here with my swollen belly and I wonder if Ivan Dixon, this arrogant alter-ego of mine, might help me.

Who is he, to me?

I squeeze the Cube.

I see the way that Tiffany puts her hand on Eleanor's shoulder and the spark of their love makes me sad, happy, and hopeful all at once. The love between a parent and child makes every other love redundant.

We board the train at Portland station and take seats in a quiet carriage. We depart, and I watch the glacier becoming more and more distant. I realise now that this huge ice mountain has been my compass all my life. It's intimidating to see it once again, in its full beauty, from the safety of a speeding train.

It solidifies my terrified realisation of where I am on this earth.

I am so very far away from where I thought I was. Gloria sits on her own a few seats down. She measures people by looking them up and down and curling her lip. I don't know if she's actually doing security or just being mean. After a few minutes, she gets bored and appears to fall asleep with her head on the table.

"Give me the mirror," I say. Tiffany does what I say and reaches inside her bag to pull out a small hand mirror in a makeup compact that she holds out in front of me. Her hand vibrates with the motion of the train. "Keep still," I say, then I quickly add "Please" and "Sorry" when I realise how demanding I'm being. I'm tired, sore, angry, and taking it out on the only person that I am close to.

I look in the mirror.

I gasp.

I still can't believe it.

I'm a pirate. I'm a survivor.

No, I am a soldier who has been injured in a battle that they didn't know they were in.

But I am not a victim anymore.

It doesn't hurt when I peel back my eyelids and push the Cube into the socket, the void where my eyeball should be. Tiffany gasps.

One rounded corner protrudes like a crude cornea. Its copper metallic finish dulled from years in Eleanor's drawer. I can blink. It feels weird, uncomfortable, my new eye waters, tears run down my face. In the discomfort, I find my resolve.

I press a finger into it. It sparks into action, beaming right into my brain. It's a stronger, more powerful connection than before.

"Earth, Sea and Sky," says Tiffany, blessing herself and lowering the mirror to her lap. Her mouth gapes open wide.

The sky crackles with electrical thunder.

In my mind, I can see the whole city, the whole colony. I can see it across time.

Ivan sits in a chair in front of me.

"I knew you'd get it," he says. "I'm so pleased to finally meet you."

THIRTY

IVAN SHOWS ME around. We are not in a real-time live discussion but he has left these notes, these messages for me. He calls them mental breadcrumbs.

"I want to show you things. I want to help explain about this world," he says. This thread jumps back and forth, he's telling me and I'm watching as an observer. I feel like it is just for me, made for me alone, not something that I have stumbled upon.

I wonder how old Ivan is. I'm not sure whether his messages are chronological, or recorded in some time before now. This makes me sad. I must find out where he is and meet him. I have so many questions to ask him. I want to meet Ivan in the flesh, if that is even possible, perhaps he stayed here in the colony and never went back.

"Shall I start with my mother?" Ivan asks, nodding his head to say yes to his own question. "If you're building an off-earth colony, she's the sort of person that you need. She won't complain about what she doesn't have, she'll make do, and in making do, will fulfil that inner part of herself. Her thrift and tenacity deeply satisfy her sense of being."

She reminds me of Eleanor, and not least because they live around the corner from one another, albeit on different continents.

"We get on great, Me and Mom," he says. "And we always have. Let me start on the ship, on my second trip down. I think this is where things started to go wrong."

Ivan tells me that you need a lot of money when you embark on making your dreams come true. But Ivan would say that, he is governed by money and success. The Professor bought a boat. It was a Danish built expedition ship that slept a hundred and thirty people. It was formerly a tourist vessel taking holiday makers on three-week polar expeditions to Antarctica.

To cater for the wealthy occupants there was a bar and a gym on board. She was named, 'New Brighton'. She was a glorious ship, taking her passengers to create a new world of their dreams. There were kayaks, a library, state-of-the-art sonar and a reinforced steel hull.

The boat reminds us of toothpaste. She sparkles white like an iceberg with a trendy blue stripe and a bright red hull. Ivan's room has a huge window and the type of carpet that he has seen on the floors of many a British pub.

I feel the motion of the ship in my legs. It sways me. I glimpse the turbulent sea through a porthole.

There is an expedition vibe going on. It's like being at university during Freshers' Week only in a huge metal dormitory. There are engineers, nurses, doctors, physicists, builders, mathematicians, chefs, a butcher, a viticulturist, and, of course, the crew of the ship.

Somewhere on board the lunch is being prepared. I can smell the watery odour of boiling salted vegetables, and the roasting of chicken. Ivan questions the motivations of the other people on the ship.

"You have to wonder exactly who goes into something like this knowing that they are never coming back. It's the one thing I never quite understood," he says. "I always worried about the human element—people changing their minds."

"Maybe they hate their lives, their families. Maybe they just want to start over, like The Professor does," I say, but Ivan cannot hear me.

"The Professor is already in the colony," Ivan continues. "At this point, I haven't seen him for a little over a year. We speak on our call once a month, on a fully encrypted quantum communications channel. The Chinese are using this technology too, but to the best of our knowledge, we are still under the radar. We don't want anyone looking at what we're doing."

"When is this?" I ask. "Is this now?" But Ivan doesn't hear, this conversation is one way only.

"I've been busy with a couple of other projects," Ivan says. "But now I'm going to see the colony with my very own eyes."

Ivan was one of the very few who would come back. The only people allowed to return are the crew of the service ships. Once you were here, you were here. There is no going back. It is in the contract.

The memory jumps. He talks straight at me into a camera. Other times I am seeing what he sees through his spectacles.

We're still on the ship, but it's later in the same voyage. Ivan has the start of a beard. A white streak in his stubble reveals his true age.

There is pumping music.

It's the ship's dining room. It has been transformed into a disco, the tables have been pushed back against the wall. A 'Happy New Year' banner is strung across the stage. Ivan is enjoying this so much. It's rare that he relaxes with people. He usually has an entourage of staff that work for him, cook for him, keep him on time, and laugh at his jokes. But here he is, on his own.

It is as if he has gone to a place where he is free of the burdens of celebrity and success. Yet still they know who he is. They have seen him on the 24-hour-news channels.

There will be no such channels in the new colonies. Ivan has seen how disruptive and manipulative they are. In fact, there will be as little technology as possible, the analogue telephone is the only concession.

Ivan has made mistakes. He doesn't want me to know, but he's laying them out there so that I don't get an omnipotent view of him. I want to reassure him, but I know I can't. He loves his mother. He loves Elizabeth. He loves his children. I know this and this makes him a good man in my opinion.

"I spent Christmas with Elizabeth. She took pity on me, invited me round to join her and our children. She let me stay over and we had Christmas morning together. It was the first time in three years we'd all been together."

Elizabeth was trying him for size. Ivan was devoted. He wants her back. If everything went well then they would be back together for good by Easter and after that there would be no infidelity ever again.

"That part of my life would be over," Ivan says, earnestly.

The next part of the memory, the breadcrumb, we watch together. Ivan made friends with the butcher, a man from the East End of Glasgow with an accent that Ivan could barely understand. His parents were dead, he was single, he had responded to an advert surreptitiously placed in Meat Trades Journal. Ivan thought he was a really good dancer and was struggling to keep pace with his moves.

He's brought his own whisky that the bartender keeps behind the bar just for him, and he lets Ivan have a dram. He wants to know how exactly Ivan is intending to make alcohol in the colonies, when exactly Ivan thought we would be self-sufficient in that respect and what spirits were going to be made.

Ivan and the Professor had discussed this in detail and crucial to their plans were the availability of good drugs and alcohol. It is in the plan, strategically researched. In their extensive research where there is no religion to enforce cultural barriers within a community then you need alternative outlets. The Professor has a proposal about a religion based on ecology and conservation that he is working on. Glorifying the earth, the sky and the ocean seems like a smart idea to Ivan.

Ivan and the butcher are dancing with two nurses. Then Ivan is dancing with the doctor, Joy Forster. She is beautiful. I can see that. Ivan is impressed with her brain and with her body.

The room is bathed in swirling orange light, casting an unworldly shadow. What would a woman like Dr Joy Forster have to run from? Why would she be leaving civilisation to start over?

He tries to justify and to rationalise her choice. Ivan could not envisage ever leaving Elizabeth and his children. But he could envision himself with Dr Joy Forster, however briefly and discreetly.

They are all jumping up and down to a song by The Proclaimers. It has become an unofficial anthem for the new colonials. It's a song they all love and they chant the words with their arms strung out around each other.

Dr Joy locks eyes with Ivan and walks off the dance floor. He follows her out into a claustrophobic corridor. She is standing against the wall leaning her head back.

Ivan presses up against her. They start kissing. They fumble along the corridor to Ivan's room and push through the door and onto the bed. Ivan pushes his hands into her trousers and up under her shirt and into her bra.

THIRTY ONE

I INSIST THAT we are discreet and take only Gloria's car. It's a small, silver run around. We listen to Sarah on the radio. She is doing a phone-in about Brighton residents' concern over a recent power outage and their increasing frequency. She tells someone from Hove that there's no point saying 'we should never have brought the beasts here', as we have to live in the now, and we have a responsibility to the ecology. She quotes from 'Earth, Sea, Sky.'

"You know the thing that you killed up on the glacier?" Tiffany asks, she doesn't like to upset me, or bring up trauma without good reason. I nod. I remember the meaty smell of its blood more than anything. I remember the cool, droplets of water on the end of Vincent's nose as his breathing slowed and shallowed. "Do you remember how they got there? Do you remember the power cut?"

"Yes," I say, but it's new information in my mind. I am bringing myself up to speed on everything that I have forgotten and it takes a while. I remember a power cut stopping everything, temperatures suddenly plummeting, people frozen to death and streets blown white with snow and ice. Three days, three is all it took to reduce Brighton to an uninhabitable frozen city.

Presumably, if we were unable to maintain power again in the future, three days is all we would have to save ourselves.

Henceforth, I realise that this is what it's really about. Mother and the Council want to keep their power. Sarah Phoenix and her rebels want to have their freedom. While all the time the glacier behind us is inching closer, shedding parts of itself into the sea, and the earth that we worship, and the air that we breath—they all want to return themselves naturally to their inherent icy state.

But what's it got to do with me?

I watch Tiffany's fingers spin across the steering wheel. In the not so distant past, breeding pairs of polar bears were brought here to ensure their survival. They were going extinct in the Arctic, at the other end of the world.

After escaping from the zoo in Roedean during the big, three-day power outage they colonised the giant sluice behind the farms. They love the frigid water, and the ice that comes down from Mount Hood and floats there. It's like their natural habitat, except they have an abundance of food. But people are paranoid.

"I remember meeting Sarah Phoenix in the Spiegeltent," I say, pushing my fingers into my eye. Eleanor has told me I should think about Vincent's mother when I am inside the Cube. Her name was Shirley Ellis. Vincent loved her very much. If he's alive, as they believe, and in the Village, then I might be able to locate them both. "But do you work for her now?"

"No, Sarah has given me the responsibility of bringing Vincent back," Tiffany says.

"Thank you," I say. "You probably don't want to."

"I do what Sarah asks of me," she says, and I tip back my head and I push my finger inside my eye. I can drive the Cube myself. I don't just have to sit back and receive information, I can direct my mind into the quantum computer and search for information.

"So you do work for Sarah?" I ask.

"I work at the club. But this. This is my life. This is all our lives." She sounds so earnest. It's lovely. I'm surprisingly calm. I don't feel her urgency. I don't feel a cause welling up inside of me. I'll try, for Tiffany. I'll try to steer my way around the Cube—find what's there.

It's hard.

It's like trying to make yourself sleep when you can't.

It's like trying to move your ears.

It takes a burst of intense concentration to move anywhere but directly to Ivan. I think of Vincent's name.

Vincent Ellis. I ask the Cube and, when there is nothing, I ask about his mother. Shirley Ellis. My internal vision spins and elongates. I see lights. There are three Shirley Ellis' living in Brighton and Hove. I'm surprised. I like the name Shirley. Never met anyone else called Shirley. One is too old. One is too young. That leaves one Shirley.

"I have her address," I say.

"Really?" asks Tiffany. "That's incredible."

"She's been in the Village for five years," I say. "I'm coming with you."

"No, this is my mission," says Tiffany. "I have to do this. You're not even supposed to be here." She's bluffing. She doesn't want to go on her own. I think she wants to be with me. She's being overly dismissive and prickly which makes me believe she wants me with her.

"You can't leave me on my own, Sarah said. Besides, I want to help you." That's all I have to say. She flicks me a smile and drives with her foot down to the Village.

The Village is a rough sort of estate. Mother would not like me going here. It's in an area close to Shoreham Docks. It's elevated, with clear views miles out to sea. As we drive into the neighbourhood there's an abandoned car with its windows smashed in. A little pug dog is shitting at the side of the road.

Daubed in red paint on the side of one house is a sign that says 'Fuck off polar bears'.

"That'll deter them," says Tiffany, but I like honesty. Everyone else is too scared to call them by their name.

"Have you been here before?" I ask. She drives carefully around the edge of the estate, but not so slow to attract attention. Shirley Ellis lives right in the very centre of the Village.

"Only to buy pot," she says. We are going to park up and hope the car is still there when we get back. Gloria waits for us, parked in a van with three more people. We pull up behind the van and Gloria comes back and slides into the backseat.

"I thought you might need a hand," says Gloria. She wears a soft cotton tracksuit in cerise pink with a matching baseball cap and large, gold hoop earrings. Her lipstick is fuchsia. She wears a pair of trainers, which she doesn't like doing, but Tiffany had explained previously that there might be running involved, so she reluctantly put them on. The sports shoes anchor her great physical strength into her body.

Of all the crazy things that I have learnt in the last few days this has to be the most abhorrent. The Council, (and therefore my mother as head of the Council) has a policy of facilitating drug users as long as they stay within the Village and do not commit crime. The Council has effectively created a free range open prison, policed by its own occupants' reliance on smack.

There are many drugs available for free at The Village Post Office, but in most part all of them are using a version of an opiate-based synthetic, made here in Brighton at the Pavilion.

"But this can't be right," I say. "It means that The Council are making people addicted." Tiffany and Gloria nod.

"Those who can't deal with living in an isolated colony," says Tiffany. "Those that show the tell-tale signs of mental frailty end up here in The Village. You either tow the party line, or you are made dependent."

"Does my mother know about this?" I ask. Tiffany sighs.

"I wondered if you might have been down on the list to come here, Robyn," says Tiffany. "But that your Mother couldn't allow it, and so she scrubbed your memory." Yet again, my mother's touch is at the centre of all activity.

"Quite simply, my love, it's Council approved, super-strength gack," says Gloria. "I tried it once and never again. You feel like you fold down into the earth, and up into the sky at the same time. You become one with everything and fully yourself. Incredible, but never again. I came close to losing myself."

Tiffany has also tried various products of The Village. People come in and trade goods, stock up for parties. It's a Garden of Eden.

"Let's try this quietly first, without them." She means Gloria's security back-up. She'd prefer to do it nicely. "When we secure Vincent, then we leave together in your car, Gloria. I'll drive."

"Okay," says Gloria. "Stay behind me, Robyn, if you can." But before we go my metal eye twitches. It wants to tell me something. We're starting to interact, me and my new eye.

Ivan, it seems, has been to the Village before.

THIRTY TWO

IN THE CUBE, the Professor takes Ivan to the home of the Principal Gyroscopic Engineer. There is rain in the air. The Professor is anxious and upset. The engineer has lost a finger in an accident. He is worried that these incidents will make people unruly and homesick. We must take extra special care of this engineer, we must love him as if he were our own son.

It's a 3D printed house on the other side of the emerging village. It's where all of the team is going to live while the main body of the city is being completed. It's base camp—a series of printed homes that won't degrade, won't age, they'll stay here reliably through the years, quite literally, whatever the weather. It's the hidden engineer behind the arty veneer of New Brighton.

Ivan looks up and down the street in the hope of seeing Dr Joy. He thinks there's a little flicker of chemistry, nothing like the love he has for Elizabeth, but an exciting flirtation to pass the time. Ivan loves the fleeting buzzy connection that comes and goes between people that you find yourself drawn to. The sex they had on the ship was incredible.

The Gyroscopic Engineer is a lovely person. He has been pulled off an oil-rig close to Tampere in Finland. The Professor wants Ivan to meet him because he is impressed with his thinking. When The Professor speaks about The Gyroscopic Engineer his eyes well up with tears. Humans try to imprint themselves on anyone they find attractive, either sexually or platonically.

The engineer's house looks uniformly the same as all of the other homes, but this one had been personalised with a pot of flowers outside. Neither Ivan, nor the Professor are sure what kind of plants might grow here yet unaided. Once a reliance on fossil fuels is terminated the team will explore using geothermal energy to grow food on an industrial scale.

As soon as Ivan walks through the door, he is hit with an overwhelming sensation of happiness. There is a smell of cotton wool and flowers. A piece of paper had been folded in two and someone had drawn a picture of a baby. A rudimentary handmade greetings card. On one chair sits a teddy bear.

The engineer beams. He has a lovely smile and a gentle face. He put his hands on his hips. One arm is heavily bandaged. He had an accident with one of the structural pillars. He has lost a finger, but still he waves away any pity or empathy that we are trying to give to him.

"I have a child," he says. "It's a small price to pay, to lose a tiny finger and gain a child."

The Professor removes his hat, which is rare, and bends down to make himself smaller.

The mother, a blonde woman around thirty years of age, lifts up a soft muslin to shield herself from prying eyes. She is breast-feeding and Ivan is stunned by the serenity of the baby—and of the mother. He tries to pull his eyes away.

"There's nothing that stirs a man more than a woman and her child," he says.

Ivan has been part of these special fleeting moments before. Even as a father Ivan had felt like an intruder into this world. He wanted it again, those days and weeks of careful meticulous dance.

"Don't stop. Feed your child," The Professor says. "There's nothing hidden here, grow us a strong child. There's nothing more natural in the world. Is there, Ivan?"

Ivan stutters to say, "Congratulat—"

"He's a father of three himself," says the Professor.

"Four," Ivan says. "Father of four."

"Nothing he hasn't seen before. He's the father of us all here, Ivan, as our sponsor."

The baby carries on feeding and the mother relaxes and introduces herself. She is a viticulturist and we joke that we need her back at work as soon as possible to make wine. Her breasts are as white as a sculptor's marble.

After the baby pulls away she dabs at a spot of regurgitated milk on the infant's sweet, red mouth with the muslin and passes the baby up to her father, the Engineer. He hauls the baby up onto his towel-covered shoulder and pats her gently on her back to wind her. He turns his back so that we can see the baby's face.

The baby loves the Professor's fleshy face. Too small to reach out and grab or even to smile she makes a cooing noise as the Professor tells her how beautiful she is. He shakes his face from side to side and the flesh wobbles.

A baby.

"Here she is, here she is," says the Professor. "The first baby born on this land." They had met on the ship, the Viticulturist and the Engineer. The timing suggested the baby was conceived on that ship. It was everyone's child. She is the child of the entire colony, proof that the urge to live, the instinct to procreate is infallible.

Life goes on!

Ivan takes the baby in his arms. His skin fizzles with electricity. He goes to the window and feels the low sun warm on his arms, and on the child. He rocks her. The last time he held a baby before this was his lost daughter, dead in his arms.

I gasp in my real world and Tiffany asks me if I am okay. I'm not okay. I'm crying. I am feeling Ivan's great, dark-black sadness.

Ivan hums her the same tune as he hummed his own daughter, born too soon. The Brahms lullaby, 'lullaby and good night, with pink roses bedight'.

Ivan is lost in the baby's blue eyes. Behind him The Professor talks. He asks what they have decided to call the baby. They call her Maud, after the land on which we all now stand, me and Tiffany included—Queen Maud Land.

"How lovely," the Professor says. "My own father never held me like that."

Me neither, I think. I don't know anything about my father.

THIRTY THREE

TIFFANY AND I walk into The Village—that early settlement of prefabricated homes built by Ivan and The Professor to house the first settlers. It is early morning and deathly silent. I hear the squeak of rubber wheels and the clank of the changing gears of a bicycle. A boy appears and cycles around us in a circle.

"What the fuck is that on your neck?" he asks, ogling Tiffany's tattoo. Even though he only looks thirteen at the very oldest, there's a flirty suggestive intonation in his voice. He teeters on his bike, balancing between the brake and putting pressure on the pedals.

"We're okay, thanks," says Tiffany.

"Just okay?" he asks, "I could make you feel a whole lot better."

"We're not buying today, thank you," says Tiffany, business-like. "We're visiting a friend." The boy laughs.

"Who?" he asks, and I touch Tiffany's arm because I don't want her to tell him. "Suit yourselves," he says. "But if you change your mind, I'll be around, stand out here in the middle of the green and I'll see you." He cycles away.

"I should have asked him which house is Vincent's mother's," Tiffany says, but I already know. I can't explain how, but I am starting to see the outline of a map in my normal vision. My balance is back, but it's brought with it a series of red, blue and yellow translucent markings that denote information. I'm visualising road turnings, place names, and a translucent grid like mapping. The Cube overlays information onto the scene, onto my life, it guides me.

"It's number sixty-eight," I say, and I am drawn over to the right. Sixty-eight is a house like all the rest, exactly the same, row by row.

These units are dented and weathered and most of them are covered in a layer of orange-hued fungus, a ginger fuzz framing their roofs.

We stand at the front door. The television is on loudly in the background. Tiffany is nervous, and she hesitates in knocking. She's frightened and I know she's only pursuing Vincent because I want her to. Because it's an unspoken agreement with Sarah—for my help, I want Vincent in return. Then I want my sister. Once they are both safe, then I can unleash what is bubbling up inside me. If it were left up to Tiffany, I think that she might just leave Vincent here. But I can't do that.

I step forward and knock. There's a scuffling behind the closed curtains and someone comes to the door. A scruffy man in a dirty vest prises open a crack in the door.

"Hello," Tiffany says.

"What do you want?" he asks.

"Is Shirley here?"

"No, she's not," he tells us. "Are you from the Council?"

"No," Tiffany says.

"What do you want?" he asks.

"We are friends of Shirley's son, Vincent. He's gone missing, and we want to ask her if she's seen him," Tiffany says, and he pulls the door open fully, revealing his stained vest and scabby arms.

"Seen him? I can't bloody un-see him."

He's alive.

"The useless lump," he says, scratching his balls.

"You mean Vincent Ellis? He's okay? He's alive?" I pounce.

Vincent is alive.

"Fucking Vincent this, Vincent that. It's all I hear, all bloody day, with her fussing over him," he says. His fingernail is in his teeth now, loosening some trapped remnant of breakfast, or dinner.

"They're together?" I ask, and I feel a sudden tremendous pang of happiness that Vincent has what he wants at last. He's back with his mother.

"They're over the road. You'll find them in that house there with the red door." He points, and I thank him joyously, but he slams the door in my face. I hop across the road, instinctively jogging, and light on my feet.

"Calm down," Tiffany says. "He might be telephoning across right now, telling them we're on the way over." I'm impatient to know what state Vincent might be in. I am delighted that he is alive. Relief floods through me, my skin heats, my chest swells and reddens, and there's a lump in my throat. I didn't let him die. I saved his life. I did something good for once. Tiffany puts her hand up in the air and points to the house, so that Gloria can see that we are on the move.

But I don't care about their plan. All I care about is that Vincent is alive! I never realised how much I loved him. I never really showed him enough warmth. I was just so nasty to him, all the time. I'm like my mother.

The red door is already open. I place my hand on it and it swings back, revealing a dark room within. There's a strange chemical smell. It's cave-like. The curtains are all shut. The Cube shows me that there are only three small adjoining rooms in these properties, so stepping inside it only takes a second for me to look around and see him.

He is lying on the floor. He is much different, but I know the shape of him, my body can sense his smell. We are connected forever, he and I, in a way that cannot be explained. His feet are stretched out in front, across the floor, and his body is tilted back and over as if he has passed out.

There is a long, gnarled scar down the front of his once beautiful face. It is mottled red and runs down into his neck. His thick black hair is gone and instead his head is covered in a badly cropped stubble where his hair has been crudely shaved off.

I kneel down gently next to him.

I touch his face.

He is clammy and hot. His eyes are swollen, but his cheeks are hollow.

"Vincent," I say, crying at the sight of him. I have found my Vincent, the stupid boy. "We're going to have a baby," I whisper close to his ear. I look down the length of his arm and his sleeve is pushed up and there's blood in the crease of his inner elbow. A needle lies on the floor.

Vincent's eyes open in a thin line. A blood vessel has burst in his eyeball and has left an ink-splat of blood in a web of red veins. I think he sees me, there's recognition, his eyebrows raise and he smiles. He is missing his two front teeth.

"I'm pregnant," I whisper. He knows. He understands. He must understand. I want to give him a picture, a scan, something tangible to give him hope, but I have nothing to give him. I touch his face. "You can choose the baby's name."

"Leave him alone," A woman shouts from the doorway. It's Shirley, Vincent's mother. I can see the resemblance. I've seen a photograph that Vincent carries. She was once beautiful, but now she's haggard and scrawny. She staggers from side to side with a dark glass bottle in her hand. I immediately regret saying he can choose the baby's name in case he calls her Shirley after this one!

"Let him enjoy himself," Shirley shouts, and she moves fast to grab me under the armpit digging her scrawny fingers into me.

"Hey," Tiffany shouts, and the other men lying on the floor start to rouse themselves to see what the noise is. One man rises from the floor and unfurls his huge body. He is more than six feet tall with a wide, flat face and thick biceps.

"Don't let them leave," Shirley tells him and he fills the doorway with his body. There's no way we can get past him. I don't think I could lift Vincent anyway.

"Take a seat, ladies," he says, and though Tiffany wants to fight, she sits down in a cautious, measured way, her eyes scanning the door and the window outside. She'll be wondering how long before Gloria and her crew kick down the door. We sit next to each other on the sofa. Shirley opens the curtains and the room fills with light. The Big Man puts his hands over his eyes. Vincent's eyes narrow and his head flops back.

In the light, I can see small blood spatters against the radiator, and on the wallpaper. Some have faded where someone has tried to clean them away. The floor is littered with tin foil and lighters and other drug paraphernalia.

When she's ready, she stands by the window, looking out.

"What have you done to my son?" she asks.

"Nothing," I say. "I care about him. That's why I'm here."

As she turns, the low slip of sun highlights the angry black bags under her eyes, the thinness of every wisp of hair. She must look twenty years older than she actually is.

"His injuries," she begins, her shoulders cave in, her body cleaves with regret. "He was brought here in a terrible state. His body and his mind. He was broken."

"I never, we never hurt him. We love him. We didn't know if he was even alive. He could have died at any time," I say. He's just lying there out of it, on the floor.

"I had to," she says.

"Had to what?" Tiffany asks.

"I had to give him something to ease his pain. He was having visions, screaming." I shake my head. "Leave him alone. Let him enjoy himself."

We sit in silence. Vincent moans to himself. Someone scrunches up silver foil. It is a little weird, I'll admit that. Your boyfriend is on the floor, and your girlfriend's on the sofa, and we're in a crack den. Yep. Pretty weird.

"This isn't what you want for him, is it, really, Shirley?" Tiffany asks. "I know it's not your fault, but if you love him, you should let us help him." Shirley rears up, venom at the ready. I thought it was great from Tiffany. Great words! But to Shirley its incendiary. I grip the arm of the sofa.

"I just wanted to be in the world. In the real world. I wanted to really be in the places that I see in my dreams, the places that I remember being in, but have never been to," she says. "You think that we are scum, losers, and that we're junkies. But we are free!" She starts to laugh. "It's you lot that are the losers. You're in a gilded cage."

"It's okay, he can stay and we'll just go quietly," says Tiffany, sensing escalation in Shirley's energy. The big man in the doorway hangs on her every word.

"We explore the real world every day. We are the ones who are truly living. We're roaming the world. In here," she says, tapping her head. "More than you ever will."

She turns back to the window.

"My son is never leaving. He's never being taken away from me again. He is staying here where I can look after him." She says. "Now leave, and don't ever come back again, because we won't be so accommodating next time."

"Come on, out," the Big Man mutters, moving to usher us out of the front door, and although Tiffany lingers, we have little choice but to obey.

Until there's a dull thud and the Big Man fits, and his arms go up to the back of his head, and he drops to his knees, revealing Gloria and three others standing behind him holding a baseball bat.

THIRTY FOUR

GLORIA STEPS OVER the Big Man's body with her long-trainered foot. One of Shirley's cronies sits on the sofa in paisley pyjama bottoms. Another stirs a saucepan of hot soup at the stove. Tiffany, spotting a possible threat, strides over and takes the saucepan out of his hands and throws it at the wall. Tomato soup splashes red and the man recoils in fear.

Tiffany is in control. I like it. They are frightened of her, of Gloria and of us. I keep watch on Shirley, who is poised like a cat. We don't want any surprises.

Vincent sits up. He's awake. Gloria kneels down next to him and Vincent says to her; "Alright, love?" I know that those short words will tenderise Gloria's heart.

"You're coming with us, Vincent," Gloria says, and the man on the sofa in the paisley pyjamas stands up and puts his hand on Gloria to pull her away. Gloria stands up to her full height. She turns around, launching a punch that connects with the man's jaw and knocks him flying back onto the floor.

"Do something," shouts Shirley, but her men are lethargic and slow. The soup stirring man gets up as if to make a move. I recoil for safety. These junkies are hard to judge. I feel like they could do anything.

"Stay back," Gloria says, picking up a ceramic vase and wielding it as a weapon. The cowering man shakes his head and puts his hands up. The vase slips from her fingers and smashes loudly on the floor. Shirley launches herself at Gloria and lands on her back, her thin mottled arms around Gloria's neck. Gloria tries to shake her off, but

Shirley bites her ear. Gloria screams in pain and rams backwards against the wall, where Shirley falls limply to the ground.

"We should go," Tiffany says, peering through the curtains. Gloria picks Vincent up in one fluid movement. She has him in a fireman's lift. His arms hang limply at first, but then he starts to kick. We didn't figure on him wanting to stay. Shirley writhes on the floor clutching her ribs.

The boy on the bicycle cycles past the front window, whistling. Across the road, the green doors are starting to open and people are coming out of their houses. The din of people asking questions and talk begins to rumble then erupt as they realise what is happening.

"We need to move, now," Tiffany says, and she ducks as a large stone bounces off the front window. "You three, get outside, keep them away," she says to Gloria's team. They go out the door and assemble in front of the growing crowd of Village residents, the angry mob of Shirley's friends.

Tiffany grabs my hand.

"Follow me," she says, and Gloria moves in behind us with Vincent over her shoulder. Shirley coughs, winded and writhing in pain, but still puts out a hand to her son.

"Vincent, no," she screams. "Please, I'm begging you, leave us alone!"

Tiffany and I step around her and we spill out onto the street. People move slowly towards us in groups. Step by step, they move in closer. Gloria's team shout for them to get back.

"Leave him alone," someone in the crowd shouts. A stone is thrown, followed by a glass bottle which smashes on the floor in front of me. There are forty, at least, we are massively outnumbered.

"What do you want to do?" Gloria asks, turning with Vincent clamped firmly against her shoulder.

"We've got to get him out of here. Got to. Open up a channel to the cars," she orders, as she takes a small handgun out of her jacket pocket and she fires one extraordinary hail of bullets up into the sky. I'm almost deafened and shocked to the core. The crowd in front of us drop to their knees. All of them crouch down, some with their faces in the grass, some hold their arms over their heads. "Go!"

Tiffany is shockingly impressive, and sexy as hell.

We run across the green. I can still hear the bullets reverberating in my head. I look behind me. Some of the mob is still down on the floor, but the rest have started to rouse. They throw sticks and stones, a chair flies through the air.

The car is unlocked and Gloria's team opens the doors for us as we scramble inside. Tiffany starts the car. Excitement and the adrenaline surges through me. This is easy. This is good. Gloria stuffs Vincent into the back seat. Both of them are big and this is a small car. We start to pull away from the kerb.

"It's going to be okay," I say to Vincent, but I hear a woman's scream. Shirley has run out into the street. She is furious, and her mouth is open. She is possessed and she will use her body to stop us leaving with her son.

"Shit!" Tiffany says, and puts her foot to the floor, tearing around in a semicircle. Shirley spins around.

"Don't run her over," I say, but Vincent has his face up against the glass and he's banging on the window. He tries to open the door.

"Lock the door," Gloria shouts, reaching across him to pull the car door shut again. He wants to go to his Mum. It doesn't matter what they do to you, or what they don't do for you, you still want them to love you more than anything in this world.

"Vincent! Vincent!" Shirley screams. She is crying. It's not her fault. She hasn't got any choice. She's had her life taken from her, her baby taken away from her, but right now we can't help her. She chases the car, she stumbles, falls upon her knees, and then she is back up and chasing the car again.

"You've got to go on without her," says Gloria to Vincent. She restrains his arms by holding him at the wrists. Vincent twists to get free of her, but she is strong and eventually he desists and a long deep sigh emanates out of his chest. Vincent releases and bangs his head backwards against the car seat.

"Fuck! Fuck! Fuck!" he says. There are tears in his eyes. He knows he has to let her go. He can never have the thing he wants the most in his life.

I can still hear Shirley's screams as we round the corner and drive out of the Village.

I'm never going to let anyone take my baby from me.

THIRTY FIVE

I SIT WITH Ivan in my mind on a chair in Tiffany's apartment. Vincent is restrained across the corridor in Gloria's flat. I can smell the salt hitting the stones and I can hear the birds, who I once thought were seagulls, but I now know are albatross, squawking and fighting for food.

Ivan is in an apartment on the seafront. He films himself with a camera. His shadow is long and soft against the back wall.

It's funny seeing him like this, because usually I see his reflection in the mirror as he would have seen himself. I notice that he has a small bend in his nose. I'd like to ask him what happened there. He's also got one eye slightly smaller than the other, which is not noticeable the other way around so I wonder if he even knows.

I used to have one eye smaller than the other.

I tighten my fingers around the Cube in my eye socket.

"When you are taking things to an off world colony like Mars," Ivan says. "You are limited. Don't get me wrong, I love the conundrum of how and what to send to get x and y done. It reminds me of a riddle my mother used to give about the fox, the grain and the chicken. She would draw it all out...."

I fast forward.

This bit is boring. Ivan loves the sound of his own voice. I think about the inane nature of recording yourself alone in a room. I think about the level of confidence and self-assured ego to believe that anyone would care what you had to say.

Certainly no one ever cared what I had to say.

Until now.

I'm learning a lot from Ivan. I pause and play using my mind. I'm not even sure how I am doing it.

"Before I split with Elizabeth, I used to like going on business trips," he says, gazing wistfully out of the window. "I would get to stay in a nice hotel. I would get to know the members of my team that I was traveling with. But now I wish that they were here with me. It would make it all bearable. If I'm not with Elizabeth and my kids, then what is the point of any of this?"

He loves Elizabeth. But in the next scene he is with the Professor watching a demonstration of reverse osmosis filtration of sea-water and he sees Dr Joy.

She is going to walk past the lecture theatre that Ivan and The Professor are in and he deliberately stops the demonstration and crosses thirty yards to open the door and call her over.

"You've got to come and see this," he says. "It's incredible."

The Professor is looking at her too. She's an attractive woman. Ivan has grabbed both her arms from behind playfully and I think she must think she's going to see something good, not reverse osmosis. But of course she is a scientist too, they all are, and they find it fascinating.

There's a weird play of brain fuelled flirting. The Professor moves in behind her.

"Allow me," he says, and he holds a cup up to her lips, and it's really awkward. I squirm watching it, as he holds up the cup for her to drink from. They're both all over her. It's uncomfortable to watch.

"Wow," says Dr Joy, "It's clean water. That's incredible."

"We want to extract the salt because it's so damaging to infrastructure, long term," says The Professor.

"We have an abundance of glacial run-off of course, for drinking water. Probably the purest water on the planet. Have you seen Subterranea?" asks Ivan.

"What a jolly good idea, Ivan. Doctor, would you care to join us? We're giving Ivan a tour of the grounds so to speak."

She goes with them. I flick to the tunnels. It is some time later the same day.

There's an entire subterranean network below Brighton. I can see them in the tunnels, wearing hard hats, listening to an engineer point out supportive structural beams.

But I can see the plans too, in the form of drawings, blueprints, cross-dimensional, inter-sectional, and multi-layered with internal pipework, concealed entrances and doors. It's all going into me. I leave mental-breadcrumbs to help recall this information next time I need it.

There is something that they call an insulated 'hive' that will eventually be capable of releasing an escape capsule into the sea. I wonder if it is still there, and The Cube tells me that yes, the 'hive' and it's selection of escape pods still exist. An additional green light system tells me that all ten escape pods are fully operational.

In the lower vaults of the tunnels, deep underground, there are huge fans processing millions of litres of freezing, clear blue water and creating energy. It zips through me. This is the heart of our colony.

I know where everything is. Everything. They've given Dr Joy a tour, but they have given me the keys to the City. It's as if I know all the levels, all the passageways, I am learning all the secrets. Everything flows out to sea.

But there's one large tunnel that goes against the current. It's wide, like a main artery, and it flows the wrong way, up and out of the back of the City toward the ice. I know instinctively that it will take me to the Pavilion.

When I get to the Pavilion, I will find out what exactly Mother does.

Ivan and The Professor are giving Dr Joy a detailed briefing on every subterranean tunnel that is being built under the new city floor. She wants to return the favour and show them a ground-breaking new technique that she has used on one of the engineers who lost a finger.

"Fascinating," says the Professor. "But first, and last, the crevasse, because this is where we got really lucky."

The Professor explains that he picked a spot where a natural fault line had fractured the glacier. A huge crevasse, a mile deep, an ice blue Grand Canyon had opened up. A full thickness hydro-fracture filled with snow. If you fell in there you were gone for good to an icy hell.

This was where it all began. The team of engineers snapped the ice off from there. They proactively melted it by altering the atmosphere. Ivan interjects because he wants Dr Joy to know that this was his concept first and foremost, taken from a series of drawings that he had started back in College.

Antarctica was going to melt, just like the Arctic was thawing. It was only a matter of time and so the idea was born. An established community already there. A secret, a group of people ready to take the human race forward, regardless of what political and scientific perils befell the rest of the world.

This new colony could save the human race. (I snort at Ivan's self-importance.) But, of course, it had to be secret.

When Ivan thought about Mars, he first thought that he would have to build contained units for people to live in—like the space station—sealed units just like in the movies.

There were many theories, but the one that kept coming back to him again and again was: if you change the atmospheric conditions, it means people can go outside and walk around and grow vegetables and farm animals outdoors. You let people really live.

But two things occurred next, like, how are you going to trial that? Where and on whom are you going to test that technology? Because if it fails then its end of days, a holocaust, you end up killing a generation of your best minds, engineers and astronauts.

Well, you trial it on the earth. You trial it in one of the most inhospitable places on the planet.

So, they say, do it in a desert. Somewhere like Mars. But Mars was being targeted by several National public/private partnerships, so Ivan turned his attention to something else.

Titan. The biggest of Saturn's moons.

Looking up at the sky, it is just a flicker of orange near Saturn. Just a pinprick, barely visible, but Ivan thought about that rocky mass of water and ice and asking, 'What if?'

Titan; Earth's rich ice twin with its lakes of liquid methane. With its cyanides, and all the ingredients and building blocks for life. In the future that we face with a fading sun, the furthest reaches of Titan will warm. There will be enormous, city-sized pieces of ice melting. Trillions of ice rocks turning to water replacing the liquid methane. Ice mountains will become gigantic oceans of water. The solar system's last sea world will enjoy its moment in the sun.

The closest thing to Titan on earth, well that's Antarctica. Just persuade a government to give you a small patch of land to experiment on, guided by the most sophisticated quantum computer that has ever been invented, and there you have it.

There you have us.

Ivan takes her hand.

"At first, the firn wanted to settle again. It wanted to pack and refreeze as nature intended. We think everything is melting because science tells us so, but leave snow here for a few minutes and it wants to run back uphill into the glacier. I see no snow now, but if my feet walk on this ravaged ground it won't take long," Ivan says.

Ivan wanted to run the entire operation off the sun. Giant solar. But there's not enough to power up any generators. It's the question that is left in the midst of everything: Power.

The aeroplanes which terra-firm the area and control the weather are flying on gas brought from Saudi Arabia.

Sure, they can see them from space, but the entire project is mired in secrecy. It is tied to the British government, tied to the United Nations, tied to Titan. There is a desire for this project to succeed in secret, without anybody knowing.

This is what excited Ivan. That they are completely independent. Once the farms are operational they won't have to even trade with anyone. They'll be off the grid.

They are in a hospital. It might even be the one that I was in. I've been in a lot of hospitals and now I recognise the difference between the weathered mint green of the hospital in Brighton and the icy fondant walls of the hospital in the Pavilion.

In Brighton they fix a broken wrist. In the Pavilion they experiment, they put things into your mind, and take parts out of your face.

Everything flashes white, and then Dr Joy pushes through some plastic doors. Ivan and The Professor follow her.

The memory slows down.

"Wrong door!" says Dr Joy, "Not in there, that's the genetics room." Two scientists in white coats and masks work silently at a bench. At the back of the room is a huge locked door with a metre long door handle and a sign that reads, 'Caution. Deep Freeze.'

They stop to look through the window.

"Who is in charge of genetics?" Ivan asks.

"That is my own private specialism, Ivan, as you know," The Professor says. "Well, my own and our team of expert geneticists that you see working here."

"Are you two going to be working in labs next door to each other?" Ivan asks, no doubt a convenient arrangement made by the Professor.

"We've got your samples in there haven't we, Ivan?" she asks.

"Oh yes, you don't let a prize stud like this wander by without taking a sample of his DNA, Joy," The Professor says. "He's our finest bull!"

"You've got five fertilised embryos from Elizabeth and I sat on ice in that little room," Ivan says. His heart picks up pace. He had allowed this, signed off and consented before they lost the baby and now he is not so sure about giving them away.

The Professor senses Ivan's sadness and places an arm around his shoulder.

"But it is mainly DNA samples for the third splice," says the Professor. "For a small gene pool, Joy, to ensure diversity, rather the opposite of breeding, we 'out-breed' by injecting the mitochondria of the third person into the embryo. Effectively the subsequent child has three biological DNA maps."

"For the sole purpose of eliminating debilitating genetic disease?" asks Dr Joy.

"Exactly that, Joy. We want a healthy, robust workforce. They're used to mitigate Huntington's disease, but we plan to make it routine, everyone here has signed up to it in their contracts. It's mitochondrial. You still look like your mother or father, but you are the healthiest, most bouncy bonny baby the world has ever seen."

They are in a white, cubed room. It is shiny and bright, so white it hurts my eyes. They wash and clean, scrubbing their hands.

"Better have you completely sanitised boys," says Doctor Joy. Then they are wearing white cotton scrubs with their mouths behind face masks. She asks them if they are ready. Another doctor or nurse comes over and issues instructions about engagement and etiquette required for viewing. They all nod.

We go through another set of heavy duty plexiglass doors and into a theatre. We hear the pulse of a heart-beat. There's a machine. There are tubes filled with dark blue blood.

In the middle of the room on a white table, a little object is held up by a metal brace. The tube of blood is filtering through finer and finer pipework until, at last, it runs through the finger and back out again unoxygenated.

It's the Finnish engineer's index finger.

They've kept it alive.

"We've kept it alive for four weeks," Dr Joy says.

"That's incredible," says Ivan.

"We brought the best brains, Ivan, who can work here undisturbed," The Professor says.

"It's working, limitless science, we've done it Professor," Ivan says, beaming, clasping The Professor's shoulders.

"It's a little gift for him, to congratulate him on becoming a new father," says Dr Joy. "Next Wednesday morning I am going to sew it back on. I'm going to make him whole again."

The engineer's finger pulses red with oxygenated blood.

THIRTY SIX

I OPEN THE front door of my house on Montpelier Road and hope for the best. I must be crazy, but we've spent some time checking that the coast is clear. There's not a living soul in this building anymore. I'm sure of it. It is my house, my home, and the place where my sister and I grew up. I realise now that I am the one who has spent the most time here. It is I who was the constant presence cooking in the kitchen.

I would have been scrawling in my notebooks while Mother was busy at work. Now, I need those notebooks back. I've left notes, important clues and pointers which I must now unravel. To anyone else, Mother included, it is just lists of what I've eaten and smells that I've encountered, but to me, it's the fabric of my life.

Gloria and I are exhilarated after rescuing Vincent. It has cemented our relationship and given us confidence about what we might be capable of achieving together. There seems a symmetry between her and I. A powerful professional connection. She can be my Professor. We talk at length about New Brighton and about what she wants for the colony.

In the cruel, fluorescent glare of the streetlight, I catch the full length of Gloria's and my own shadow. We seem to move in slow motion. Gloria is so much taller than me, and I'm skinnier now than I have ever been in my life, bar my emergent and beautiful pregnancy bump. I look at my thin pale body and I am not the same person that I recognise as myself.

On the coat peg in the hallway hangs the waterproof jacket that I had thrown on to meet Vincent the morning the ship ran aground. I hold its sleeve to my chest. I was so innocent then. Dare I think that, in my enforced state of ignorance, I was happy? I was angry with Vincent that morning, but happy that he'd called. As I ran out of this door, I'd had butterflies in my stomach that I might bump into Tiffany again.

We enter cautiously inch by inch. I'm not to switch on the lights. I'm only picking up my notebooks discreetly, while Gloria peruses my mother's private files. I don't need my old clothes. I am wearing leather trousers that Gloria has given me, biker boots from a second hand shop in the Laines and a black jacket of Tiffany's. Gloria wants to take one of my mother's power suits from her wardrobe. We're meant to be in and out of the house within five minutes.

Upstairs there is a sound. It's the echo of a television set.

It's coming from my sister's bedroom. She must be here!

Instinctively, (more like foolishly!) I run. I can't help it. I run up the stairs, taking two at a time. Gloria does not pause, she follows me.

"Wait," she whispers. She's my guard. My sister is going to love her. She'll take care of my sister too. I push open my sister's bedroom door.

"Alice?" I ask. It is dark, except for the glow of a television set which is on in the corner of the room, playing Superman, the original film version. I walk into the room. I see the bed. It's been made. The sheets are perfect, they have not been slept in. The curtains are pulled closed. In the corner of the room, shrouded in darkness, is a lounge chair.

As my eye adjusts to the darkness, I can see that there is someone sitting quietly in the chair watching us.

"Alice?" I whisper. The light clicks on. Mother has turned on a black spindly spotlight that sits on the table next to her. She is wearing a black dress with black stiletto shoes.

"Robyn," she says. "I've been expecting you."

THIRTY SEVEN

THE FIRST THING to say is that I don't look like my mother. In fact my mother looks more like Vincent which will sound weird, but they have the same characteristics and the same colouring.

No, I didn't go with Vincent because he looks like my mother, I never chose him at all, and I never chose her. You don't get to choose your family. Isn't that what they say? At least she didn't abuse me. But of course she did. Does. If Gloria wasn't standing right here beside me then she'd be able to control me again.

"You look really angry, Robyn," Mother says. She just leaves that sentence hanging there, under the weight of which I may crumble or as she expects, I will become defensive, then emotional and then crumble. Mother has had her hair cut into an asymmetric bob which covers her left eye. She holds a pair of thick, black sunglasses in her hand as usual. She often places the end of one arm in her mouth when she's thinking.

I choose not to answer. Perhaps there is more of her in me than she or I realise.

I am able to scan the room with the Cube. I know—it's amazing. It's like I can see inside everything, as if I am in the situation, but am watching from afar at the same time. I don't let mother see the Cube beneath my patch. My sister is not here. But someone else is here. Other people are in this room.

I look against the back wall and there is the man from The Astoria in the long black coat. The man I thought was a dealer.

"Robyn," he says, to acknowledge me and I see that standing next to him is a policeman, and next to that another policeman, until I see that there are seven policemen standing along the back wall of the bedroom. Gloria spins around taking in the scene. They've been silently waiting. Can they see me like I can see them—inside some sort of Cube device?

"I don't blame you for being angry," Mother says. I remain still. I listen. She is still my mother, and she still holds some currency. I still love her, and she has something that I want. My sister, Alice.

"I'm just trying to do what is best for everybody, Robyn," Mother says. Her face has softened and she leans forward, and casts a shadow of her outline, until she is the silhouette of a mother, full of hope and potential.

"We just came to find Alice," Gloria says, stepping in front of me, trying to take control.

There is a long pause. I can hear Gloria's impatient breath. She's not one for a stand-off, she's more of an action woman. There is the sound of more boots on the stairs. The front door has opened. There's a flashing blue light now emanating from the street.

We are trapped.

The open door fills with the faces of more policemen.

"Wait there one moment," says long black coat man.

"Why don't you ask yourself where Alice is, Robyn?" Mother says. She is a smart cookie, my mother, I'll give her that. I know there's no chance of an actual conversation when she can get inside my head and mess with me so easily. She's not the leader of the Council for nothing. She does this to people for breakfast. The question is whether to play into her hands and respond in the way that she has planned. She is always ten moves ahead. I'm not going to do that. I am not going to fall for her traps.

"I've asked myself that many times. And now I'm asking you," I say.

"Come and sit down next to me," she says, and pats a spindly stool next to her. Gloria steps forward and puts her hand on my shoulder.

"No fucking way, Mummy," she says. "She can hear you fine from over here."

There's a silence again. Even Gloria is mesmerised by my mother. She is the woman that Gloria wants to be, and yet Gloria hates her in equal measure. There's a special world of hate reserved for mothers who don't love their children.

"Okay," says Mother. "Robyn, I love you so much. It might not seem like that right now, but it is the truth. These people that have taken you are not to be trusted. You need to trust me now." I so want to believe her. She's my Mum. I step forward to sit on the stool.

"Robyn," says Gloria, but I have come to sit next to Mother and she holds my hand.

"The truth hurts, Robyn," says Mother. I can see soft wrinkles and smell her expensive perfume. "That's a fact. I have done everything I can to protect you from that pain. I am going to give you one last chance. You come back home to live with me, and we'll start again. I'll help you to forget everything that you've seen and we can go back to exactly how it was before."

"No, Robyn," says Gloria. "No."

"I have to make difficult decisions in my job, but I swear it's for the good of you, and the good of your sister and the good of everyone in this town. It is extremely complex and I have to find a very difficult balance. Ignorance really is bliss, Robyn, and that can be my gift to you. I will look after you always. I'm your mother." The policemen watch in stillness. "Please, Robyn, come home for good."

I want to be with Mother and Alice. I love them.

"And Alice?" I ask. Mother puts her hand on my shoulder and gently massages me with her fingers. She touches me. I can't help but feel loved.

"Yes. If, and only if you agree to come home, you can be with Alice again, all of the time."

"Why are you keeping us apart, Mum?" I want her to give me the right answer, the answer that explains everything that I have learnt about my mother, and that excludes her from wrongdoing.

"Robyn, the truth is only something that will hurt you, and I don't want to cause you any more pain."

"But why?" I ask.

"I'm going to give you one last chance for things to go back to the way they were before." One last chance to go back to the way things were before I knew what I now know. I look at Gloria and I know that if I choose to go with Mother that Gloria will disappear into the Village, or worse.

I know that if I stay with Mother, that she will eviscerate my memory of everything that I have learnt.

Two things twitch. The Cube in my eye trembles with rage, and the baby in my womb flutters with love.

I can't stay with Mother.

"Let Gloria go," I say. "And I'll stay with you."

"I'm not leaving you," Gloria screams, getting fisty and putting her arms up ready to fight.

"Show her to the door," Mother orders. The police congeal around Gloria in one mass and lift her so that she's partially visible being held aloft like a groom at a wedding, and passed over their heads, still struggling, from one to another out of the room and down the stairs.

"Tell the radio presenter, Phoenix. Tell her that I'm coming for her next," Mother shouts and I flinch. I look away to conceal my face. I can't let Mother see how disturbed I am. I go to the window and draw the curtain open to watch them slacken Gloria off, and throw her into the street. She's missing a shoe. She turns to shout. Her hands are on her head in rage. A policeman orders her to move on and by sheer numbers she has no choice but to walk away.

The long black coat man opens up a doctor's bag and produces a very thick needle.

I won't have much time.

What I am capable of?

But this is my home. I know it so well.

"Mother. Please, can I ask you one thing?" I say. "I want to know the truth. Even if it is painful, I want you to tell me. Please."

"Are you sure?"

"Yes," I say.

"You're so grown up. I'll manage it afterwards, Robyn, so that you won't know for long."

"But not in front of them," I say.

"That's enough, Pinkie," she says to long black coat man. "You can let the men get back to duty. We'll call for them should we need them again. Keep two at the front door, please. Bring the car around to take us to the Pavilion. I don't want to wait around."

It takes a few minutes for the house to empty out. In those minutes I am in the Cube. There must be something. There must be a way out. Please, show me. My mind races. Where I am looking? What I should be looking for? My heart races. I notice that I am beginning to sweat.

"Are you ready?" she asks me. "I'm not going to sugar coat this, darling. I'm just going to say it out loud, and let it land where it lands. Okay?"

"Fine," I say, while my breathing is speeding up.

"I was always fascinated by the way you managed it," Mother says. I don't what the fuck she's talking about, but she's headed into my head again. "You were quite small. Four years old I'd say. At first you played with her in the garden and when I called you in for your dinner, you asked me if Alice could join us."

Now, I really don't know what she is talking about.

But here we go anyway. She's gone all glossy, lifting her head with her bob, bobbing. Here's what it's like to have a sociopath for a mother. She thinks she knows me more than I can ever know myself, and her criminal acts against me have ensured that I can never really be one hundred percent sure of my own mind and of my own memories.

"So, I laid the table for a third person," she says. "We had table mats with images of London on them, which you liked and you would point at the red bus and say to Alice; 'We're going to London', or 'It's raining in London, we need an umbrella'."

"No," I say shaking my head.

"That's right, when I asked you what you were playing one day, you said, 'I'm going to London to find Alice.'"

I know what she's doing, but it can't be true. I'm not that mad.

"But of course Alice wasn't there," Mother says. Hammer blow. I feel dizzy, overcome. What is going to happen now? I want to sit down, but I daren't, in case that man sticks me in the neck with a syringe. She's fucking lying.

"No, this is bullshit, this is one of your lies," I say under my breath.

"Alice wasn't at home, Robyn, because Alice is not real. You don't have a sister."

"Shut up!" I shout.

"Alice was, and sometimes still is, your imaginary friend."

"Shut up! She's real!" I scream, and I vow that the next time I see Mother I will be armed.

"I am in awe of you, Robyn. I always knew that you had such tremendous potential," Mother says, and she trembles, ever so slightly, with delight.

THIRTY EIGHT

I CAN'T PROCESS what she has told me. Her words stick in my throat. I stand for a time, rocking back and forth. I accuse Mother of lying. The men are close by with the apparatus to restrain me. Mother has asked them to wait. She's giving me the chance to calm down of my own accord. She's up on her toes, she's worried things might get out of hand. I bet she regrets letting her minions leave. But I have two important secrets myself. This baby who drives me, and this Cube that fuels me.

"Call up the chaps at the door," she asks. "Get them back up here."

How many men does she need to restrain me?

Why so many?

"Your car is arriving," says Pinkie, the long black coat man. I see it pulling up on the road outside. It is slick, black and futuristic. It's not something that you would usually see on the roads of Brighton. It's military, reminiscent of the vehicles the day that the ship ran aground.

"I'm going to be sick," I say, dry heaving, and coughing up bile onto the floor.

"Take her to the toilet," Mother says. "Through there in the bathroom. Robyn will show you." She points down the hallway. I am seeing jagged white lines in my peripheral vision. They are vibrating. They are connecting me to my home. They are tying my fears into the fabric of this house.

As I am led out of the room by a policeman I can see the needle is at the ready to subdue me.

Enough is enough.

Inside my head the Cube short-circuits.

It feels sticky and hot inside my furious brain.

I am coming up on something.

I see the reflection of a street lamp glint off the surface of the needle just before I come to the boil, and just before mother's lamp suddenly fades.

"What's happened there?" Mother asks, tapping its shade while I walk down the corridor accompanied by two policemen. I bite the inside of my cheek just enough to bleed, and dab it with my index finger.

At the bathroom door they try to accompany me inside.

"Please," I whisper, showing them a streak of scarlet blood on my finger. "I'm on my period." The fools are startled by the blood and immediately relent. Mother would be furious.

"Don't lock the door," one says. I go into the bathroom. My own bathroom. My toothbrush sits in a white plastic cup where chalky toothpaste has pooled in its bottom.

I focus.

All the house lights go out. I send them out. Then...

All the lights in the street pop. Poof. Gone. Yes, me again!

All the televisions, radios, traffic lights, and the cheap illuminated signs on Western Road shops turn off.

I lock the door.

It's pitch black, but I know my way around. I know this room.

I run the hot tap, I take the shower off its hook and leave it running, at full steam, swirling around on the floor like a snake.

"Are you alright?" The policeman whispers as I squirt a bottle of something, shampoo or shower gel, I can't tell which, onto the wet tiled floor and then I grab another and do the same.

"What's happened to the lights?" I ask.

"Open this door," whispers the policeman, most likely talking quietly, so Mother doesn't know they let me out of their sight.

I open the window. There's a bolt that stops it from opening fully, but I frequently remove this unbeknownst to Mother. She probably thinks it doesn't open. I'm thinking how wrong she is as I climb out onto the kitchen roof. I put my feet down. I'm outside. The wind is firm. I duck down and push the window back, almost closed and jam down the bolt back into place. I push my face into the gap.

"One second," I say to the policeman. "I'm almost finished." I might sound distant. I've got to try. I'm shaking.

"Hurry up," he says, but I am already gone. In the cold darkness, I watch every footstep across the flat roofs.

I don't have very long. Ten? Twenty? Thirty seconds?

Between next door's roof there is a low brick wall and gutter. I climb over easily, and the next, and the next. The houses are silent. I hear some voices, a cough from a bedroom, a toilet flushing, and a cat's eyes flashing.

The darkness is magnetic. It sucks me in. It's all around me. There is no moon, no stars.

I've done this before. This escape from the bathroom window, it's how I know what to do, how I know to get to the end of the terrace and climb down onto a shed. I have never been chased before. I have never been in fear of my life.

I trip on something. A sharp tile maybe, right across my shin. It sears in pain, a great heat. I clasp my shin but I have to go on.

There is a noise behind me.

They are in the bathroom. I glance back. They have torches, of course they have bloody torches, they're the police.

I keep moving. I can't hear them on the roofs.

I hear the smash of breaking glass. They've broken the window. He's running his torch around the frame to get any glass shards out and then I hear boots on the roof behind me.

I have to go on. Three to go. There's a gap a metre wide where an alleyway runs between the terraced houses. The Cube directs me, lighting my way from inside myself. I have to trust it, I do trust it. I run and I jump. I land on my feet and then fall onto my knees. It hurts. The police are getting closer. I think I can hear breathing, a whooshing sound of men's breath chasing me down.

I glance behind again. There are flashlights all over Mother's garden. Dark figures are climbing in the gardens, going over the fences. I can see the flashlights trailing up into the sky.

There's shouting. A whistle blows. A dog barks. They are coming my way.

I am fucking petrified. I want to piss myself. I want to jump off these fucking roofs and fly away into the sky. Shall I stop and hide? I could turn, try a window and hide inside a neighbour's house? No, surely they'll find me. Us. My baby and I.

The booted footsteps are getting closer. The closest one blows his whistle and the torches pause and resume refocused, and faster.

Three houses to go.

A man screams. I can't stop and wait to listen, but I know that a policeman hasn't seen the drop. He's fallen straight down, he's screaming in agony. It would be enough to give a nasty break. The chasers fall back, but there's only respite for a second. It seems to spur them on.

I'm at the last house and I stumble and find the garden shed adjacent to the roof. I drop down onto it, and then onto a large bin and then onto the ground. I can hear a motorbike engine fizzing over. I go to the far end of the garden, brushed by shrubbery that catches and pinches me, and where there is a back gate out into Temple Street.

The police are already at the southern end of Temple Street and seeing me sends them into a frenzy. They start to charge.

But just as we had prepared, Gloria is waiting for me on a motorbike. My Gloria, my saviour.

"Get on," she says, and she revs the engine of her motorbike as I throw my leg over. She looks in all directions at once. The police are zombie-like, clumping together to mindlessly attack. I cling to her as she opens up the throttle and hammers out of Temple Street in a streak of burning rubber.

THIRTY NINE

IN THE CUBE, Ivan turns, and I see Elizabeth for the first time. Elizabeth.

I want to cry.

I know her. I don't, but I do. Can you know someone just by seeing them once?

She has a gap in her front teeth. It is lovely. It is meant to be lucky. I have a tiny little gap in my front teeth too. I feel like I am looking at a more feminine, more mumsy version of myself.

"Why are you wearing those silly glasses?" she asks.

"I am recording everything, for our children," Ivan says.

"It was bad enough when you used to be on your cell phone all the time and now this obsession with filming everything,"

"This is important work," Ivan says.

"This is your new preoccupation," she says, fixing her lipstick in an ornate mirror. "It's fine. I'm used to it." He takes off the camera glasses and throws them onto the table and I see the room at an angle. It's a hotel room. I can see that little cardboard sign hanging from the back of the door that says, 'clean my room'.

"My only obsession is you," he says. Cheesy! But I can feel his sincerity—he means it. He stands up behind her and presses his body against her.

"Ivan, let go, we agreed we were just going to be calm this time around, okay?"

"It is going to be different this time, I swear." I hear Elizabeth take a long deep sigh. That's never enough for someone like Ivan. He wants vials of each other's blood hung around necks. Names in tattoos running across his heart. He feels deeply and insatiably and sadly, whatever he has is never enough.

I pause him.

If only he could do what I am doing now and see himself. Perhaps he would be able to take time to look inside himself and appreciate everything that he has going for him.

I haven't got much, but what I do have I value dearly. I value Tiffany and Gloria and Vincent and this baby I am growing. My sister, Alice, I value her as she is, and I am going to fight to get her back. I don't believe my mother's lies.

I wonder if my mother was ever like this with my father. She never mentions him. I asked her, especially in the time before I stopped questioning. I was always asking about him. Then there is the memory of the burial at sea and I'm not entirely sure whether we did bury him at sea or whether that's been put there as an artificial memory.

I let the Ivan scene play again. He looks more tired, maybe older.

Ivan is being intense with Elizabeth. He is demanding a kiss but wanting sex. She doesn't want to kiss him, because she knows it will lead to sex and she doesn't want sex right now. But he just takes it as rejection. He requires a display of love from her. What an exhausting menace he must be to poor Elizabeth and I realise he is stupid in love—stupid not to realise that this is how you push someone away. Elizabeth is here for now and although I can't see inside her mind, I expect she'll put up with this for a time and then she will be on her way again.

He'll be angry and devastated, and she will be free. Who could blame her?

The door opens and the children come in. The same three children from my first memory of Ivan. They are older now than they were when I first saw them. Ivan puts his glasses back on and I see the room from his viewpoint.

The middle boy and the little girl are dressed the same. I recognise the clothes they are wearing because I had the exact same clothes; a brown wool jacket and a red and yellow tartan scarf.

The girl stands with her arms held out away from her body to show her Mother the strange outfit that Ivan has made her wear.

Elizabeth examines a thin line of tiny suckers that the girl has across her forehead. They are connected on a string-like piece of wire that connects down her back into a little black battery pack that flickers with a green light.

"What is this Ivan? It's not going to hurt her is it?" Elizabeth asks.

"God, no! The device records changes in the temperature of the skin and brain waves that's all, and brain activity through the skin. A programme matches these small changes with a list of prescribed emotions, and then we can match the visual memory with a series of basic emotions."

"Christ, Ivan, she's seven years old,"

"She's going to love it, it's perfectly safe. You're making history. It's going to be fun, isn't it, sweetie?" Ivan picks up the little girl and extends his arms so that she is above his head. I get this instant sense of déjà vu, like that has happened to me.

I can smell him, my Dad. There's a musky aftershave and underneath the fresh zest of soap. Vincent's Dad smelled of sweat, not a disgusting smell, just citrus soap with the freshness of outdoor work, of digging and lifting and carrying. Ivan doesn't smell of work like that. He's too organised to allow his smell to become feral.

There had been an absence of staff in this scene, but out in the corridor they emerge like beetles, they have been waiting. There is the snap of a camera, the hiss of cabling snaking across the floor from camera to lighting. Someone scribbles a note on a clipboard. Elizabeth shies away, retreating back from the action. I can see in her eyes that already she thinks that she might have made a mistake getting back together with him.

An assistant introduces herself and takes Elizabeth by the elbow. We watch the children in the tartan scarves walking down the long hotel corridor.

A man has a handheld computer. We don't have them at all in New Brighton, nor do we have the mobile phones which every person in Ivan's world seems to be using at all times.

"This is great," he says. "We've got a little bit of anxiety coming through as they walk down the length of the corridor,"

"Anxiety?" asks Elizabeth, horrified.

"That's perfectly natural, children always have this reaction when they walk down enclosed hallways, even with all of us here, it's instinctual."

"Bring them back please, I don't want them being scared." Elizabeth shouts, and she's broken free of her handlers and is marching down the corridor, "Milo, Ivy, hold each other's hands please."

"Mom, I'm not scared," says Milo. Well, his recordings would suggest otherwise, but in front of all of these people, he doesn't want to look like the frightened one.

Elizabeth takes them both by the hand.

"That's enough. Thank you. We're going outside," she says, and the crew tentatively detach themselves from their recording devices. A man wearing a black T-shirt with a boom microphone leans against it and takes out his mobile phone. They wait for a sign from the only person who can tell them what to do, their boss, Ivan. But the only person he really wants to impress is Elizabeth, who, yet again, is astounded by his activities, and not in the right way.

I am smacked by a whoosh of wind from a red double decker bus. We are outside the hotel. The street is crammed with traffic. There are black taxis like the ones we see on the TV.

We are in London.

At last I am in London!

It really does exist—somewhere.

I feel like I want to leave Ivan and his crew, it's so vibrant, so energetic that I don't feel stuck in Ivan's memories. I feel like I could jump into one of these taxis and be whisked away wherever I choose to go.

I want to tell Vincent that I made it.

But I can't. I am locked into Ivan, I am one with him. The emotion that I can feel from him is one of excitement. I wish I could tell him to stop all of this and take his wife and his children to a quiet park and sit listening to them talk. I wish I could tell him that if he doesn't stop pushing and shoving he's going to lose his family.

Why do I even care?

He is showing me this for a reason and in a way he is kind of saving me.

A large sign reads: The Royal Garden Hotel, Kensington.

We stand underneath a canopy where taxis pull in to pick up and drop off. A woman gets out of a taxi with triplets, three girls who all look the same. They have expensive-looking brown leather luggage.

The air is laden with winter—of mushy leaves drying out into something far crisper and more sprightly. I guess there is an invisible fog of car fumes and dust. I can't taste in this world, I can't smell either. I can see the warmth coming out of people's mouths as white plumes. The cold is spiky and immature. I guess one thing I know for sure, one thing anyone who has grown up where I am from knows, and that is the cold in London is amateur. It's nothing at all. 'T-shirt weather' I joke to myself.

Ivan turns around just as an old fashioned brown-liveried coach pulls up to the hotel.

"It is perfect," he says. As I see it, I know this coach, it's the coach that I got on my first trip to London, when we went to the Natural History Museum with the school. Ivy and Milo board the coach. Ivan and Elizabeth follow, but sit in the front seats and let the kids run amok up the back.

The seats are made of brown velvet. There are little orangey curtains that you can pull to guard yourself against the watery sun.

The coach sets off from the hotel into the street.

Bizarrely, we pass one of the buildings from Brighton seafront, the Royal Albert Hall, double the size and bold as brass in the middle of London – astounding!

"I love that building," Elizabeth says.

"I know you do," Ivan says. We sit in traffic. Exhaust fumes whistle. There's a gentle hum. Someone from the crew knocks on the door and provides two lunch boxes for Ivy and Milo.

The sky darkens.

Outside, is it raining? No, it's hail. No, wait—it's snow!

The coach pulls up outside the most magnificent building I have ever seen in my life, with its contrasting stone brick work and grandiose towers. The Natural History Museum. We get off the bus, and walk through a gate in the wrought iron railings and up the steps.

There is no queue for us, no waiting, we are ushered through as the first flakes of snow start to land and melt. On the ice rink outside the museum, children can't believe it is snowing and they skate with their palms open wide to the heavens to catch it.

"It won't settle," Ivan says, but of course I know that it does, and that when we leave, we will run around outside and have the most amazing snowball fight that I've ever had in my life. Me and Ivan and Elizabeth and Ivy and the boys.

FORTY

I SIT IN a Café overlooking the sea in Saltdean. The Brighton skyline splinters through the fog, though it looks a lot smaller now than I once thought it was. The sea is actually bright blue here and only a few hundred feet out to sea, a pod of Minke whales spout water into the air and their silky backs turn over in the froth. It is so beautiful here, unspoilt. We, humans, should not be here with our toxic disregard for life.

Gloria settles me like an aged great aunt on a day trip from the old people's home, and then sits back at the other table. We pretend that we are not together. Rather, she is here to meet her friend, who can help us. She rubs my shoulder, gives me another tissue and goes back to him. He's six and a half feet tall, with huge biceps and a shaved head that reveals wrinkles of muscular flesh at the back where the neck meets the crown. Vincent would describe him as a brick shithouse. He takes off his thick dark glasses and lovingly tucks a loose strand of hair behind Gloria's ear.

If you are in trouble here, I don't know exactly how long you can evade the authorities before you end up in the Village. Clearly, I've not managed it for long myself before. In my case, how long before I end up forgetfully passive, because that is what will happen to me again. She won't kill me. She will silence me, and perhaps this time for good. How much more can my brain take before it breaks?

I have been crying.

I know! But she's still my mother!

My fingers tremble around the coffee cup, spilling liquid into the saucer.

My mind is riddled with images—pictures of the people that I love. My people. Are they real, or not? My sister had a habit, a little quirk; she sometimes put her finger over her drinking straw pulling it out of the glass, holding the liquid inside, then sucking the drink from the bottom. It's so real. I couldn't have made that up, could I?

I suppose it would be convenient to me that she lived in a world where she never went out, and never met anyone else apart from Mother and I. According to Mother, of course, she facilitated my fantasy. But I wouldn't, I couldn't make up a detail like the straw. I have never seen anyone else do that.

I ask Gloria if she knows my sister.

"I hardly know you, love. Never mind your sister," she says. I can tell that she thinks I might be mentally unstable. That makes her like me more, and I think she respects me and what I've been through. I also think she believes Mother and that she feels terribly, dreadfully sorry for me. She is disappointed too, because she had marked me out as a leader, a saviour. I can smell her sour disappointment.

I don't know what is real anymore.

Could Mother have implanted artificial memories of Alice to cement my mirage? So that she became more real over time. The pain in my chest is real. I don't have anything of hers. I want to go back home to our house to look into her bedroom and see her things. I don't even have a home anymore. I need to smell Alice's smell. That's something that you can't lie about.

The waitress brings more coffee and bangs into the table and spills even more into the saucer.

"Sorry, I didn't see that," she says, shaking her head. They are all going blind. They are all banging into tables, and shielding their eyes from the meagre bit of daylight that we get.

There's such a likeness, now I see it, between Gloria and the ranger she is lovingly tending to. They could be brother and sister. They hold hands across the table and he moves his chair ever closer to sit next to her and put his arm possessively around her. She likes it. She looks into his face and they kiss.

I don't feel grief. I just feel shocked. Can I believe my mother? My body acts like it must believe her. I'll call my baby Alice, whether it is true or not. I search the Cube for Alice, but she has gone, without a trace.

There's no record of my mother having another child except for me. Because my mother carried me and birthed me, that much is on record. She must have agreed to carry me then for some reason other than wanting a child.

Gloria stops kissing the ranger and they come to my table. The ranger shakes my hand. He has a kind face now that I see him close up. He is older than I thought, but his body is what people would describe as being in great shape.

"I've reported the motorbike stolen to the police. It might be alright. I suppose they know who you are anyway," he says.

"Thank you," I say.

"No, please. Anything that you need," he says. "I support you." I wish I could be what he wants me to be, but it hurts too much. Perhaps it is the truth that he wants, like we all do, but I feel it deeply, these strangers stringing out together in a line to help me. Gloria puts her hand flat on his chest and gazes into his eyes, fluttering her eyelashes. She's chipped her nail varnish from the night's activities fleeing from the police.

"Tell her," she says, to the ranger. He coughs to clear his throat. I sense his nervousness in the way that he stares at the floor before he speaks to me. I've never experienced reverence of any kind before I find it confusing.

"Gloria tells me you've got access to a cubic computer."

"I had to tell him, Robyn, I owe him the truth," Gloria says. I nod. I haven't heard it called that before, 'a cubic computer'. In fact no one ever mentions it in mixed company. We don't use computers here in daily life. They are a mystery to us. In Ivan's memories they are all around, people use them every day, small ones, big ones, computers that are like telephones, in your watch, in your refrigerator.

"It's okay, tell me, please," I say to the ranger.

"You know the metallic entrance plates that we'll need to access the Pavilion?" he asks. I realise that they are planning on going to the Pavilion.

"No, I don't," I say. "Tell me about them."

"They're everywhere. You can find them all over the city, mainly as access points to the grid," I look blank. The grid? He senses my ignorance. "The grid is a name for the network of multi-level tunnels that run under the city."

I do know about these.

I searched for 'ranger' in the Cube.

Faces flick through my mind and I land upon his face quickly. I see his name, his age, his wife, and his children. There's a look of the Professor running subtly through all of them. Everyone looks the same.

I wonder if Gloria knows that he is married. I don't think that I am ever going to mention it to her. He is handy, this bloke, he's a good resource for us.

"They don't work from fingerprints, they work on DNA," he says. "They can recognise micro particles of DNA signature from one contact."

I hadn't thought of this, but it's why my Cube has started working without me touching it, just by being in contact with my flesh.

"But how's it working with my DNA?" I ask.

"Either it has been set up for you as an individual person, and in some cases there can be a familial DNA which is strong enough,"

"Your mother?" asks Gloria. "Your mother must be using a Cube, and you can get access via her."

"Yes, your mother or father or a sibling. It would have to be someone very closely related to you. Your immediate family."

"About time your mother gave you something useful," Gloria says. "She'll be livid if she thinks she's given us so much information."

"They're made from Tantalum, and they have an eternal charge. It's incredible. It's astounding that we once had the technology to produce them," the ranger says.

"We know about the tantalum. What about Pavilion access?" Gloria asks. She is set on going there but without my sister to rescue then what is the point?

"If your Mother realises that you are accessing the Cube, then she might block you." I know that hasn't happened yet. But I need to ensure access and we need to operate underground without detection.

"To access the Pavilion without alerting security, you need the DNA of a high ranking Council official,"

"Like a swab?" asks Gloria.

"No, you still need the finger connected, the scanner needs to read a person's flesh."

"Thank you," I say, and I finish my coffee. "Thank you for all of your help." I can think of one way to get hold of senior official's flesh.

The ranger gives Gloria the keys to a clapped-out white van. It displays a workman's livery in red swirly writing and on the side panel it says; *H. White and sons, Brighton's Finest Tilers.* He's lined up three such vans.

We drive along the cliffs back into Brighton in our liveried van.

"Search yourself in that thing, and you might be able to find Alice from there," says Gloria. She's being kind. I wish it were that easy. I have already done it and found nothing, but to please Gloria I do it again. Why do I want to please Gloria? I feel like she's the sort of person who would risk her life for me, that's why. She already has.

So, I think about myself, and I say my name over and over in my mind.

"Robyn Lockhart. Robyn Lockhart. No. Robyn Elizabeth Lockhart." My real, full name, never used.

Robyn Elizabeth Lockhart.

Then it appears suddenly in my consciousness. It's a series of sheets of written information, some scanned and printed lists.

I read the entry. My address and my mother's name. There's the name of my school. There's a hospital record. In fact there are many hospital entries. There's an admission record at the Pavilion. I can't drill in any further on that record.

There's another piece of paper.

It lists my age as twenty-seven years old.

But I am only twenty. It must be someone else. I look again. But it is face, my image. It is me.

What the fuck? I'm twenty, and only just twenty. I was a teenager only a few weeks ago. Gloria asks me if I am okay. I'm not okay. I bolt upright.

"I'm twenty seven years old, Gloria," I say.

"That's fuck all," she says, sucking a blue ice-lolly.

"I mean, I am twenty-seven years old."

"I heard you the first time, and it's still nothing. You're just a baby. I'd give my left tit to be twenty seven again."

"Did you know?" I ask.

"I thought you were nineteen or twenty. That's what I've been told."

"Twenty-seven," I say, pulling down the sun visor to look in the tiny mirror at my good eye. "Do I look twenty-seven to you?"

"Even if you are, and I'm not saying that you look like you are, twenty-seven is nothing, babe."

"Mother lied to me."

"Quelle surprise!" Gloria says.

"They've stolen seven years of my life, Gloria. I thought I was a fucking teenager." All those years have disappeared in seconds. I wanted to do so much. I wanted to go to university. I wanted to get a proper job, move out, move in with someone. I wanted to make mistakes. I wanted to be wrong, get it wrong, learn to grow up myself not suddenly be here now.

I hold my head in my hands.

"Even if you can remember those years, Robyn, they'll be fucking awful," she says. "Good riddance. Don't look back. We're changing the future you and I. That's what we're about."

My anger rears up inside me, intense heat drives my chest red. My mother is going to pay for what she has done.

FORTY ONE

WE ARE IN the downstairs room of a pub near the station. It has dark wooden tables stained with streaks of sticky beer. Now I understand why every shop, pub and house has a basement, because we don't exist on one linear level, our city crashes vertically through the floor, layer after layer downwards.

"I should have done something to stop him," says Sarah Phoenix. She stands, delivering her words. People are mesmerised. I feel the weight of their pain, they are all missing somebody. She has their hearts. I want to know more about her and her six flame-haired children.

Inside my head, The Cube searches, bringing up files. I can lock on and scan her face. Her information is suddenly with me. I know where Sarah Phoenix lives, her exam results, and the ages of her children.

Then suddenly I know her sadness. Her husband is alive, but they do not see him anymore. He's in The Village. I suppose he might be one of the men that we disarmed. There are many men like him.

"He was unable to cope," she says. "He wanted to travel, he needed to leave here, he became claustrophobic. It was the stress of bringing up his children here in the same place that he believed was trapping him, that tipped him over the edge."

It is usually a great panacea. When people focus on the mundane necessities of child-rearing they forget about—what is it that they forget about? More likely they tolerate the simulation of their existence. People say you feel things more when you have a child, but you don't need a child to feel. Having a child makes you feel fear. It makes you afraid.

But sometimes feeling fear makes you go the other way. There's a yearning for the truth, a rebellion that will not quieten down. It might be spontaneous, but it is rarely organised. It butts up against the established status quo, it really is the only time that the Council takes note and acts.

You can do anything, go anywhere, think anything—but when you start displaying a questioning attitude then you get flagged. Within The Cube, it's actually a triangular pixel of code that becomes attached to your home address. This triggers further investigation from The Council. After that, it doesn't take long. There are warnings, but eventually problem individuals end up medicated at the Pavilion.

"My husband is gone," Sarah says. "Made lost by the Council. Taken from me."

I know that she seeks vengeance, but that her intent is not as sharpened as mine, that her boundaries are not as limitless, that she has more to lose, and less to fight with.

He is dependent on free, Council-prescribed super smack. No one could face calling it 'Ice' under the circumstances. Its proper name is Hentanyl, known by people in The Village as 'Hent'.

Her story hits me hard.

I absorb this information immediately. For everyone else, these stories would trickle through over years as rumour. They have time to process, time to filter, time to think. Not me. I don't have the luxury of time. My baby grows bigger by the day. I have to act now, before I am consumed with fear.

I have no physical home anymore, no sister to drive me on, only my home here amongst these Scarab rebels, marked by their tacky beetle tattoos, who have freed me and taken me in.

"I can't risk being sent to The Village myself, for the sake of my children," Sarah says, as people nod in agreement. "I have to keep them out, keep them clean."

"All this suffering," Gloria shouts. "We need to show them we have rights. We have a right to leave!"

"What changes can be made when generation after generation is wasting away?" Sarah asks.

"The time is coming to take action," a man in the audience shouts. Gloria shakes hands with someone at the back of the room. Gloria is important in this community. She has gravitas, a confidence in her stance as she towers above her contemporaries. The Scarabs use the image of a beetle. They are listed in the Cube as an organised crime group.

I search for Gloria in my Cube, but of course Gloria is not her real registered name. I search under the address where Gloria and Tiffany live and there's nothing, no triangular pixel. I look into her face and then I find her, years ago, looking much different. She has made herself anew.

These new friends of mine are operating at great risk. I've met them only for a short time, but the brief intense nature of our meeting feels like they are friends that I have known my whole life. I trust Tiffany and Gloria with my life.

Vincent sleeps on a bench at the back of the room with Gloria's coat over his legs. He shudders from time to time as you would expect from somebody who is about to require another dose. We don't believe that they will be looking for him, rather that he will run back to his mum, to Shirley and her maisonette of delights if he gets half a chance.

We are going to hand him over to someone who can look after him, get him straight and safe while we concentrate on the business in hand.

Gloria taps me on the shoulder.

"Robyn, this is Mo. He's going to look after Vincent for a few days. He's a doctor," she says, introducing a tall, thin, dark skinned man. He looks like one of the willowy figures that I saw in passing on the refugee ship.

"I'll do my best," he says. He's with Nat, the woman I met once before at Eleanor's house and the nanny to Sarah's children.

"The time for action is now," Sarah says, slamming the table to a burst of angry applause. Gloria brings me back to Mo.

"You already met Nat didn't you? She's actually a nurse," says Gloria, and Nat smiles, but turns to Mo and talks in another language. It isn't Spanish or French or any of the languages that I have learnt through artificial memories.

"I'm sorry," I say. "I don't understand." Mo clasps his hands in front of his chest and bows his head.

"It's nothing," he says, but Nat mumbles words in secret. What has this got to do with me? Gloria has turned away to applaud Sarah. There is an energy in this room that is making me sweat.

Nat is looking at me. I feel the pressure of her eyes upon me.

I hear a voice say, 'she shouldn't be here.'

"Ignore them," Mo says. The material of his clothes reminds me of the fabric I saw on the refugee ships.

I feel queasy. Here, in this dingy pub function room, people know more about me than I know about them. I am momentarily disarmed.

"What did she say?" I ask.

My back prickles with tiny little beads of sweat, though I am cold. I look at Mo. He looks at me. Nat won't make eye contact with me. They don't trust me.

"She wants to know if it's true about your mother?" Mo asks.

"What about my mother?" I ask. People have stopped and turned to look around at me. Tiffany and Gloria stop to turn around to look at me.

"Leave her alone," Tiffany says, but I feel the weight of the room, of their stares. My vision flares, lights flickering, dots joining together, information flashing inside my eyes, inside my head. I feel dizzy and take a step back and half a lager shandy tips over and frees itself into the swirling carpet silencing the room.

Now everyone looks at me.

"I think you should have checked, Gloria, before you brought her down here. We've got some people with very strong feelings about the Council. Obviously, after events of the last few days, Robyn is likely to draw unwanted attention," says Nat.

"That's why we need to be here," says Gloria. "She's a victim of her mother, as much as any of us are. Worse in fact. You should have seen what they were going to do to her."

"We don't treat people like this. It's true. She is her daughter, but she has also been abused by her mother," Sarah says. People gasp (embarrassingly!) and there's a kind of energy in the room, a surge of anger and emotion. Hands are clasped. Heels stamp the ground. It's really raw. Chairs are forcefully shoved in under tables in a very British show of disdain. Tiffany and Gloria close ranks in front of me, as if to protect me. Inside my head, inside the Cube I can see the plans of this pub outlined in blueprints, and behind the floral carpets I see an entrance to the tunnel system and far away in a safe disused space where Mo has set up his makeshift hospital.

"I'm not like her," I say.

"If she is your mother then you don't belong here," Mo says. "I'm sorry to say it but you don't. The things she does and the things she represents are just too bad."

"I know a lot of things," I say. I scan Mo's face but there's no record of him, in fact a red light triggers the word, 'illegal'. "I know there's a tunnel right under our feet, and a secret entrance. I know that you came here on a boat. You arrived a year ago. I know that you hide in those tunnels."

"I guess you're your mother's daughter," he says.

I turn to face the room.

"I'm not," I say. "I'm just like you."

I flick up my patch and look straight into Mo's eyes.

I blink.

My eyelid flutters down over the Cube. My eye socket feels full and warm. My tears moisten the Cube and it takes on a glistening, watery quality. I am not as I was before. I see them all standing there with their mouths hanging open, looking at me. I must look intense. I guess it looks grotesque in a way, some kind of Frankenstein.

"I am not with Mother," I say. "I am with you."

"It's the Cube," Nat says. "She's got the computer." There's the hum of shocked chat at the back of the room:

"How can she use it?" someone whispers.

"You'll look after Vincent," I say, and Mo nods.

Gloria moves behind me, her statuesque figure at my side. I offer my hand to Mo.

"I trust you and you will trust me," I say, not giving him much choice. In the back of the Cube somewhere there is an odd ping.

"Robyn's mother has systematically abused her," Gloria says. "Robyn is one of us."

"You have nothing to fear from me," I say. The odd ping rings through my head once more, getting closer. "I just want my sister returned to me. That's all."

Sarah makes her way through the crowd towards me.

"I can help you," I say to Sarah. "I'm going to help you. I'm going to stop my mother."

They crowd around me, keeping their distance. I feel their excitement and their fear.

Sarah holds out her hand to me. I take it. I feel the softness of her palm, and witness the harshness of her pain. Gloria and Tiffany exchange a look. They are proud, they came for me, they had a plan. Did they recruit me? And bring me here for this purpose? To displace my mother? I know now that they did, and that they have tried more than once.

They start to applaud.

Sarah embraces me.

These people are going to be my new family.

But there's that worrying ping again.

Before I can enjoy the warm applause that starts around the room, a man stands up at the side of the room. He is dressed in black, brown hair and eyes. He looks normal enough until he pulls out a small handgun which looks incongruous in the surroundings of the pub.

"Sarah," says Gloria, "Sarah, behind me now!" But it's too late. He pulls the trigger and Sarah flies backwards across a table, clutching her shoulder.

I am washed in Sarah's blood. It's in my mouth. The pinging rings non-stop through my brain.

Above us we hear the noise of heavy boots massing together and running fast down the stairs.

It's me. I know it's me. They've tracked me somehow through the Cube and I have brought them right here.

FORTY TWO

I AM DOWN on my knees over Sarah. Blood seeps out of her, I can feel it on my legs. The blood looks red against her pale skin. She has an ethereal unworldly look as though she is already an angel. Her breathing is loud and guttural. Amidst the chaos, she smiles.

I throw out a block in the Cube to scramble my signal, and to stop them from tracking me. It's easy when you know how. But it's too late. Do they know it was me that led them here?

Gloria turns over tables. People are carrying furniture to stack it against the door. There's a racket of noise clattering outside trying to get in.

"Get that fucking door barricaded," Gloria shouts. People scream. Gloria directs people around the room, but we are unarmed and ill prepared for this onslaught. It's my fault. If I hadn't antagonised Mother. If I'd have gone with her, this would not be happening.

"Leave me," Sarah says. "I command you to leave me."

"I'll never leave you," says Gloria. "Put some pressure on that!"

The shooter's body lies on the floor, his neck is shucked like an oyster, the life popped out of him. Whatever promises my mother made to him are now meaningless.

"It is my will that you leave me here. Get into the tunnels," Sarah says quietly, life draining away from her.

"No, absolutely not. I'm bringing you to safety," says Gloria.

"Look after my children," she says, and I am astounded by the violent sadness within myself. I begin to cry. I think about my beautiful sister's face. I see her sweet, honest smile. I feel loved when I am with her. She's gone too. It's as if she, Alice, is dying here in front of me, along with Sarah. It's all my fault. I have brought death to these people. I have finished off the rebellion. I am my mother's daughter, after all.

The Cube is washed with my tears, and I clearly see that there is a tunnel entrance beneath our feet, and that Mo is opening the trap door entrance.

"Look after your own children," Gloria says, trying to move Sarah, but she contorts in pain and she spits up blood. I check the Cube again to make sure that they can't ping me anymore.

"It's up to you now, Gloria. You and Robyn will know what to do next," Sarah says, and her neck goes limp. Gloria calls Mo, the doctor. He runs towards us.

Tiffany helps Vincent down through the trapdoor. Our only chance is to run and escape through the tunnels. Tiffany holds it open while people jump down and away.

I watch Mo come towards us. He takes a stethoscope from his coat pocket. The noise that the police have been making outside stops and it is suddenly calm and quiet. I hear their boots retreat back up the stairs.

They've gone completely silent.

We all freeze.

Gloria looks up at the barricaded doorway.

"Fuck," she says.

"Run," whispers Sarah, before a huge blast rips through the room. I hear a tremendous explosion that lacerates through my ear drum, then a pop, and a high pitched ring. Fire singes my head. The side of my face is sand-papered by tiny wooden splinters. My clothes are gone from the left side of my body. They hang like rags.

I can see smoke. I hear wails.

A hand takes mine. It pulls me along the ground over lumps of fiery smashed wood and broken glass until I fall straight into the earth. We land together in a lump.

It's Tiffany.

"Can you walk?" she shouts. I can, and she slips her fingers through mine and we run. We don't stop and we don't look back.

FORTY THREE

I AM BACK with Ivan.

I can hear the slow drawl of a siren somewhere down below us in the distance. Ivan stands at a window the size of an entire glass wall. We are high up. There are droplets of water, perhaps remnants of a rain shower still smattering the glass outside. There are skyscrapers across the block from us. In the distance we can see the Statue of Liberty. We are in New York. Ivan undoes his collar around his neck. He feels congested around his chest, and short of breath.

Everything is so close up here. I could hit these other buildings by throwing a stone but we are so high I feel like we exist in multiple levels, ground to sky. I can see into the apartment across from us. A woman watches a television. Her face plays the reflection of blue and red light. It's a plush apartment, there is real art on the walls, a large rug made from animal skin across the floor. The chair she sits in is designer chrome with soft brown leather pads. She holds her head in her hands. I can't see the tears, but I still know she is crying. The door opens behind her and I see the light of the hallway. A man takes his key out of the door, an overcoat hung over his arm. He drops everything and they run to each other and embrace. I can see their backs heaving and their shaking heads. He holds her head in his hands. They are a long way away, but I can sense their devastation.

The images are flickering in and out of vision. Ivan tampers with something in the glasses' arm and the image returns to focus.

A neon sign a few blocks down flickers erratically, and then sparks fly from the left hand corner and the thing shuts down and goes off completely into darkness.

I realise that Ivan is not only older, but he is much thinner too. His thin skin is pulled taught over his cheekbones. I can see the shape of skull at his temples. He was never fat, but thick set, squat and strong. Not anymore.

He is not well.

Something moves behind Ivan in the reflection. He turns around. A woman sits behind a mahogany desk. Her back faces us and she too is watching a huge television screen. On the screen a press conference gets out of hand, and a fight breaks out between the people present. Security officers have to pull a man away from the person speaking at the lectern. They are all wearing suits. I realise the speaker is the President of the United States.

The footage jumps to soldiers marching, and convoys of khaki coloured trucks. On a scrolling bar along the bottom of the screen I read, 'unprecedented mobilisation of troops'.

"You've got to get your children, Ivy, and you've got to get out of here. Your mom too," Ivan says. "You can't stay here."

Ivan is desperate. He has to move them. He can't leave them to take care of themselves. Ivan hasn't told them about the cancer growing inside him.

They found it in his colon first, something small, something operable, but it didn't stop there. It has moved fast and, just like his Mother told him, he should have been more careful about all the radiation he exposed himself to. He remembers her warning him of the cancers that the first astronauts ended up with. 'Invent something to stop that,' she had told him. If only he had listened.

But it's too late now, the doctors think. He won't tell Ivy. Most people survive now. What's the point in worrying her? He'll live if he can keep access to treatment, and if things change so much and he can't get the treatment that he needs, then he will be in trouble.

"We're going up to Canada on Friday," she says, and turns around. She must be forty years old. She has a well-maintained blonde bob, a slim toned body and a sharp navy business suit. She drinks whisky from a short, chubby crystal glass.

"That's the wrong direction, Ivy. I've made arrangements. I've told you, so many times," Ivan says.

"You're not in charge here anymore, Dad," she says, and drains her glass. She stands up and walks to a bar at the far end of the room. "Do you want one?"

"You don't like me to drink," Ivan says.

"I don't think it matters now," Ivy says.

"Sure," he says, and he undoes his top shirt button and takes off his jacket and walks to sit in a beautiful velvet lounge chair in front of Ivy's desk. Ivy pours the drinks. The television rolls on and on. Ivan picks up the remote control to silence the television. "You need to look after your mother. That loser she's with isn't going to be able to do anything for her now. Do you understand?"

"Don't use this to get at Mom, Dad!"

"It's not about me, she needs to be looked after."

"She's being looked after better than she ever was when she was with you."

"A retired teacher isn't going to be able to fucking manoeuvre through this!"

"She's coming to Canada."

"Is she going to Canada with him?"

"With me," Ivy says, and she gets up and goes over to retrieve the rest of the bottle of whisky. He never was a drinker, Ivan. It was a vice that he just didn't have. So I know this is bad, or he's bad, or he's changed. They fall silent amidst the electric noise of the building creating a paranoid claustrophobic hum.

The loop jumps.

Ivy puts on her coat. It is a camel coloured trench-coat with stitched pockets and brass buttons. The lining is purple silk. It looks very expensive. Ivy and Ivan have drunk most of the bottle of whisky. They have softened. She is no longer angry with him. He is no longer trying to score points about Elizabeth's new husband.

I never thought of that before. That he might have named her Ivy after himself.

I never saw her, the little girl, as a person before. I just saw her as an extension of Ivan.

He asks if she remembers something that he told her when she was small. A story he made up for her about a little girl who lived at the bottom of the world, where it was covered in ice.

"Of course I remember, it was my favourite story, I'd make you tell it to me all of the time."

"Well, it's true, Ivy," Ivan says. "It's not a story, it's real."

"The little girl in the ice at the bottom of the world, building a new colony with her friends,"

"Yes," says Ivan.

"What's true about it, Dad?" Ivy smiles, her eyes have opened, and smile lines embrace him. She doesn't believe him, she believes that there is an essence of truth, a little seed, a metaphor, a life lesson that he is going to impart now in these difficult times.

"All of it. It's real."

"Okay, Dad," she says, touching his face. I get a clear memory of him putting his face into her hair when she was a little girl and inhaling. A love so strong. "I love your imagination, and what I love the most in the face of all of this, you never stop dreaming. You're my inspiration."

"No, Ivy, it is real. I built it. With the aid of the British government." He grabs her wrist as she turns away—just like he did once to her mother. "I built a secret colony in Antarctica. We broke ground in 2036. It was an experimental base for terra-firming Titan."

"Dad!"

"We modelled it on Brighton."

"We'll have to go for a holiday then, God knows when any of us will ever have a holiday again."

"There's no God down there. It's got its own religion! But, yes, exactly. I am preparing flights to Uruguay and from there, a ship. We'll go there, all of us."

"Shall I take my bikini?" Ivy mocks.

"Don't mock me. I am serious. We'll all be back together, and your Mom can bring her boyfriend, I don't mind, I just..."

"When Ruben got up in front of the board and told them that you had lost the plot, I was the one that backed you up. I backed you, Dad. Every time, I fucking backed you. When the shareholders finally got rid of you, when they got what they wanted, and kicked you out, I still stood by you."

"What?" Ivan can't understand her outburst. He's never really understood women very well. As far as he is concerned, he is trying to help her. It makes perfect sense to Ivan.

"Now, when I need you..."

"That's what I'm saying, I know you need me."

"I fucking need you now. Right here! And you are coming out with all this fucking make believe bullshit, when I need you to help me."

"It's not bullshit, Ivy," Ivan says.

"It's always, always the same."

"I'm trying, I really am."

"Whatever bullshit experiments you've been doing over the years on company time, you are not in control of those anymore, even if you had done something down there, you think it would still be going now? You think no one would know about it? When everyone knows fucking everything? I can't even take a pee in my own toilet without my insurance company analysing my urine every four hours. Four hours! You are telling me that you have a secret fucking ice castle in the most inhospitable part of the planet."

"Yes. I am telling you exactly that."

"So, I'll look on my phone right now, and I'll look at Antarctica and I'll see it, right? From the images from our own satellite,"

"No, it's a scrambled frequency, it's terra-firmed, it's constantly under cloud cover, it warms the area, raises the temperature, it's a secret, no one knows about it. You won't see from any satellite image. It's in collusion with the British Government. I signed the Official Secrets Act back in 2036. It's safe from climate modification, it's built to be so."

"Of course," she says, sarcastically.

"We can fly the day after tomorrow,"

"It's convenient that no one can see it," she says.

"Cloud layer, it's a bonus, I guess it's kept it under cover, literally, all these years," Ivan says. Ivy removes a solitary hair from the lapel of her coat.

"I am not flying anywhere with you, Dad," she says. "You get one offer to come and live with us in Canada, and that's it. I mean you, and only you, so don't bring some girl with you who is my age, it's just embarrassing." Ivy picks up her briefcase and heads for the door. He grabs her arm again.

"You have to believe me," Ivan says.

"I want to, Dad. I really want to."

"Come with me. You and I, we'll go there together and I'll show you and then we'll bring the rest of the family down, if you want to."

"All those years I waited for you to take me somewhere. I'd have gone anywhere with you. But you never did, you were never there, and now it's too late."

"Ivy," he pleads.

"I can't possibly go off on an expedition to the south pole with you, Dad! I'm the CEO for Christ's sake," Ivy shouts at him. Look at what he has saddled her with, great riches and great responsibility. She softens. She thinks he's finally lost it. "You go, you tell me what it's like now, and then I'll come afterwards."

"You will? You're not lying to me?"

"Never," Ivy says, and they leave through the office doors arm in arm. "Have you got time to come over to eat?"

"What are we having?"

"Aubergine parmesan, I think."

"Did I tell you that your brother and I had steak last week, real steak! In a place in Brooklyn."

"Well go to his house to eat then," Ivy snaps.

"I didn't mean it like that."

"Steak is against the law, you want to go back inside?"

"That's on appeal, as you well know, I did not embezzle a penny." He pats her hand. She looks like my sister now when I see her from this angle. The same triangle between nose and the corners of her mouth.

"I know you didn't, Dad," Ivy says, raising her eyebrows. A large security guard takes her briefcase and walks with them to the lifts.

"I know you don't believe me, no need to patronise an old man, but I'll show you."

FORTY FOUR

A MONTH OR more has passed since I've known that I am actually twenty-seven years old.

A month since I got someone killed.

A month since the people I cared about were blown up and attacked because of me.

In that month I have worried more about the passing of time than ever in my life before. Eight years of my life are missing. I am older than the friends that I believed were my contemporaries.

It's long enough to know that Mother can no longer track me or she'd have been here by now.

I have an anxious gnawing sensation that leaves me gripping table-tops for balance. It won't leave me. Everything is transient. Suddenly everything teeters on the edge of extinction. I will never get those years back. I'm a decade closer to old age. Overnight, I lost my youth. Sarah Phoenix lost her life.

"Where do we bury the dead?" I ask.

"Fertiliser, honey, we recycle everything here," Eleanor says. "Under normal circumstances, you'd end up feeding the tomatoes in the polytunnels."

"You shouldn't be here," I say. "It's dangerous. You should go back to Portland." We are in a tunnel that reminds me of a tube station in London. Rather it reminds me of a fake memory of a tube station in London. It arches in the same way, except the platform is much wider and instead of a train track a river of crystal blue water runs through it. It's the meltwater from Mount Hood. It is pure to drink.

"Some of the old religions are coming back. Their ways are being smuggled in with the refugees. They are doing some very odd traditional ceremonies up there on Mount Hood," she says, force feeding me a mouthful of vegetable soup.

"I'll get you killed if you stay here with me. I'm cursed."

"Cursed? Bah!"

"Not cursed then, bad luck. Aren't sailors meant to believe in bad luck?" I ask. My physical injuries are superficial. But inside I don't feel right. I wonder where Tiffany is. I sit here, waiting for her to return.

"Sometimes the families scale Mount Hood, carrying their bodies on their backs and leave them out there in the open for the animals and the elements," Eleanor says, but I've already seen this.

I remember being small. Just a girl, standing on the deck of a ship, a black ship, and Mother squeezes my hand. She is crying and the person we are burying is my father, or at least he's my mother's husband, and I have a suspicion, an unspecified feeling that he was not my biological father.

"If I die, I'd like to be put up on Mount Hood like that," I say. Because there is no Alice, and because there is no Sarah, there is no one to stop Mother, and she will keep coming for me until I am dead in body or in mind, so I don't care whether I live or die.

"Don't be so morbid," says Eleanor. "Look at this lovely baby we're growing in here." My belly is becoming round and swollen. The bump is showing. My greatest fear is that Mother will take this baby from me. She'll take my mind and then she'll take my baby. Cut it right out from my belly. I've got to get away.

"Do you think the baby's okay?" I ask Eleanor.

"Of course. The baby is more than okay. The baby is brilliant." She says. 'It's not your fault. We gave you that Cube. We should have thought about it being pinged. It's not your fault and Sarah would never blame you."

But I blame myself. I cuddle the baby in my belly.

I realise that if you have access to the Cube there are many other radio waves that we can possibly access, but don't. They are there for the listening. Where on earth do they originate from? The compass in my Cube spins out of control in confusion. But I know that everything other than here is North.

I look at a small crumpled map of Tiffany's that she had in her pocket on the day of the attack. It's tissue-thin paper looks like it's come out of a very old diary. I keep it on me now. In case something happens, I want to have something of Tiffany's on me.

On this map, the real Brighton doesn't look far.

You would go up into the Southern Atlantic Ocean, I suppose, and make land along here, I trace my finger over what might be Argentina or Brazil. I'm not a sailor, so I don't know whether you just kick right off into the middle of the ocean. You might sail up hugging the coast so that you had plentiful access to food and drink. That would make sense to me.

I would not cross to the coast of Africa, something instinctive tells me not to go that way. I would instead go up as far as New York and Connecticut and then make the crossing of the Northern Atlantic Ocean, like the Titanic. No. That is a very bad example. It's possible that if we make it to New York, I could see Ivan there. Or his daughter, Ivy. I suppose that once we are out of here we can radio for help from South America.

We would make a safe passage across the Northern Atlantic Ocean and stop perhaps, at Cork in Ireland where I have an Artificial Memory of going on holiday. That must be an actual real memory from one of Ivan's children. He must have gone there.

I can't think of anyone else who will know or understand what has been happening down here except for Ivan. He won't be happy. This is not what he intended. We don't know what governments are even aware that we are here. We don't know if the rest of the world knows about us at all, or what is being done to us.

England is so small.

Brighton—the real Brighton—must be so warm, tucked into that little bit of sea channel opposite France. I expect you can go swimming in the sea there.

Tiffany arrives back from Dr Mo's makeshift hospital. She doesn't stop, she drives on, helping people though most believe this is a lost cause. They believe we should surrender and make the most of our limited lives. She's helped to move people around the tunnels. Many have fled out of town, up behind the farms. Others are still in custody. She doesn't like it when I talk about escape. She shuts down the conversation. She feels guilty about those who have died already. But I can't stop thinking and planning our escape. I've become obsessed with thinking about taking Tiffany away on our own. I want to be with her. I want to get us on our own, somewhere safe. I am desperate for that moment, for that intimacy. I'm ready.

"Where do you think you were born?" I ask her. She stands at my side and looks at the map. She points her finger at North Africa, it lingers to the right, to the East. She's careful not to touch me now, when I want her to the most.

"Eritrea," she says. "That's where my parents or ancestors were from, I think, Eleanor is sure of it. She says she can see it in my cheekbones. She has seen a lot of people come in by boat. But that doesn't mean I was born there, or in fact, that I have ever been there at all. I could have been born at sea for all I know, or I could have been born in America or Brazil, and what would that make me?"

"A mermaid," I say, and Tiffany laughs, and I want to talk more about her, and make her laugh and see her smile, but the sadness creeps back into me just when I'm starting to get Tiffany where I want her. I can't help it. "Did you ever meet my sister, Alice?"

"I hate these tunnels. They make me so claustrophobic," she says, shaking her head.

"Did you ever meet her?" I ask.

"You ask me this every day."

"Well, answer again," I say. "Of all the times that we have met, and of all the times that I have forgotten, did I ever introduce you to Alice? In any of those times, you're sure you never met her?"

"No, Robyn. I'm sorry," she says. I was so sure that she had. "You talked about her all the time but I never met her."

I want to see Alice in the Cube.

I search for her face.

I search for her name.

I search by address and I search the hospital records and there is nothing. I snap back into the tunnel.

"What about a photograph? Have I ever shown you a photograph of her?"

"No."

"Well how do you know what she looked like?"

"I just imagined that she would look like you." I can feel my ribs poking me in a different way. I am changing. If Tiffany has never seen Alice then maybe Mother was telling the truth.

What's the point in anything?

Tiffany stands up and moves away from me. She's pushing me away. Why would she want me now? Now when I have lost everything and am about to give up altogether.

I'm not strong.

I'm not special.

I'm not who they thought I was, and Tiffany knows it. I'm just a regular person. I'm just a loser who has ruined everything.

"Oh, Robyn," Eleanor says, pushing more soup into my mouth. "This baby is what we're about now. We're going to be alright, we're going to look after one another."

"I came to tell you, Robyn," says Tiffany. "Vincent wants to see you."

"Vincent?" I ask. My Vincent! "He's well?"

"I must tell you, he's very different to how he was before."

FORTY FIVE

"I USED TO come here as a child," says Gloria, leaning against the Victorian stairs and elaborate gateway made of some sort of resin compound. It's a simulacrum, a copy of the original, masquerading as the real thing. It will never rust, degrade or fall apart. We are somewhere underneath Brighton Aquarium.

"Did you always know we weren't really in Brighton?" I ask Gloria. There are black circles under her eyes. She hasn't slept properly since we lost Sarah.

"No," she says. "I used to think we were really in Brighton. I only realised when I was ten years old. I had a memory of a holiday to Wales and something about it just wasn't right. I told my mother. I kept asking, when we'd been there, who I had been with, if I had gone with the school, had my mother gone too? It just sort of seemed to land in my mind and I rejected it, so my mother told me. It was the same year that I stopped believing in Father Christmas."

We walk past the tanks filled with the ugly, jelly-white fish of the Southern Atlantic Ocean. The intercom announces that the sharks will be fed in fifteen minutes. Gloria pushes a door that leads Tiffany and I into a room behind the scenes, at the back of the aquarium. Tiffany and I can look down into the tanks from behind and watch the visitors peering, elongated from this angle, at the fish.

Life continues in spite of everything that has happened.

At the end of the room is another door. It has an oval arched doorway and a circular hatch lock that you would find on a boat. It reminds me of a lock that I had seen on the ship that ran aground. Gloria turns it. The door pops open with the hiss of released gas.

We walk through it into a tunnel. The floor is bare concrete. This is more like the structures I expect to find behind the Victorian façade. Gloria has a flashlight. I am starting to lose my bearings, then the Cube takes over and I see structural outlines in blue dotted lines. I turn on the lights, a strip of LEDs that run the length of the tunnel as far as my eye can see.

Gloria backs against the wall. Tiffany does the same.

"It's okay," I say, "I turned them on." They both stare at me.

"You did?" asks Tiffany, and I say yes.

"Turn them off again," says Gloria, and I do, and in the darkness I hear them gasp.

"Turn them on," Tiffany says. They are wide eyed. I am too. I always wondered what my purpose was, what was my thing? Was I just a passer-by in my own life or was there something more that I had to do.

"Through here," says Gloria, knocking on a door that I can see from the Cube leads into another chamber, which in turn leads on and on underneath the eastern side of the city. This city is only five miles long and two miles wide. Ten square miles. That's nothing. It's tiny. How big is a city meant to be? Outside this we are set in two hundred and fifty square miles of terra-formed land, shielded by the cliff edge of the glacier on one side and the sea on the other.

We're shrouded from above by a thick layer of cloud that never breaks up, never moves away. It is like a permanent marshmallow ceiling. We never see the sky. Only in the far distance, sparkling and tantalising.

We are tiny and insignificant.

The door opens and there is Dr Mo ready to greet us. I thought he might have been dead. I thought I might have killed him too. I watch his eyes to gauge his reaction to me but he does not react. He looks out into the corridor and then steps back inside to allow us to pass inside into the chamber. Pleasantries are gone. The Scarab rebels scuttle around now.

The room is dark green. The paint flaking off. Artificial light stares aggressively down at the concrete floor. There are no rugs, no carpet and no soft furnishings. Along the left hand side are a series of doors. Each has a letterbox sized opening. A nurse pushes a bowl of food through one such opening.

"I was a doctor," he tells me. "In the old world." I want to ask him about the old world. I want to know what it is like.

"Is he ready?" Gloria asks. There are books piled up on the table. One thick red tome says 'The Bible' in gilded lettering.

"What's this?" I ask, holding up the heavy volume in my hand. He smiles and widens his eyes. "What's funny?"

"It's just that most people in the rest of the world know what the bible is. It's a religious book of the Christian faith. This one," he holds up another book in lettering that I cannot read. "This one is the Quran, and this is the holy book of the Islamic faith. These are the two biggest religions in the world."

"Bigger than Elementology?" I say. I bless myself, "Earth, Sea, Sky." I do believe in the elements, I believe in the earth that keeps us alive. He smiles again.

"Elementology doesn't exist outside of this place. The world has no idea about it." He nods toward The Bible. "When our patients are coming off Hent, we encourage them to read some of these words to help them through, there's a lot in there which can nourish the soul."

"Where is Vincent?" Gloria asks, impatient. She doesn't like to hang around, and says that we need to keep moving.

"He is over here. He is ready," he says, and leads us to the last door.

The heavy metal door is wide open.

I look around the corner into the cell and I see Vincent.

He sits on the bed. It's an old fashioned camping bed.

He's looking at the floor, and then suddenly up at me.

I shiver. My mouth is dry.

His head is shaved. He is completely bald and completely naked. He has no eyebrows and no hair at all on his body. There is a deep scar running down the lower half of his face into his neck. He is pale white.

"He asked me to shave him. He wanted to get rid of every hair on his body. He says he wants to purify himself. To be completely clean. I did what he asked."

Vincent stands up to full height. His naked body is carved out of white marble like some ancient statue.

"Fucking hell," says Gloria. "Isn't he cold?"

"You always keep me waiting," Vincent says. The relief surges through me. He is alive. He is going to be okay. More than that, he is reborn as something new. I go forward to him, but I'm tentative, like when you approach a big dog.

I take his hand and put it on my belly.

"This is our baby," I say. Tiffany can't watch. She has hung back from the door. She doesn't want to see. Gloria does want to see.

"We're leaving," I say. "It's all being arranged. You can't stay here now. You'll be rounded up, and sent back to the Village. You'll come with us, see your baby grow up in the real world."

"I've got things to do here first," he says. "After I have done those things then I will come with you."

"You will?"

"Yes, I will," he says. "Are we all going?"

"Yes," I say.

"And your sister too?" Vincent asks, and I don't want to give him bad news. He doesn't know. He doesn't know what lies Mother has told me.

"No, Vincent, she isn't. I know this sounds weird, I can't explain it, but I made her up. She was something that Mother cultivated in my mind to keep me occupied."

"What are you talking about?" he asks.

"My mind has been tampered with, for years, Vincent, and I think one of the ways that I coped with what was happening to me was to imagine that I had a good and loving sister who loved me in return."

"You do," he says.

"I would have told you that, Vincent, when we were together," I say. "I would have told you all about her, like I told Tiffany."

"Are you talking about Alice?" he asks, his eyes are screwed up, confused. Gloria has come inside the room and started pacing around.

"Yes," I say. "She's just another part of my brain, a sort of artificial memory, a creation."

"Alice is real," says Vincent, confused. "Of course she's real."

"Alice is real?" I ask.

"Your sister, Alice, is a real live person. I've met her so many times, Robyn, she's my friend," Vincent says. Tiffany appears at the door. "Who told you that she wasn't real?"

"You've met her? You've met Alice?" demands Gloria.

"Mother," I say. "Mother told me."

"The sister's real," Gloria shouts to Tiffany. I am in shock. I am exhilarated. I am excited. I feel like an idiot, so easily played. I am so stupid to let her slip away so easily.

Vincent spits. He jumps up onto his camp bed and bounces up and down like a madman. The scar across his face looks vivid. His eyes are wide and his teeth gnash.

"You've been had, Robyn. Your mother is lying!"

"She's real! She's real!" Gloria shouts, throwing her hands up into the air.

"We're not going anywhere without Alice," Vincent shouts.

My sister. My sister is real and I am going to get her.

Mother is going to pay for what she has done to us.

FORTY SIX

ELEANOR MEETS A retired group of coastguard alumni once a week. I would like to be part of an alumni, a circle of close strangers held together by common learning, or college, or recounting of a shared experience, a place in time that I can remember properly, clearly, in a linear fashion.

This time Eleanor gives me a little butter on the end of a silver spoon. The butter is speckled with what look like herbs. They are herbs. I taste the butter. It's just a little as she wants to be careful with me. I had forgotten it was so bitter. It is such a luxury to forget a detail and then remember naturally as your day unfolds, when something triggers that memory. How wonderful.

The bitter taste, a bit green apple, and an equal bit citrus, takes me back to Eleanor's conservatory and her food and the exploding petals going up the wall. It is frightening and exciting all in one go. We took those safe spaces for granted; those homes, apartments and boring bungalows. How lucky we were to have the illusion of safety.

I have something specific in mind this time; Ivan. I need to locate him, so that he can help us escape. I think that he might know that I exist, or if not me, someone like me.

I don't need as much as I did before. My neural pathways are open now, raging with adrenaline and cortisol and other pregnancy hormones. I am an underground train network of rage, love and hope. I take the special butter just to give me a little boost, a small sharp jolt to get me where I need to go.

I have never done this before with the Cube inside my head. What I am doing is an assisted meditation.

There are books about what you should do and feel in the first flushes of pregnancy. No coffee, plenty of sleep, yoga, mindfulness and folic acid supplements. I should be attending classes; pregnancy yoga, pregnancy pilates, having my bump painted in the rich colours of a lady bird. Instead, I am doing this.

Eleanor has brought military grade waterproofs for our proposed journey. They flop like an empty skin over the chair. I will need something that can accommodate my growing bump.

I hear the waves crashing. I'm inside my head, I'm inside the Cube. I am everywhere. I look around, I'm still inside the tunnels, it must be a wave of meltwater crashing through the sluice. But it is calm. There is no discernible change in the channel.

I hear the waves crashing again. Then I hear the harsh wind driving them on.

Inside the little map that I've been looking at, all crinkled and rolled up, the sea swooshes and sways. Huge tornadoes gather and, seen from above, giant twisters spin across the ocean.

Is this real?

Tiffany leans in out of nowhere.

"Are you okay?" she asks. "I'm not sure this is a good idea." Her tattoo moves, the sea froths, and a huge rip tide cascades up the length of her neck. I hear it crashing forward. I put my head on Tiffany's lap, close my eyes and then there is only blackness.

At the end of the blackness is a light. I am in a tunnel. I'm riding a rollercoaster. Everything is white on black. Around me are icons, figures, pirate's faces, skull and crossbones and jolly skeletons. I am not scared of them. We rattle along towards the light through the dark black tunnel.

And smack, I am out and thrown up into the air hurtling, parachuting through bright white light. The air against my face makes my cheeks ripple. I parachute slowly to the ground.

I land in a chair opposite Mother.

She is crying,

"I'm so very sorry," she says. "I tried to make it nice for you. We needed your genes. We still do." Up she gets and walks towards me, holding out her hands. I edge away from her and the chair back breaks, snaps off and I reel back. I fall through the chair, and then through the floor, the floor opens into a ceiling and the ceiling collapses around me, there are wires from the strip lighting sparking, and thick dust from the ceiling tiles and bricks.

I hit something hard and cold and blue.

Ice.

Millions of years of compacted ice, flat and smooth, to slip down like a giant petrified slide. I whoosh down fast on my backside. The noise of the slide is of a fast ice screech. I can't stop and I'm going too fast, until at last, the angle evens out and jettisons me into a rounded ice cave where I whizz up and around its periphery before stopping spinning in the centre.

I'm not alone in the cave.

Ivan and The Professor are talking.

They are two old men now. Their backs have arched gently in the shoulders. The Professor still has a full head of thick hair, though it is now pure white. He always wore a hat when he was younger. What year are we in?

The question becomes for me, not where are we, but when?

Their voices are the same but wrung through with tinny treble. The Professor's face with its excess flesh is so very wrinkled. The floor is smooth and cold and blue. There is something different this time?

It's not like I am watching. It's the sharp shock of the cold. It's the hardness of the ice. It feels like I am right there, right here, with them not just witnessing Ivan's memories.

Ivan and The Professor stop when they hear me scrambling to my feet on the ice.

They look at me directly.

They can see me.

The butter from Eleanor is magnificent.

"Who are you?" asks Ivan.

"Robyn," I say. "Robyn Lockhart."

"How did you get in here?" asks The Professor. I point up, but it is now a blue arched ceiling. It is vivid and hard and I can only describe it as being stuck in a frozen wave. Yet it is bright and the clarity of my senses, the air in my lungs, the dryness of a small breeze on my cheeks is so vivid. I can't describe it any other way. It is hyper-real.

I am inside the ice.

They turn back to the work in hand. They stand over a Perspex tube fixed into the ground. The tube is, in turn, attached to a large cog, a pulley that moves. They are bringing something up from the ground. Small mineral deposits hardened inside a tube, no bigger than a pencil are being extracted.

"It is fascinating, Ivan," says The Professor, and he unclips a tube of sample earth and holds it up in the light.

I want to stay, but I am falling, moving forward in their time to a restaurant by the sea front. I know this place! It's the Brighton Beach Club. It's a great name for a restaurant that hangs over some of the coldest, most frigid water on earth. It is very posh. There are long leather banquets in burgundy. Bronze lamps hang low over the tables. It glows orange. There is a roaring fire. It is more hunting lodge than beach club.

I hang back this time. I don't want to intrude into their memories. I want to watch. The Professor's arms are splayed open along the back of the banquet. He sits in the middle of a semi-circular table. He calls the waiter over and instructs him to bring another bottle of wine.

The Professor looks seventy years old. Other diners, a Norwegian couple with their once common, now soon to be extinct locks of blonde hair talk about The Professor. They smile. He's important here. I sense the whole restaurant knows that he is eating here.

A young man is with them. He must be The Professor's son. He looks like him, with the same dark, almost wet-looking hair and dark brown eyes. He has the same brooding, ample brow and robust cheeks. The waiter brings over the wine and I realise he looks like the son too, and in fact, looks very much like Vincent used to before he went mad.

It's already started.

In one generation alone.

Does Ivan know?

Usually, I'm locked to his viewpoint, synced with his thoughts and emotions and so I concentrate more, I calm down and I listen to Ivan. When I finally get to him, I feel his breathing, it is faster than it used to be, perhaps irregular? Then I understand that no, Ivan is not about to have a heart attack, he is agitated.

He looks at the waiter, and he looks at The Professor's son and he casts his eyes around the restaurant to look for anyone else who is under thirty years old.

There's a huge burst of laughter at the table.

I look into the face of the doctor, Joy Forster, from Ivan's perspective and his old recording camera glasses, and she laughs gently. Her eyes are framed with lines marking the passing of time. Both Ivan and I see now that she and The Professor are together. Joy touches the boy's head. He is her son too. She has been with The Professor for a long time. I wonder if Ivan knew about this back in New York City but it certainly feels new. How does he feel? Ivan feels embarrassed. It is the abrupt unripe sensation of being the last person to know. Ivan tries to swallow it down, to make it look like he knew all along that The Professor and the doctor were a couple.

"I always knew that you two would end up together," Ivan says, but he thinks about a time on the boat, thirty years before when Ivan and Joy were together. He wonders if he should have made more of a play for her after they arrived. He actually wonders whether he and Joy would have been a success as a couple, knowing now that he never got Elizabeth back. Having lived with the fact that Elizabeth married someone else, a lowly first grade teacher with no money.

There was something there between them. On the boat they had been hot, and intensely connected. There still is something there, and that's why she looks uncomfortable at times and breaks into laughter. But how would it have ever worked between them? Joy left the old world behind and her demons and regrets and started again down here. How Ivan could ever stay here and leave his children. He could never ever have done that. But there's a connection and Ivan feels it every time she puts her hand on The Professor, as if to say, 'I am with him, I chose him, leave me alone.'

Or is she saying, 'don't leave me alone.' Is she saying, 'I want you, Ivan'?

I love Ivan when he's like this.

It's like he won't be beaten down. He often thinks that he's got a chance with every woman, even though he's an old man now, be that an old rich man. Despite his cancer and his loneliness and his desperation to help his family escape from whatever it is they have to run from; that there is life in the old dog yet, that Ivan is not beyond making a play for his best, oldest friend's wife.

We jump forward in time. We are still in the restaurant. It is late. There's a pitch-black sea outside. It is impossible to see the horizon. Behind them dim street-lights emit only a tiny flicker of light. The Professor has declared a black-out. The reasons why are two-fold. One, there are concerns about sufficient energy supply in the colony; and two, The Professor is worried about news Ivan has delivered from the old world.

Conflicts, civil movement and famine, backed up by plentiful copies of the world's newspapers—print outs from the internet. The Professor hasn't seen the internet for years. He doesn't miss it. The problems are real. The Professor was never going back—ever. For him, this future is what he escaped from.

The meal is finished. The wine bottle is gone, emptied and replaced with short coffee cups and a swirling fragrant brandy in front of The Professor. The son kisses his Mother and makes his excuses to leave. He shakes hands with Ivan. After he leaves Ivan sits upright. He's angry, he wants to share his annoyance.

"I thought we'd agreed that there would be no religion here," Ivan says.

"Well, they started to need something, Ivan. I underestimated their ability to be free thinkers. They want to be led. I'm rather pleased with Elementology," says the Professor laughing.

"It is very frightening, Ivan," Joy says. "But we feel so safe here in New Brighton. We are completely excluded from all of this going on in the world."

Ivan looks grave. He doesn't like to be the bearer of bad news, he likes to be the solver of problems.

"It's only a matter of time. The United Nations know that you are here," Ivan says.

"But the people don't know, Ivan. We are a tiny peaceful outpost busy minding our own business." The Professor strokes Joy's face. "The world's Governments want us to quietly succeed. This is about cultural preservation."

"For now. The world has changed, Hilary," Ivan says. I don't think of him like that, with a name. Ivan thinks that Hilary is a girl's name and it always tickles him. He sits back. "I can't continue to resource things in the way that I used to."

"Ivan," says the Professor. "Whatever is the matter?"

"I'm not in charge anymore. I don't have the reins of the company," Ivan says, shaking his head. The Professor leans in to him and squeezes his shoulder.

"This is our special experiment, Ivan, our legacy. No one can take this from us. Ever. We did it."

"Hilary, I want to bring my family down here," Ivan says.

"We talked about this, Ivan," says The Professor.

"This is my life too," says Ivan. He wonders again fleetingly if there is something strange going on with the young people. Another waitress walks by bearing a resemblance to the waiter and to The Professor's son, and to The Professor himself. Why do they all look so similar, especially when they had planned for genetic diversity?

"We can talk about it, sure, we can talk it through," The Professor says.

"I want to bring all of them, get them to safety."

"Ivan, have you told them about us?" asks The Professor. He blinks repeatedly—waspish, anxious little flutters that give away his discomfort.

"No, of course not."

This was a lie. I saw Ivan tell his daughter. The truth is that even if he told someone, no one would believe him. His daughter made Ivan feel that he was washed up. That he had made some bad decisions and been removed from his position of power. The Professor doesn't know this. He thinks that Ivan might still be Ivan the powerful.

"I thought you said that your son, Milo, was in politics now?" asks The Professor.

"There are other colonies here now, in Antarctica, on this very land. Not just scientific bases, big colonies of scientists and I am telling you that it is just a matter of time before this all comes out," Ivan says.

"And your daughter, Ivy, is very well known, I understand," The Professor says.

"Things are changing fast in North America. Nothing is safe as it once was. The world that you knew when you left doesn't exist anymore," Ivan says, and Joy puts her hand up to her mouth.

"That's horrible," she says. There's a silence that extends into several uncomfortable seconds. "I think about my old friends so often and I wonder, well I hope that they are going to be okay. My brother, he might have a family now. He lived in Florida."

She crosses herself. She touches her head, her stomach and her left and right breast. It's like we do in Elementology but slightly different. Ivan shakes his head.

"Florida has changed," Ivan says, and smiles to make Joy feel better. "He'll be okay. They're doing better down there."

"How many people are you proposing to bring down here?" asks The Professor.

"Twenty-two," Ivan says.

"You want to vanish twenty-two members of one of America's best known corporate families?"

"I've got to get them out."

"Where will you say they have gone?" The Professor folds a napkin, laughing. Joy is silent. She looks away from the table, says 'excuse me' and goes to the bathroom.

"They will have gone into exile," Ivan says.

"Surely, people will look for them? Newspaper reporters? Or the tax man? Or your shareholders?"

"I'll come up with something. I did for you, didn't I?" Ivan says, perturbed, and The Professor nods slowly, a new kind of understanding emerging unspoken between them, both knowing the game, calculating their next moves.

The Professor does not want Ivan down here.

Ivan remembers the shocked look on The Professor's face when he arrived at the dock, unexpectedly. The Professor came down in one of a fleet of SUVs, the same cars that now look completely outdated to Ivan, compared to what they have in the real world. The Professor was outwardly warm and friendly but repeatedly asked Ivan; 'What are you doing here?'

Ivan had made his fortune by being able to read people.

"And what if they don't want to come? What if they don't want to leave their gilded New York and California existences? Their personal trainers, and their nannies, and their corporations and their mistresses?" The Professor says this while looking down at his own chest, shaking a crumb from his jumper.

Ivan knows that they have to leave New York one way or another. He also knows that The Professor does not want him here. He doesn't want a threat to his crown. The Professor has become the most powerful man in the colony, and he does not want any challenge to his position, not from Ivan himself and certainly not from Ivan's precocious progeny.

Ivan wants to tell Joy about his cancer. He wants to give her one last chance to persuade The Professor. He wants one last chance to kiss her again. To have her come to his room late at night. Oh, how he would love that, behind The Professor's back.

The Professor turns his shiny knife over and over on the table.

Ivan is going to give The Professor one last chance, and if he fails to accommodate Ivan's wishes then Ivan will have no choice but to activate his insurance policy. An insane biometric insurance policy that will destroy everything that The Professor has been building for the last forty years.

FORTY SEVEN

I'VE STILL GOT my key to Jan's cafe. I let us in, and close the shutters, leaving only a dim emergency lighting strip, which gives off a dull, electric blue light.

David Sykes's skin looks puckered, pale green in this light, as though he is about to vomit. I only need to know one thing, it's the thing the Cube can't tell me; why has Mother done this to me?

"Gloria's like a genie, isn't she? She just appears out of nowhere," I say, feeling nervous.

I've never tortured anyone before.

There is no going back now. He cries. It's a breathy, whiney cry that steams up his wire-framed glasses.

Gloria moves around the table, bending over, and at first glance it looks like she is just tidying up, as usual, as if she were a waitress here, sweeping and mopping the floor after a busy day like I used to do. I can smell the disinfectant, a bitter cocktail of bleach and pine.

But she's not cleaning up. There is a bucket, and there is disinfectant, and there is a thud as she dumps a large metal bolt cutter onto a table.

Outside there is the sudden squawk of a group of lads going past on their way to a nightclub. They are rowdy, drunk, and shouting.

David's eyes flick left to right. He is obviously thinking about shouting out to the lads. A stupid idea, but one he tries anyway. He's got a rolled up pair of Gloria's sports' socks stuffed into his mouth, so that his lame attempt at a shout becomes little more than a muffled grunt.

As soon as he does it, he panics, and when Gloria stands up to her full height and picks up the bolt cutters, a dark shadow leaks out across the groin of his beige chinos. He starts shaking his head.

"No," he says, through the socks.

"They don't care about you, David. They just want to get fucked out of their brains. They can't cope, you see? They know that we're not in Brighton, not really, and they make peace with that reality through a liberal smattering of recreational drugs and alcohol," I say.

He trembles violently. I guess he is wondering how you can be so wrong about a person. About me. I haven't told him what I want from him yet. I feel like he needs to spend a little bit more time with Gloria before I tell him what he needs to do.

Gloria tries to turn on the coffee machine. It's a vintage Marconi, an original from Italy, it must have come across on the boats. It is temperamental and likes to be handled in a particular way.

I get up and go behind the counter. Jan has stuck postcards to the wall from places all around the world. At one point, I thought that these postcards had been sent in by regulars who had gone on holiday. I thought it was a kind of tradition. I realise now that you can buy these from a shop in the Laines. They are real. They are vintage too, bought in bulk, remnants from real places, real holidays in the real world.

"Move over," I say, to Gloria.

"Does he want one?" Gloria asks, raising her eyebrows at David.

"No, he's just pissed himself," I say, flicking the power on the grinder that gargles noisily into life. I chink the lever twice with my index finger and the coffee comes out and fills a perfect sphere. I whack it up into the machine.

"Can you do me a double espresso?" asks Gloria, as I fill another one for myself. I'll make my own super strong with plenty of sugar. I used to like lattes and milky coffees, but now I could not think of anything more safe or sanitised.

"I thought you were laying off the caffeine?" I ask.

"I need it," she says. "I need something."

"Have you got all of the cleaning products?" I ask.

"Yes," says Gloria.

"Plastic sheets?"

"I'm going to put it into a bucket sat on top of a plastic sheet, so there shouldn't be much to wash up," Gloria says. I don't want to leave any mess for Jan. David tries to stand up with his chair attached, making a huffing sound, but Gloria has tied him up in such a way that he can't straighten his legs.

All it takes is one deep cough from Gloria for David to freeze and sit down.

He didn't deserve this. None of us did. Least of all my sister and I. We have been experimented on for most of our lives. Who else was being treated in the same way as her and I? We couldn't be the only ones. I know now that Jan has a daughter in the Village. Her only child.

It makes me feel so sad. It sits like a sharp edged nut in my oesophagus. It is a pain and a sadness that is with me all the time. I can't shake it off. I can't forget. It makes funny jokes turn sad. It makes every memory sentimental. It makes every smile a joke.

My mother was never there. Rather, she was always there but she was a controlling and cold presence. She didn't ever really love us. Am I even her child?

The child growing inside me is mine. I am her Mother, and I know instinctively that I cannot be my own mother's child, because she would not have been able to do this to me. The coffee machine starts to fizz. I look at the bag of beans on the counter.

"How do we produce this much coffee?" I ask Gloria, and I press the button and wait for the machine to spur into action. The hot water has to pressurise inside the machine so we wait.

"Can you ask the... the cube thing?" says Gloria.

"No. It doesn't work like that." I hold up the bag of coffee beans with wording written in Spanish. "Where the fuck do they get all this coffee from? I mean per person, four cups per day, every day. It's real coffee too. We can't produce it in polytunnels."

David quivers.

"Forget the coffee, Robyn. How can we produce this much beer? Or wine for that matter? From the farms? From the polytunnels? Who do they think they are kidding?"

"We must be importing the coffee in from somewhere else, from outside," I say, and just then the machine rears up and pushes steamed water through my coffee grounds. It is very noisy. It will give David some hope.

Gloria's tiny cup looks minuscule in her long fingers. She empties three sugars into it and stirs. She leaves a thick smear of red lipstick on the cup and then sets it down. She leans into the mirrored fascia of the coffee machine and wipes the corners of her mouth with her little finger.

She stands up tall.

"Are you ready?" she asks me, and I drain my cup and nod.

Gloria bends down to pick up her bolt cutters. As she does I see her Scarab tattoo—a black beetle pokes out on her lower back. It's ready to climb up her spine. I'm thinking about getting one of these tattoos too when the time is right. I don't want to give things away to Mother too soon. It will be a permanent reminder in case anything happens to my brain.

Gloria stands up quickly and leans on the table, resting the bolt cutters in her lap, near her own cock for dramatic effect. She lets them lie there open like sharp scissors and pulses her hips back and forward so that the cutters bounce on top of her genitals.

David looks as though he's been left out in a storm. I'm not sure which orifice the water is coming from; eyes, mouth, ears, pores, or dick.

"I'm sure this wasn't what you had in mind for our second date, David," I say. "I'm sure you had other ideas. I know you like me. Even if I've only got one eye. Not sure you got the memo, but I'm not nineteen, as Mother might have told you. I'm actually quite a bit older than that. I expect it will put you off me."

He's shaking.

"I am going to ask you a question now, and depending on how you answer, that is going to influence how the rest of this conversation goes. If you lie, I will know. I only want the truth. Do you understand?"

He nods.

"Do you know my true age?" I ask confidently, as if I am operating a lie-detector, but there's no machine and no methodology, just a very angry Gloria and a sharp, hydraulic piece of portable equipment. He is squinting because either the question is too hard or sweat is stinging his eyes.

"Take your time," I say. "It's important that we get this right."

If he knows my age, then he's admitting that he is in cohort with my mother, that he has been colluding in my oppression and that is going to make me very angry.

"If you don't know then you will be of no use to me whatsoever," I say. "In which case Gloria and I have agreed that we will take you out past Saltdean, out past the farms to the borders of the sluice where we'll break your ankles and leave you out for the Polar Bears."

Gloria slowly taps the glass face of her watch.

David makes the last exasperated gasps as if he's running a marathon or ejaculating. Then he starts to nod violently up and down. I remind myself that these fuckers followed me and killed Sarah Phoenix among others.

"That's a relief, David," I say. "It really is a relief, because if there is one person in this world who doesn't want to watch you having your penis sheared off with Gloria's bolt cutters, it is me."

He breathes rapidly in big gasps, great rasping gulps like people do in films when they are about to pass out.

"Don't worry, David. I'd have brought my nail scissors if I was going to cut off your penis," says Gloria, and I do, surprisingly, have a small spontaneous chuckle at her remark.

But it's not his fault. It's my mother's fault, and whatever else is at large here. He doesn't deserve this and I know it's wrong. But I need answers.

"I'm going to make you more comfortable. Not that I can trust you, but I want you to trust me. Okay?" I ask, and he nods. "I'm going to take this out of your mouth." I take the balled up socks and pull them out of David's mouth and rather than shouting he coughs his guts up.

"I am angry with you, David, because I believe when we went out, you knew that I was being heavily medicated and that I was not in control. I believe you knew. I think you were happy to take advantage of me."

"We had a nice time," he says in a weeny voice. "Didn't we?"

"If you consider drugging someone and then spending the evening with them a nice time, then yes, I suppose we did."

"I didn't fucking do it, I didn't fucking do anything, I was just following your mother's instructions."

"And thought you could have sex with me at the same time."

"No, we went on a date. I didn't try anything untoward with you," he says, and I suppose he didn't. What's the problem with having your food ordered by a man, being followed to the toilet and told you've spent too long in there? Where's the issue with him colluding with your Mother to have full control of your life?

"Did you know I am pregnant? I was pregnant on our date. I've probably been pregnant for four or five months now. Did you know?"

"Well, Robyn. I never wished you any harm."

"Because I didn't know that I was pregnant."

"I liked you that's all,"

"And you work for my mother,"

"I never wished you any harm,"

"You could have helped me, you could have warned me, we were on our own together, you and I, and you kept up the pretence," I say, and I am astounded at just how calm I am. I can't lose this argument anyway, not with Gloria here. The cards are stacked against poor David, but I really think he was complicit—he still is.

"Look, I can't be bothered to argue this out with you. You're a sad piece of shit, David, if you think that sitting opposite someone who doesn't know where they are, or what day it is constitutes the start of a meaningful relationship."

"I would have brought up that baby as my own," he weeps. I've offended him. The thought of him with my child makes me shudder.

"How very chivalrous of you, David. Fortunately, if I have anything to do with it, you will never see my child. If you ever want to see the sky again, you will follow my instructions to the letter."

"I never wanted to cause you harm," he weeps.

"Shut up," I say. "Now, where is my sister?"

"I don't know."

"Of course you do," I say, and I make a pinching motion with my thumb and index finger. "I know about the computer. I know you have access."

"I don't have access to anything. I'm just a junior administrator. I don't know anything about your sister." Gloria throws her espresso cup hard at David and it bounces off his skull. He looks stunned. I am shocked by the prelude to violence.

Gloria is really going to do this.

I am really going to do this.

"David, I'll fucking snap you in two, now start talking," says Gloria.

"She's at the Pavilion," David says, sobbing. But of course I know this already.

"How do I get into the Pavilion, David?" I ask, because I know from common sense and from what I glean from the Cube, I can't just walk into the Pavilion and take my sister. We will need insurance, and David, to help us access the Pavilion. He shakes his head.

"I wondered why someone would take off a little finger when the thumb is so much more integral to the hand," I say. He should be happy that we're not going to take off the dick. We're not animals, he would die. I know that they have been removing and reattaching body parts here for some time now. We are going to take David's thumb, and we will keep it on ice. If he does what we ask and gets us into the Pavilion without any questions asked we will give it back to him and he can have it reattached. I've seen the great work of Dr Joy Forster and her incredible stitching.

"Are you going to hurt me?" David mutters. Gloria has momentarily gone out the back of the Café to retrieve her ice box. It's where we are going to keep David's thumb. We need a very clean incision. We're lucky that David has such spindly fingers. Gloria toyed with using a scalpel but with not having any specific medical training she opts for power over precision.

David's pupils dilate and he slides back a little bit in his chair like a jelly off a plate. It must be the Hent we gave him starting to kick in. I take no pleasure in watching someone else's pain. I never asked for any of this.

"Amputation can sometimes have unexpected benefits," I say. David's head bobs left and right on his pencil-like neck. I lift up my eye patch. I move my head from side to side so that David can get the full extent of my new look.

"Like it?" I ask.

"What the fuck is that?" he says. "Your eye! It's made of gold."

Gloria stretches her arms out and clicks her fingers. They give a satisfying pop. She puts on her red plastic reading glasses for close work.

"You won't feel a thing, my love," says Gloria. "I'm quick and I'm clean."

And she is.

I look away. I am ashamed to do this to him. He doesn't deserve this, even if he is a perverted old snitch. I push my fingers against the Cube in my eye socket.

The Cube tells me how to get to the Pavilion. It tells me the quietest entrance. It tells me exactly where my sister is and I can see her, or imagine her, lying on her side in a hospital bed.

All we need from David is some DNA, attached to an actual human finger, and we don't want to transport the whole thing of David. The mouth that questions, the eyes that stare, the heart that wants to report everything back to Mother. One finger will do the job just fine.

I hear a snap, and David screams.

"We're coming to get you, Alice," I say. "I'll be there soon."

FORTY EIGHT

GLORIA DRIVES TIFFANY and I to the Pavilion in the tiler's truck that she has borrowed from the ranger. The windscreen wipers have carved out a clear oval free of the splattered mud that covers much of the rest of the vehicle. It has a double passenger seat, so Tiffany and I can both ride up front.

We're in a convoy of three trucks, one 4x4 SUV with a reinforced pneumatic lift, six motorbikes and several cars. Others, hundreds of normal people, and the entire ranger service, will meet us at the Pavilion. Confirmation of my sister's existence fills us all with hope. Tiffany squeezes my hand.

We can do anything with the right tools. Gloria has furnished me with a double-barrelled shotgun procured from a ranger. It's a twenty gauge, similar to the one that I had with Vincent, but as an added bonus Gloria has sawn off the ends of both barrels so that it fits snugly inside my coat.

The owner of this truck is a friend of Gloria's. He is a manly paramour who prowls the bars of Brighton and the air-thin extremities of our community with equal vigour. There's been a polar bear in this truck, a dead one or at the very least, the pelt. I recognise the smell of damp fur and blood.

We stop around a hundred yards from the hospital, at the top of a steep hill. There are plenty of Victorian-style houses. They are obviously replicas, actually built with plastic and some sort of wire frame and painstakingly 3D printed to look exactly like the originals in the actual street in real Brighton, thousands and thousands of miles from where I sit.

I've got to wonder why bother with the pretence. Why not just build all the homes like they did in the Village? A basic uniform, durable unit that was fit for purpose. Why pretend that we are anywhere but here? The whole pretence of Brighton seems like the work of a mad man.

We remove David from the boot and a tabby coated cat panics in horror and scatters itself across the bins at the front of a house. The cats are on high alert. They are a tasty snack for polar bears. Several have been eaten, though they are fast and wily, the beasts are fast too. The Council advises keeping your cats inside at night.

We are not worried about being seen. I'm certain the powers that be suspect we are coming. Mother will know that I am coming.

We have wrapped David's hand in thick bandages. It looks like a dirty boxing glove. He is still high on Hent. I stay in the car while Gloria makes him walk. He is shaky on his legs, but he is able to put one foot in front of the other.

This is a pretty normal sight in Brighton; someone walking inebriated towards the main hospital.

Gloria points him in the direction of 'Accident and Emergency'. It's a main road, well-lit with speed cameras regulating traffic to a crawl. If he falls, he'll be picked up before he bleeds to death on the street. If he keeps his mouth shut about us then he'll get all of his phalanges back.

His fingers are in the ice-box on my lap. Once his digits enable us to enter the Pavilion and access the correct corridors and leave again with my sister, we will get those fingers back to him. We've already labelled the box with David's address and large red letters that read 'Handle With Care' and 'Keep Refrigerated'.

It has been agreed that we will enter the Pavilion covertly. Tiffany and Vincent will work together to locate my sister and take her to safety. At the same time Gloria and I will lead the Scarab rebels to find Mother and deal with her once and for all. We expect that they will defend the Pavilion, that they will fight back with everything that they have.

Gloria gets back into the driver's seat. She's playing pop music quietly in the background. As we drive away I can see David behind me in the passenger mirror. He staggers into the middle of the road. The shoulder that carries the damaged hand is tilted down sideways, off-kilter, like a Halloween zombie.

This is such an awful thing to do to someone. I would never have done this had it not been necessary. I think of what could have been. I think of a sedated, mind-addled me, married to David and it conjures so much fear in me that it excuses anything that I have done so far, and anything that I have to do in the future.

"It's a long drive," says Gloria. "Get comfortable. Close your eyes if you want."

As we pull off, a passer-by in the street takes David by the shoulder and guides him back onto the pavement. For all the bad, there are so many caring people here. Tiffany closes her eyes and leans into me, but I stay awake.

Sometimes I don't even have to touch the Cube with my fingers anymore. If I concentrate very hard and by that I mean I have to almost feel the outline of the Cube in my head and then focus the muscles in and around my eye socket, then I can access it. It's a bit like when a personal trainer asks you to pull in your core. It's a muscle that I am not used to using, but every time I do, it gets easier, more natural.

It feels like it is becoming part of me. Gloria has thick, black-rimmed spectacles for driving. She looks like a politician. For the first time I can see her in a position of authority. People would listen to her. She brakes as we approach a red traffic light.

The light should change green. I think the light should turn green. I want it to change green. Inside and out I see lines of connectivity. I see the cabling of a motherboard, it looks something like the inside wiring of a television.

The traffic light turns green.

I made it happen.

In the passenger seat next to Tiffany I settle my head against the rest. I close my eyes.

The soft tissues of my eye contract as I squeeze the muscles around my eye.

We are out of Brighton already. We hurtle along a black tarmac single-track road. Outside, like ghosts fluttering, I see the outline of row upon row of giant polytunnel.

I close my eyes and go into the Cube to look at the Pavilion. I have looked at nothing else for days. I don't recall ever having been in a building that big. The Pavilion is sprawling. It is well equipped—more futuristic I suppose, or you might say technical.

The Pavilion is like an architectural version of Ivan. Of course I am thinking about memories of being inside the Pavilion, the feel of it, the aura, and the environment. The medical smell. The claustrophobic sensation of hours spent with medical earphones on. The repetitive laying down of memories in sound and vision. The swallowing of large amounts of medication in slick oval pills which sometimes caught in my small throat. I flinch.

"Are you okay?" Asks Gloria. "You were dreaming."

"I was living a nightmare," I say, and turn into Tiffany for safety. When I search the Cube for files about the Pavilion, I understand what it might look like, having never consciously looked upon it from the outside.

From the blueprint I comprehend the scale of the Pavilion. It is like an iceberg. There's a piece that clings to the earth like an angular cement block, but that is nothing compared to what is beneath. There is a lesson there I'm sure. For no town, no city, no life was ever just what is seen above the surface.

But though it will take us more than an hour to drive to the Pavilion, I can see that there are underground tunnels which connect it to Brighton, to Portland and to other venues on our spot of conquered Antarctica.

I wonder if Mother travels here every day. I am confused, because when I believed I was only a child—and this was only last month don't forget—I thought that Mother was always around, looking after me. Now I'm not so sure. It is possible that she wasn't at home as much as I thought. I am twenty-seven years old after all, and more than capable of living on my own.

Gloria speculates that Mother will get the express train. She won't drive. Tiffany thinks that Mother mainly lives at the Pavilion. We haven't seen another vehicle on the road at all.

I'm not sure either how much time my sister lived at home with me and how much time she spent away—presumably at the Pavilion—as a patient or a willing guest, I have no idea. But I'm going to find out. I'm going to find everything out tonight, one way or another.

FORTY NINE

BEFORE THE PAVILION comes into view, there is a preliminary check-point where Gloria winds down the driver's window.

"Tiler," she says matter-of-fact. The security guard looks at his clipboard. He ticks a column on his list and lets us in. Apart from the polar bears there are no criminals in our world. We don't ever have a crime wave. Dissenters are dealt with efficiently. Angry people like Gloria, Tiffany and I don't just drive up to the Council and demand answers.

"Through the next checkpoint, and then follow the road to the left. Park underneath the building in the service tunnel, please," he says, but of course I know where we are going.

Vincent and the ranger have already parked up their motorbike and join us in the back of the truck. We review the plan. We will enter the building together. Once inside I will locate my sister. Tiffany and Vincent will leave with my sister, ensuring her safety. They should not wait for Gloria and I. They should not return. Once we have secured Mother, I will power down the Pavilion. I will lock every door. I will seal inside every soldier, every policeman who tries to hold us down.

Gloria and I will stay on to deal with my mother. I have planned a route for us. The ranger has left a vehicle outside the perimeter fence, that Gloria and I will find our way to. Failing that, I have mapped the underground tunnels and trains and have a longer, more treacherous route planned for our escape.

We have a thirty-minute head start on our amassed troops. Mother has an army of soldiers. We have teachers, waiters, nurses and rangers. We may be diminished, but fate is on our side. This is our destiny.

The Pavilion is the colour of concrete. There's a glass structure that covers it, web-like. Now that I am here, it is much bigger than I thought. In part, it looks like a section in the centre has been gouged out. There are many windows, long, thin and uniform. It looks to me, in the never ending darkness of our days, like a science fiction prison ship has collided with the planet Mars.

The ground here is odd. Not what I expected at all. In fact it reminds me of a Wild West movie. It's a rocky plain, strewn with tufts of hardy plants here and there. I wonder why Mother didn't have it planted up. Maybe because this is the business end. If you want the fantasy, then go to the seafront and parade up and down with the penguins. If you want the inner workings, the truth, then come here.

My heart thumps in my chest thinking about Alice and Mother.

Mother's going to kill me.

Or I am going to kill her.

At the second security check point a police man steps out in front of the car. He's wearing a classic police uniform with a helmet and shiny buttons. Why no soldiers? It seems too easy. Perhaps Mother is expecting me.

The policeman motions for Gloria to open her window with his long finger. I clutch the box containing a small piece of David.

Gloria opens her wallet and shows the policeman her driving licence. It's her real name, which I've seen before is not Gloria. It is too small here to assume an alias. If you were committing a crime or pretending to be someone else, somebody would know who you are, know your sister, or your mum.

The policeman winks. He is a Scarab, one of Gloria's friends from their secret group. He's the inside man on duty tonight, specifically to allow us entry to the main campus of the Pavilion. He raises the orange striped barrier and we drive through.

We're in.

Gloria holds my face and glares at me.

"Are you ready?" she asks. We park the truck and leave it open. I see my hand trembling on the door. Tiffany sees me, and touches my hand to reassure me. She believes in me. I'm panicking about how we might escape if we've got to run and I also worry that I don't know if I can do this. Why me? Why not someone else? Someone stronger?

"Be careful," says Tiffany. "I love you." My heart swells, and hopefully soon I'll be able to love like a normal person. But right now, I have something I have to do first.

I remember that the only person who wishes to do me and my unborn child harm is my own mother. My coat drags down to one side with the weight of my shotgun. I remember that I have made the decision on what I need to do. She is the person that I am most afraid of. She is the person that wishes to cause me harm and if it comes down to it, then she will never leave this place alive.

My sister will get up and walk. I will disconnect her from whatever bullshit equipment she is wired to. I am sure of one thing and that is that there is nothing wrong with my sister. Just as my mother has muddied and confused my mind, she has made my sister sick. For whatever reason, we are yet to find out, she has made her ill and me mad. I will take my sister's hand and we will walk away together, to freedom, to be ourselves, our true selves, whoever we are.

FIFTY

THERE ARE FIVE of us. The door we have chosen is a side entrance. There is no one around. The double doors are smoked glass and are shielded by a cement overhang. I expect that there must be cameras, so I switch all cameras off. Using the Cube, I overlay the Pavilion with the blueprints of its inner workings. I am getting highly adept at using this technology.

Gloria opens the ice box and takes out David's thumb and index finger. She gives me the index finger.

"Hold that," she says. It feels like a small carrot.

The entry pad is metal. Gloria points to it. It has a single circle carved into the middle. Now I see it, I realise that I have seen these all over the place, all of my life. This technology hides in plain sight, just like Gloria and I are now.

I hold up David's finger. It is already yellowing, like a wax replica. Gloria has the thumb, holding it with her little finger sticking out like it's a cup of tea. I press his finger into the circle. The circle lights up white and the doors open.

"Look at that," says Gloria. "We didn't need the thumb after all."

The concrete external structure gives way to luscious, white, glossy walls. Have I been here before? It's familiar. It's the smell that gets me, that triggers me into remembering; it smells of dust and, weirdly, pottery—the art room at school. There was something so comforting and warm about that room. The feathers, the paint, the objects so alive.

There's a noise.

The doors close behind us.

They clamp together and all sound silences. I wasn't even aware of the thrashing noise of wind outside until it stopped so suddenly. We are insulated. The ranger carries a toolbox full of guns. Gloria bends to unzip her new automatic weapon from its carry case. I take the sawn off shotgun.

"Which way?" Gloria whispers.

"Down," I say. "There are stairs, further along here on the left. Follow me."

Off we go, Gloria's feet are light and fast. I wish the others could move like her. She's like an athlete. There's a door on the left. The Cube gives me the direction, like a piece of luminous blue string that I can follow.

Another noise.

Footsteps this time.

Someone is coming.

We pile into the stairwell and down we go, not looking back. Gloria gestures for us to flatten against the wall. She seems to look backward, forward and presently all at the same time. Looking over the banister the drop is so long that I cannot see the bottom before it fades into darkness.

The footsteps in the corridor pass us by. It's crucial that Tiffany and Vincent take my sister away safely first, because I need to deal with Mother and I can't do that if Alice is still in this building. I have explained this to Tiffany.

The footsteps are back. A nurse opens the stairwell door and looks inside and sees us. She tries to back away but we can't let her go and call the alert. No one wants to hurt her, but she might get us killed. As she turns to run Vincent strikes her on the back of the head with his rifle. The ranger pulls her body into the stairwell. Tiffany checks her pulse.

"She's alive," says Tiffany.

"Bind her," I say, and the ranger gags her mouth with the ripped sleeve of his T-shirt and then ties her hands and feet with rope that he has carried around his shoulders. Tiffany is shaking.

"I had to," says Vincent, the scar across his eye twitches.

"You did the right thing," Gloria says. Tiffany is here to save my sister, not to assault innocent nurses. The same nurses that I turned the other cheek as they removed my eye. I wonder if this is how it started with Mother. One action takes you over the line, a second and third drag you down. I must focus.

"This isn't easy," I say to Tiffany. "But I need you. Bring the nurse with us."

We all move down the stairs, we go down one level. I go inside The Cube. Alice's room is only thirty metres away. I look for Mother. She is here at The Pavilion, just like I hoped that she would be. She is lower down, deeper into the earth.

My sister is on the floor below us. I can see her in the Cube. The Pavilion is a squat rectangular building and on each floor there is a main corridor that runs around the centre of the building in a loop. Off this loop are minor tributary corridors the lead out to hospital rooms or offices.

We peel off the main corridor into a smaller tributary. Now, this I have been in before—or something exactly like it. I have very vivid memories of staggering through a corridor the same as this looking for my sister.

I found her that time.

I hear myself screaming over and over again.

I can still feel the pain.

We have to be quick. We need to be in and out with Alice. By the time Mother realises that she has gone, it will be too late to stop the boys leaving with her, but perfect timing to rouse Mother from her pit and snare her into the sights of Gloria and I.

Would I let Gloria kill Mother?

Perhaps.

It depends, I suppose, on what she's got to say for herself.

I am going to see my sister. I put out some lights so that the corridor is darker, and it glistens like the outer sheen of a smooth metal. We fill the corridor, the five of us. We push through some outer barrier doors into the main corridor. I register these doors.

They close in the incidence of fire, they will shut and lock automatically putting a barrier between the people either side.

We carry heavy weapons, we trudge in boots that Gloria doesn't like to wear, but I deem necessary. The material of our work suits rub and sounds like we're putting up a tent.

Is anybody watching us? This is too easy. Let them watch. We're ready.

I am frightened. I am scared. I am so excited to see her, finally, that I might burst. I want to hold her close and fast, I want to take her hand and the two of us run away. Just us: My sister and me, we could run.

Gloria is ahead in the corridor. 'Is this the one?' she whispers. We work symbiotically now Gloria and I. In a different life we could have robbed banks together, or been magicians on stage.

The doors bear a combination of letters and numbers; 3V, 4V, 5V. My sister is in room 8V.

Each room carries the same metal plaque that we used to get into the main building. I point at the ice box that Gloria has been carrying and she drops it down, opens it and gets out David's index finger.

8V.

My sister's room.

Alice.

Gloria holds David's finger up against the metal plaque, the circle lights up and the door opens. Gloria holds David's finger up to her lips in a gory gesture to keep quiet.

I go inside.

Someone is on the bed, they lie on their side, facing away from me. It's like a dream I had before. It's like a memory, real or fake, of being here before looking for my sister.

I go to the bed. I sit down quietly behind her. I know her smell. I know the way that her hair, usually so straight, kinks around the back with the promise of a curl.

I touch her hair.

I touch her shoulder then she jumps and looks around behind at me.

"Robyn," she says. "Is it really you?"

"Yes," I say. "I've come to get you. I've missed you so much." We are both choked with tears, but I can't let go now. I can't cry, I have to stay in control. We pull away, face to face, touching, disbelieving that we are together again.

She puts her hands on my face and touches my cheeks as if she is seeing me for the first time.

"Your eye," she says.

The eye that she regards me with, though, is not my own, as I had expected. Her eyes are green. I look into them and they are pure and clear. She isn't blind at all. Another of Mother's lies.

"You can see?" I ask, disbelieving.

"Yes," she says. "Of course I can see."

I take her hand in mine. In my head we are girls again. We are playing, we are fighting, we are sitting next to each other eating our sandwiches and kicking our heels together. How could I ever have thought she wasn't real?

We hold each other for a long time, but not long enough.

"There's no time to talk now, but I love you," I say. Now that I have her back, I have someone else to deal with.

I sign to the boys to lift her up but I am shocked when I see Vincent and Alice, they lock their heads together with tears in their eyes. They smile and holding each other's faces. She touches his scar. We put the nurse into Alice's bed and pull the covers up over her.

"Let's go," says Tiffany. "They'll know we're here by now."

The ranger carries Alice. In his big bulky arms, she is a waif, a ghost trailing a white sheet behind her. Vincent stalks behind on his skinny legs, a shotgun in his hands. They pass through the set of doors leading to the exit.

Up in the ceiling I short-circuit a wire, it doesn't take much for it to glisten and spark. I do it again and again as if I am popping bubble wrap. In moments there are flames. I put my hand out to stop Gloria.

There's smoke and fire and the barrier door crashes down. A water sprinkler starts up.

"My make-up is going to run!" says Gloria. Vincent, Alice and the ranger are on the other side. A fire alarm starts to screech.

"We shouldn't leave without you," Vincent says. But he is. He has to leave without Gloria and I.

"You must," I scream. "Get her out of here!" He steps back. He bangs the door and kicks it. I can't see him through the door. I can only hear him. They won't go back the same way. They go down and down and down, and come out into the sluice and tunnels where no one will look for them. That way they will be far away from the fighting.

Gloria and I peel backwards down the corridor, deeper into The Pavilion, straight towards the direction that Mother will be coming from. Something tells me that this time Mother won't be alone.

FIFTY ONE

IVAN WANTS ME.

My attention is being drawn to something that he thinks is important. I go into his mind. He is in a house.

He stands in front of a huge bay window overlooking Hove lawns. Life goes on below, people on bicycles and people walking dogs, throwing balls. I can see Ivan's reflection in the glass. He is the same age as his last message. It's the same trip, some days after their conversation in the restaurant.

This is the first house they built along the front. I remember looking at it from outside with Ivan, marvelling at the detail, how real it was, and how true to the spirit of Brighton and Hove, and to England and to every old building in England. Built traditionally, espousing the characteristics of the period, keeping them safe, like a living museum.

Outside a hurricane blows. Freezing snow and rain hammers against the windows. Horrendous weather.

On the wall is a large oil painting of The Professor, stroking a pug. Why are all dogs either Pugs or Alsatians? In films, I've seen so many kinds—so many breeds, but here, in town there are pugs alone, and on the farms there are Alsatians.

The Professor looks austere, accomplished. He is the man whose twenty foot high bronze sculpture adorns the seafront.

He is the founder, he is the father of us all.

"This is not about you, Ivan," says The Professor, standing up behind his desk. "This is about cultural preservation. While you lot kill each other over water and oil, we will preserve the traditional values that you have lost. When the ice melts, we'll already be here. Completely self-sufficient."

"I am going to contact the British Government and ask them to intervene in the running of this colony," Ivan says, standing upright and tall looking out to sea.

"I suggest, Ivan, that you work with our scientists to disable the technology that you have activated, or whatever it is you are claiming that you've done, before everyone freezes to death!"

"You can't leave all these people to fend for themselves, Hillary. We'll both be dead soon, and what then? I can't fund this anymore. It's over. I've been frozen out. I can't send anymore supplies. How are you going to feed these people?"

"I don't know how you could link yourself biometrically to the main computer. How did you do it?"

Ivan shakes his head.

"I did it long before we even started all of this. You don't think I would spend all that money and entrust everything to you. Your only hope is to get me and my family down here or I will call upon British armed forces."

"You'll do no such thing," The Professor screams. A huge clap of thunder booms through the sky.

"What on earth is that? What have you done?" asks The Professor. They should not get weather like this. The colony is a tightly terra-firmed micro-climate, there are no extremes of weather, storms and heatwaves are not on the agenda here.

"You can't go on without me, Hillary, and I need to safeguard the future of this colony. You need my DNA to restore the terra-forming processes, and I will not give you that until you agree to bring my family down here."

"No, Ivan. I'm going to safeguard the future of this fucking colony," he shouts, and the door opens and in walk six armed soldiers dressed in black.

Ivan has built-in a security device into the quantum computer. It needs Ivan's DNA to function or critical running elements of the programme will be terminated. It means that, without Ivan, the computer won't be able to continue its programme to moderate the weather.

"You don't understand. You either do what I say, or the computer goes off and within weeks, even days, the terra-forming stops and you will be plunged back into the natural habitat of the Antarctic," Ivan shouts, and he backs into the window. The men have surrounded him and they are waiting for The Professor to speak, to tell them what to do. Each of the men has some element of The Professor's dark facial characteristics.

"I'll be very clear. This is your last chance, Ivan, to cooperate," The Professor says, but Ivan scans the faces of the young soldiers and he pulls away in disgust. The Professor can't have done this, surely, he could not have spliced his own genes into every baby that's being born here?

"Why the fuck do they all look like you?" shouts Ivan, pointing, spitting, a cornered animal. "You've gone fucking crazy. You should not have done that."

"Why do you think?" The Professor says, laughing, smiling at his boys. The Professor nods his head at Ivan, and the boys know what to do. They have already been briefed and they close in on Ivan.

I can't see anything and then it seems that Ivan is punched so hard the glasses fly off catapulting across the floor. Eventually they stop, I see black, then white, the picture is gone, and I can hear the muffled sounds of Ivan being hit.

I can feel his fear. Ivan's adrenaline kicks in frantically. This is it, these men mean business. Ivan tries to look away. He searches for something to hit them with. One man takes hold of Ivan's throat with both hands. What Ivan feels when he looks at this man, apart from pain, is shock.

The moment is here and Ivan knows it. I want to go in there and pull the men off him. But I can't. This isn't now. I'm not there.

Ivan's eyeballs burn. They are filled with his own heart, with pressure like they are going to pop. His heart flips because he is panicking. His heart is like a fish on a hook.

"Stop," I shout. Gloria puts her hand gently over my mouth. If Ivan could get his hand up he could punch these men, but his arms are weak and this man is too strong. Then Ivan feels another set of hands holding his arms down, pinning them to the sides of his body. He forces Ivan down. He can't fight back.

This is it.

Ivan manages to get one fingernail into his arm and he scratches as best he can. The man's skin goes up under Ivan's nail. His eye catches Ivan's, but he doesn't even flinch. He's not laughing, none of them are, they are diligently, intently squeezing Ivan out of this story. The Professor, Hilary White, is a betraying murderous fiend.

"You bastards. I gave you everything," Ivan says, his words broken, laced with saliva, barely audible.

It happens quickly, but seems like forever. Every movement is in slow motion. There are sparks in Ivan's vision. White sparks.

Ivan thinks about his children and wonders about his baby that didn't make it. The loss of that child was too much for him and Elizabeth, and it began the end of their love.

"I'm here," I say. "I'm with you, don't be afraid."

Ivan can hear The Professor. He's not going to make it. This is it. Ivan cries. His body is exploding, no imploding, into itself. Ivan knows these men that are murdering him. They are like the first settlers, the friends he met on the first boat over, the men that he interviewed, the people to whom he gave this chance.

"I gave this to you," Ivan says. No one can hear but me, and he's talking not to these specific men, but everyone in this colony to whom he gave a new life. "I gave you this colony. You came to me, you came up to my face and called me Sir, and thanked me."

"Take him to Catalina Island. Sink the ship. Issue the mayday," says the Professor and Ivan hears The Professor's footsteps walking away as he drifts into painlessness. It is the last thing that Ivan ever hears. "And make sure that you take the whole arm, and rush it to Dr Joy Forster at the Pavilion hospital, we're going to need to preserve at least some of him."

The last thing I hear from Ivan is this:

"Elizabeth. Elizabeth, I love you. It was always only you."

Then Ivan feels no pain. He feels nothing at all. His body is warm on the floor. I try to pluck the Cube from my eye but Gloria stops me. I want to throw it to the floor, but sinews have attached and I can't remove it without pain. It is a part of me now.

I fall to the floor and wash my face in my own tears.

My father is dead.

FIFTY TWO

THIRTY SEVEN MINUTES pass, to be precise, before the fighting starts. We hear it above our heads. Shots are fired. There's an explosion and then there's the familiar rumble of boots. I cannot help them outside. I cannot trap the soldiers in here, some things have to be, have to happen. When we take Mother it will weaken them beyond repair. This we do for ourselves and we do for those who have died at her hands.

Gloria and I descend the stairs at pace. I surprise myself. I was never fit, but now I'm pregnant, I seem to have power beyond my expectations. There are people above us on the stairs. Several times we have to retreat and hide in a corridor to let soldiers pass by. We choose our battles. We are saving ourselves for Mother.

I am locked onto her in the Cube. I can see her moving around and though we are actively trying to create a coming together of her and I, I am shocked when I finally spot her.

When I see Mother, she is moving at speed. I can't ever remember her going to aerobics, or keep fit or coming into the communal swimming pool to teach me how to swim. But boy, can she move! She is graceful. It's as if she's on wheels.

It's her. Her skin, and her hands. Oh, to see her once more as I used to see her, before all of this. But I can't unsee what she has done.

She has soldiers with her, three trained fighters, but I have Gloria and I have The Cube. We don't want to be cornered, so we wait in a cupboard by the lift. I feel her coming, rather I see her as a red dot coming up in the lift.

She gets out with three soldiers. As they step forward Gloria swings out, and just to show she means business she bangs one of the soldiers in the face with the butt of her gun. Blood splatters all over Mother's white pant suit. Surprisingly, they are not expecting this and the second soldier brings up his gun fast but Gloria is faster, readier and hungrier, and she peels off a volley of shots from her automatic. The soldier's chest clamshells open right in front of me. It smells of liquid iron. I don't turn away. I show no weakness, because I have none. I have no purpose other than Mother. She had a choice, but there is no turning back now.

It appears that by scrambling pings into the Cube since they killed Sarah Phoenix, I have kept myself hidden from Mother, and I do have an element of surprise after all. I can beat her. I can do the right thing. I will save my sister.

I recognise the third soldier, it's Pinkie—the long black coat man. I've seen him again and again. He is panicked, his eyes flick towards the dead body on the floor, and he fumbles to draw a gun, but so do I. I have my gun pointed at Mother's head.

"Who is my real mother?" I ask. I spit it out, half-wanting to hold her. I still want her to love me. Why has this happened to us? A small part of me wants her to say that there's been some terrible mistake and that we're all going home now for tea. Why can't we talk to each other, love each other? But it's too late for that. She's had her chances.

"I am," says Mother, panting and covered in blood. She holds her hands up in surrender, then wipes blood from her mouth.

"Tell me and I won't kill you," I say. Gloria moves in closer to watch my back. I feel her stiffen. She takes out a small handgun. The semi-automatic is noisy and messy. She has paid the price for our freedom.

"Move over, Robyn. I'll do it for you. No one should have to kill their own mother." Gloria stands in front of Mother, towering over her with a pistol aimed right at the centre of her forehead.

"Thank you," I say, and move aside and Mother suddenly trembles. She has realised that I'm not her little girl anymore. I am not used to seeing her like this. She's frightened. She *is* capable of fear. She stands upright. I can hear her breathing. She's just witnessed Gloria obliterate someone in cold blood. She deserves to be this scared. I'm in control of her. I have control over her now, and over what happens next.

"I do love you," she says. "I've always looked after you, day after day since you were little."

"Who am I?" I ask.

"You are different. You are special."

"You'll tell us or one of your cronies will tell us once we've put you to rest."

"It's hard to explain."

"Try," says Gloria. "And make it quick."

"I know you know, Robyn, about the colony, and I wish I could have been more open with you, but you are very sensitive, I had to protect you."

"I know more than you can ever imagine," I say.

"The founders of our colony made provision for genetic diversity among the population to safeguard future generations. It was meant to eradicate genetic disorders amongst other things."

"The third splice, I know about that. So what, who, was I spliced with, what's the big fucking secret?" I ask.

"You weren't spliced. In fact you are one of the very few people here who have not been spliced."

"So?" I ask, she's beginning to make me angry. She's trying to delay, trying to waste time until help turns up. I plan our next route in the Cube. She's not getting away now.

"Do you know the name Professor Hilary White?" she asks, and of course I do, it's the Professor, Ivan's partner and founder, the brain behind the colony.

"Yes, I know him." The noise upstairs is intensifying. There's an explosion and rapid bursts of gunfire. The lights flicker—and it's not me doing it.

"Instead of splicing randomly selected genes from our pre-approved stocks, he spliced his own DNA into the entire population. Every pregnancy, every child."

"Why?"

"Why? Power, madness, who knows, but I am trying to clean up the mess that he has left us in," she says.

"What mess?"

"We all inherited something else from him. It's the eyes. We're all going blind. All of us."

"You?"

"Yes, I am descended from Hilary White, your friend here with her gun in my face, what's your name?"

"Gloria."

"Gloria, I can see you are too. Vincent is," Mother says. I can see that they look alike. I've thought that for a long time. That's why the Finns look so different.

"It makes us what? You and I?" asks Gloria.

"Well, biologically, we're sisters. Half-sisters," says Mother. Gloria is repelled. She drops her aim for one moment before pulling it up hard and fast in rage.

"I don't believe you," she says.

"It's true," I say, thinking about the genetics room and The Professor and a lifetime watching people who all look the same and don't look like me. I put my hand out to lower Gloria's gun.

"Over the generations his genetic imperfections have bred in. There's almost no one left who is not a carrier, we've stopped the third splice completely but his genetic code is so rampantly spread throughout the entire population that it can never be eradicated," Mother says.

I don't want to believe her but I've seen them. The endless sets of thick black sunglasses strung out across the beach, in the dark and even at night. The people with glasses, the people with vision problems, were so common that it couldn't be anything else but true.

"I'm going blind," says Mother, matter of fact. "Keratoconus. It is slow moving in my case, but I'll get there."

I don't want to comfort her. I'm torn, but I hate everything about her. I remember that she is a cruel and evil woman. She's still my mum.

"So, what about my eye? It was for you, wasn't it?"

"No," she says, stumped for the first time. "Maybe."

"Stop lying to me, Mother. Enough is enough."

"You are special, Robyn," Mother says. "You are genetically different, original. You were created from a fertilised embryo kept on ice, donated by a supporter of the colony."

"Who?" I ask but already know.

"It was the financial sponsor of the colony, an entrepreneur called Ivan Dixon."

"And my biological mother?"

"His wife, Elizabeth. I don't know anything about her. I can't tell you much. I gave you her name as a middle name, Elizabeth. I did that much, and I love you, Robyn, I really do."

"Put the cuffs on him," Gloria says to Mother, pointing at the long black coat man. Mother does as she is told and removes his handcuffs from his belt and clamps his hands together around a metal pipe inside the stairwell. Gloria pulls at them to make sure that he is restrained.

"We don't want him following us," I say. "Mother, you are going to take Gloria and I downstairs and show us exactly whatever the fuck you are doing down there, and once we know that we can make an informed decision about your future."

Mother laughs. Her laughing makes me so sad and angry that I see stars and fuzzy white lines. I want to kill her. The soldiers didn't deserve what Gloria did to them, but it's survival of the fittest now.

"Alice is gone," I say.

"Gone where?" asks Mother, panicked. "Where is she?"

"Too late. She's free and away. You are never going to see her again. She is being taken to the coast as we speak and on a boat away from here." It sounds so luxurious. If nothing else, I have freed Alice from this fucking bitch.

"No," she screams. This is the first time I've seen her truly upset. She's agitated, she licks her lips, her eyes dart around looking for an escape.

"It's true," I say.

"You can't," says Mother. "I need her here."

"Show me. I have a right to know why you've been experimenting on me all of these years." I push her back into the lift. Soldiers are coming, I can hear them getting closer, but we'll be ten floors below by the time they arrive, and I will have disabled the lifts.

We descend. The three of us in the lift at close quarters. Gloria is staring at Mother, and I think in one way she is admiring of her.

"You are making a big mistake," she says. "Alice is very ill, she needs hospital attention."

"She's not ill at all, and neither am I. It is you that is ill, with your failing eyes and your faulty genes. No offence, Gloria."

"None taken," says Gloria.

"And innocent people like Gloria here, who have been unwittingly drawn into this."

"I didn't start this," says Mother. "I am trying to solve it." I don't believe her. She wants the power. She took my eye, mutilated me, scrubbed my memory. She made me forget I had fallen in love.

The lift stops.

The door opens.

I scan the room. There is a faint sign of life. It is a small and fragile signal.

"They found early on that the first generation, the children of the early settlers, did not necessarily share the intelligence characteristics of their parents. They didn't think about the lack of adequate education systems. There was a lack of teachers, or possibly a lack of external stimuli, so The Professor invented the genius gene, and spliced it into all new embryos. And it worked. But of course, there were side effects. None of that is my fault."

The first colonists had come from the finest universities and research institutions. They were highly educated, but what of their children? The next generation, without the support and processes of the education system, were not as brilliant as their parents.

We walk into a laboratory. In the centre is a raised stage, and in the middle of that a big glass box the size of a large car.

"What's that?" I ask.

"Well, that really is The Pavilion itself," says Mother. "It's the brain centre of the quantum computer that allows the colony to function. Without it, we would be plunged into regular Antarctic conditions."

We circle the box, it is frosted, or coated in condensation and I can't see inside.

Gloria is close behind Mother keeping a watch on her.

"So you bred Alice and I to be biometrically matched with this computer?" I ask.

"I didn't just breed you, I wanted to have children."

"Why?"

"Women want to be mothers of course," she says.

"No, why did you breed Alice and I differently?"

"What do you mean?" Mother says, and I stop and I lock eyes with her.

"Yes you do. You know exactly. Why you breed two children from fertilised embryos donated by Ivan and Elizabeth Dixon." The condensation inside the box is clearing and I am beginning to be able to see inside.

"Gosh," says Mother proudly. "You are clever."

"I know everything," I say. The box is clearing almost completely now so that I can see inside. On one side is a seat with what looks like some sort of harness. On the other is something else that I can't make out. Something that looks like a piece of leather suspended on a table.

There's a bang.

Gloria is down. Behind her stands David Sykes, still gaunt and pale, his eyes pink from crying, holding a length of copper piping in his hands. Shit.

There's blood coming from Gloria's temple as she lies motionless on the floor.

FIFTY THREE

MOTHER'S BEHAVIOUR NEEDS no further explanation. She needs Alice and I, because of something that is inside us, locked inside our cells. It's what we were born for. To think that for all this time, I wondered about the purpose of my life.

We are the cog, my sister and I—the crux of the colony without which the sun doesn't shine, and the water does not flow, and the radiators do not heat. We are the only people here without whom the clouds will simply blow away and let in that never-ending night, that will chill the town right back to its frozen bones.

This Cube in my eye gives me access to the beating heart of this colony. It is the engine, it is the brain, and it is my inheritance.

I thought I might see my father. I thought that he might be here, that I might walk on the beach with him, that he might see me and recognise me and take me to New York City, or to London, or to the real Brighton.

I thought he would introduce me to his other children—now grown—my brothers and sisters, and say, 'Here she is, at last.'

I thought he would help me find my sister, Alice. I dreamt that he would get hold of my mother and tell her that she didn't know who she was dealing with. He would demand that she return Alice and save us both.

I'm soon to be someone else's Mother, and already I feel the responsibility for my child's life. She depends on me.

I don't understand the science, but even more urgently than ever before, I need to get my child away from here, and Alice too, because as long as we are here, we are commodities, at risk of being enslaved, imprisoned, made addicted and mad.

"All you had to do was take turns sitting here with your sister and everything would have been fine. But you wouldn't," Mother says. In the distance the noise of fighting roars on. I hope Vincent and Tiffany are far away with my sister.

The mist inside the box clears and I see that on the table is a human arm. The skin is old and mummified. It's the colour of caramel. The muscle has wasted away and the skin sags in folds. Where the elbow should be is a series of wires and tubes filled with blood, pumping and aerating the arm. The hand is clenched, holding something tightly.

"He gave us everything, your biological father. He gave us all of this. A utopia. But he added a huge caveat; we could only have it on his terms. When Ivan tried to blackmail The Professor, The Professor called his bluff."

"Hillary White murdered him in cold blood," I say.

"Inside," says Mother. "Come on." She points at the chair. David has taken Gloria's gun. I don't have any choice. I'm going to be locked in here with Ivan's arm. David is inside the box with me, he's delighted to be in charge.

"I tried to help you, Robyn." He smells of disinfectant. He opens a head brace of some kind and pushes me back into the seat. He holds me high on my waist, his fingers sweeping my breasts. In front of me, the arm twitches. I see a finger move. Ivan's wedding ring is still on the hand. It's the most gruesome thing that I have ever seen and yet I want to touch it. I want to touch my father's skin.

I sit back in the chair and instantaneously know that my sister, Alice, has sat in this chair before me. This is where she has been, all those hospital appointments, she has been here, a biometric key to the city. If only someone had shown her how to use it.

"There's nothing left, out there. Get on that boat with your friends if you wish, but there is nowhere for you to go. The old world does not exist anymore."

I shake my head and think of my sister being free. I think about my baby, and me growing fatter and more pregnant stuck in this Perspex box underground with my dead father's hand.

"The hand is dying," Mother says. "How long do you think we've been here? Your little cube didn't tell you?"

I shake my head. David tightens the straps around me.

"Ivan died more than one hundred years ago, Robyn."

She is lying. "I don't believe you," I say. "Another one of your lies."

It can't be true. One hundred years and only earlier today I had believed that I would meet him. It means Elizabeth is gone. The rest of his family is gone. There would be no one to go back to. No one to find. No one to be reunited with.

In front of me there is an electronic board with the day, the month and the number 2174 written on it.

"You won't recognise the number," Mother says, noticing my confusion. We don't count the years like that here. But out there, in the Old World, the year is 2174."

"This colony was established in 2036," says David.

"The world outside this colony is unrecognisable, Robyn. Refugees try to get here every day. What do you think they are running from? You could have been the Queen of this colony. You could have had it all."

She folds her arms, and turns her back on me.

"Strap her arms and legs, David," she says.

"Yes, Ma'am," he says, but his arm is thickly bandaged, he is pale and weak and struggles to restrain me with only one hand.

"I might need a little bit of help," he says, calling to Mother, who turns sharply. She'll be thinking she should have chosen someone more capable as her aide.

"Do I have to do everything myself?" she says.

"In Ivan's time this colony was tiny," David says, under his breath. "It has evolved for one hundred and fifty years. It's peaceful here. It's safe. The colony works. The world outside is chaos, Robyn. Utter anarchy."

"When his hand dies," Mother says. "The computer will shut down, the terra-forming programme will stop. We've already had emergencies as a result of this hand decaying."

She's talking about the polar bears escaping from the zoo. She pulls a monitor cable down over my head and affixes it to my temples with small, red suction pads.

"How can you do this to me?" I ask. She is unmoved. I realised that I loved her, more than she ever loved me. I am fuel. I am petrol. I am the tool of her power and she has used me.

"If the weather goes down, then we won't get everyone out in time. We don't have enough boats. We estimate that twenty thousand people will die if we revert to the cold. I'm sorry it had to be you."

"What happens if I die?" I ask. The thought of a glorious exploding suicide crosses my mind, taking me, and my mother out with it.

"It doesn't matter," she says. "We can keep your blood pumping, keep part of you alive enough to operate the computer. Ivan has been dead for a century already. I'll be sad, of course, but it's for the greater good."

She's not lying now. I've given her a chance to repent and explain herself to me, but she is so bent on her course of action that I know for sure that she cannot really love me.

She's up close into my face and I see her wrinkles, the Professor's jowls beginning to swell and sag. She's attractive, her dark hair is only now starting to prickle with white. But she's nothing like me. She smells of the soldier's blood, in which she is still spattered.

"Did your eye heal well?" she asks, compassionately like a real mother lifting up the patch. She sees the Cube instead of an empty scarred hollow. She gasps and pulls away.

She wasn't expecting that. She didn't know. She knew I had it, had followed me, but had no idea what I had done with the Cube, how I'd symbiosed it into my body. How I had become one with it, fused my brain to its power.

I don't explain that her tying me into this chair has been a fool's errand. I don't explain that I know this computer better than she can ever dream of knowing it.

"I know how to work this machine," I say. "I've been working on it already." She's stumped and freezes. Slowly her eyes open wide as realisation seeps through her body. I release the suction pads off my temples and they start to fall away.

Mother starts trembling. It's panic taking hold of her.

My hands are tied in with leather buckled straps.

"Undo them please, Mother," I say, and when she lingers unable to decide whether to untie me or leave me tied in, I send a bolt of electricity to my bindings and the buckle on my left wrist harness first curls and then melts. There's a powerful connection in this room. I am brimming with potential. I reach over with my now free hand to undo myself from the second binding. Mother takes a step back.

I lift up the head piece. Gloria mumbles. She is coming around.

"David, do something quickly," says Mother.

"What the fuck is happening?" says David.

"Where are the soldiers? David, just do something!" Mother shouts.

David tries to exit the Perspex box and with one glance from my eye, and a surge from my brain, I pull the doors snap-shut on him. David is caught by the head in between the entrance doors. I can move them so fast it is imperceptible to the naked eye. He wriggles like a little worm.

Open. Shut. Bang! He's caught again.

Mother's mouth hangs open. Alice and I are close, but there are differences too, and I am much less tolerant and better trained and dextrous when it comes to the usage of quantum computers.

David squeals in the door. It has badly hurt him. I open the door a fraction and then I pull it shut hard and at speed back on his head. He falls silent.

I'm not even sure what I should do with Mother, if she tries to physically attack me then I am in trouble, that's if she wants to take my hand off now. I would fight her for it.

While I am thinking about Mother, I open and snap shut the doors again and David Sykes falls to the floor like a knocked out drunk. His head bounces.

Mother stares at me. She is breathing uncharacteristically heavily and her shoulders lurch up into her neck, and her mouth takes on a roundness as she tries to regulate her breathing. I think I might have killed David but I am so mad about Mother I could kill anyone.

Yes, I am a monster.

I kill the lights.

It is pitch black.

I release myself from the chair. Mother tries to run away, but she can't find her way in the darkness and David is clogging up the doors. I close them again as fully as I can with his body in the way just to make sure that she can't get out.

What has she made me into?

When all I want to do is go to pregnancy yoga and prepare to be a mother myself? What sort of role model is she?

I turn the lights on.

I am standing by Ivan's arm.

Mother is still. She was trying to squeeze through the door to get out, trampling on David, she now stands on top of his body. She is frightened of me.

"What does this feel like?" I ask, and I am honestly interested in what it must feel like to be so powerful and yet so scared. She has denied me so much, that I have never learnt loss, I have never learnt power or control over myself or even over my own memories.

"Now, Robyn, calm down. I am acting in the interests of the entire colony. You wouldn't want all those people to die would you? Neither would I, and that's why I did what I did."

"Where do you think you're going?" I ask. "Sit down."

"Do you know what it took to offer up my little girls for the colony?" she asks, and I don't know what it took for her, but I know what it took from me.

"Sit in the chair," I say. She doesn't want to. "Sit in the chair," I say again. I persuade her to get into the chair by staring hard. That's a sign of my new power. I tie her in and put the red suckers on her temples. She shakes her head. Before I put her into a continuous dream state I tell her: "You defile his memory. He gave you all of this and you abuse his body in return."

"Please, please," she begs me. "What about all the little children?"

But what about me? What about the grown up children made mad with falsehoods and mistruths.

"I'm leaving, and I am taking him with me." I disconnect the arm. I'm not sure how so I pull at the wires and there's resistance somehow. I hear a crack and peel outside and the fierce physical displacement of the glacier makes the entire laboratory shake. But I could be imagining it, such is the power of my anger towards Mother that I feel like I could displace a glacier, I feel like I could make the sky roar with thunder.

"Don't, Robyn. Please," Mother says again, immobile, passive and desperate.

But the resistance in the hand itself rattles me. I stop trying to untangle the plastic veins and wires and suddenly the fingers open up.

Ivan's dead hand kept alive only through wires pumping blood and air is responding to me.

The Cube that he was holding slips out and onto the table top. I pick it up and secure it. It's like mine, but shinier, newer. I've got both now, his one in my hand and my own inside my head. He holds up his palm with five fingers outstretched.

I can hear him say; "If you love me, put your hand on mine." And I place my palm open against his.

His hand is unexpectedly warm. I wallow in the sensation of touching him. His hand is soft and baggy with skin, but it is him and I know that it is him.

I close my eyes. I imagine that I am back with him in the bedroom where I first ever set eyes on him. Where he smelled his own daughter's head and thought that he might cry from the intensity of that love. It is a sweet innocent love, that endures forever.

His fingers close around mine. Our fingers are locked together as if in prayer. His nails are tissue thin and the cuticle has grown long, taking up half the nail itself. I am holding hands with my father. He is holding me. Does he know that I am here? If he feels nothing else then I hope that he feels my love.

I will leave him here in peace. I won't take him back. I'll let the computer slowly unwind and unravel along with him. I push his Cube back into his grip. I'll let them go down slowly together. I hold his hand.

I take his ring, a solid gold band, which is thicker than anything that I have worn before and heavy in the way of real metal. It is his wedding ring for Elizabeth, my biological mother. It's a ring that he stills wears all these years after her death, all these years after she stopped loving him.

The ring comes off easily. I push it down onto my index finger, and it's far too big so I take it off again and wear it on my thumb where it just about fits.

Mother is trembling. I put her into a long, anxious sleep, where she'll see demons and regrets and where she'll sweat cold, locked here in this box. When they find her here she won't be the woman that she was.

I decide to give Mother a short Artificial Memory of mine, and I play it over and over again. I set the computer to play it for Mother non-stop.

The memory is mine;

It is of me running, brutalised to a hospital bathroom and viciously unwrapping my own bandages to reveal an empty hole where my eye should be. I play it over and over and over again. Only I can unlock this box, so here she will stay for some time to come trapped inside my memory. I work undisturbed, even by the noise of the fighting up above, to attach Mother to the nutritious drip that has been feeding my sister.

I watch as Mother closes her eyes, deep in the memory, she gasps, her hand comes up to her face and she screams. Tears pour down her face, but it doesn't stop there.

She does it again. She gasps, her hand comes up to her face and she screams. And so it continues.

"I loved you," I say, to both of them; to my mother and my father. "Goodbye."

FIFTY FOUR

DOWN AND DOWN I go until the passageway turns cold and filled with ice water as turquoise as a precious jewel. I don't follow the run-off to the sea, I go the other way, back toward the glacier where no one will be looking for me.

The fighting continues at the Pavilion without us, slowing drawing to a close. A few of the soldiers fight on, as do I, shutting down their resources from within my mind. It is only time now before they surrender and we take control of the Pavilion and of the City of Brighton and Hove.

I manage to rouse Gloria and she travels steadily with a gauze, stolen from Mother's stash, plugged to her head. I saw the white bone inside Gloria's head where her eyebrow had opened up. She is unsteady on her legs and slows me down but I cannot leave her.

I use the Cube to plot a direct route through the crisp white tunnels, and hours later we emerge, shivering, exhausted and exhilarated from an entrance near the sluice. There's a communications box that the Finnish gypsies use to switch the electric fence, and I trip the switch, hoping that they will come to investigate.

They do. Paranoia about the polar bears is high, and they don't want to leave any holes where bears can get into the farms. In the distance, I can see the foot of Mount Hood and beyond that it reaches up never ending into the sky.

The Finns that arrive are not my friends, but I ask them to take me to Lena and Erik, who being the most upstanding of individuals, are known by all Finns. As they cart us across the farmlands in a truck, I marvel at their blonde hair, diametrically opposed to Gloria's dark locks, and I wonder what else is out there in this world.

FIFTY FIVE

WE ARE EIGHTY miles from Brighton. No one will see us leave the coast of Antarctica. The ship is ready. The crew is a team of eight retired coast guards each as vibrant, white-haired, and cynical as the next. Eleanor captains the ship. She wears her crisply laundered uniform. We have provisions and water for three months at sea.

I may never see New Brighton again, but perhaps one day I will see the real thing. Perhaps one day, we will run this boat onto the pebble beach there and jump ship during the night and disappear amongst the punks and drunks.

I'm unsure what to expect out there. We will get help and resources for Alice. I still need to save her, but in a different way. She will stay behind with Vincent to build a better future. She is needed there, one of us is. We are conjoined with the land, Alice and I, one of us must stay or everyone will perish. I guess Mother's plan worked, in a way.

Vincent brought my sister to the dock to say goodbye. I will see her again when I bring help. She grows stronger every day. She no longer looks like a skeletal version of me. After we hugged, she dried her eyes and slipped her fingers through Vincent's like I once had.

Vincent's hair has grown back into a thick crop of stubble, but as pure white as Mount Hood. He dotes on my sister. He has the family that he always wanted. The unconditional love he needed.

Gloria, my brutal, unremitting saviour leads us now. She is our Queen and will lead our community into the future. There is blood on her hands, and she will do whatever is necessary.

Eleanor calls me to the bridge. I was holding Tiffany's hand as we lay next to each other in a bunk. We have left the coast behind and have a full view of the horizon all around us. We are out of sight of land. The ship decelerates suddenly. Eleanor has powered down our speed.

We climb the metal steps up to Eleanor's bridge. The ship's radar beeps and pings with dots ahead. The sea is a blue-grey pond. It's flat and pocked with an occasional, white-tipped swell. My legs stutter and sometimes wobble. I've never been to sea before.

I see it.

I see them.

As far as the eye can make out there is a fleet of ships, glowing orange with rust as the sun catches their metal. An armada of junk boats, trying to get to our colony. There are hundreds of refugee boats containing what might be thousands and thousands of refugees.

"What shall we do, Robyn?" asks Eleanor.

Behind or ahead? Backwards or forwards?

"We're not a secret after all," Tiffany says. Out there, whatever is there, they know about us.

Shall we go back or shall we go forward?

I feel something inside my body. A tingle. I feel my baby inside me, too soon to feel her move but still I know that she is there driving me on. She is growing, my child. She's a child of all of us; my sister's, Tiffany's, Ivan Dixon's. And she is mine. I choose life. I choose the truth.

But there is something else, something different, wider, and greater in the Cube.

I am tuning into the frequency of something infinite. It is the frantic static of the real world. There are multiple messages, radio waves, data and languages coming to me through the Cube.

It is breathtakingly powerful, beautiful and cruel. It is the world. Out there.

"Full steam ahead please, Eleanor," I say. "Let's go home."

ACKNOWLEDGEMENTS

With thanks first and foremost to the wonderful Vicky Hague for her unwavering support. There is no one else in the entire world that I would like to be in lockdown with.

Huge thanks to Sean Coleman. It is an honour to work with you.

Thank you to Richard Skinner and Matthew Smith for their support and guidance. Thanks to my early readers Dan Dalton, Sue Saunders, Suzanne Holland, and Lucy Flynn. Thank you to my wonderful Faber alumni Alison Marlow, Giles Fraser, Kelly Allen, Trisha Sakhlecha, Maria Ghibu, Alice Feeney, Daniel Grant and Anjola Adedayo.

In researching this book I want to thank a number of people who advised, and provided ideas and guidance; Ben Ayme. Sebastian Weidt, University of Sussex. Sarah Gorrell, Kwali Kundalini and Lena Koskela. Christine D'Ercole for keeping me sane in lockdown.

Special thanks to the Langley massive, and St Bernard's Convent girls for continued support.

ABOUT THE AUTHOR

Helen Trevorrow is a graduate of the 2016 Faber Academy creative writing programme. She studied at Leeds University and has worked in marketing and public relations in London.

Helen's debut novel In The Wake is a feminist crime thriller about family, unrealised trauma and alcoholism.

Helen has ghost-written many articles for newspapers, magazines and websites.

She lives in Brighton, Sussex with her wife and child.

CPSIA information can be obtained
at www.ICGtesting.com
Printed in the USA
LVHW042042090322
713030LV00023B/848/J